The Vows That Break Us

Katie Hayoz

Zoyah/JFF Publishing

First published 2024 by Zoyah/JFF Publishing

First edition

Cover art by Emily Wittig

Contents

This book includes scenes that involve kidnapping, the devil, and death.

The Devil sidled closer and whispered in her ear, "You are not strong enough to withstand the storm."

She whispered back, "I am the storm."

—origin unknown

THE VOWS THAT BREAK US

BOOK TWO of DEVIL OF ROANOKE SERIES

KATIE HAYOZ

Prologue

Redd

Some secrets are meant to be kept.

Agnes, the woman who pretended to be my mother, repeated this phrase to me over and over. It was her rote response any time I had questions. Questions like who I was, where I came from, or why I was different. She refused to give me answers because, she insisted, she wanted me to have the luxury of *not* knowing. By withholding the truth, she was supposedly giving me a gift.

I never forgave her for keeping those secrets.

And I never stopped seeking the truth.

Now I've found out who I am, where I'm from, and why I'm different.

The answers have come at a cost.

My body floats lifeless on the surface of the pond while the crowd beyond it cheers, their faces masks of hatred.

This place is darkness, evil, chaos, fury. This is where I was born.

This is also where I died.

1

Eleanor

Eden: 1589

All my life, I'd thought myself clever—the pranks I pulled on my mother, the schemes I'd devised to survive. But the Devil was so much cleverer than I.

The scene in which I found myself proved it.

I'd saved my Virginia. From the moment of her birth two years earlier, I'd done nothing but worry for her life; now it was secure. Yet in saving her, I'd killed young Walter and bound myself and my neighbors to the Master forever.

The Master eased Virginia from my arms as I lay weeping in the mouth of the Fire Pit, Torment wrapped around my shoulders. My daughter—my beautiful, sweet daughter—rested her rosy cheek upon the Devil's chest and he hugged her to him as though she was already his. How did I get here? How was it that a trip to the New World full of promise and hope ended up as a fall into Lucifer's twisted paradise? How did a simple desire to save my child from starvation turn into a pact with the Devil himself?

I deserved this. I'd introduced Evil and the Master to Roanoke. I'd encouraged others to use the Devil's masks to steal and slaughter. I'd taken pleasure in other people's pain. Aye, I'd lost those I loved, from my father to Ananias to Manteo, but was that punishment enough for a life of such sin?

Torment dug his hooked teeth deeper into my skin, his mink-like body a perfect fit around my neck. His venom forced disgust and despair to burn through my blood.

If not before, now I was paying my due. And then some.

"Eleanor?" The Master gripped my shoulder and shook me gently. "Eden is sated. 'Tis now time to celebrate."

The Master's mask had become one with his skin, rough and worm-eaten though it was. His black eyes stared down at me, their evil depths glittering in the orange glow of the pond.

I looked about me. The barren trees which had been snarling like ferocious beasts now grew green leaves and settled down until they were still. The dirt at the Master's feet was no longer dry and cracked but covered in moss, lush and springy. The river ran clear and shiny; fish leapt in and out of the water. It had stunk like rot, but now the thick, sweet scent of flowers perfumed the air.

It was heavenly once again. It was just as the Devil had promised it would be after Eden swallowed a youthful sacrifice.

"I hate you," I ground out. The Master wrapped his fur-clad hand around my own, pulling me to my feet. His breath was warm against my ear as he whispered, "No, Eleanor. You hate yourself."

Ah, how that forked tongue pronounced the truth.

Mere steps away, Dyonis Harvie howled and wept, his once friendly face now so contorted with pain that it took me a moment to realize he was no longer wearing his mask.

I'd brought this misery upon him. I took his only child to save my own. I'd snuffed out Walter's flame so that Virginia's would continue to burn. As for mine? I'd long ago lost my own light. I was the infinite black of a deep well on a moonless night.

Emme and Elizabeth and the others held Dyonis upright as we all made our way through the forest and to the village square. Our masks were removed and dropped along the way, like breadcrumbs of evil showing our path. Soon enough, we would discover that it did not matter where we left those vile instruments; they would always appear again, grinning at us somewhere in our homes. But now, here, we quickly dropped them, hoping to shed our malefice as a snake sheds its skin.

The others' faces had changed since the sacrifice had been made. Tears blurred their eyes, horror harshening the curl of their lips, the flare of their nostrils. It was not the first time we'd seen death, nor the first time we'd killed, but never before had we murdered one of our own. Never before had we taken the life of a child.

Never before had *I* taken the life of a child.

My backbone felt like string and more than once I collapsed, only to have the Master prop me up again. He all but dragged me to the village square.

A feast was set upon long tables, fish and meat grilled to perfection, candied fruits and thick puddings in painted porcelain bowls. Large pitchers of ale and wine and clear river water beckoned to all who were thirsty, yet we adults let our tongues swell to sand in our mouths rather than take a drink. We let our stomachs rumble in hunger rather than eat the victuals of celebration.

The children, however, stole sweetmeats from the platters with greedy fingers. They ate and drank and danced.

No one dared look at me. Not even in hatred. That would come—oh, how that would come—but at that moment I was nothing but a specter. I curled in upon myself, such agony twisting my heart that the scene around me blurred to black.

Soon, I felt the cool edge of a cup pressed to my lips. The brew inside smelled musty enough to bring tears to my eyes. I looked up and into the Master's face. He no longer wore his wooden mask, but a simple bandeau of leather. His black eyes sparked with warmth, and a small smile turned up his lips. "Drink, Eleanor. Complete the binding and suffer no more."

I shook my head, hugged Torment tighter around my neck, and pushed the cup away.

But he once again pressed it to my lips, his voice and eyes growing cold and hard. "'Tis not a request, but an order."

The brew was icy and stung the back of my throat, numbing the very core of me. I swallowed, then gulped down more. I wanted to feel nothing. I *needed* to feel nothing.

In the end, he had to pry the cup from my grip.

After I had finished, Virginia reached for the vessel. "Not for you, Virginia," said the Devil. "Even I am not so cruel as to bind a child to me for something a parent chose."

Then the Master gave Virginia her mask. He twirled one hand in the air and a wooden face appeared, red sap running from the corner of the eyes, yellow teeth sharpened to points. "*This* is for you, my dear Virginia. You've earned it," he said.

She lifted it to her face and sighed in pleasure.

"Welcome to the fold," said the Master. He conjured masks for the other children, but none were as magnificent as Virginia's.

None made my blood run as cold.

The Master became my nemesis the moment he had asked me to sacrifice my own child. Seeing the mask, I understood that he would not stop his twisted games. He fully intended to get Virginia into his clutches, to bend her to his will.

I vowed then and there I would never let that happen. I vowed to protect and keep her. Never would I leave her, lost and alone, for the Master to manipulate. Never would Virginia belong to the Devil.

I'd saved her life. Now I needed to save her soul.

2

John

Eden: Present Day

I've done it. I've done what was asked of me and redeemed myself of any wrongdoing. I've proved my loyalty to Eden. To my village, my people, my home.

Next to me on the bank of the pond, behind the trio of hellhounds, stand my grandfather and the Master. Looks of approval dress their faces. Word will get back—to the Council, to Clara, to everyone—that I am a worthy scout. It is the recognition I've always wanted.

I should feel joyous. Or, at the very least, relieved. Instead, it is fear that grips my heart as I watch Deception, the water dragon, rise up behind Redd. It is guilt I feel as the Master approaches Redd and with his thumbnail taps the crescent-shaped birthmark at the edge of her jaw.

She does not flinch. Her shoulders are squared, her dark eyes intense. Though she's dripping wet, she looks every bit a force to be reckoned with.

"Welcome home," he says to Redd.

"You," Redd breathes. "I saw you, in my mask."

"And I saw you." The Master winks. In his human form, he's graceful and captivating. His eyes shine from behind a black band of leather; his black, red, and blond hair is a glorious mane upon his head. His smile is warm and almost sincere.

Grandfather, too, smiles. His teeth glint in the fiery glow of the pond. "We've been waiting for you to come back to us for a very long time," he says to Redd.

Aye, that is the truth. More than four hundred years have passed since my grandfather and the others left Roanoke to heal in this Devil's paradise called Eden. More than four hundred years since Eleanor Dare tricked them all into a pact by killing Grandfather's child instead of her own. More than four hundred years since my family has wanted revenge for that act.

Revenge that is now within reach as Redd is of Eleanor's blood.

So long ago, Eleanor's trickery started a never-ending cycle of sacrifice that offers us youth and health and the possibility of eternal life. One life for the good of many. And though we have never forgiven Eleanor for her act, this pattern of give and take has become the keystone of our existence. It is a way of life that I was taught to respect and appreciate. A life of abundance and beauty that outshines the darkness forever lurking outside our door.

But to survive, we must occasionally welcome that darkness inside. We must treat it as our guest and smile into its craggy face and house it and feed it. And we must do so without regret.

Deception tilts her massive head and exhales, releasing enough vapor that, for a moment, I can't see Redd in the cloud of it. Any worry, any instinct Redd may have that warns her to get out of Eden, will now be smothered by Deception's breath. We do cruel things here in Eden but avoid cruelty itself; Deception's presence is used as solace to those who would otherwise have reason to be afraid. And though Grandfather's hands are not pushing Redd's head underwater right now, Deception is not allowing her to figure out that later they might.

Nor does Deception allow Redd to be properly alarmed when Grandfather produces a set of manacles and clamps them onto her wrists.

My gut twists.

As a boy, I would fish in the river with friends—Brian and Henry and Clara—splashing and grabbing the silver salmon as they swam by. We would climb the twisted branches of the trees in the forest, reaching for the sky encrusted with stars. We'd pry Malice pearls from their shells along the riverbank and stroke their rippled surface, gasping at the strength of emotions they procured. It wasn't until I was a scout, trained in slipping between worlds, knowledgeable in the ways of the darkness that I kept one of these pearls on my person. Arrogance. A pearl of sparkling silver that I clung to whenever I saw Henry and Brian laughing together at private jokes, drunk on floral wine, oblivious to just how stuck we were in our own town. Idiots.

By then I knew how entrenched we were. Clara knew, too. We both had felt the darkness's clammy hands guide our own. We'd both seen beyond Eden's borders. And yet our shared experiences were what drove us apart. She welcomed the tasks and was always searching for ways to get further tangled in the

Devil's embrace. I, on the other hand, was always quietly hoping to squirm my way out.

Never had I truly tried.

Then Redd Winter came into my life.

Redd is here because I brought her. I knew from the moment I began to look for her out in the Beyond that I was leading her to her death. I did it for Eden. For all of us. But now…now my stomach roils at the thought of what will happen if she's forced to stay.

I need time. I need to get the Council to agree to plant the Eternity Flower in the Beyond before there is any talk of feeding Redd—body and soul—to Eden.

"What are these?" Redd slurs her words as she eyes the manacles.

I open my mouth to speak, and Deception narrows her beaded pupils at me. Deception needn't remind me: I know that Redd will not heed my warning, will not understand it.

"Redd." I want to say *run!* but the word dies on my tongue. Redd has no chance of escape. Not now. Plus, I've already made Grandfather wary with my actions. He will only listen to my arguments about the flower if he trusts me. And he will only trust me if he knows I want what is best for Eden.

"Redd," I start again. "They're pretty bracelets."

Grandfather's chin lifts at my response. For the slightest of moments, his reaction pleases me.

Redd's t-shirt and shorts stick to her like a second skin. She studies her encased wrists, the eyes that were so full of intensity only a moment before now dulled with Deception's drug. "They are." She looks up and around her. "And so is this place. It's beautiful."

Of that, there is no doubt. Eden is not beautiful; it's magnificent. Above us, the stars glitter in the onyx sky. Below us, the orange algae flutters like flames under the water of the pond we call the Fire Pit, mist hovering above the surface like smoke. The heavy white blooms of Eternity Flowers crowd the banks of the pond as well as the river that winds through the dense forest and into the village. Even Deception is a sight to behold, her black serpentine body swaying, a jagged line of teeth lining her maw, bright algae hanging from it like a beard.

When I was a child, this beauty was enough for me. This *place* was enough. As I wish it would still be. I love Eden above all else. And yet I despise what I must do to prove that love.

Redd shakes her head. "It's so gorgeous, John. It's even better than you described."

"We must be getting back." Grandfather announces. "There are plans to be made."

The Master turns to my grandfather. "Indeed, Dyonis. Make your plans." He laughs and the air shimmers until he's no longer there.

Redd blinks at the spot where the Master stood. "This place really is magical," she breathes, her voice full of wonder.

Deception disappears under the surface with barely a splash. I hold out a hand to help Redd further onto the riverbank. She wraps her fingers around mine, the chain on the manacles clanking against the metal cuffs. Even after being in the cool water for several minutes, her skin feels hot to the touch.

Grandfather watches stiffly as the hellhounds approach Redd. Chaos greets her with a green tongue to the face, while Evil and Fury sniff. She pats and scratches Chaos, grinning as the hound's fur changes color with each movement.

"I thought he was a monster, but now that I really see him, he's…he's amazing," she says. Already her eyes are clouding with mischief.

"Chaos!" I scold. "Enough!"

The hound steps back and whines his disappointment. Redd shakes her head. "You might be amazing, Chaos, but you're also a stinker."

"Come along…" Grandfather hesitates before saying her name. I know it's because Dare blood runs through her veins. It is almost impossible for him to address a Dare without cursing.

Redd misunderstands Grandfather's hesitation. "My name is Redd. Redd Winter."

"Winter. Odd choice of a name." A muscle ticks in Grandfather's jaw. "Come along."

"Can I…" She blinks at Grandfather, a troubled frown forming on her lips as if she can't remember—not unusual for someone drunk on Deception's breath. But the frown is gone as quickly as it comes. "I want to meet my mother."

"'Tis late. Any requests you have must wait until morning." He smiles at her, though it is watery. "Have no fear. Your mother will be here when the sun rises."

He whistles at the hellhounds. Evil and Fury follow him as he steps into the fog of the forest, but Chaos stays on the riverbank, his tail thumping against the mud. "Chaos!"

Grandfather shouts. The hound looks up at me, his orange eyes bright in the darkness.

"Go on," I tell him. He hurries after the others.

I look at Redd. "You're here."

"Yeah. I don't know why we came in separately. Why did we?"

Deception has hobbled her memory. We did not simply come in separately. I actively tried to keep her out. I'd taken her mask so she could not enter through the underwater tunnel. So she'd stay safe. And now, if I told her that she was in danger, she would not even listen. Could not listen. I avoid the question and ask one of my own. "How did you get in?"

"I swam." She smiles with such pride it makes my own lips twitch.

"You swam? It takes at least four or five minutes to swim through, Redd. And you had no mask to breathe with."

"My mom..." Her smile falls. "I...I mean Agnes...she trained me to hold my breath. Five minutes. Now I know why: to come here!"

My heart quickens at that. I'd always understood one could only make that passage with a mask. *She could leave.*

My mask and an Eternity Flower are both floating on the rippling surface of the Fire Pit where the river pours into the pond. I pick them up and grab her upper arm, shoving her towards the deep part of the water. Deception's breath might have Redd fooled, but not me. I could drag Redd back to the Beyond.

She looks at my hand as if it's a strange creature. "What're you doing?"

"John!" Grandfather steps out of the fog and back onto the riverbank. "John, what is happening here?"

I stand there, uncertain whether to take a step further into the pond or out of it. Grandfather alone couldn't stop us if we swam into the pond and headed toward the tunnel. But how in Satan's name would Redd swim with her wrists bound? And would she even go with me, or fight to stay?

Devil's curse.

"Redd is a little unsteady on her feet," I tell Grandfather, giving him a knowing gaze. It's not a lie, as she *is* intoxicated from the poison of Deception's breath. I loosen my grip.

Redd eyes me, her brows twisted in confusion. "These flowers," she gestures to the massive white blooms of the Eternity Flower lining the riverbank. "The scent is so...so strong. I can't sense anything else..."

"You'll get used to it," I say helping her off the riverbank. "It's everywhere in Eden."

We follow Grandfather and the hellhounds over the carpet of forest fog toward the village. Above us, birds sing. Their gold and silver feathers shine under the moonlight as they hop from branch to branch. We walk upriver, the sound of the rushing water drowning out any possible conversation. I know this path by heart, every tangled root to step over, every nest to point out, every burrow to peer into. And every evil spot to avoid. As we get nearer the lichen-covered mound that houses the Cave of Dread, my mouth grows dry and my hands clammy. Grandfather passes the giant boulder blocking its entrance without so much as a glance in the direction of the place of torture. I do not follow him directly, but curve to the left, giving the foul cave a wide berth.

Finally, we step out of the fog and onto a grassy knoll dotted with wildflowers and a sleeping flock of sheep. Chaos howls and runs towards the quiet creatures, who bleat and panic at his presence. Evil and Fury play along, hemming them in so the poor sheep have nowhere to escape.

"Stop it," I yell to the hounds. They obey, but the sheep won't be going back to sleep anytime soon.

Grandfather grunts. He continues to lead us toward the village.

A gentle breeze whisks over us and I look at Redd, still wet from the pond. "Are you cold?"

She purses her lips as if she's thinking about it. "I don't think so. I don't know." Then she studies the manacles around her wrists once again and giggles. "These really are pretty."

The ground rises and falls and, there before us, is the village. Moonlight washes away the pastel colors of the buildings, painting the hundreds of thatched, half-timbered homes a silvery grey, their windows glowing. From here, the square is also visible, the gargoyle fountain bathed in a garland of candles, and the white spires of the Devil's cathedral glittering as if made of precious gems.

"That cathedral," Redd gasps.

The ornate building houses the library, the Council headquarters, a gathering hall, and the Master's private sanctuary. Aye, we call it a cathedral. But it is not the place of worship she might understand. Or at least not one to the deity some of those from the Beyond revere.

"So the guy who disappeared like that—" she snaps to make her point "—what's his actual name?" Redd's dark blond waves are beginning to dry, and a strand blows across her freckled face, creating a thin stripe of a mask so much like the Master's.

Belial, Satan, Lucifer, Beelzebub...the names come to mind, but I do not voice them. I am not ready to tell her who he really is. She would not believe me, regardless. Deception has made sure of that.

But I don't need to answer; she's too distracted to wait for a response. Instead, she stage-whispers, "And what's with the superhero mask?"

"The Master has always worn a mask," I say. "Always. We do not question it."

Redd's eyebrows lift in surprise. The truth is that we do not question much of anything. Not only are we taught not to, we instinctively avoid doing so. Because when one asks questions, one gets answers. Here in Eden, it is often better to stay ignorant.

We head down the hill and into the cobbled streets of the village. Even for the late hour, it is unusually quiet. No one is out for a nightly stroll, and no one is drunkenly weaving through alleyways. Grandfather must have pulled his rank as Governor and created an early curfew upon Redd's arrival.

Redd's eyes are wide, an enchanted smile on her face. To her, the village must seem quaint and charming and exotic. We slow our steps so she can get a better look as we follow the sputtering flames of the streetlights until we reach home. The house I share with Grandfather, Grandmama, and Thomas is fat and painted a pale green. Pink rose bushes line the front walk while white

Eternity Flowers sit under the windows. They are planted in front of every home.

"This is your place?"

"Aye."

She looks pointedly at the dark wood of the door where a brass plate is nailed above a knocker shaped like a lion. *Harvie,* is the name engraved into the metal.

"You said your name was John Smith."

I tilt my head. "Harvie. It's John Harvie."

I wait for her to get angry, but instead she laughs, Deception's heady elixir still running through her veins. "I knew it! I knew John Smith wasn't your real name. Dammit. I should have bet with Shay on it."

I wipe my boots on the mat and begin to step over the threshold when Evil pushes past me. He huffs, smoke escaping his nostrils. My stomach turns as I breathe in his sweet odor. I thought I'd overcome the weakness that was growing inside me, but here in an enclosed space, I realize now that it's back. I've been away from Evil for too long. I swallow back bile and wipe a sudden sheen of sweat from my brow, hoping Grandfather won't notice the hellhound's effects on me. It means my heart has softened to a sauce once again. It means I've failed to be the stone-hard man Eden asks me to be.

Redd, too, looks peaked in Evil's presence. The hound snorts, then heads down the hallway. Grandfather stops Redd before she steps into the house. "You follow me."

Before I think to hold my tongue, I ask, "Where are you taking her?"

Grandfather scowls at me. "Her quarters."

He means the holding cell in the root cellar behind our home. Grandfather keeps those who've disobeyed Eden's laws there until the Council has decided their fate.

The sweat upon my brow worsens. Of course. She's a prisoner of Eden, not a guest. I only hope Deception's breath holds sway over her long enough for her to believe the conditions are comfortable.

"Aye," I say, then turn to her. "The lovely guest chamber. You'll like it."

She blinks and smiles as Grandfather leads her around the house.

I close the door behind me. The moment my steps echo in the hallway, Grandmama comes rushing out of the kitchen. She wraps her arms around me and squeezes. "We're so proud of you, son. You did it. You brought the Dare girl back to Eden. You've saved us all."

I stiffen in her embrace, thoughts of sacrifice and Redd ruining the moment of joy. She lets go of me. "I'll get dinner on."

"Nay." I shake my head. "I must speak with Grandfather first."

"But I'm hungry!" Thomas whines, stepping out of the kitchen. "And the food is ready."

"Oh, my poor little brother," I say. "Good thing one cannot die of starvation here."

"Beelzebub's teeth, you're annoying," he says, trying to hide his smile.

The creak and slam of the back door come from behind Thomas. My brother straightens while Grandmama hurries into action and slides past him back into the kitchen.

"Dyonis," she coos to my grandfather, "John would like to speak with you."

"Nay. Not 'til I've had a drink." Grandfather bangs around. When he comes out into the hallway, he has a small earthenware cup and a glass bottle of milky liquid in his hands, and Redd's bag over his shoulder.

"You," he says to Thomas. "Upstairs. We'll call when it's time to sup."

"But—"

Grandfather lifts an eyebrow and Thomas moves. At thirteen, he knows better than to argue, so he simply drags his feet as loudly and slowly as he can as he goes up the stairs.

I follow Grandfather to the great room, where all our discussions seem to be held. My stomach is twisting into knots, but the only outward sign of my fearing our conversation is the sudden appearance of a shiny cockroach scurrying over the floorboards. A Worry. I swallow and look at Grandfather to see if he's noticed. But he's preoccupied with his drink.

He sets the bottle and cup on the small wooden table near his armchair and throws the bag to me. "Get the girl's mask. I need it."

I set Redd's bag down and instead tug the monstrous thing from my own. "Here."

A look of pride fills his face. "You'd already taken it from her? Well done, John."

I do not clarify that I had taken it *before* entering Eden. That she did not need it to get in...nor would she need it to get out.

He heads to a cupboard at the back of the room, the wooden doors latched shut by a demon's tail knotted between the handles. He brushes a finger along the tuft of fur at the end and the tail wiggles then unknots. It is more secure than any lock as it will only open for Grandfather or the Master.

Inside is a deep recess, lined with bits of fur and scarlet streaks of dried blood that come from the Devil himself. There are already a few masks inside. The identities of the owners are confidential, but I do know that among them are Virginia's and Eleanor's. This is the only spot in the village, and perhaps the world, where a mask will stay locked up, away from its owner. He adds Redd's, then closes the doors, the demon's tail knotting itself again after a tap from him. "There. She cannot leave."

"And what of Eleanor and Virginia?" Only hours before I'd been sent on my mission to find Redd, Virginia was brought before the Council for questioning. It was the first time I'd ever laid eyes upon her in person. She crossed the square head held high, back straight, despite the slurs spat at her by those she passed.

"They are not your worry," says Grandfather.

He points me to a tall chair, one that faces the hearth but in no way is comforting, the imps carved into the back poking and digging into one's flesh. As a child, it was the chair Grandfather sat me in for "a talking to" or Grandmama had me stand on to stick pins into fabric for new clothes as I grew. I slide onto the wood, the pointy little faces rubbing against my spine. Despite the roaring fire before me, a slight shiver runs over my skin. This chair is exactly like the one in which I recited the creed over and over and over when I first became a scout. *The price of life is a soul. One life sacrificed saves so many. Love Eden above all else. What we do we do for the good of Eden. The Council and the Devil are your masters. Listen and obey. Listen and obey. Listen and obey.*

"You must know—" I start, but Grandfather holds up a hand. He settles into his massive wooden armchair, pours himself a shot of the liquored syrup, and heaves a sigh.

I hear the clicking of claws on wood and then Evil enters the room, his blue-black fur a shadow in the firelight. The hound settles down at Grandfather's feet. His orange eyes stare up at me, then close as Grandfather strokes the top of his head. Finally, Grandfather tugs at the black rancor Malice pearl hanging from his left ear and levels me a look. "Now. Speak."

"I believe we can save Eden. Save everyone, even Redd—"

"You're on a first-name basis with the Dare girl?"

"You're the one who told me to seduce her."

"And did you?"

I look away. I cannot allow him to see that it was *she* who ended up seducing me. "She is here, isn't she?"

"I almost believe you wish she was not. Do I need to question your loyalty? Again?"

My recent night in the Cave of Dread comes to me, unbidden, and I must take a breath to steady myself. "I am loyal. My hesitation has nothing to do with my loyalty. In fact, I want what is best for Eden. And there is a better way. A way to save this place without further sacrifice."

He grunts and fills his cup again. "This girl will be what saves us. For a very long time."

"But we can be saved *forever*. Agnes was growing the Eternity Flower in the Beyond."

"Agnes? Still alive?" He shakes his head. "Impossible. And growing the flower outside is also impossible."

"I saw her. And I saw the flower."

"You saw who you thought was Agnes and what you thought was the flower. You saw what you wanted to see. You seek to be a good man, John. Then you must understand that what we do...how we survive...'tis good. Or rather...the good outweighs the bad in the end."

"But that is my point, Grandfather. With the Eternity Flower in the Beyond, we could leave Eden. There needn't be *any* bad. I can assure you: I saw Agnes. I saw the flower. I have no doubt."

"Your task was to bring back the girl. You did that. Forget the flower."

"I cannot. I beg of you, it is—"

Grandfather sets his cup down with such force that the liquid sloshes over the lip. His voice grows hard, the volume just above a whisper. "Do you not think that in more than four hundred years we've attempted to grow the Eternity Flower beyond our borders? Do you not think that we looked for a way to move forward without taking another innocent life? Are you so arrogant that you believe yourself the first to seek a way around this?"

"Nay, but the solution has always evaded us. Except now there is a precedent—"

"We have our solution: the girl. Instead of five or ten years, her death will assure us a hundred. The Eternity Flower in the Beyond is simply a wish, John. Not a reality."

"But you're wrong, Grandfather." My words tumble out before I think of what I am saying. I hold back a gasp as his eyes fill with rage. No one questions Grandfather. No one.

A loud scratching noise and a long howl come from the back door. Fury. Grandfather is keeping his anger in check, but I know he is livid for the hellhound to be seeking him out so quickly. Evil leaves his place by Grandfather's chair to see his canine brother.

A purple vein in Grandfather's neck pulses as he stands and moves toward the window. The glass in the panes is wavy, and the nighttime lights outside seem to ebb and flow like water.

He sighs. "What does the girl know of our world?"

The change of topic throws me off guard. I'm expecting immediate push-back, not conversation. I swallow and think. "She's aware Agnes gathered children, though she does not understand why. Agnes told Redd she was her mother, but I convinced Redd to seek visions in the mask for the truth. It was enough to drive a wedge between the two and enough to get Redd to want to meet her true family. I promised she could." I hope my voice does not reveal how much I want to make good on this promise.

He nods. "'Tis how you got her here. Clever."

I'm about to tell him about the other reason Redd was compelled to come—to seek out Minnie's daughter—when Fury's scratching and howling reaches a crescendo.

"For the love of Lucifer," Grandfather swears and stomps down the hallway to the kitchen. I hear the back door open and Grandfather scold Fury in low but dangerous tones. When he comes back to the great room, Evil in tow and a new bottle of liquor in his hands, the only sound from outside is the tiniest of whimpers.

I've gone this far in questioning Eden's ways without severe consequences. I decide I must go further. I must get Grandfather to open his mind to other possibilities. "I understand that growing the flower outside of Eden and sending people into the Beyond may not punish the Dares. But do we really want to keep on sacrificing lives to survive, Grandfather? I know it weighs upon you. It weighs upon us all. We could be free."

"Free." He snorts and takes a long drink of the liquor.

"You've always told me that the only reason we stay put, the *only* reason we sacrifice a life, is because we have no other choice. This would give us a choice, Grandfather. We owe it to the village to see this through. Agnes is alive and well. She still looks young. And Redd...when she did get hurt, she healed rather quickly. All of this is proof that the flower grows well enough to sustain us on the outside. Let us plant it there. That is the first step, Grandfather. I believe we must take it."

Grandfather studies me. The vein in his neck is less evident and his jaw less tense. Absently, he pets Evil, stroking the soft triangle of the hellhound's ear over and over again. "You will not let this go, will you, John?"

"Not if it will allow us to live differently. You taught me to love Eden above all else. This...this would be for Eden. How could I go on without trying?"

"You are doing this for Eden? Or for the girl?"

"Always Eden." I do not finish with *and the girl.*

His eyes are no longer filled with anger, but determination. "Fine. Tomorrow afternoon you may leave. You'll see that the flower will not take root. That you've convinced yourself of a fairytale."

"I need Redd's help. I must recreate exactly how she and Agnes planted the—"

"If you go, you go alone. 'Tis that or nothing."

"Then I shall leave yet tonight—"

"Absolutely not. You've been gone several days. Your body needs time to recuperate. Returning to the Beyond now would hasten your illness, possibly to a dangerous level."

"I'm willing to take that risk—"

"NAY!" His voice is like thunder, his jaw rigid.

I stand silent, swallowing down the lump in my throat. This is his way of telling me he cares. I give one quick nod, and he visibly relaxes.

Had Redd not surprised me by coming into Eden, I would have gone right back out with a flower. Any danger would have been worth it to keep another sacrifice from happening. But I understand Grandfather's worry. "You'll give me time, then? You won't sacrifice her?"

He blinks. "Eden is still in full bloom. She wouldn't be sacrificed until it starts dying, regardless. That could be days or months or years."

"And should Eden begin to wilt tomorrow?"

"You know the Harvest takes some time."

"But will you give me a chance?"

Grandfather's jaw ticks as he stares at me. "This would be a very special ceremony. 'Tis not prepared in a day."

Hope and fear rush through me in equal parts. I'll have a bit of time if so, but in that time I must succeed. "Aye. I understand."

"If that's settled, let us eat." He starts to rise from his chair.

"There's no reason to keep Redd prisoner," I say.

He stops halfway into a standing position, then slowly settles back into his chair. His voice is overly calm. "She won't go willingly to sacrifice."

"But when I've planted the flower, she won't *need* to go to sacrifice. And it could be months or years before a new Harvest. It is not right to imprison her for such a period when she's done nothing."

For the longest time, Grandfather says nothing. The only sounds in the room are the fire crackling and Evil's heavy breaths.

"Her mask is locked away. She cannot get to it." I clear my throat. "There's no reason to keep her in a cell."

Grandfather scoffs. "Still so soft, John. You worry that when the effects of Deception's breath wear off, she'll see her predicament and suffer."

"Eden is not a cruel place, Grandfather. Not when it does not have to be. The Master made this place his paradise. He sees enough suffering in Hell. Remember you just said that the good outweighs the bad here. Show me this is the truth. Show me you're a governor who rules with compassion."

He pours himself another drink, lines deepening in his brow as he thinks. "So you want to allow her to roam Eden, free as any other inhabitant? You want Eleanor and Virginia to go free as well? To get their kin back, regardless of all the chaos they wrought?"

"I want the cycle to end, Grandfather. It is as simple as that."

More silence, then a nod. "The village could use a diversion. For no matter how short a time. But then you shall agree to this."

He makes a clicking sound at the back of his throat. A second later, a scampering noise comes from the chimney, and a squirrel pops out her head. Beady black eyes fixed on me, Secrecy chitters softly as she enters the room, her fluffy tail shivering like a feather-duster.

Grandfather says, "No mention of danger or sacrifice, John. The girl is to know nothing."

I nod, then feel a tugging at the back of my tongue and Secrecy's cheeks puff up as though she's been gathering nuts. She scales the wall to escape through the open window.

My throat tingles, but the sensation will go away soon enough. I know because it's not the first time Grandfather has bound me to Secrecy.

Grandfather stands. "Tell your grandmother to set another place at the table. I'll go fetch the girl."

A grin spreads over my face as he leaves the room.

And here I thought miracles did not happen.

3

Redd

Eden: Present Day

The guest room is probably the most beautiful place I've ever stayed in. It's all lush velvets and velour, satins and silk. Pink and pastel green tones make up the décor, like private rooms for royalty. There's a dressing table holding a fancy antique porcelain bowl and pitcher, a gilded mirror hanging above it. The giant four-postered bed sits under a canopy of tasseled drapery. I sink down into the mattress. It's soft and giving under my weight. From the multi-paned window high up in the wall, moonlight shines down onto me, licking the golden bracelets on my wrists. But when I look down at them to admire the craftmanship, something about them niggles...

My head starts to swim and the room goes blurry around the edges. I feel drunk. Or possibly high, though I've never been, so have nothing to compare it to. God, I must be more exhausted than I thought. I begin to lie back to rest my head on the pillow, but before I can, the air before me grows dark with smoke.

A second later a man—the one they call Master—is standing before me.

"Hello, Redd." He turns in a circle, taking in the sight of the room. In the moonlight, his naked back looks like a battlefield compared to the smooth skin of his shoulders. Two long lines of nasty scars reach from his shoulder blades almost down to his waist. He's wearing nothing but trousers, black boots, and a dark strip of a mask stretching over the bridge of his nose. His perfectly tousled hair is streaked with blond, red, and black and grazes his shoulders. His lips curve into a smile, and I can just make out the top of an eyebrow sticking above the mask. The fact that he's wearing a mask should put me on edge, but it doesn't. It isn't scary.

I feel safe here. In Eden. With him.

I try sitting up straighter, but my whole body feels like Play-Doh.

"May I?" He motions to a spot a couple of feet away from me on the bed. I nod. As he sits, the mattress dips. The ever-present scent of the Eternity Flower is now replaced with his own personal perfume—winter wind, charred earth, and fall leaves. With my sixth sense, I get nothing from him.

"What's your name? What should I call you?" I ask, my words slurring slightly.

"Everyone in Eden calls me 'Master.'"

"Master is an odd name."

He laughs. It's a laugh made of silver. Of glitter. Of tinsel. Of everything shiny and festive and cool. I want to listen to it forever. "I have many names. All of them odd. But here it is Master."

Whatever. If that's what floats his boat. "Okay."

"How do you like Eden so far?"

"It's beautiful."

He tilts his head just so, and a soft ray of moonlight makes his eyes gleam. They're dark and deep and absolutely freaking amazing.

"I must admit I could have kept everything easy," he says. "But Chaos is not the only one who likes to stir up trouble. And my coming here will make the next day or so very, very interesting. It is an affliction of the modern world and I have spent too much time there: we must always be entertained." He reaches over and knocks one finger on my temple, the way my friend Shay does to her brother when trying to get him to see sense. "Look around you, Redd."

I do. I see the beautifully decorated bedroom. See the latticed window. See the golden bracelets on my wrists. "I am. It's gorgeous."

"Nay," he says, his voice harder. "Look again."

I blink and the room has transformed. I'm in a basement, lit only by moonlight that barely makes it through the tiny, dirty window high in the packed-dirt wall. The dressing table and chair are really two dusty wooden crates, and the mirror a battered copper pot hanging from a rusty hook. What seemed like a four-poster-bed is actually a cage, the mattress a thin, lumpy thing stuffed with hay. But what shocks me the most are my bracelets. They're not bracelets at all; they're giant, old-fashioned handcuffs, the chain between them thick and heavy.

Panic makes my breath catch and my chest ache. "What the hell is this?"

The Master nods. "Now you see it."

"I don't understand. Get me out—"

The sound of a bolt sliding shuts me up. The Master sighs. "Ah. Not enough time. I'll have to have my fun another way. Yet now you may get glimpses from time to time. And use your blood-ties, Redd. You're stronger than this; Deception should never have gotten one over on you."

"What? What are you talking about? Help me out of these!" I lift my wrists. But it's too late. The air shimmers and then he's gone.

The door opens. Dyonis stands there, an annoyed look on his face. "Come and sup with us."

Anger spikes through me but I'm still woozy and so it doesn't have the kind of power it normally would. "What's going on, here? Get me out of these cuffs!"

Dyonis stops short in front of the cage, skeleton key out. I see his Adam's apple bob as he swallows. "Eden's beautiful," he says slowly, carefully. "You are safe here."

"If I'm so damn safe—" Wait. What was I going to say? My brain feels as foggy as Eden itself. I take a breath, trying to calm myself. Why am I so tense?

Everything goes dark for a second and then Dyonis is taking some bracelets off my wrists—"we'll need to get those polished"—and leading me out the door, up some stairs and into the night. "We'll sup and then move you to a different chamber. A better one."

"Oh," I say. I kind of liked that room.

He leads me to another door. This one has warm, yellow light spilling out of the small window.

"How are you finding Eden now?" Dyonis asks me as he turns the knob.

I nearly trip on the flagstone threshold, and giggle at my clumsiness. I can't keep the smile off my face. "Beautiful," I say. "Eden's just beautiful."

4

Eleanor

Eden: 1590

We built our own cottages when we arrived, laid stones for cobbles and designed a magnificent building reminiscent of a cathedral, though its glittering stone would never reach the Lord's eye. Our labor had been minimal as devilry was magic, and Eden provided everything with ease. What should have taken years to create took only weeks and the village already looked like an established town, complete with a bubbling fountain, a footbridge, simple paths, and a sprawling farm. To the east of the heart of the village, the river rushed furiously over rocks and roots and boulders, the glorious white blooms of Eternity Flowers lining its banks. The river led into the forest, where the trees were dense and gnarled, the wildlife abundant. A blanket of mist covered the spongy ground until the whole of the forest became tinged orange from the glowing water of the Fire Pit where the river spilled like smoke into its mouth. To the west of the village was a series of rolling hills.

Six months after the sacrifice, I could no longer stand the hateful stares of the others, nor the mournful look on Dyonis Harvie's face. I left the village to build my new cottage as far from the Fire Pit as possible. Emptying my home of my meager belongings, I led Virginia up the western hillside. It was late spring. The winter in Eden had been beautiful but odd. Snow had fallen in feathery clumps and the pond became a slick of ice, but the temperature had not gotten near freezing. The trees had gone bare of leaves, but not of fruit, and while most of the flowers had closed into tight fists, the Eternity Flower still bloomed, glittering with frost and dusted with snow.

But while winter had been pretty, the nearing of summer here was glorious. Small buds were bursting into giant blooms, and the leaves on the trees were such a bright shade of green they looked painted on. The birds that had been lethargic and mournful over the winter now stirred in spring, their songs growing louder and longer as the season wore on. Young saplings provided a thin layer of shade in the morning sun, its brightness made more prominent by the shimmering haze that seemed to always surround Eden. My sweat dampened Torment's fur, his body snug around my neck, and ran down the knobs of my spine. It slickened the palm that held Virginia's as the heat grew. We walked higher into the hills and came across an expanse of land that I'd never seen before.

When Virginia's life had been threatened, I'd searched every bit of Eden for a way out. I'd explored the hellish paradise from one end to the other only to find it ringed in an impassable wall of fog. Eden had simply ended.

But now it seemed that the renewal of life brought with it acres of new land. A plateau of wildflowers abutted a rise in the hills, where caverns and cliffs overlooked the village below. Behind that, the clouds themselves created a cottony impasse. I chose a spot among bluebells where water trickled from the rocks and meandered through the weeds down the hill until it spilled over the side in a torrent directly into the river below. Instead of the sickly-sweet scent of the Eternity Flower, the air smelled of grasses. I could almost trick myself into believing I was in a peaceful meadow back home in England and not here in an unknown place right under the Devil's thumb.

As Virginia chased after butterflies, I gathered long sticks to build the wattle. The work should have been grueling; my hands should have been chapped, my back sore, my thighs aching. But each time I threaded one stick through the frame and twisted it around like rope, twenty more were suddenly layered beneath it. Timber cut like butter, and stakes sunk effortlessly, as if pulled into the ground.

I'd gotten three walls together when the Master appeared from a ripple in the air. "My dear Eleanor, why have you left the comfort of the community?"

"'Tis no comfort. Not for the likes of me."

"Ah." He smiled, the curving of his lips suggesting sympathy. "They have yet to forgive you."

"They will never forgive me. Just as I will never forgive you."

"I do not need your forgiveness."

"Good. You'll never have it."

"Oh, come, Eleanor. Stop blaming me for your choices." He saw me bristle at his words and laughed. "The others lie to themselves. They think they hold the moral high ground. Yet, I can assure you, any one of them would have done the same had it been their own child to be given to Eden."

He ran a hand through his mane of tresses and tipped his face to the sun. As always, a band of leather masked the bridge of his nose and around his eyes. "Such a lovely day."

"Too warm for my taste," I said, wiping sweat from my brow. In truth, I enjoyed the heat. I liked how it made my skin tingle and my breath slow. In a place where I often felt deadened, it made me feel alive.

Yet my hatred of the Master made me disagree on even the pettiest of things.

"That so?" His lips widened into a grin. "And now? Is it more to your liking?"

A cool breeze fanned my face and danced over the field. Goosebumps rose on my skin. I shook my head. "Too cold."

He chuckled. It drew Virginia out from where she was playing in the tall grasses and flowers.

"Master! Master!" she shouted. My stomach plummeted at the sound of joy in her voice. It was the same each time he came around; the sight of him filled her with happiness. She released a butterfly she'd caught in her hands and ran directly towards the Devil, arms outstretched.

I threw my hand out and grasped her dress as she passed. She stumbled backwards before reaching Lucifer. He raised a pointed eyebrow above his mask when I lifted Virginia and hugged her to my chest.

"Why are you here?" I asked him.

"I thought you could invite me in for a drink."

"I haven't four walls, let alone a tankard of ale."

"Not so." And with a flick of his wrist, my unfinished cottage became a proper home—the walls daubed and white-washed, the roof thatched, and the windows fitted with shutters. The Master's magic was different, more powerful, than the kind any of us villagers could wield here. While we were limited to only growing or expanding our resources, he could create something from nothing.

Inside the newly erected house were three chairs and a table, cups and a fresh pitcher of ale, waiting alongside a platter of bread and cheese. Virginia squealed and climbed onto one of the chairs, her pudgy legs swinging back and forth as she waited for me to serve her.

As I poured her a cup of ale, the Master strolled inside, his demeanor at ease. "Leave us," I told him, my voice as hard as I could make it. "Go torture other souls."

His laugh boomed throughout the room. "This is why I enjoy your company, Eleanor. Because you still pretend you have power over your life."

Torment dug his teeth further into my skin. I welcomed the discomfort.

The Master filled his own cup and ripped the heel off the bread. He stuffed it between his perfect lips then tore off another piece for Virginia. She beamed up at him. I snatched the bread from her fingers, and as her mouth began to turn down into a frown, I handed her a new piece, one unsullied by the Devil's hands.

That just made him laugh louder.

He then took a swig of ale and grimaced. "The taste of your anger is ruining the ale, Eleanor."

I lifted my cup as if to toast him. "May you choke on it."

With a snap of his fingers, several Eternity Flowers sprouted up in front of the windows, and a tall potted one appeared in the room, filling the air with its powerful scent. He poured himself more ale and took a long drink. "Better."

"Better!" Mimicked Virginia, finishing her cupful.

I left mine untouched. I was no longer thirsty. And my ale would taste foul regardless, seeing as it came from him.

He sighed as if he thought me dramatic. "So, shall we discuss the village?"

When I did not answer, he followed up with, "I've decided to let you all govern yourselves."

Now it was my turn to laugh. "How big of you."

"The others have already begun organizing a Council. You should be on it."

"I want nothing to do with governing this hellscape."

He leaned forward and took a curl of Virginia's hair between his fingers. My lungs grew tight as he tugged it, ever so gently. Virginia giggled. "If you have no say in governing, then you have no say in what is fed to Eden." He turned his black gaze to mine. "*Who* is fed to Eden."

I had been reaching for some bread, but my hand stilled in the air. "I saved Virginia."

"Aye." He nodded. "You saved her once. The question is: Can you save her again?"

The first Council meeting took place in Dyonis Harvie's home.

Dyonis had built a manor house with the kitchen to the back, the living areas near the front, and sleeping chambers above. It had been completed before Walter's death, and back then he'd waxed on about the future and founding a new family. It was his dream to have dozens of children running around and a wife to raise them right. He still missed his Margery but had wanted another companion. In the early days of Eden, before that fateful night, his smile had found me often. Often enough that I knew he'd considered it possible that one day we'd make this our home together.

Now, however, when I knocked upon his door he spit in my face and cursed me. Evil sidled up next to him and my heart pinched at the sight of the beast. Evil used to be my friend. Now it seemed he had taken to Dyonis Harvie. He growled and snuffed out a stream of gray smoke. I narrowed my eyes at the hound. It was enough to send him back into the bowels of Dyonis' home.

I stood straighter. "I'm here to put my name forward for the Council."

"Nay. You've no place here, foul witch." He glared down at Virginia, who was hiding her face in my skirts. "You or her."

"The Master himself insisted we make our way down here." The words brought a flash of anger and fear to his eyes. I tucked my hair behind my ear, revealing the crescent mark of the Devil's fingernail near my jawline. "Or would you go against the Master's will?"

The hatred in Dyonis' eyes burned brighter. He tugged upon the Malice pearls hanging from his ears but swallowed and stepped back to let me inside.

It was the first time I'd used the Master's name to influence another. The first time I'd drawn attention to the fact that I seemed to be the Devil's favorite. Bile rose in my throat as I did so, but so did a twisted sense of pride. I hated Satan with every fiber of my being, and yet I realized he was my sole protector.

"You stay here," I told Virginia. She sat on the long bench in Dyonis' hall, hugging Sloth to her chest. The cat was a massive lump of violet-colored fur and shiny black claws. All manner of creatures roamed about Eden. Sloth was a favorite of Virginia's, as he could sleep through anything, allowing her to carry and play with him as if he were a doll. Apart from the Powell's babe who was still in swaddling, Virginia was the youngest child in the village. She was also the only girl, so she spent more time with Eden's pets than she did the other children.

I followed Dyonis down the hallway. He obviously did not use his magic to clean, as dark spots of Contagion stained the corners of the ceilings. Contagion spread everywhere if one did not scrub it away daily. Its musty smell permeated lesser-used rooms and seeped into everything, like damp used to do back in England.

The din of conversation echoed through the house, abruptly stopping the moment I arrived in the great room. The villagers crowded inside blinked at my presence before hatred drained the color from their cheeks. Only Emme and Elizabeth gave me softer looks, pity shadowing their brows as I caught their eyes.

Twenty-four of the twenty-six village adults were in attendance—Winefrid Powell and Joan Warren had stayed back to watch the children. Dyonis called the start of the meeting and asked those who wished to be on the Council to put their names forward. A bitter debate ensued before six of us were finally agreed upon. It was we who would decide the rules of this new society, make the laws, grant titles, mete out punishments. Back in England, Queen Elizabeth was ruling with an iron fist, and so here, too, the women wanted into the game. Though my place was gained easily due to fear of the Master's reprisal (Griffen Jones was forced to cede his seat to my demand), the seats that Elizabeth Glane and Emme Merrimoth occupied were hard-won. Every man—even beetle-brained Humphry Newton—thought himself above the female sex. But it was the women who bore children...and children who kept Eden, and us, alive. Therefore, some of the seats were reserved for females.

The most powerful position was that of governor, the leader of the Council, who had final say in any decision. Dyonis, it was decided, would hold that position, here as he did in Roanoke. Yet Eden was nothing like Roanoke. The tightly-knit web of fear that had been cast over us all since the sacrifice had now begun to loosen. We were comfortable. Well-fed. Safe from attack. Drought and war were no longer our concern. Because of this, we could envision a better future.

"But for how long?" asked Jane Pierce. "How long before we must give another child to Eden?"

The questions snapped that net firmly around us once more.

She crossed over to the window and looked out the honeycombed glass. A braid of blonde hair tumbled out from under her coif and over her shoulder, the reddish light of the setting sun painting it fiery. "We'll wake one morn and this—" she waved her hand to indicate the lush trees and grasses outside "—will be dried up. How do we know when that will happen?"

"We must understand the cycle," said Cutbert White. His lips twisted around a meat pie, one of many that Winefrid had sent along with her husband in lieu of her attendance. Cutbert, being the glutton that he was, had already eaten half of them.

I shook my head. "I'd venture there is no set cycle. The Master takes pleasure in our unease. He knows we can never fully relax with the threat of sacrifice lurking over the village."

"That would make sense." Cutbert nodded and wiped the grease from his mouth. "Yet we must be prepared."

"Or...unprepared," added Emme.

Eyebrows shot up in confusion all over the room.

"Mayhap the Master wouldn't ask for a sacrifice if there was none to be had."

"What exactly are you suggesting, Emme?" Dyonis asked. We'd dispensed with formal address between adults weeks earlier, when the Devil had told us he'd had enough of the *Mistress so-and-so* and *Master something-or-other*. He was Master. The only master in Eden.

"That without children we cannot offer youth to Eden. Simple as that."

We all shifted on our feet or in our chairs. Lewes Wotton looked aghast. "This is meant to be our paradise. I'll not sheathe my rapier. No Council can make me do so."

"Rapier?" Dyonis looked pointedly below Lewes' beltline. "You mean to say your half-sword?"

The room erupted in laughter, but the giggles and guffaws stopped just as suddenly as they had come upon us. Dyonis' face slackened in shock, and I knew he was appalled with himself for being able to make a joke when his son had died so horribly only months before.

"It could work," Emme continued. "Eleanor snatched away any chance of reversing our pact with the Master yet in doing so she also proved 'tis possible to alter that pact."

"No children to offer could alter the pact again," said Lizzie Viccars. "Or...it could bring us quickly to our deaths."

"A solution that could be for the best," Jane posited.

That raised hackles; after everything we'd done so far, after all the fighting, all the disease...after Manteo's death, after Walter's death, was it right to wish for death now? But it was easy to talk of no longer offering sacrifice or of giving in to death. Talk is always easy.

'Tis the doing that is the hard part.

"Regardless, 'tis a moot point, as we have children among us already." Christopher Cooper lifted a thick eyebrow. "When the time comes, which child will give his life for Eden?"

All eyes turned to me.

My voice was steel. "Nay. Not Virginia."

Edward Powell's voice came from the back of the room. "Virginia is the natural choice: the one the Master asked for in the first place."

His words were true enough and held no real malice. Yet as the room erupted into a boom of agreement, my blood boiled.

I would allow no one to threaten Virginia. I lifted my chin and sought Edward's face in the crowd. "One might say your newborn, Samuel, is the natural choice. For he's the youngest, and 'tis youth that Eden craves."

Edward stepped forward until he was directly in front of me, his hands fisted as if ready to strike. "I won't see him drowned."

Emme put a hand on the man's shoulder. "The Council will decide the sacrifice when the time comes."

"And will that choice be respected?" Edward asked, his glare burning through me. "Or will Eleanor drown whomever she sees fit?"

Though I had not put on my foul mask since the night of the sacrifice, the pull of its evil strength was constantly tugging at my soul. And now I gave into the temptation to use fear as an ally.

"Aye," I said, my voice steel. "Mayhap I will."

The collective gasp that followed brought a bitter smile to my lips. I would never be forgiven for my act. I would never be liked or cared for again. But I could command respect, no matter how begrudgingly it was given.

There were more insults thrown. We were not strangers to death; our arrival at Roanoke had acquainted us intimately with the Reaper. However, it was one thing to lose loved ones to unforeseen circumstances or hardship. It was quite another to choose a loved one to murder. We were new to it then, so our guilt was natural, expected. Yet even after decades...after centuries...the task never came easy. No matter how much we told ourselves it was for the good of all, sacrifice would always be accompanied by a heavy sense of guilt. The Devil made sure of it.

The anger in the room was enough to get Fury scratching at the door. But once the ruckus died, Dyonis took control of the meeting and dismissed all those who were not on the Council. We were to stay and write up a draft of village rules.

Though Dyonis kept his stance tall and his tone firm, the truth is we were all on unsure footing when it came to creating a semblance of society here in Eden. What would be the consequences of certain acts in a place where physical pain and death were off the table? In fact, was violence even a crime if a knife in the gut was only a problem because of the stain it would leave on one's chemise? The sole way to die was to be sacrificed. Yet there are worse things than death; the constant weight of guilt in my heart andTorment on my shoulders were proof of that.

We were still discovering Eden's intricacies. We had yet to spend any time in the Cave of Dread or the Garden. No one had been sucked into the quagmire where Misery made his home. And even fewer had been caught longer than a day or so in an Enticement's web. We understood that the definitions of crime and punishment on our official documents would change many times over the centuries to come, so to start off, we kept things simple.

As for the sacred covenants of marriage or baptism...or the sins of adultery, fornication, and lack of attendance in religious service? Did they matter in a place where God did not exist?

Our old beliefs could not be shed as easily as our pasts.

While our deity had disappointed, we could not altogether dismiss what we'd understood as God's rules. In a world where one's future rested upon the birth of babies, in a world where the men outnumbered the women by two to one, fornication was encouraged. Pregnancy out of wedlock was nothing to be ashamed of. Marriage could come after. However, the bond between husband and wife was still a sacred partnership, and a way to carry on the family name. Adultery would not be punished, but it would be frowned upon—even if we were now baptized in the Devil's blood. We may have been godless, but we were not completely without morals. It was, we decided, what made society tick.

Truth be told, it was heady to decide how others should live their lives. Halfway through the meeting, the Master's songbird, Conceit, perched on the windowsill. His iridescent feathers puffed up, his glittering beak parted, and he regaled us with a song. Already, this nascent form of the Council fed him well. He grew fat on our self-importance; so much so, that when he took off, his weight troubled his flight.

We were idealistic, still hopeful that we could make Eden the paradise we'd dreamed of. And we were convinced we knew how. After forming a rough set of rules, we made a covenant to keep the details of what was discussed in the Council between us.

From the open window, Secrecy scampered into the room. Tail twitching, she watched and listened, never blinking those ink-black eyes, gathering our words. By the time she left, her cheeks were bulging.

I could feel it, like a pin at the back on my tongue—all of us on the Council were now bound to the beast. We could not betray the confidences that took place when we met.

When the Council finally parted ways, I gathered a sleeping Virginia from the hallway, leaving Sloth to snore alone. She settled into my arms with a soft sigh, her head nestled into the crook of my neck, under Torment's chin. I started the trek through the village and up the hills to my home. The stars were brighter than any lantern, the moon a glowing orb. My path was lit by the shimmering veil of mist that hung in Eden.

Before long, I heard the swooshing of footsteps in the long grasses behind me. Elizabeth and Emme were rushing to catch up. They glanced furtively back at the village as I stopped.

"Afraid you'll be seen with the infamous Eleanor Dare? As far as I know, we made no rule against talking to the village outcasts. Unless you all created an addendum after I left," I said.

A glimmer of embarrassment flashed over Emme's round face, but Elizabeth was unruffled. "No addendum. But 'tis true, being near you is not a good look as of late."

"Was it ever?" I asked, stroking Torment's fur. The two women laughed.

"We'd like to talk." Elizabeth stated.

I hesitated. Eight months earlier, these women were good friends. We'd gossip over glasses of perry, dig in the river for Malice pearls, or play cards until late into the evening. But since the night I traded Walter's life for Virginia's, they'd not once shared more than fearful looks with me. I knew what I had done was not only bad, it was unforgivable. Yet the Master had been right; the others were fooling themselves if they thought they wouldn't have done the same. It would only take a moment's introspection to make that clear—something no one in the village dared attempt.

"Fine," I said, turning back to climb the slope to my cabin. "I'll pour us some perry."

We hung our coifs and cloaks and I tucked Virginia into bed. Once the glasses were filled with the pear liqueur, Emme leaned forward, her heavy breasts pressed against the wood of the table, her copper curls shining in the brightness of the lantern. "We'd...we'd like to make amends."

My heart expanded so fully, I thought my ribs might crack. I missed these women. Oh, how I missed them.

Elizabeth tucked a long strand of dark hair behind her ear. She sat tall in her chair, thin and willowy where Emme was round and stout. "I know the heartache of losing a child. I lost three already back in England. 'Twas the reason my husband left me."

It was something she'd never shared before. I knew that her husband had vanished. That she'd been left to struggle on her own and came to Roanoke as a servant for Minister and Mistress Payne—neither of whom were in Eden, thank the Devil.

I swallowed down my bitterness. "If you know, then why did you judge me so harshly for saving Virginia?"

She shook her head. "You are still the one who got us into this predicament, Eleanor. And the sight of you...you...drowning little Walter..." Tears filled her eyes. She sighed and started again. "'Tis a sight one does not forget."

Emme cleared her throat and gazed blankly at the wall. I imagined she was trying to scrub the memory from her mind as one tries to scrub dirt from a doorstep.

"Does anyone else in the village feel they can forgive?"

The blush that rose in their cheeks told me all I needed to know.

They were alone in their ability to forgive me. But there was something else they were not telling me.

I took a sip of perry, its sweetness clinging to my lips. "I sense a caveat."

They shared a glance. Elizabeth looked me in the eye and said, "Any friendship between us must remain secret."

I could not help but laugh—a sharp, biting laugh that was usually reserved for the Devil himself. "Oh. I see. My treatment bothers you enough to offer me pity, but nothing more."

"Because of the Master, your role in ruling the village came with ease, but you saw the fight we had to put up. We cannot do anything that might jeopardize our places on the Council. Dyonis would not deal well with our acceptance of you."

I downed the last of my perry and stood. I wanted to hug them and cry and bring them back into my life, whether it be under the shadow of secrecy or out in the open. I had never been a solitary creature; these past weeks of ostracism had been slowly grinding my soul to dust. But stronger than any of those desires was my pride. It was a snarling beast living inside me.

I tore their coifs and cloaks from the pegs on the wall and shoved them toward Emme and Elizabeth. "If you cannot come here in broad daylight with the whole of the village knowing, do not come here at all."

"I pray you, Eleanor," Emme reached for me, her stubby fingers settling on my shoulder. "You needn't suffer loneliness for eternity."

I pushed them out the door, shutting it firmly behind them. When I turned, Virginia was standing near the hearth, rubbing her eyes.

"Mama," she said. "Can't sleep. Hold my hand?"

My hurt and rage at Emme and Elizabeth's words dissipated immediately. I tucked my daughter into bed, kissed her forehead, and lay next to her, wrapping my long fingers around her small ones.

I needn't suffer loneliness for eternity, I thought. *I needn't suffer it at all. I have company; I have Virginia. And she'll always be mine.*

5

John

Eden: Present Day

Though we break our fast in the kitchen, the other meals of the day are taken round the heavy oak table in the dining hall. Having sped down the stairs the moment Grandmama announced it was time to sup, Thomas is there with us now, stealing a slice of lamb from a warming plate. He wipes his fingers on his breeches and stands at attention as Grandfather enters with Redd, affecting innocence. I roll my eyes and gesture to my own chin. *You've got gravy there*, I mouth, holding back a laugh.

He wipes his chin with his sleeve as we all take our seats. His gaze is something akin to worship as he watches Redd unfold her napkin and set it on her bare legs. Thomas has combed his hair for this occasion, but the coppery strands still bend in disarray.

Grandmama introduces herself to Redd. "I'm Isobel, John's grandmother." She tilts her head to Grandfather. "And you've already met my husband, Dyonis."

Redd leans in and says under her breath, "Your *grandparents*?" It takes me a moment, but then I understand the incredulity in her voice. In the Beyond, elders look aged. In fact, in the Beyond they die while still rather young, usually under a hundred years of age, but look as if they'd lived a thousand. Here, elders like Grandfather who are well over four hundred could pass for forty on the outside.

"My dear guest—" Grandfather starts.

"Redd," she insists. Her voice is still slightly murky; Deception's effects have not yet worn off.

"There are rules you must abide by while here."

"Of course."

"Our people get ill when they pass through to the Beyond."

"The Beyond?" she frowns.

"Beyond Eden," I explain.

Grandfather continues. "Our people cannot live outside of Eden. The adults realize what this means, but the children"—he glances at Thomas "—the children do not." Narrowing his eyes at Redd, he adds, "Do not speak of the world outside our borders with affection. Do not torture our children with adventures they cannot attempt. Understood?"

"Uh, yeah. Understood. But John left Eden—"

"Now is not the time to discuss the intricacies of the illness."

Thomas shifts in his chair. "I'm no longer a child, Grandfather. She needn't hide things from me—"

Grandfather silences Thomas with a sharp tone. "No questions, boy. Not a one."

Redd shrugs. "Oh, it's fine—"

But Grandfather cuts her off. "Nay," he says.

Thomas doesn't ask questions, but he can barely sit still, fidgeting as we eat. I know he wants to hear about my mission, about the Beyond, about Redd, but in front of Grandfather and Grandmama he must pretend ignorance as to what really goes on beyond our borders. I will fill him in when we're alone.

Redd looks at him. "You're the brother who's good at cards?"

His face lights up. "John talked about me?"

"He said you beat him at Maw."

"You play Maw?"

I cut in. "She's better at it than you are, Tom. She utterly ruined me."

Thomas smiles as he addresses Redd. "Then I challenge you. After we sup?"

Grandfather scrapes his knife across his plate, the grating sound loud enough to make us all flinch. "Our guest will retire after we've eaten. She's had a long journey and needs her rest."

"Oh, I'm fine, I..." Redd's words die out at Grandfather's stare. Her hand flutters in the air before her, like she wants to reach out and touch him, but she pulls it back and onto her lap. "I guess I could get some sleep."

Once we've cleaned our plates, we all retreat upstairs to our sleeping chambers. Grandmama takes Redd to hers. She and Grandfather sleep in separate chambers most nights, although occasionally when I wake and pass Grandfather's room, the bed will have not been slept in. I'll know if he spent the night with Grandmama or if he snuck off to be with his mistress by what Grandmama serves to break our fast. Warm bread and freshly churned butter means one thing, while cold porridge and bitter ale mean another. Tonight, with Redd sleeping in Grandmama's chamber, Grandfather is forced to share his own.

Soon we are all settled into bed.

Darkness and moonlight press against the windows as I hear the faint echo of Grandfather's snores coming from down the hall.

I pick at a thread on my quilt and gaze at the stars, unable to sleep. A slight creak announces someone's presence in the hall. I sit up, squinting in the dimness to see the door move. My heart drums, imagining Redd entering my room, wild hair tumbling over her shoulders, moonlight shining through the thin fabric of her shift. Every muscle in my body tightens in anticipation. I suck in a deep breath, waiting for her to enter.

But it's Thomas' voice that comes to me in the darkness. "John? You awake?"

My body deflates and I sigh. "Aye. Come in."

I gather my thoughts and wave a hand over the wick in the lantern on my nightstand. A flame sputters and brightens to reveal Thomas in his night clothes, eyes shining with curiosity. He steps inside, carefully shutting the door behind him.

"You want the gift I was to bring back for you," I say, gesturing to my bag.

"Nay." He grins. "Or rather, aye, I do want it. But I'm here to talk about Redd. Tell me everything. Leave out no detail." As he's speaking, he rummages through my bag for the book I bought. It explains how those outside of Eden view our elders' past. In the Beyond, their disappearance is considered a mystery: The Lost Colony of Roanoke. Of all the possibilities as to their fate, none posit a pact with the Devil, so none have guessed at the truth.

Thomas absently pages through, then pauses and clicks his tongue.

"Look at this." He turns the book in my direction. The heading reads: **Virginia Dare: First English Child Born in America.** *Eleanor Dare was with child when she boarded the ship to the Americas. She and Ananias Dare gave birth to a girl on 18 August, 1587...*

Thomas points to a sentence further down the page: *Another baby was born shortly after to Dyonis and Margery Harvie.* Shaking his head, he says, "Grandfather would be furious. They don't even say if it was a boy or a girl. For all that Uncle Walter is a martyr here, he's nothing out in the Beyond."

"Do not let Grandfather see. He's in a foul enough mood as it is."

"Aye. Why is that? You seem to have fulfilled your mission, so why does he act as though a Nuisance has crawled under his collar?"

My own skin itches at the thought of the Master's tiny six-legged pets. I absently rub a hand over my neck. "Because he believes I tried to keep her away."

"And is that true? Did you?"

"I did. But, like most everything of late, it did not turn out as planned."

"You like her. Redd. You like this girl. And Grandfather knows it." He shoves at my feet so there's room for him to sit on my bed. "I've never met someone raised in the Beyond before. She's quite intriguing."

"And beautiful," I add, hugging my knees to my chest and leaning against the headboard.

Thomas nods.

"And headstrong."

"Ah." Thomas smiles. "I can see why you'd fall for her."

"I haven't fallen for her."

He snorts and rolls his eyes in response. We're quiet a moment and then he says, "I heard you and Grandfather talking."

"You eavesdropped."

"I abhor being uninformed. And if I did not eavesdrop, I'd not only be uninformed, I'd be downright ignorant. The little scraps you tell me are not enough to subsist upon."

I laugh, but there is little humor there. "Ever notice Verity has no place in Eden? No one grows fat upon the truth here."

"Ever notice how well-fed Evil and Fury are?"

I swallow. Not only are Evil and Fury well-fed, but so are many others. I once glimpsed Grandfather changing his chemise and saw a Grudge clinging to the skin of his torso. The leech was bloated almost beyond recognition.

Thomas's mouth turns down. "I've never felt I belong here. Perhaps none of us do. It's as though our souls are as stagnant as our aging. Or, rather, our aging once we reach adulthood."

I close my eyes. He's never felt he belonged because he was stolen from the Beyond as a baby, though he does not know that. Luckily for him, he was brought in to populate our community, not to feed it. Yet even if his sentiment is not from being birthed on the outside, he's not wrong. There's a superficiality to our existence here. Aye, we do not die young.

But we also do not live. Not in the way they do in the Beyond. And yet, given the opportunity, would we truly choose such a fleeting existence, no matter how lively, over our own?

Tom pokes me and my eyes fly open. "Is it true what you told Grandfather? That Agnes is alive? That she was growing the Eternity Flower on the outside?"

"Aye."

"And she's been able to live in the Beyond without sacrifice? Could we?"

"That's what I am hoping. I'm unsure if it would sustain us for eternity. But it would give us time. And a choice. We've never had a choice to live any other way."

"I'd give anything for a choice," says Thomas. "I cannot pretend to love it here. Not when I know there is a different world out there. Not the cesspool of a world the Council wants us to believe in, but the real one. Full of skyscrapers and machines and pain and joy and adventure and death. I want to see more of it."

I give him a sad smile, remembering the one and only time he tried to step foot into the Beyond. It was in my early days as a scout, and one of the first times I was to go out alone. As I was preparing a sack, my brow slick with sweat, nerves making my hands shake, Thomas would not stop badgering Grandfather to let him go with. He is so unlike me: I obey without question, always afraid of Grandfather's anger. Thomas, however, often seeks out Grandfather's fury; he's spent many weeks confined to his room with one of the pets, or forced to carry out menial tasks, unnecessary except for penance. This particular day, however, the increasing stack of punishments did not deter Thomas and even Grandfather gave in.

"Satan's scourge, be done with it then! Go on! Accompany your brother. I have warned you, Thomas. The outside world will descend upon you with such violence, I dare say you'll run back with your tail between your legs."

Thomas had terrified me. The moment we stepped through, I knew something was wrong. He fell forward into the reeds, landing on the embankment of mud and sand, moans of agony escaping his lips. Before my eyes, his limbs began to wither.

I was in pain myself, but in the few times I'd left Eden, never had I experienced what Tom was going through. Panic and tears blurred my vision as I rummaged through my bag to gather petals. I squeezed the nectar onto his tongue and, though it slowed the shrinking of his muscles, his eyes were still wild with pain.

"That's enough." I lifted him off the ground.

"Nay! Just a little while longer," he begged. But it would take more nectar than I had with me to ease his suffering. And seeing him in such torment was too much. I dragged him back through the watery tunnel, back to the Fire Pit and onto the bank of the pond. In Eden once again, all pain, all injury disappeared as though nothing had happened. He leaned his head against the rough bark of a naked tree and wept. "I want to go back."

The desperation in his voice nearly brought me to my knees. But I held his shoulders and assured him "one day," knowing that it would never happen.

When we got back home, Grandfather did not belittle Thomas or even ask how it went. Instead, he took one look at our white faces and prepared us both a strong posset. As he put the warm mugs into our hands, he barked, "We will not speak of this to your grandmother. She's enough to worry about. And we all know 'twill not happen again."

We drank before the fire, silent tears running down Tom's cheeks.

I had thought that would end his fascination with the Beyond. But, instead, his interest in the world outside of Eden increased. Those few minutes—no matter how painful—were precious to him.

"Then you'll be leaving," he says now. "To plant the flower."

I nod, my chest constricting. I know Grandfather said Redd would be safe, yet a needle of terror pierces my heart. He agreed, but it was no promise. If I do not come back in time with proof the flower can be planted in the Beyond, Redd will pay the price. And if not Redd, one of the children of Eden.

He lowers his voice. "You do not want her to die."

"No," I say. "I do not."

He rubs a hand over his hair and nods. "That Grandfather is allowing Redd to get to know Eden and not stay locked in a cell is a hopeful sign, John. Will she meet Virginia?"

"If the Council allows it. I imagine it would be rather complicated. She's seen practically no one for eighteen years." I rub my throat, where I can still sense a lingering tingle. "And, of course, Secrecy would be involved. I do not see Grandfather letting her talk freely."

"Grandfather lets no one talk freely," Thomas scoffs. "Clara will be tasked with keeping an eye on Redd in the meantime."

"Aye. We'll have to do our best to keep Clara's claws from sinking in too deep."

"That may prove impossible." He lifts an eyebrow. "Do you think now that you're no longer engaged to her, she'll be partnered with someone else?"

"Most likely. Brian or Henry. Unless one of the older generations asks to wed her."

"Or unless you are able to make the flower flourish on the outside. Then her life—and everyone's—would no longer be based upon so few options. Then the world would be open to us. Damn the Council."

"Shh." I put a finger to my lips but cannot hide my smile.

"I mean it." The joy that lights his face fills my heart, and I know I must succeed at procuring this future without sacrifice and heartache and walls of fog.

Not only for Redd to live, but for Thomas to thrive.

6

Redd

Eden: Present Day

I wake up woozy and disoriented. My head spins and my tongue feels thicker than the padding in my push-up bra. Like a hangover despite me not having gotten drunk.

I'm in a four-poster bed, in a whitewashed room, with thick, polished beams running across the ceiling. Filtered light comes in through the glass of diamond-shaped lead lattice on the windows. Paintings that look like something out of classical mythology line the walls in gold frames, each one with a strange creature as its subject. I blink at them: a mink-like creature with hooked teeth, a massive forest-green lizard barely visible among trees, a tangle of glossy webbing encrusted with spiders that look more like jewels than arachnids.

And then I remember: I'm in Eden. I'm in the town where I was born, the magical town the woman I've always called Mom tried to keep secret from me. I made it. I freaking made it despite her trying to thwart me.

Anyway, this place is amazing. It feels familiar even though I've never been here before. I'd say it even feels *right*, but there's still a teeny-tiny part of me that doesn't quite trust all the perfection. There's a scratching in the back of my brain, like a memory that won't come up. Something that makes me uneasy.

So now what?

I take a deep breath, and even here inside the house, the scent of the Eternity Flower is so overpowering that it gets caught in my throat and nose and nearly makes my eyes water. When I arrived last night, it was like a muzzle on my sixth sense. Even through touch, it was almost impossible to get a true feeling for others' emotions. I wonder if everyone in Eden is extra sensitive like me. Maybe all these flowers are a way to keep that overwhelming sixth sense at bay. A way to be *normal*.

Is that proof I'm here among family?

Hang on, Redd. Before I start dreaming of calling this place home, I've got things to do, like finding my birth mom and Minnie's kidnapped daughter. Then, I'll need answers to so many questions. Like why did Mom—well, Agnes—kidnap any kids in the first place? Are they all here, or only Minnie's daughter, Autumn? And why did Agnes kidnap me from my birth mother and flee Eden?

My whole life, I'd known Agnes was hiding something big. I could taste the lies and fear in her words and actions. And now that I know she was afraid of me finding out the truth, everything should make sense. But it still doesn't. There's something big I'm missing. Something else that played into her terror. I intend to find out what.

Last night, Isobel gave me a linen shift to sleep in. Now, I shove the patterned quilt off my legs and look for my shorts and top. I don't see them anywhere. Instead, there's a chemise, petticoat, heavy blue skirt, and lace-up bodice set out at the foot of the bed. John did tell me and Shay that this place was old-fashioned.

I sigh. *When in Rome...*

There's a basin of water on the dressing table. As I approach, I realize it smells like roses. Finally, some other scent than the Eternity Flower. I wash up and dress. I struggle with the skirt ties but finally get them on right. The bodice, though, is a disaster. I put it over the blouse but can't seem to tie it on in a way that doesn't make me look like I just rolled out of bed.

A quick knock comes at the door, and then Isobel is poking her head into the room. I know she's John's grandma, but she doesn't look a day over thirty. And John's granddad looks not too much older than that. I could see them being young grandparents if John was, oh, *two*...but he's *my* age. Either they have an extremely talented plastic surgeon on call, or their tap water comes from the fountain of youth. Maybe that's part of the magic here.

"Oh! I see you found the clothes. Good." She opens the door further and steps inside, her mouth twisting as she takes in my shoddy dressing job. "Why don't I help you with that?"

She bustles over and starts yanking on the ties of the bodice until it bruises my ribs and somehow manages to both squash and uplift my boobs. "Better." She smiles and smooths out my hair with her hands. "But you're missing your coif."

In record-breaking speed, she braids my hair and wraps it into a flat bun. She picks up a small, embroidered bonnet-like thing that I'd missed from the bed and sets it on my hair, knotting the ties at the back. I turn around and she tugs at the corners of the material hanging over my jawline. Her hand stills as she spies the fingernail moon birthmark. For the tiniest of seconds, I think I can almost sense her emotion, a mix of rage and satisfaction. But the odor of the Eternity Flower gets caught in the back of my nose and makes my heart race.

I sway and she steadies me. "Not used to the stays, are you? They can be rather tight."

One...two...three...four... I count to calm myself, like I always do. *Five...six...seven...* I swipe my hands on my skirt, my sweaty palms sticking to the fabric.

"Aye. There we go." She drops her hands. "Go on, take a look." She nods to the spotted mirror hanging over the dressing table.

I take a deep breath and step closer. A giggle bursts out of me before I can stop it. Isobel frowns and I bite my lip, holding back more laughter. My normal look is wild hair, T-shirts with ridiculous graphics, and cut-offs. Even when I dress up for work, it's a version of the same theme—nicer T-shirts, hemmed jean shorts, waves tamed with a hair band. This...this is next-level weird. I look like I stepped right out of the thirteen original colonies. I look wholesome and innocent. If Shay were here, she'd die laughing. Actually, no. If Shay were here, she'd have a blast dressing up like this. *And* she'd figure out a way to make colonial seem sexy.

"Come, break your fast. Then you may get acquainted with Eden."

"Where are my clothes? And my backpack?"

Isobel purses her lips as I open a door of the massive wardrobe in the corner. But I don't see my backpack or clothes among starched white blouses and petticoats. I shove things around, looking for the creased picture of Autumn as a toddler. It's not there.

There's nowhere else in the room for me to look.

Everything of mine is gone. They didn't even leave me my toothbrush or a pair of underwear.

"I had stuff," I say, trying not to sound as panicky as I feel. "It's all gone."

"I must ask you to stay in the clothing I've given you," Isobel says. "Our way of life is different from yours. 'Tis to be respected."

"Except it wasn't just clothes. There was a picture…" In it, Autumn was a baby with rosy cheeks and corkscrews of blonde curls, but I was hoping her face would jog a memory. When I showed it to John, he *said* he didn't recognize her, but I know that was a lie.

"I pray you, remember what Dyonis said last night. Much of the outside world is not to be spoken of or shared here. Everything will be returned to you when you leave Eden."

I blink and swallow down a sense of unease. *There's nothing to worry about. Eden is beautiful. You're safe here.*

I'm not sure why I'm so bothered by the missing photo if it's not gone forever. And I did know that this place was old-fashioned. I guess I don't like that someone went through my things. "Sure. Yeah. I get it. But I would have handed stuff over. No need to take it without asking."

Isobel never really looks me straight in the eye for long. Her gaze shifts to the side as she responds with a nod. "As I said. All will be returned."

A sudden flash hits and I glance down at my wrists. I can feel the heavy weight of old-fashioned manacles clamped over my skin. *What the...?* Must be left over from a dream. But it makes the hair on the back of my neck stand up.

Time to move on to the good things. The reason I'm here. "I can't wait to meet my mother. Can I do that after breakfast?"

"Not directly after breaking your fast."

"But I've already spoken to Dyonis about it. He said I could see her today—"

"And you shall. But she needs time."

"What? What do you mean?" *Does she not want to meet me?*

"She has not truly been a part of the community for years. She has been...isolated. Secluded. She's barely spoken to anyone since you were taken. You cannot simply show up at her cottage." Again, Isobel's eyes slide off my face to look at my birthmark instead.

"But I thought she knew John went to get me." Panic and anger fuel me to move. I move towards the door. "I'm going to find her. I have to see her."

Isobel steps in front of me, resting a hand on my shoulder. "Have patience, child. You do not want to shock her. Or break her state of mind. Allow the Council the time to prepare her. The news will be given...gently."

Disappointment and worry sit like a boulder on my chest. Does this mean she's unwell? God, did Agnes stealing me away do that to her? "But she's the reason I came here in the first place."

Isobel's fingers squeeze my shoulder with the gentlest of pressure. "You needn't worry, my dear. You will see her. I imagine by the end of the day, you'll find yourself in her arms."

The image brings tears to my eyes. I blink and twist my mouth into a resigned pout. "Okay. But if evening rolls around and I still haven't met her, I'm going to find her myself."

Isbel nods. "Of course. John can introduce you to Eden this morn." Following her down a narrow hallway, I try to get a glimpse into the other bedrooms. John's is one of these. I can't help but wonder what his space looks like. If it's as sparse and old-fashioned as Isobel's or if it's cluttered and modern like most boys'. But the rooms I pass are simple—beds with quilts, candles on the nightstands, no curtains, just shutters to keep out the morning light.

Downstairs is different. Still-life paintings on the walls, silver candlesticks, large bouquets of the Eternity Flower brightening the corners of the rooms. Everything wooden from the doorframes to the mantles to the table legs and chairs is intricately carved with faces or flowers or strange beasts. I pause for a second as we pass a large room with massive wooden chairs and a large carpet. Masks like the one that was in my metal box leer at me from the chimney breast. The cheeks and chin and nose are all worn to a shine, the wood is so used. Wild animal hair of black, white, and red frames the faces and shadows darken the empty holes for the eyes. They are ugly and terrifying, not something you'd normally put on display. But nothing about this place is normal. Case in point, the magical hound named Evil that's curled up on the carpet before the fire, smoke escaping his nostrils with each breath. He opens one eye as we pass, the bright orange iris like an ember in the silvery-black charcoal of his coat. My stomach twists at his look. While Chaos is cute, *this* dog is creepy.

The kitchen, too, is decorated. It's not a huge space, but the beams and brightly painted floral bouquets adorning the ceiling and walls remind me of the rooms pictured in history books. A fire roars in the fireplace, a large pot hanging from chains above it, though, oddly, the place doesn't feel hot or stuffy. There's a cast-iron stove as well as what looks like an old-fashioned bread oven in the wall. For once, a different smell overpowers that of the Eternity Flower: freshly made bread. It's divine. We enter the room and I see there's a nook to my left, where both John and Thomas are sitting at a table piled high with bread and butter and honey and meats and cheeses. They each have a tankard of something in front of them, and as I walk in John sets his down heavily, his eyes round with surprise.

"Redd." His Adam's apple bobs as he takes in my appearance. "You, uh..."

"Good morrow," says Thomas, around a mouth full of breakfast.

John stands, tugging at Thomas' sleeve. Thomas stands, too, and grins, eyes ping-ponging between me and John. John's no longer wearing jeans and a tee shirt. Both he and his brother are in dark brown breeches, stiff jackets, and over that, some kind of vest.

We all sit down. "John," I say. "You're staring at me."

Thomas snorts and then buries his nose into his tankard.

Isobel glares at him and pours me something from a ceramic mug. "I certainly didn't raise my boys to act so poorly."

John's cheeks flush. "I apologize. You look lovely, Redd."

Thomas's eyebrows come together. "You look like—"

"Like a proper young lady," finishes Isobel, her voice hard as steel.

I take a drink of what's in my cup and nearly spit it out. It's extremely bitter, but also kind of sweet and bready. John's lips curve into a secret smile. "Small ale," he says. "Coffee is not drunk much here."

"Orange juice?" I ask.

Now his smile grows wider. "Even less."

The drinks are lacking, but the bread and butter are amazing.

I can tell Thomas wants to ask me things but every time he leans forward and begins to open his mouth, his eyes dart to Isobel and he stays quiet. I think about not letting kids know about what exactly is beyond Eden. After all the years of Agnes keeping the truth about this place secret from me, I'm not sure I'm okay with keeping the truth about the world secret from them.

"So tell me all about Eden," I say to John.

"As I said before, Eden is magic. You cannot create something from nothing, but if the basics are there, you can alter whatever you wish." John gestures to the piece of bread on his plate, which has a bite out of it. He scrunches up his eyes and, all of a sudden, the piece is whole.

I laugh. "Okay, that's pretty cool."

"It comes in handy when Grandmama doesn't make enough. But it rarely tastes as good as the original."

"These boys are spoilt, I tell you. Every day, fresh food from scratch. Such a luxury."

John nods. "True. Most of the neighbors do not bother with homemade. Cutbert White's family has continually conjured their meals for over twenty years!"

"That's why they are always trying to secure a dinner invitation elsewhere. How many times have they eaten here this past month? Four? Five?" Thomas bites a hunk of cheese, then continues, "They have a nose for Grandmama's pot pie. Somehow, they can smell it baking from across the village. We know that on those days they'll suddenly show up to chat not long before we sup. Once they are here, it's rude not to extend an invitation."

"For the love of Lucifer, you exaggerate, Thomas." Isobel's tone of voice is stern, but she's smiling.

For the love of Lucifer. What a weird expression. Why use the Devil's name? I'm about to ask about the phrase, but by the time I open my mouth to do so, I've forgotten why I thought it was weird in the first place.

Eden is beautiful. All is good. You are safe here.

"Can anybody do magic?" I ask. "Can I?"

"It may be difficult since you are not an inhabitant of Eden," Isobel says. "The magic does not take hold straight away."

"You could still try, however." John pushes his tankard towards me. "I'm running low. Imagine it full."

I close one eye. Then the other. *Imagine it full,* I tell myself.

John shrugs as the vessel stays empty. "Ah. Well. It's perfectly understandable that you aren't able—"

Suddenly, ale fills his mug and overflows onto the table. We all jump back as it dribbles into our laps. Isobel gasps. John looks at me, his hazel eyes wide. Then he laughs. "You're a daughter of Eden, no doubt there."

"Ha! I did it! What other things are magic?"

John picks up the bread knife and lifts his chin toward Thomas, who sets his hands facing upward on the table. John drags the blade across the fleshy parts of Tom's palms. The skin splits and blood flows out, thick and red. Thomas lets out a howl.

"Oh, my God—"

But then Thomas laughs and wipes his hands with his cloth napkin. While the cloth stays stained, the gashes disappear, his skin perfect and unscarred. He's still laughing as I cross my arms and scowl at him.

Isobel takes the knife to a large porcelain basin and pumps the handle of an old-fashioned faucet. She eyes it while the pipes gurgle, and then water spills out into a continuous stream. "Do not fret at the boys' theatrics. There is no physical pain here," she says as she washes the blood off the serrated blade. "And wounds heal in less time than it takes to make them."

Thomas nods. "We feel...uncomfortable...but we don't feel pain."

John picks up the cheese knife. "Would you like to try it?"

I look at the blade, not sure I'm ready to test this particular brand of magic on myself. But then I hold out my hand. John wraps his fingers around mine, his grip solid and warm. As the point of the knife pierces the skin of my palm, I suck my teeth, expecting pain. But nothing comes except a sudden feeling of warmth along with a thick ribbon of blood. John wipes it away with his thumb. As he does so, the skin knits together. No cut. No scar. No pain.

"See?" He bites his lip.

"Wow." I scrutinize my palm. John's hand is still on my own. That, along with the discrepancy between what should be there and what isn't, makes me sweat.

John drops my hand, a shadow crossing over his face. "Truth be told, there are places we can suffer." Then he shakes his head and gives me a small smile. "Outside Eden, we feel pain. The first time I went out, when my leg cramped up, I screamed in agony. Now I realize that was only a taste of what pain can be."

"Your grandfather said something about it being difficult to leave. How often do the people here go outside of Eden?"

"Most don't." John's eyes flick to Thomas and then back to me. "There are only a handful of us who travel beyond the borders."

I feel my mouth drop open as I try to imagine, first, never leaving my hometown and, second, never having a headache or a sore throat or stomach cramps. "Does that mean there are people here who've *never* experienced pain?"

John nods.

"Wow, really?" I look at Isobel. "What about you? Have you?"

"The women here are all familiar with monthly discomfort...and the difficulty of childbirth, of course."

"But why would—"

Her cheeks go pink and she hurries to add, "Otherwise pain is not something I know."

"In the Beyond you get hurt all the time, do you not?" Thomas asks me.

"Oh, I don't know about *all the time*. But I can tell you I wouldn't cut my hand without feeling it, that's for sure."

"What about elsewhere? Griffen Jones cuts off his own feet out of boredom sometimes. He says he likes the way it feels when they grow back. Would you do that if—"

"That's enough of that talk, Thomas," Isobel scolds before I can ask any questions. She then turns to John. ""I've already told Redd that she will need to wait to see Virginia until later in the day. Perhaps you can show Redd her birthplace in the meantime. The Council will ring when they're ready for you."

"Aye. Allow me to give you a tour." John stands and holds out a hand to help me up.

"I'm coming with," says Thomas.

"Nay. Your tutor will arrive soon, Thomas." Isobel frowns. "And do not bother your brother."

"Oh, I'm used to Thomas being a bother." John ruffles Thomas' hair. "Come find us once your lessons are done."

As we follow the long hallway to the front door, I whisper, "Does someone here actually cut his feet off?" to John.

He chuckles. "Lunacy burrowed into Griffen Jones' brain years ago. Since then, he does all manner of odd things."

I don't even know how to respond to that. Shay, who is always up for a good horror show, would probably ask to see the spectacle. But just thinking of it makes my stomach queasy.

We step outside the front door. I squint in the sunlight and gaze around me. The village looks different in the daylight, as if its magic is evident. A shimmering golden mist hovers in the air. I reach out, wondering if I can catch the shiny particles, but my hand goes right through them. "What is this?"

"We call it the Veil." John gestures to the glittering air. "We don't know what it is. It simply is."

"So...the magic, this place? It just...is? No explanation?"

"In Eden, one is supposed to accept things without question." Bitterness fills his voice.

I think of all the times I wanted Agnes to answer my questions and all the times she refused or acted as if I was being unreasonable. "My mom...er...Agnes...wanted me to do the same."

"Aye. Agnes was raised in Eden. It is no surprise," he responds. He leads me through crooked cobbled streets, and we walk through the cool shadows of the half-timbered buildings. The homes remind me of rainbow sherbet—all creamy oranges and strawberry pinks and pale limes. With the bright blue sky above, the golden glitter of the Veil dusting the air, I feel like I'm in a fairy-tale snow globe.

"I like your brother," I tell him as we pass under a row of flowering trees.

John smiles. I realize that in the short time I've known him, he hasn't smiled enough. When we were coming to Eden, worry weighed him down. Today, though, it's a different story. I reach out and touch his arm, hoping to sense what he's feeling.

But all I get is the taste and smell of the Eternity Flower.

Which sucks. Without my sixth sense, I don't know who's feeling what. And not knowing...that kind of terrifies me. But I could never read John well. I catch his eye and he smiles again, wider this time. God, I want him to be a decent guy. *Please let him be a decent guy.*

This is how life is for most everyone, I think. Never sure. Always wondering. Praying. Pinning their hopes on soft looks and sweet smiles.

I smile back; it feels like I'm jumping into the unknown.

We pass a few people whose eyes nearly bug out at the sight of me. They stop walking as we stroll by, whispering among themselves. I smile at a dark-haired woman in a starched white coif and get a blink and a giggle in response. A man wearing a full-on lacy collar and velvet jacket raises his eyebrows so high as he looks at me that they nearly touch his hairline. He seems to catch himself, though, and bows his head as we pass.

"Forgive them." John hooks his elbow through my arm in what seems like a protective gesture. "Your being here is quite unusual. We don't get visitors to Eden."

"What? Never?"

"Never."

I think he's exaggerating, but then we step into the village square. A market is set up, with all kinds of food and goods. There are about two dozen stalls, and maybe a hundred people in the square all together. Between the laughter, the shouting, the sound of several musical instruments, and the banging from what seems like a forge just beyond the market, the noise is deafening. But the moment we exit the shadows, the chatter turns to whispers and the whispers to sighs until the only sound is the rippling of water from the fountain.

The villagers step back as we weave through the square. I smile and nod, hoping to get them to warm to me. Somewhere in this old-fashioned village is my family. I want to be welcomed here.

"Aren't you going to make introductions, John?" A young woman behind a stall of fabric leans forward as we pass, her gaze full of curiosity. "Earlier this morn the Governor informed us Virginia's girl was here."

John stops. "Aye. This is Redd."

"Beelzebub's teeth!" The woman gasps. "You share Virginia's likeness."

"Really?" It's almost stupid how happy this makes me. "What else can you tell me about her?"

The woman's face goes pinched. "Oh, I am not one to ask."

John clears his throat, reaches over and plucks some green wool from the stand. Holding it up, he says, "Is this all you have?"

The change of subject seems to relax her. She waves her hand distractedly and the small square of wool grows so that its length spills out of John's hands and onto the display.

John grins. "Redd, meet Jane Newton. Her talent is conjuring from fabric that's already been woven. No need for a loom."

Jane sizes me up once again, then hands me a length of soft blue fabric. As she drags her fingers along it, it quadruples in size. "You can use that as a shawl. The blue will set off the lovely dark brown of your eyes."

I wrap the material around my shoulders. "Nice," I say. "How much?"

"We don't use money here," John answers. "We don't need it."

Jane nods. "At some point the sheep will need shearing so I can gather more wool. John has a way with the beasts. He can come calm them for payment."

"Well, thank you," I say. "It's beautiful."

"I've worked hard at getting it right. Despite what we're told, not everything conjured comes easily." Jane gives me a wide smile and points to the far end of the square. "You should try Michael Myllet's baked goods. They're not conjured at all, not a one. Though his spices may be. Many of us have tried different pursuits over time, but he's rarely veered away from baking, so he's had hundreds of years to perfect his recipes."

"He can't be *that* old," I laugh at the exaggeration and she gives me an odd look.

John's cheeks suddenly rival the red of the strawberries in the next stall. "Perhaps another time, Jane."

As we step away from the stall, I whisper to John, "Was I wrong to ask about Virginia? That got strange."

He shakes his head. "No. But it is highly unlikely anyone will talk about her with you just yet. Not until the Council has set up a meeting between the two of you."

"Well, it's good they don't gossip but still. It's not—"

I don't get to finish my thought because the villagers choose that moment to stop ogling me in open-mouthed amazement and instead come forward, full of excitement. John and I are stopped every two seconds by someone wanting to get a good look at my face. John introduces me to a dozen people, all with names like James or Elizabeth or Mary or Henry. Everyone I greet is young. I'm used to spending most of my time with senior citizens, but there are none in the square.

John's right. No one answers any questions about Virginia. But the villagers in Eden smile at me and grip my hands in greeting like I've just saved their lives.

It's so weird and unnerving...and wonderful. I feel my heart cracking open with each new introduction. The people seem eccentric—the odd clothing, the stiff language—but warm. I know I need to find out the truth about this place, about Agnes, about Virginia, about Autumn...but I can't seem to use my sixth sense, and nothing puts me on guard. Agnes' words of warning seem ridiculous now.

There are only a few kids out. A bald little baby who can't be more than a few months old. John calls him Clarence and tweaks his nose. A girl who's just beginning to walk. A couple of adolescent boys playing tag, jostling everyone as they rush past.

Thomas comes along, his hair a mess, his eyes wide and full of mischief. "I gave Goodwife Warren the slip."

"Of course you did." John shakes his head.

"Let us take Redd to the waterfall!" Thomas bounces on the balls of his feet.

"Redd?" John turns to me.

I'd rather see Virginia than a waterfall. But if that's not possible just yet, I guess it'll have to do. Besides, Thomas is nearly bursting. I've never seen anyone so excited about a waterfall. "Sure. Sounds good."

John leads us away from the square, through several alleyways until the houses are no longer packed together but scattered between fields of wildflowers and vegetable gardens.

We keep walking, the air shimmering in the sunlight. As the last few homes fall behind us and a grassy hill rises in front of us, Thomas looks furtively around him. We're the only ones here.

"Tell me about the Beyond," he blurts out. "What's it like outside of Eden? I want to know."

John groans. "Tom, I've told you already—"

"No. I want the truth." He points to me. "I want to hear it from her. Is the world outside so horrible? Violence and war and illness and death?"

"I...uh..." I lick my lips and glance at John. His look is pleading with me to agree, to tell his little brother that the society I live in sucks. And yeah, in a lot of ways it does. But it also doesn't. "Yep. It's all those things."

At Thomas' stricken look, I add, "But it's also full of love and beauty and fun and adventure."

"I *knew* it," says Thomas.

"You've really never been outside this village?" As magical as this place is, I can't imagine never leaving it.

The two of them share a look I can't interpret. But then Thomas shrugs. "Soon I'll be able to go. I hope."

"You will." John's words are like steel.

We're climbing the hill now, on a worn path through the grass.

"Are you afraid of dying?" Thomas asks.

The question throws me. It's not something I ever talk about with those closest to me, let alone someone I've only met the day before. "Uh…I don't think about it a lot. Or I try not to."

"You don't?" John seems genuinely shocked. I can't sense his emotion, but the look on his face and the tone of his voice spell it out. "I would have thought otherwise."

Maybe, unlike most everyone I've encountered, both he and Thomas talk about it in depth. Maybe it's a thing in the village. They use the same strange expressions, though I can't seem to remember now why I find them weird. Strange wording, maybe? Anyway, there's a structured sense of community here that makes me wonder. "Is Eden home to some specific religion? Are you all part of the same church?"

Thomas snorts. "Not unless you consider small-mindedness and self-preservation a religion."

I lift an eyebrow. "Actually, that sounds like plenty of religions."

"You are quite the cynic," says John, his smile softening his words.

"In some ways." When I was little, Agnes tried different religions. All sorts. She spent time in Catholic confessionals and Baptist revival meetings. She studied the Koran and took classes on the Torah. She meditated. She prayed. It was like she was playing a game of hide and seek with God and couldn't find his hiding spot. I hated it. Every time she'd introduce me to a new belief, my mouth would go dry and my skin would feel itchy. No matter how hard I tried, I couldn't sense the Almighty Being.

Neither could she.

We never did find God. But our Sundays were spent with an angel—Minnie. She taught me that love didn't have to be skittish or stern. That family doesn't have to be blood. And that loss batters one's heart, but it doesn't stop it beating.

Now, Thomas, John, and I cut across a plateau where goats are nibbling at weeds and brush. In the distance is the sound of water rushing. It grows louder as the terrain goes from grassy to rocky and we end up next to a waterfall. It towers above us, the full height of the hill. I watch the curtains of water. They fall a good two hundred feet. Here, at the bottom, white foam froths in a tiny natural pool then snakes over boulders to meet up into one fat flow of the river below. Sunlight hits the fine mist in the air, creating a shimmering rainbow.

If anyplace ever felt like somewhere I'd find God, it's here.

"This is my favorite sport in all of Eden." Thomas rips off his shoes and starts unbuttoning his vest and jacket. "You are going to love this, Redd!"

John's already taking off his shirt. I look at his muscular frame and hold back a grin. If it involves John getting undressed, I agree. I'll love it.

I take off my own shoes and untie my overskirt, figuring we'll be getting wet from the spray.

Thomas whoops and begins the climb up the hill to the top of the falls. John and I follow, John in nothing but his breeches, and me in my petticoats. Sunlight plays on the muscles in his shoulders and brightens copper tones in his chestnut hair. Despite our being barefoot on rocky dirt, the ascent is easy, and we reach the top in a handful of minutes.

The curtain of rushing water shoots directly out of a cavern in the cliff face. We scramble over spiky shrubs and smooth boulders until we're near enough to touch the water. It's much cooler here, and the sound is nearly deafening. Green and black mosses blanket the rocks jutting into the spray. Vines with serrated leaves cling to the wet cliffside. It smells like damp and rust and springtime all at once. We're so much higher than I imagined. I look down at the swirling water below and my adrenaline spikes. I don't want to get too close to the edge.

That's when a female voice shouts from behind me, "Belial's buttons, you Harvie boys are predictable. I knew I'd find you up here!"

I turn to see a willowy blonde coming up the path we just took. She's wearing only a shift, her bare thighs flashing in the sun as she climbs to reach us.

She goes directly to John and rubs a bit of dirt off of his cheek, her thumb lingering on his skin longer than it needs to. The gesture makes my stomach twist. I don't want to be jealous. But she's half-dressed and standing under the sun in a way that John can surely see right through the linen of her chemise. And if I'm totally honest, it's a good view.

"Clara." A look of irritation crosses John's face but is quickly replaced by a benign smile. I'm not sure if the irritation is at Clara, me, or the fact that he has to yell over the rushing of the waterfall. "Meet Redd!"

"Redd! Welcome to Eden. I'm delighted to make your acquaintance. Glad I sought you out. Despite being John's next-door neighbor, he did not even bring you over for proper introductions," she complains directly into my ear.

"Wonder why that is." Thomas' voice is so tart even the rushing water doesn't soften it.

Clara narrows her eyes.

Something about her gives me a sense of déjà vu. She's all fine bones and delicate features—a small curvy mouth, high cheekbones, feather-like lashes. Despite her lack of clothing, she holds herself like she comes from privilege. Like she's used to getting what she wants. She reaches for my shoulders and pulls me into her arms for a hug.

I swallow a sharp blade of unease that's formed in my throat. With the damn Eternity Flower everywhere, I don't get a clear sense of Clara's emotions. Yet the taste of malice coats my tongue as she tightens her grip.

I disentangle myself from her arms, uneasy. But then an errant curl falls in front of her eye and my unease is replaced by excitement. I suddenly know why she seems familiar.

Oh, my God.

Clara is Autumn. Minnie's daughter.

All the times I looked through photos at Minnie's place, all the stories I heard about little Autumn, when she first sat up, how she crawled backwards, how loud her screams were when she was hungry—and, of course, the story of that day on the beach when Minnie and her husband fell asleep only to wake to Autumn gone—all these bring tears to my eyes. I'm so relieved I hug her again, squeezing her tight.

She lets out a strangled laugh, but hugs me back.

I've found her. Minnie is going to be so happy. Her daughter is here. She's alive and well.

I'm no longer jealous, but thrilled. It doesn't matter that I tasted malice when she hugged me. My sixth sense is warped here; it's officially time to ignore it.

Besides, when we break apart, I see that she's beaming at me.

"Clara," I say, but think *Autumn*. Her eyes are exactly the same shade of sky blue as Minnie's.

Thomas waves a hand and yells, "Enough with the introductions. Time to dive!"

I'm sure I heard that wrong. "Wait...dive?"

"Aye. Dive the waterfall."

"You mean fall jumping?" I burst out laughing. "Absolutely not."

"Oh, come now," whines Thomas. "You simply must. It will not be nearly as fun without you." Despite his height, he looks so much like the kid he is right now with a pouty mouth and crossed arms.

John looks at his brother. His voice booms over the cascading water. "You must understand, Tom, in the Beyond a dive such as this could hurt one."

I scoff. "Hurt? You mean maim or kill. My brains would be splattered all over those boulders below. And I've got lots of brains, so it would be a mess."

The corner of John's mouth lifts into a half-smile. "Is that so?"

"Yep. Brains galore."

"Then you are intelligent enough to understand we are in Eden. And cannot get hurt here," Clara adds.

John nods. "Trust me."

"Yeah, well, that's just it. I don't trust you."

"Trust the magic," says Clara.

"I *really* don't trust magic."

"The magic works on you, Redd," Thomas points out.

"A knife slice is not exactly the same as jumping several stories." I take another glance down at the frothing water, careful on the slick rock and mud under my feet. "No. Hell, no."

John shrugs. "Understandable. You can watch us from—"

But before he can finish his sentence, Clara shouts, "Off you go!" Her hands fly out and she shoves me. Hard. With the roaring chutes of water just below, my reflex is to reach out to the closest thing, hoping to stop my momentum.

My fingers wrap around John's upper arm as I pitch backwards. But instead of stopping my fall, he plummets over the edge along with me.

7

Eleanor

Eden: 1592

The Master was gone for long periods of time but, in those early years, when he came back to Eden he spent evenings at our cottage. I do not know where he slept—or if he slept—but from the moment the sun began to set to the moment the moon rose high in the sky, he was in front of our hearth, relaxing in my rocker and sipping my ale.

Every minute he did so, bile burned the back of my throat. I hated him and wanted to him to leave. I often attempted to refuse him entry. But he paid me no heed. And, in the end, I gave in. He was the reason we were spared the malice of the other villagers. He controlled everything.

Virginia was giddy when she heard his playful knock upon the door. He often brought gifts when he'd been away a while, providing an easy way into my little girl's heart. He'd give her all manner of things: from carved figurines that moved as if imbued with life, to special storm stones that created rainfall, to a baby water dragon named Deception—the scaly black pet was too young to come into its powers and still small enough to be kept in a serving bowl. At first, I forced her to refuse these gifts. But then I relented as I saw my bitterness only managed to endear the Master to her further.

Everyone in the village was discovering his or her aptitude for Eden's magic. Like most of us, my handle on it was nothing spectacular. I could use it without difficulty, but my conjuring never improved or enhanced my subject. Virginia, however, had a way with plants, and the flowers she conjured from seedlings were magnificent. When the Master entered our cottage, Virginia would conjure lily of the valley, tucking a few springs into his hair. He allowed this. In truth, when she did so, something about him changed. The cold black of his pupils sparked warmth, and the harsh curve of his lips softened. For those few moments, his beauty was not only terrifying and imposing—it was genuine.

During those visits, Virginia's adulation and innocence cracked open the hard shell of the Master's exterior, giving us glimpses of the quivering being underneath.

One night, Virginia stroked the scales on Deception's head and asked the Master why he never showed his full face. The small dragon leaned into Virginia's hand but kept its beaded pupils on the Master. Torment cuddled tighter around my neck, and Sloth, that lazy feline, opened one sapphire eye. The fire crackled and popped as we waited for the Devil to speak.

His mouth tipped into a frown and he stared down at the rough wood of the table. I thought he would not answer when he finally said, "I was one of God's beloved children once."

"I've heard of God," Virginia offered excitedly. "God will come for us. Goodwife Warren teaches it in our lessons. She says once we all repent our sins, the Lord will open Heaven to us."

His eyebrows shot above his mask. "What sins have you to repent?"

Virginia shrugged, cheeks burning. By now she understood what others in the village had insinuated, though they did not say it outright—that her very existence was a sin. Blinking back tears, I focused on my darning. I poked the needle through the ripped stocking, while magic tugged the thread.

The Master turned to me, his voice low and mocking. "I leave you to govern yourselves and the Council appoints a misinformed religious flax-wench as teacher?"

I kept my eyes on the stocking, on the hole that needed repairing. Joan Warren taught the children simply because she'd volunteered to do so. There had been no discussion around the post. It was clear now that there should have been.

He continued, "Let it be known that any more talk of Heaven in the classroom will get Goodwife Warren's tongue ripped out."

I nodded once. Joan would listen. I had no doubt the Master would make good on his threat.

Turning his attention to Virginia, the Master tapped the tip of her nose. "Your tutor's head is addled. She knows nothing more of the Lord than you do. But tell me, Virginia, does life displease you here so much that you await Heaven?"

She vehemently shook her head. "Nay. Goodwife Warren tells us of Heaven, but it sounds tiresome. No place for children. I prefer it here, with Deception and Mama and you."

The corner of his mouth lifted into a sardonic smile. "So your tutor must have told you that God banished me from Heaven?"

"She said your pride and arrogance forced the Lord to smite you to the underworld." The adulation that filled her voice proved Joan Warren's lesson had gone completely misunderstood by her pupils.

"Alas, the Lord has difficulty with opposition." The Master scoffed and looked at me. "Mayhap you'll tell me, Eleanor, how to parent an unruly child? When your patience grows thin with Virginia's antics, do you pull her closer, show her more love? Or do you push her away?"

My heart began to race, but before I could answer, Virginia squared her shoulders and said, "She does neither. I'm no unruly child."

I laughed and gave her a wink. "'Tis true. Virginia is a good girl."

"Ah. I must agree." The Devil nodded. "I, however, was an unruly child. Very unruly. And when adolescence took hold, I became positively insufferable. I believed myself more intelligent, more beautiful, more daring than any other angel in God's family."

"Were you?" Virginia asked.

He grinned. "Aye. I was. But 'tis not the way of things in Heaven to put oneself above the others. Not unless you are God Himself. So, I was punished."

"Deserving, then," I quipped.

The gaze he turned upon me was cold enough to raise goosebumps. He unbuttoned his chemise and drew it over his head. His perfect form was marred by violent pink scars running down his back. "Deserving? My father ripped out my wings with his bare hands. He threw me down from the heavens, banishing me forever... What shall Virginia expect should she cross you? Will you throw her into the quagmire Misery calls home and allow the beast to suck sorrow from her bones and savor her tears?"

Virginia gasped. Her lip wobbled as she widened her eyes at me. I glared at the Devil. "Beelzebub's teeth! Stop scaring the child!"

I ran a palm over my daughter's plaited hair and cooed, "I would never, my love. The Master is trying to drive home a point, but he is doing so rather poorly."

After a moment, the child was back to her curious—and impatient—self. "What does any of this have to do with your mask?"

"Aye. The mask." He put a hand to the leather strip as if verifying it was still there. "'Twas a woman—isn't it always?"

I let out a sound between a grunt and a snort. All manner of men were the same, be they angel or Devil, blaming women for their problems.

Virginia set Deception's bowl on the floorboards, slid off her stool, and settled at the Devil's feet.

He continued, his tone growing wistful, "That woman is an extremely powerful angel named Nature. Humans call her *Mother Nature*. But she is not nurturing like the human name evokes. In fact, she cares very little for humans, very little for life outside of her own. She adores beauty, creation, destruction. She is vibrant, unpredictable, unfettered."

Here he stopped and said to Virginia, "Somewhat like *your* mother."

I did not lift my eyes from my darning, for I knew he wanted me to. Such blatant flattery. What game was he playing?

"Nature told me I was the most beautiful being she'd ever laid eyes upon. She had a way about her that made me feel so...alive. You've yet to experience the pleasures of the flesh, Virginia, so you may not understand. Volcanoes erupt under Nature's touch. Windstorms flatten entire islands when she sighs..." His grip tightened on his mug of ale, the veins in his hand bulging. "I did not fret when I was thrown out of Heaven; for I knew I had no need of Heaven if Nature was by my side. She was Heaven in living form."

I watched the Master's chest rise and fall as he breathed. He did so as though the memory caused him physical pain. For the briefest of seconds, I almost felt pity for the Devil.

"But she was loyal to the Lord. Furious that I'd risen against Him," he said. "Even more furious that I then expected her to choose between us."

I threaded another needle with a flick of my hand. The rip in the stocking was larger than I'd realized. "Did she choose?"

"Nay." A sad smile worked its way across the Master's face. "So I stole her away with me."

"You kidnapped her?"

"I believed we'd be happy together."

My pity evaporated. "Of course you did."

"I created Eden for *her*. But she was not here long." He kept his eyes on the fire and said in a low monotone, "The Lord sent an entire army of angels for her."

"They brought her back to Heaven?"

"Aye. But not without a fight." The Master slowly took off his mask. Underneath was such a sea of scars it took my breath away. His face was rippled with ridges and welts; it was discolored and shiny. His eyes, those piercing onyx eyes, were not dark irises as I'd thought. Nay. They were two spheres made of ink-black shadow, like the deepest part of caves. At the bridge of his nose was a wound that gaped open, the blood there congealed and fresh though the injury was centuries old.

Virginia pressed her lips into a flat line. I paused in my sewing and stared.

"My father took my angelic sight. 'Tis impossible for me to see goodness now without cruelty. To give love without pain. My heart has turned as monstrous as my face." A heavy sadness weighed down the Master's words as he slipped his mask back on. "And Nature has never called me beautiful again."

For a moment, the only sound in the room was the crackling of the fire. Then Virginia reached up and took his hand, squeezing his fingers. "I find you beautiful," she said. "I would always choose you. And so would Mama."

I pricked my finger. Blood beaded up, staining the wool. The stocking was ruined.

"Enough. Time for bed," I said as set down the darning and tugged Virginia's hand from his. "Now."

"But Mama," Virginia started.

"Nay. The Master is not a friendly uncle or a kindly cousin, Virginia. He needs to stop acting as though he is." I lifted my chin and spat out, "Remember, he is the Devil."

The darkness behind his mask sparked with amusement. "Aye, I am. Remember that, Virginia. And remember that your mother already chose me long ago."

8

John

Eden: Present Day

Redd and I tumble over the edge of the falls, headfirst. I twist to wrap my arms around her, her head jostling my shoulder, her fingernails digging into my skin. Her lips open but I do not know if she's screaming as it's impossible to hear anything over the deafening crash of water. My stomach twists and jumps, landing in my throat. My ears pop and my eyes tear up from the lashing of the wind.

I've dived the waterfall countless times. It's always been a rush. Always a handful of seconds where, even in Eden, I feel truly alive.

But this time is different. Better. Because I'm sharing it with *her*.

Redd is tight in my embrace. We're flying. Together. And, for a moment, it's bliss.

At the bottom, we slice into the surface of the water, the impact forcing us apart. Our bodies slam against the boulders half-buried in the silt. My neck, shoulder, and elbow crack loudly. There's no pain, just a slight itching as the bones meld back together.

Redd is face-up in the water, crying. I calm her and help her out of the natural pool, pulling her until we're crawling onto the grass. She's shaking so much her teeth chatter. Above us, Tom whoops in joy as he jumps. Clara lets out a high-pitched squeal. Then, a few seconds later, the hollow crunch as they both hit the rocks. Blood splashes.

Redd screams, her dark eyes wide. But both Thomas and Clara sit up with grins on their faces. They crawl out of the water laughing.

Redd stops screaming and stares. Then, her eyes crinkle and her mouth spreads into an astonished smile.

And I love it. I love how she beams over this simple feat. How that light in her eyes seems brighter and her smile is so large it makes my heart crack. Eden's magic has always been a part of my life. It simply *is*. Yet to see Redd experience it as a novelty is a kind of magic in itself.

She grips my hand and tugs me until we're both standing. A patch of sunlight shines on her head, lighting up the gold and brown strands of her hair. She looks like an angel, those ones in old paintings and tapestries that glow under an aureole of light.

"Oh, my God. That was crazy," she says. "Do you think we can do it again?"

9

Eleanor

Eden: 1593

Virginia was just as shunned as I.

She was treated like another of the Devil's pets, one that hid fangs and claws under her innocent appearance. Winefrid Powell sometimes looked upon her with sympathy and let Virginia play pat-a-cake with her youngest, but only if she could keep an eye upon her. The village boys did nothing to include Virginia in their games. Early on, when she approached them, they would run away. Sometimes, I would call them back and insist they include her, though not always. It filled the greedy hole in my heart to have her to myself. But by the time she was six years of age, they were doing much more than running when they heard her approach. Now their words and actions became cruel. I could no longer sway Virginia's attention and stop her tears through finger puppet shows and kisses on the forehead. Now their barbs began to pierce her heart. She'd come home, spirit cowed and eyes swollen.

It fired a rage in me that burned so hot, hell was a cool drink of ale next to my vengeance.

I decided to deal with the situation in two ways. First, to fortify Virginia. And second, to scare those foul-faced boys into submission.

One fall morning after the other children had sent her home, I took Virginia to the area where the riverbank was slick with shells. We walked hand-in-hand through the growing mist of the forest floor. Above us the trees had turned fiery red and blazing yellow, deep orange and pastel pink. Here, in Eden, their leaves did not fall until the first winter snow. They only changed color to remind us that time was passing. The air was slightly cooler, enough for a shawl around the shoulders, but the sun still shone as if it were mid-June.

We pushed through the line of Eternity Flowers clinging like an illness to the riverbank, their sickly-sweet odor turning my stomach. The amphibian Repugnance blinked one eye at us, then the other, before sinking into his muddy hovel, his slick hide covered in venomous lumps.

I gathered my skirts in my hand, sat on a flat rock, and hugged Virginia to me. Tears still trickled down her cheeks.

"Why do the others hate me? What have I done?" She kept her eyes on the river water, shimmying and bubbling at our feet.

"You have done nothing, my love. Nothing except live."

So I told her what had happened four years earlier. I told her about Walter. I had to explain exactly what death was, because—miraculously—it had not touched us since that day. The taunts the other children used on her had always gone misunderstood, but now I saw her face pale as she put it all together.

"You *are* the 'murderous witch' they talk about in rhymes." Her gaze rose from the water to meet my own. Horror filled her eyes.

Torment kneaded his paws on my neck, and I felt warm blood trickling over my skin. I raked my fingers through his fur until he gurgled with pleasure. "I did it to save you, Virginia. I hate myself for what I've done. But I did it for you."

She wriggled out of my arms to scoot to the other end of the rock. "The Master—"

I cut her off. She had genuine affection for the Master. I needed to shake her faith in him. It was time she knew the truth. "The Master wanted me to choose you. He wanted me to drown you, my very own child. He wanted you dead, Virginia."

"Nay. He loves me."

"He loves power. Nothing else."

"Nay," she spat.

"You cannot trust the Master. He is a liar and a cheat."

Tears filled her eyes and anger thickened her voice. "You. You are."

"And I would cheat again if I had to," I said. "I would do anything to save you."

"I hate you."

Though her words tore at my soul, I nodded. I reached down and dug my fingers into the damp dirt at the edge of the river, pulling out a sleek, gray shell and rubbing it clean with the pads of my thumbs. "Hate me if you must, but you are alive because of me. Do not let shame cow you, Virginia. There are other emotions that give strength and purpose. Cling to them instead. They will allow you to keep on."

I pried open the Malice shell. A slimy tan mess sat thickly inside like a pudding. I tickled the tongue and it lifted. Underneath sat a dark red pearl.

Virginia's curiosity got the better of her, and she leaned closer. "Which is it?"

"Resentment," I explained. "If we find a scarlet spite pearl, they will make a perfect pair."

My own Malice pearls weighed heavy on my lobes—silvery arrogance and black rancor. They kept me grounded. Ever since I'd put them on, I'd felt solid. I no longer had days in which I sensed I was completely disappearing.

I washed the slime from the pearl in the river. "Hold out your hand."

I dropped it into Virginia's palm and immediately her skin began to flush with fever. Sweat dripped down her forehead though the chills began, her whole body shivering in spasms.

She turned her hand over to drop the pearl, but I was faster than she. I put both hands around hers and squeezed. "Ride through the feeling, Virginia. You are a good girl, but you are not irreproachable. If you do not squirm away, eventually you will no longer be ill."

I held her hands together while she moved in and out of consciousness. After a while the fever and the trembling stopped and when she opened her eyes, I knew that her feelings of shame and horror were replaced by something else. Something stronger.

I took my hands from hers and we looked down at the pearl sitting in the pleats of her palm. It caught the sunlight and reflected color onto her skin.

"You are now equipped to face the others in the village." I scanned the river's edge for another Malice shell that looked like it might carry treasure. "But let us find a companion for this one, shall we? If not scarlet spite, ivory ire, or golden wrath would be pretty."

"Nay," she said, clutching the bead. "I do not want a pair. I want to wear this one on a chain, close to my heart."

I nodded. "Then you shall."

In the distance, I heard the echo of boys' laughter. It was time to do the other task I'd decided upon this morning.

"Why don't you run back to the cottage? I believe I have the perfect chain for your pearl in the jeweled box on my chest of drawers. Gather it and make a necklace."

She hesitated, a dark frown on her face. "What will you be doing?"

I tried not to let my gaze flicker in the direction of the Fire Pit. "I have an errand to run."

"I do not like what you did. To Walter." Her words were cutting. The usual softness of her soul did not shine through.

I swallowed back fear; I'd wanted to fuel the fire of her hatred towards others by giving her the pearl, not me. Never me. Yet, I gave her the briefest of smiles. "I would be worried if you did."

Still frowning, she shuffled off and disappeared into the forest. I gathered up my skirts to stand, but as I did so my hand brushed against something on the rock. There, empty eyes skyward, fat teeth in a silent grin, sat my mask. Eden's magic was not the kind that allowed one to snap her fingers and make an item appear...even one's own mask. Unease snaked down my spine. This was the Devil's work. He must have had an idea of what I intended to do.

I did not care for his foresight. It meant he knew me too well. Even so, I wrapped my fingers around the wooden face, pressed it to my own, and strode off towards the sound of boys playing. Towards the Fire Pit.

When I reached the area where the mist was tinged orange, I saw them pushing and shoving each other near the mouth of the pond. It looked as though they had been playing cudgels because several sturdy sticks were abandoned on the spongy ground. Now, however, they'd moved onto a different kind of sport. Were we in Roanoke—or even England for that matter—the boys would not be playing at all, but working for our survival. Here, it was all fun and games.

I was about to step out of the trees when I heard it:

Eleanor, Eleanor, murderous witch

In cold-blood she made the switch

She set the bait

And sealed our fate

When she put Walter in the ditch

I felt dizzy with horror and understood Virginia's shame. As the boys chanted, Robert Ellis was shoving young Ambrose Viccar's head under the water. The floating blond strands of hair brought me back to that fateful night when my hands were on little Walter's head. Bile rose in my throat and I nearly retched. But then the mask took hold and the feeling of shame warped into a thirst for vengeance.

I sensed an opportunity.

"I'd be more careful where you play," I said, stepping into the sunlight. "The Fire Pit is the one place you can die in Eden."

Four heads turned my way, the color leaching out of their faces the moment they set eyes upon me. The masks were familiar here in Eden—everyone had one. Yet it was quite different to see them as wall hangings or in the mirror than it was to confront a mask in use. Purpose brought out its ferocity. And my purpose was to terrify.

Robert snatched his hand back and little Ambrose coughed and sputtered as he lifted his face from the pond. The moment his eyes caught mine, he scrambled backwards, further into the depths.

The five boys stared at me. Through the mask I could hear their heartbeats, taste their fear, and sense my own growing power. It was horrible...and absolutely divine.

"What is it you're playing at?" I took another step closer. By now, I was near enough that they'd see the blood sap running from the mask's grimace, see how the wood had fused with my own skin. I no longer wore a mask; I was, in fact, a monster.

It was Johnny Prat who answered. He was in the midst of adolescence and the pitch of his voice changed with each word. "We're...we're playing at sacrifice."

"Ah. And the rhyme you were chanting?"

Their tongues stayed pinned.

I was now close enough that I could reach out and touch Robert. He was a tall boy, with ruddy skin and an arrogant attitude. He was the oldest and the leader of the group. "In this scenario, are you meant to be me?" I asked him.

His eyes darted everywhere—to his friends, to the woods beyond, to his own hands—except to me. I gripped his shoulder and pushed until he fell to his knees. The mask gave me more strength than I would have thought possible.

The other boys stood as still as death, fear rooting them to the spot.

"How about I play my own part?" Pond water seeped into my boots and soaked the bottom of my skirts. My one hand stayed bolted to his shoulder while the other rested upon his head. My fingers wriggled like worms in his dark hair before I gripped the strands and shoved him face-first into the Fire Pit. As he struggled for air, I chanted:

All ye young, you take care
She'll set her hands upon your hair
With her schemin'
She'll stop you breathin'

I let him up, and as he blubbered, I finished, "*Don't you anger Eleanor Dare.*"

They all watched, wide-eyed, as I ripped off my mask. "You boys had better be kind to Virginia, or the next time this will not be a simple game."

I felt elated and vindicated. No one would exclude my daughter again.

My mood changed the moment I left them behind and stepped into the woods. There stood Virginia, a look of pure horror dressing her face.

"My love," I said. "You were to wait for me at home."

Her fingers went to the red pearl that she plucked out of her apron pocked. "I...I could not remember where you'd said to find the chain." Her voice shook.

"I see." I pointed to the boys back at the Fire Pit. "They'll welcome you now. I've made sure of that."

I opened my arms and beckoned her to come for a hug.

But she turned on her heel and ran.

10

Redd

Eden: Present Day

I just jumped a giant waterfall, landing on a sea of boulders, and survived. More than survived. I walked away without a scratch.

And I did it five times.

As Shay would say, *Un-fucking-believable.*

I was terrified at first. And when I hit the ground, bones against boulders, I was sure I was dead. I was sure we were *all* dead. Except that it turns out John was right. I *can* trust the magic.

I'm still blown away by that realization.

The four of us—me, John, Thomas, and Clara—competed for best form. Forward dives. Backward dives. Flips. We tried it all. Hands down, Clara is the most daring. And Tom the most enthusiastic. But from take-off at the waterfall's edge to when he slices into the pool below, John makes every moment a thing of beauty. He does it with the skill of an Olympian. It's magic...without the magic.

We're exhilarated from the jumps but also exhausted from the climbing. So now we wring out our wet underclothes, then sit on the grass that blankets the area where the pool turns into the river to dry off in the sun. Apart from a few exchanges regarding the best ways to throw oneself off the top of a waterfall, I haven't talked much with Clara yet. I'm hoping to get a chance to do so now.

But we aren't even settled yet when a furious shout rips through the air.

"THOMAS HARVIE!" A stout woman wearing a giant scowl and an embroidered coif marches towards us. "We've not yet finished our lessons!"

All the color drains out of Thomas' face. "Goodwife Warren."

"I'll not tolerate you sneaking off, young man. Now come back or the Governor will hear about it. Then you'll have worries." Goodwife Warren lifts an eyebrow at Clara. "Speaking of the Governor, he was looking for you, Miss Archer. I'd no idea you were here playing harlot."

Two pink spots brighten Clara's cheeks. "When did the Governor ask for me?"

Goodwife Warren sniffs. "Only moments ago. He and your mother spouted some nonsense about the Council needing your assistance."

Clara scrambles up, fastening her skirt and bodice. She hurries off even before putting on her hose or shoes. "I shall see you later, Redd," she calls out as she goes.

"Come," Goodwife Warren orders Thomas.

"I was about to show our guest around Eden," he says. "We rarely have a guest. Surely this opportunity is better than any lesson."

"Hi." I stand and hold out my hand. "I'm Redd Winter."

She looks at my hand then lifts her eyes to my face. I don't need my sixth sense to read the hatred in her stare. "Oh, you may use as many false names as you like, my child. But I know who you are: you're a Dare. Dare is a foul word in the village."

I drop my hand and feel my face heat up with shame, though I don't even know why.

John hops up. "Goodwife War—" he starts, his voice sharp.

"Tut!" she barks. "No talking back to your elders. Have you forgotten your place, John Harvie? Because I have not." Starting back the way she came, she motions for Thomas to follow her.

Thomas sighs but dresses quickly. "Redd, we've much more to do. I've yet to beat you in Maw."

"You're on," I hold up my hand for a high-five. His brows scrunch together so I mime what to do. A second later, he's high-fiving me like a pro. "Perfect!"

He grins, his whole face glowing with pride. It's nice to know that a simple gesture like that can bring him such joy.

When he's out of sight, I turn to John. "I'm a Dare?"

"Aye. Your mother is Virginia Dare. Your father—her husband—was William Wythers. But no one ever called her by his surname. She has always been a Dare."

Dare.

So that's what that was—I remember the letters in old-fashioned script, embossed on the metal box I found the mask in. It wasn't a challenge. It was a name. *My* name.

I like it. It's a good name. *Ahredden Dare.*

"I take it she's not friends with that Warren lady." John had told me before coming that there was a long-standing feud between his family and mine. I hadn't realized that it might be something bigger. Thank God the others in the village seem to be nice.

He snorts. "Few would call Goodwife Warren a friend."

"I can see why."

"And William? My father? He's...dead?"

"Aye. He died just after you were born." John sits on a flat rock that juts out over the rushing water. "I wish I could tell you more, but I am not the one to ask."

"That's why I'm impatient to meet Virginia." I slide next to him. "I mean, I've been having a crazy fun morning, but until I meet her, it's just passing time."

He nods and for a minute we're both silent, enjoying the peace of the moment after all the earlier excitement. We dangle our feet into the river, the water curling around our ankles. It is swift and cool and soothing. I listen to the water and feel the warmth of John's body close to mine.

I follow the flow of the river with my eyes, into the woods where the torrent becomes a silver ribbon twisting through the underbrush, flanked by hundreds of Eternity Flowers. Above the layer of mist, there are beeches and cedars and pines, the foliage a glistening green.

"It's pretty here," I say. *Eden is beautiful. You're safe here.*

"Aye," John agrees. He still hasn't put on his shirt, and despite the pretty view of the river, my gaze keeps going back to his chest. "The river is as much of my life as is breathing. I grew up learning to fish in its waters, digging for Malice pearls on its banks, drinking the nectar of the flower that thrives on its edges. I used to come here, to this very spot, after my scout training to get away from it all. There is nothing quite as calming as the sound of a river."

He nods his chin to an obese toad the size of a bulldog half-hidden in the muddy bank. "That is when Repugnance is not disturbing the peace with his incessant croaking. It happens too often. Thank the Devil he's silent today."

"Every time we moved, Agnes made sure we were near water."

"You moved house often?"

"Every year. Agnes didn't like the mask showing up. So we ran from it."

He nods. "Except that mask was meant for you. And you cannot outrun your birthright."

"I guess not." I think of the way the sun sparkles on the water rushing behind our house in Hidden. Of how the sound of it lulled me to sleep. I swallow down a shard of regret. What if we hadn't run? Would I have been sleeping to the rushing of this river instead?

"You've lived all over the Beyond?"

I laugh. "No. I mean, I've lived in most of the Midwest, but there's a lot of world out there that I've never even glimpsed. What's the farthest you've been?"

He shrugs. "To find you."

"And that's further than most people from Eden? They really don't ever leave?" I trail off at the look on John's face. Sadness? Hope? Anger? God, I'm useless without my sixth sense.

John turns to me. "Do you enjoy fishing?"

The change in topic throws me. "Uhh..."

He closes his eyes and within seconds, shiny silver fish are swimming at our feet. The scales of one slide along my toes. I yelp and lift my feet out of the water. We look at each other and laugh.

Then John jumps into the river. The water is up to his thighs and the current is strong enough that he sways with the movement. "They sense when you want them, and they come. Simple as that." Before he even finishes his sentence, his arms are filled with a wriggling mass of salmon, their scales like sequins.

I smile. God, this place is awesome.

"Everything is that simple here," he adds, the words sounding more rote than real.

He lets the fish drop to the water. They flip about and then swim along with the current.

I feel my smile falter. "My mom...Agnes...ran away. It can't be *that* perfect."

"No. You're correct. It isn't perfect," he concedes. "But Eden has its moments. Remember that. I hope you need never see the darkness here. I hope all you ever see in Eden is beauty."

"Um...I hope so, too," I say.

He frowns at my response, back to being the overly serious John that I knew back home. To knock the grim look off his face, I concentrate...and then suddenly there's a loud splashing. Fish soar out of the water and pummel John like a punching bag before falling back into the river and dashing away.

"Satan's scourge!" he half-yells, half-laughs. "That was uncalled for!"

I'm giggling so much I can barely catch my breath. When I finally do, I say, "I guess magic isn't that hard."

He shakes his head, but his lips stay upturned.

"The morning is nearly gone. We'd better move on."

By now my chemise and petticoats are dry. I gather my outer clothes from where I left them earlier, tying on the petticoats, the ribboned stockings, and shoes. But when it comes to the bodice, I get it tangled. Again. So I try magic. The laces tighten, but somehow, even using magic, I manage to tie it wrong.

John lifts an eyebrow. "Do you need a hand?"

"Yeah. The magic is defective when it comes to this."

He chuckles. "The magic was refined by the Master. Apparently, his knowledge of womanly things is lacking."

"He's got special powers? Like, superpowers?" Makes more sense that he wears a mask like a superhero.

"His power is beyond my comprehension." John comes behind me and runs his hands along my spine, lining up the eyelets for the laces.

I intend to ask more about the Master, but at John's touch, goosebumps pebble my skin and my mouth goes dry. My heart hammers as he fingers the stays of the bodice, the stiff material tightening further over my breasts with each new tug.

"Looks like you know your way around 'womanly things,' John. Helped a lot of girls back into their clothes?" I tease.

I hear him chuckle, but he doesn't give me an answer. After tying the final knot, he clears his throat. "There."

I lift my coif off the ground, plop it on my head, and promptly realize I have no idea how Isobel got it to stay there. So I turn and hand it to John. "Now this," I say, then add, "Please."

He's not as adept at braiding as his grandmother. Instead of working at top-speed, John crisscrosses sections of my hair slowly and carefully, his fingers more often than not getting caught in my mass of waves. Finally, he tucks my hair under the cap, pulling the drawstring tight to keep the locks in place. "All done."

I shake my head and the coif stays in place. I turn around. "How'd you do that?"

"Magic," he grins. His eyes meet mine, the kaleidoscope of green and brown and amber like an autumn forest. I wouldn't mind getting lost in that forest. I watch his lashes shadow those eyes as his gaze drops to my mouth and stays there.

Warmth spreads from my face to my limbs, then pools into my core.

"Ummm..." I have no idea what I want to say, until he dips his head and I think, *Oh, God, yes*. The smell of him surrounds me—summer rain and fresh grass—along with nectar of the Eternity Flower. Suddenly his lips are on mine, soft and warm and insistent. He rests his hands on my hips, sending another wave of desire through me, and deepens the kiss.

It's sweet and sexy at the same time, the gentle way he pulls me closer, the hot impatience when his teeth tug my bottom lip. I'm about to lose control and pretty much pounce on him when there's a shout behind us. John startles and I nearly jump out of my skin. We step apart as a squirrel shoots past so quickly it's nothing but a gray blur. A tall, unkempt man with wild hair and an even wilder beard chases after it, shouting, "You cannot run forever!" The rodent and man disappear into the woods, darkness and fog swallowing them.

"What was that?" I ask.

John's gone stick-straight, like he was caught with a hand in the cookie jar. And I suppose, in a way, he was. "That was Griffen Jones."

"The guy who cuts off his own feet?" I squint into the forest, wishing I'd paid more attention when he'd run past.

"Aye." His face reddens and he runs a hand through his hair, the chestnut strands flopping right back into his face. "What would you like to do now?"

He's cute when he's uncomfortable. My lips are still tingling from our kiss. I almost suggest we go back to what we were doing, but instead I shrug. "Something less adventurous than waterfall jumping."

"There's the farm? It's one of my favorite places."

"Perfect," I say. "Lead the way."

We go through the village to catch the river as it loops back around itself. There, we cross a stone footbridge. It's the kind of thing you imagine seeing in a fairy tale, with the river rushing under it like quicksilver and the trees above a lacy canopy of green. A bird flies overhead, its beak a shining gold. Ahead of us is what looks like an orchard and, beyond that, a large farm. As we walk towards it, hot pink butterflies dance in front of us as if they're showing off.

John rolls his eyes and mumbles, "Braggarts."

It makes me laugh because that's exactly what they seem like.

He opens his arms wide and spins, a happy grin on his face. "This is Eden. No cars. No machines. Just nature at her loveliest. What do you think?"

"I don't know. I'm missing the pollution."

His lips turn down. I try not to remember how nice those lips are. "How can you—"

I hold a hand up. "Kidding. It's called a joke."

He pauses, then says, "Not a very good one."

"Hey!"

His laugh scatters the Braggarts. The sound of it warms my insides. I'm not sure who this flirty John is, but I like him.

We reach the orchard and weave our way through rows and rows of trees. There's every kind, from avocado to orange to cherry to plum to pineapple and a bunch of others I can't even name. "Wow. This is...wait...is that a mango tree?"

John nods. "The Master occasionally brings in seeds to add to the varieties. Every one of these gives fruit year-round, despite the season."

"Even in the dead of winter?"

"Our winter is not so dead. We've snow and ice, but it rarely gets cold enough for more than a light cloak."

"Cloak?" I laugh. "You guys really are retro."

He stops in front of a massive tree, its branches thicker and wider than most of the others. Its bark is so dark it looks black, and the spiky leaves are ivory. Clusters of something cling to the branches; they look like almonds wearing shell capes.

"Conviction. A favorite fruit in Eden. It's excellent with a bit of salt."

I wait for him to say he's joking, but he doesn't. Instead, he reaches up and twists one off the branch. When he's gotten the nut out of the shell, he hands it to me. "No salt, but you may still like it."

The second I crush it between my teeth, I'm positive I've done the right thing coming to Eden. It's the same taste that coats my tongue when I'm with someone who's a hundred percent sure of themselves.

I scan the other trees. There's a weird scraggly one with prickly pods hanging from its branches. I walk over to it and see a broken pod on the ground. A shiny reddish nut is peeking out from inside it.

"Doubt," John informs me. "I don't like it. It's bitter."

"And that bitterness lingers at the back of your throat, doesn't it?"

His eyebrows come together. "Aye. You're familiar with the taste?"

"I am," I whisper. My heart starts beating faster as I turn in circles, trying to pick out the weird trees. There's one with long pods that look ready to burst. "What's that one?"

A blush creeps up John's face. "Lust."

"Have you had vanilla in...in the Beyond?" I use his term for anything outside of Eden.

"I have."

"That's how it tastes, right? Lust. Like vanilla?"

He hesitates, but nods. "Aye."

And then we're going from tree to tree. The ones that aren't typical are all trees named after emotions...and their fruits all taste and smell exactly how I experience them when I sense other people. The whole time, my heart keeps racing. I'm not crazy. I'm not a freak. *I'm not alone.* Someone else—no, not someone else, a whole village of people—knows exactly what moods taste like.

Tears prick my eyes. Freaking hell. I'm getting all choked up over some tree nuts.

"Are you all right?" John frowns.

"Yeah, I'm good." I can still taste the Conviction on my tongue. I feel the corners of my lips lift upward. "I'm more than good."

I'm home.

11

John

Eden: Present Day

I show Redd more of Eden. The whole time, I'm trying to forget the feel of her lips on mine, but I cannot.

For the love of Lucifer, I am, as they say, smitten.

I shake my head, trying to rid myself of romantic thoughts and instead focus on what needs to be done. To save Redd and to save Eden.

That alone is better than an icy shower to get my head straight.

Redd points to a tree with twisted branches, its fruit encased in a tough green shell. "Jealousy," I say.

She grimaces. "Ugh. I don't like that one."

I nod. "Aye. Though it is nowhere near as pungent as the fruit of the Odium tree."

"Oh, yeah. That leaves a bad taste in my mouth for while," she says, but now she's grinning.

"Have you ever tried this?" I ask Redd, plucking a small, fat, rosy-colored nut from a delicate clump of growing Bliss. Its casing is so thin and fragile it needn't be shelled to be eaten. She lifts her gaze to mine and my breath catches. Her eyes are dark as shadow, but sometimes there's a golden light behind the darkness.

"Nope. What is it?"

"Try," I urge her.

She places the fruit between her lips. The moment it hits her tongue, she closes her eyes in ecstasy. "Joy," she says with a laugh. "Pure bliss."

I shake my head in disbelief. "I should not be surprised you're familiar with it all. You are Virginia's daughter." I shouldn't be surprised. Of course, being a Dare—being one the Master's chosen family—would give her certain advantages. Like knowing how Jealousy or Odium or Bliss taste without ever having picked the fruit from the tree.

We leave the orchard and head to the farm. As Redd giggles at the antics of the goats, my head spins. What am I doing? I'm here showing her Eden, falling further under her spell, and pretending all is well. I should be out there, planting the flower. But then again, once we plant the flower outside, perhaps I will no longer have the possibility to show Redd any of Eden.

Will it cease to exist?

It may. Because to survive without sacrifice, we'll need to leave this place behind.

For the first time since I realized that living outside might be a possibility, a huge wave of regret washes over me. As much as I hate Eden—Devil knows I hate it—I love it even more. I do not love what it feeds upon, but I love how the Veil makes the air sparkle. I love the way the Caul catches the rosy light of the setting sun. I love the fog of the forest floor and I even love the scent of the Eternity Flower. I love each and every creature in this cursed place, from the tiniest Nuisance to that grand goliath, Deception.

I know these creatures can exist on the outside. That is what they were created to do. But it feels sad to think we will no longer be together here in the Devil's paradise.

For the love of Lucifer, John, stop it. Every action involves a choice.

And sacrificing a life for Eden is one choice we must cease to make.

We walk back over the footbridge. Instead of turning towards the heart of the village, I follow the path that leads through the forest and to a crook in the river. Here the Eternity Flowers crowd the bank. "I'll be going back through the tunnel later today," I say as I step onto the spongy soil. My feet sink down, water seeping into my shoes.

She pushes a stalk aside to follow me directly onto the riverbank. "Wait. You're leaving me here by myself?"

"You'll be safe."

"But you just got here."

"I have a mission."

Her mouth quirks up. "A mission? Who are you, James Bond?"

I don't know who that is, so instead I answer, "I'm going to transplant the Eternity Flower in the Beyond. Like you and Agnes did."

"Planting a flower is a mission? Wow. Guess you *aren't* James Bond." I feel she's poking fun at me, but am not sure how.

"If I can get it to grow out there..." I start. I cannot tell her why. It is not only because I'm bound to Secrecy, but because I do not want her to know. *Ever.* If all goes well, she won't know that she was intended to be a sacrifice. "Let us simply say it's vital that I get it to grow in the Beyond."

"It's just like any flower." She shrugs.

"Is it?" I drop to my knees and scrape away at the mud and grit that surrounds the roots of one of the Eternity Flowers. Behind me, I hear Redd sigh, "It's going to take you years at this rate."

"We could speed things up with a bit of magic."

In a matter of seconds, she's on her knees next to me.

We both concentrate and the next time we scoop at the riverbank, our fingers go through the ground like it's pudding. She laughs, especially when we create a much larger hole than our work merits. What should take a long time only takes a minute.

Once we have the flower unearthed, roots and all, Redd says, "Okay, that was more fun than digging up a plant should be. Now what?"

This Eternity Flower is small for Eden, yet it still is half my size. I tip it, set it gently on the ground and say, "Show me how you and Agnes got it to survive."

12

Eleanor

Eden: 1594

Virginia's anger at my actions with the boys at the river colored every day with tense words and sharp gazes. It was months before she stopped recoiling from my touch or turning away as I spoke or refusing to allow me to tuck her in at night. Each day without her love, Torment's teeth sunk deeper into my flesh and the ache in my heart grew stronger.

I watched the winter snow fall like puffs of dandelion seed on the tree branches and blades of grass until the whole of Eden turned a sparkling white. Virginia made snow angels all on her own, getting up and running off elsewhere if I attempted to join her. I did not attend the winter festivities to drink mulled wine and watch the ice sliding races. Instead, I watched from afar as she flew down the western hills on frozen paths as if she had wings. I even spied the moment when she put the boys in the village to shame as they dared her to walk on the layer of ice that had spread across the Fire Pit. I stood there and watched as she stepped onto that deadly pond and did an elegant turn, like one of the queen's own dancers. She called the boys "chicken" when they didn't follow. From then on, she had their respect.

Finally, the following spring, she tired of her grudge.

And when the flowers should have been growing bigger, the grasses growing greener, my conscious growing lighter, darkness settled upon us. The trees lost their leaves and the river water turned to blood. The sun no longer felt warm and heavenly, but like a firebrand when we set foot out of home. The grass went from green to yellow to brown. Fruit shriveled and rotted; the crops in the fields turned to dust. Even the animals changed. The silver and gold of the songbirds' beaks tarnished and they flew away, their good-bye melody so sad and throaty it brought tears to my eyes. The chickens disappeared but left their feathers behind, as if they'd been wearing a coat made of plumes. The sheep were gone as well, their wool drifting about like clouds.

Eden shed her glorious façade to reveal an ugly hellscape. Contagion spread from its contained spots in corners and crevices to cover whole walls with lacy patterns of mold. Its musty odor settled over buildings, while the reek of sulfur rose from the ground. It had been less than five years since this had happened. Less than five years since we'd had to make a sacrifice. But now it was happening again.

Every day, I scoured the cupboards for something to feed Virginia, but even our preserves had evaporated into thin air. The only time she'd ever gone hungry, she had been too young to remember. Now, she was complaining her stomach was in knots. She'd lost her rosy complexion and the light in her eyes had dimmed. It brought back the horrific memories of those last days in Roanoke when I watched her suffer and worried there was no way to save her.

"This is the Master's doing," I said.

"Nay. The Master will help us. You'll see." Virginia never failed to defend the Devil, even when he least deserved it.

"Aye. He will. But at what price?"

We hoped it would pass. The Master did not come to claim a prize and so we prayed to our non-existent god that if we stuck it out all would return to normal. But as the days passed, our suffering worsened. Nearly five years and we'd had nary a headache, but now even breathing was torment. When it was clear the situation would not change on its own, Dyonis called a Council meeting.

The meeting took place in an upstairs room of the Devil's cathedral—a grand edifice made of glittering white stone, though now it was spotted with black Contagion. The Master had had some say in the cathedral's design; the jeweled windows and heavy tapestries brought to life scenes from his past and our present. We sat around a cherry wood table that Christopher Cooper had carved himself, with Eden's magic lending a hand. The oiled surface distorted our reflections in its shine, though the days of suffering and starvation that Eden had put upon us were beginning to show. It was possible our reflections weren't distorted at all.

"Five years. Walter was a martyr for us all and we've only gained five measly years out of his death. A pittance." Dyonis was pale and thin. His dark hair had lost its sheen and his hazel eyes sunk into his skull. He spat at me, the muscles in his jaw twitching. "Are you happy, Eleanor? Was it worth five years to you?"

I closed my eyes and did not answer him. He did not truly want me to. Because I would have said yes, that even giving Virginia one more day was worth anything to me.

He shuddered and when I lifted my lids, I saw that he was crying. It was silent and only lasted a moment, but it broke my heart. I stroked Torment's soft fur and allowed the creature to snuggle tighter around my neck.

"We've a grave task ahead of us," he announced once he'd regained his composure. "Are we to sacrifice another child for another handful of years?"

"If we don't, we'll die, Governor. And most likely be sent directly to hell." This from Jonathon Tydway. He, too, looked like a hollowed-out version of himself. His beard was unkempt, his skin mottled and dry.

"Mayhap 'tis best if we do die. Mayhap 'tis fitting we go to hell," Dyonis breathed. Yet it held no conviction. And no one offered agreement. Suffering will break even the most lofty of ideals. Aye, we all wanted to curl up and die, but quickly. Not this prolonged agony. This, we'd do anything to end. But we were not naive. Nor were we innocent. Heaven would not be waiting for us on the other side of Death's door. We worried hell would not end our suffering but increase it.

"We would doom the village if we died, Governor. Doom the other children."

Dyonis nodded. "Well, then. We must choose the child to give his or her life for us all."

"How do we know who is old enough to no longer be desirable as a sacrifice?" Jonathon put a hand to his beard. It was matted and bare in places, so unlike the perfectly tapered point he usually wore. "The Ellis boy is already sixteen years of age. I believe we can take him off of our list."

"A pity," I said underneath my breath. I could still see Robert chanting those awful words about me as he'd forced young Ambrose Viccars' head under the water.

Christopher counted boys off his fingers, each word an effort. "The Prat boy is now thirteen, the Viccars' boy the same. And then there's William Wythers, who has just turned eleven."

"That leaves the Powell children and—" here Elizabeth looked down at the table with watery eyes "—Virginia."

"Edmund Powell is the youngest," I stated, ignoring Elizabeth's words. "Born over the winter festivals."

"And why is it that the only children who've been birthed since we arrived in Eden are all Winefrid Powell's offspring?" Dyonis' voice was tight. He sat straight as an arrow in his chair, but I noticed the tremor in his hands. He was trying to project power and leadership, yet this task was eating him up inside.

As it was for all of us.

"It wouldn't have to do with the supposed idea that the Master would free us if we had no children to give, would it?" he eyed Emme, who'd suggested it the night the Council was chosen.

"I believe 'tis more a matter of each woman not wanting to bear a child only to hand it to Eden," she answered. Her cheeks were no longer round and rosy, but sallow and sagging.

"Yet we're all counting on Winefrid to do so."

The truth was that each woman hoped the fate would fall to someone else, anyone else. And if that someone was Winefrid, so be it. So long as it was not us. Not our children.

Emme pushed one of her limp curls under her coif. "Only four couples here are married, Governor. Mayhap—"

Dyonis shook his head. "Do not tell me there has been no opportunity for the others. Clement always has his weapon at the ready, Lewes will stick anything that's breathing—or not, and if Audry's legs spread any wider, she'd split to become her own twin. Now how are the women preventing these births?"

None of us spoke. It was a woman's secret, and in a place where there were so few of us, it was important to keep our secrets intact. But Emme, Elizabeth, and I knew; each petal of the Eternity Flower was shaped like a cup—the outer ones were large enough for use as a barrier to pregnancy as well as to catch one's courses. The proof that Eden was a man's paradise and not a woman's, was in the fact that this kind of worry still existed.

We entered into a bitter debate. Who to give to Eden? Once again, Virginia's name was put forth, and once again I fought tooth and nail. It was only when Dyonis threatened to make the final decision on his own, that I came up with a solution to save my daughter.

"And who is it who will take the child's life?" I asked. "You, Dyonis? Will you drown another just as Walter was drowned?"

"Aye, if Virginia is that child." But even though resentment burned through him, he was still a good man. Who knew if he would stay that way but, for the moment, he was simply a grieving father whose anger at the unfairness of his loss was directed at Virginia.

"You say that now, but try living for eternity with the blood of an innocent on your hands—even one you have hatred for. I can tell you, Dyonis, the taking of a child's life? 'Tis the kind of thing that embitters the soul. There is a reason Torment has chosen my shoulders as his permanent perch: my misery keeps him sated."

And that is how I saved Virginia once again. By offering my own foul hands to make the sacrifice. It was a task that had to be done, and everyone—from the Council to the children—needed a scapegoat to detest. I was already in that position. If it gave Virginia life and gave the others some semblance of peace, I was willing to stay the outcast.

The next morning, I was awoken by birdsong. Outside the window, the trees were green, and the air fragrant with pine and the scent of the Eternity Flower. I heard the river rushing in the distance and the clucking of chickens running through the yard. All was normal again. All was right. A loaf of fresh bread and honey sat on the table. I spread the honey onto a thick piece of bread and handed it to Virginia as she stumbled out of bed. Her face was once again flush and healthy, her eyes still crusted with sleep but once again full of life.

As she ate, I moved outside to sit on the log that served as a bench. From this vantage point, I could see the village below. Smoke curled up from the chimneys, bringing with it the scent of bubbling stews. The trees were lush under the golden layer of mist and the sound of laughter rode the wind all the way up to my cottage. Torment loosened his grip on my neck and settled onto my lap instead, his head and paws resting on my knees.

I allowed a single tear to run down my cheek before steeling myself and swallowing my feelings.

The whisper of footfalls came from the cottage door. I did not turn to Virginia, did not glance her way. Softly, I said, "Do not call on the Powells."

"Why is that?"

"They'll be mourning the loss of little Edmund today. It's best to stay away."

Silence. Then, "Mama. You did not..."

I turned quickly, startling Torment. He gripped my knees with his claws, drawing blood. "Aye. I did, Virginia. I murdered that babe with my own hands."

Virginia stepped backwards and clutched the Malice pearl on the chain around her neck. "You're a monster."

"Call me a monster. Call me what you will, but I had no choice. 'Twas you or he. 'Twas he or we all died." I took a deep breath and balled my hands into fists. "I may have pushed him under the water, but I am not alone in my guilt. No one stopped me. No one even tried. They all value their own lives more than the life of one little boy."

"I hate you." She threw the rest of her bread to the ground. Torment scurried over to nibble on it and it disappeared behind his rows of teeth in a matter of seconds.

"Oh, Virginia. Do not condemn what you cannot understand."

She began to cry and, Devil help me, I did not go to her. I could not. While I reasoned away my sin with words, my heart was so heavy I dared not move.

13

Redd

Eden: Present Day

I look at the flower, it roots hanging off the end of the stem like a mud-colored jellyfish. It's freaking huge. So much bigger than the one Agnes and I constantly replanted.

"I pray you, Redd. Tell me all you know about planting the Eternity Flower." The intensity in John's voice gives away just how important the whole flower-on-the-outside thing is to him.

I've been having fun, but his question makes me think of Agnes and bitterness sucks some of the joy out of the day. "Why? Why do you want to grow the Eternity Flower out there?"

"We suffer on the outside," he says. "It helps."

"With what?"

"Pain, for one."

Agnes has always been more worried about that flower than anything. She doesn't just need it for pain. It's a deeper need. It's almost like she lives for it. Maybe the Eternity Flower isn't everywhere to dull the villagers' sixth sense. Maybe it's everywhere because they're all *addicts.*

"Is it an opioid?" I ask.

John shakes his head. "It's something unique."

"But like a drug, right?" For a split-second I think of Agnes and wonder how she's coping without the nectar. I shove down any guilt that tries to surface. At least now she'll be forced to quit.

"It's more than that." His hazel eyes are now pleading. "Redd."

"Fine." I relent. "I'll show you."

I start with the tangled mass of roots. "You need to be gentle. Separate each one but treat it like it's made of glass and could break any second."

He watches my fingers like his life depends upon it.

"Then you tuck the ends into the ground, like this," I say, patting dirt over the roots bit by bit. He helps, his movements careful. It takes a lot longer to replant the flower than it did to uproot it since we're not using magic.

When our hands touch, something flashes through my mind. I hear John's voice—"You cannot enter Eden"—and at those words, rage rushes through me, strong enough to make me gasp.

"Redd?" his eyebrows dip in concern.

Holy hell. What's wrong with me?

"What is it?" He frowns, making his dimples evident. My anger falls away as quickly as it came. I don't know what that was. I mean, I'm here, in Eden. So obviously, I wasn't left behind.

"Nothing." I shake my head.

Right. The flower.

"The next part is the worst," I continue as if nothing happened and drag my fingertips over the prickly stem. "You basically do this until your fingertips look like hamburger meat. Agnes never explained why."

Here, in Eden, there's no pain when I do it. And my skin heals with every pass.

But John's nodding. "Aye. I understand now. Then what?"

"We stick by the plant. Make sure it doesn't droop," I say, remembering the horrible nights when we first arrived at a new place. "It usually perks up within an hour or two, that's the sign it's doing well. Then, later, the petals double and the leaves brighten." I don't tell John because I hate to even think about it, but sometimes we slept next to the flower, on the dirt, until Agnes decided it was healthy enough to be on its own. When I was really little, I remember it taking more than one night, sometimes two or three. Afterward, my fingertips would be infected—red and burning and puffy. It always went away. I always healed quickly enough. But I hated it.

And part of me hated her because of it.

John studies the replanted bloom. It's leaning to one side. "That seems simple enough. In the car on the way here you said something about pricking yourselves regularly on the flower's spines? Even after planting."

I scoff. "Um, yeah. I'd do it every day." Agnes forced me to.

I push more dirt over one side of the roots to make the flower stand straight.

"Thank you for that, Redd. I..." He licks his lips and turns away, his chest heaving with a huge breath. When he looks back at me, he smiles, those dimples even deeper. "Let's see if you've inherited Virginia's talent."

Just her name makes my heart swell with hope. "What's that?"

He sits back on his haunches and shakes the dirt from his hands "We all have special affinities with Eden's magic. Grandfather moves things with ease; Thomas is a fixer, excellent at puzzles. Grandmama excels at cookery. I'm good with Eden's pets—"

"And diving," I interject.

His mouth kicks up. "And diving.... Virginia is a gardener."

"That's her job?"

"No. We don't have jobs as such. But Virginia's able to grow all manner of plants from tiny seedlings into robust, healthy blooms. The fruit grove? If the stories are correct, she took what were a few trees the Master had planted and turned the place into a vast orchard over the space of an afternoon."

I think about the rows and rows of trees. "Wow. She grew that?"

"Aye. And much more."

"Okay, so you think I can grow things? I mean, I didn't grow anything back home." No. I wrecked things.

"Perhaps," John says. "We know the magic works on you. Now to see if you've an affinity like your mother."

My *mother*.

The word alone makes my eyes mist. I'm so ridiculous.

I figure I'd better start small, so I eye the ground cover. Peeking out from under clusters of leaves, dozens of tiny, crimson buds stay hidden in the shadow of the Eternity Flower.

Spreading my fingers over the soil, I close my eyes. Unlike when I filled John's cup or when we dug the hole, this time my blood seems to warm as I imagine my magic traveling up the flowers' stems and into the petals.

John gasps and I open my eyes.

The scarlet blooms are now everywhere, like a carpet of red confetti. They've doubled in size and are no longer hidden. Instead, they've pushed their way into the sun by climbing the Eternity Flowers, their silvery leaves wrapped around the stalks like curled ribbon.

And those Eternity Flowers...they now stand much taller, the blooms the size of basketballs.

"Whoa," I breathe. I'm used to breaking things, not growing them. This feels so much more...healthy.

John laughs. "You are a Dare, of that there's no doubt."

This time there's no shame that comes with the observation. This time, I feel my face flush with pride. I wonder what else I can do.

Just then, a bell rings in the distance. John sighs. "We must go. The Council is meeting and they'd like to see you."

"Council?"

"The Council of Elders."

I nod. "How old is *elder*?"

"Old. Very old. They founded Eden."

"Oh. When was that?"

"In 1590."

I giggle but he doesn't even crack a smile.

I say, "You're joking."

I wait for John to tell me that he's messing with me. But instead he responds with, "No, I'm not."

14

Redd

Eden: Present Day

Before John can move away, I squeeze his arm. "Wait. Are you seriously trying to tell me there are people here who are over 400 years old?"

"Aye," he says, his eyes meeting mine. "There are."

"John."

"Redd?"

"Do you think I'm an idiot?"

"I can assure you, I do not. The Eternity Flower is named as it is for a reason. Here, we live forever."

And even with the overpowering scent of those flowers everywhere, even with how absent up my sixth sense has been, I know he's telling the truth. I taste it, smell it, even feel it like a gentle caress. *This. Is. Messed. UP.*

"Whoa. Whoa, whoa, whoa. That's not magic. No botanicals can do that. That's..." I shake my head. "Impossible."

One side of his mouth lifts in a small smile. "Redd, in a matter of seconds you've grown flowers to thrice their size. You've healed from a knife wound and dove from a waterfall without so much as a bruise. From that to immortality is...well...a small jump."

Then his smile drops. Weird. Why would John be sad about immortality? Or maybe it is a sad thing to be immortal. How would I know? Despite having embraced the *not getting hurt* thing, I'm really having a hard time wrapping my head around the whole *living forever* thing.

Suddenly, a thought hits me and I stand so quickly it gives me a headrush. "Oh, God, no. Are you...how old are you?"

"I'm eighteen."

"Eighteen decades...?" I'm not into old dudes, no matter how hot.

The smile comes out again, and this time it's as bright as a sunbeam as he laughs. "No. Eighteen years. I'm your elder by mere months."

It's stupid how relieved I am by this information. I mean, it's not like we're together or anything. But in the back of my mind I think, *maybe we could be.*

"The Council will want to speak with you." John starts walking, and I follow behind.

"What else haven't you told me?"

I can't see his face, but his voice breaks when he says, "A lot."

"Really? Great. Just great."

"In my defense, you would never have believed me."

"I would now. So start talking."

The same squirrel from earlier scurries past and up the gnarled trunk of a tree, chittering the whole way. John freezes until it's out of sight. Then he turns to me. "There are some secrets I cannot tell you."

"Can't or won't?"

"A bit of both. However, you will not be in the dark forever."

"No. I won't. Because you're going to tell me." I lift my eyebrows. "You can start by saying why you lied about recognizing Clara in the picture I showed you before we came into Eden. She's Minnie's daughter. She was kidnapped, John. I know it and you know it."

He blanches, then chews on his lip for a while. Finally, he says, "It's delicate, Redd. Joyce Archer raised her. She, in the most important sense of the word, is her mother."

"But Clara wasn't just adopted. She was *stolen*. Clara should know that."

"Perhaps..."

"Who is Clara?" I ask, thinking of how she looked at him and talked to him earlier. A little too honeyed. "I mean, to you? Are you close?"

"Clara and I have always known each other." He rubs the stubble that's beginning to show on his chin. "However, Clara is close to no one. Not now."

"Something happened?"

"Her father...he...died. She cannot hate him, so she hates everyone else."

I have a sudden rush of sympathy for Clara. *Autumn*. "Then maybe she'd be happy to know she has another family out there."

"That kind of information is not easy to swallow." He catches my gaze. "You of all people should understand that."

It's like a punch to the gut. Yeah. I do understand. All too well. Anger bubbles at the thought of Agnes lying to me and to Minnie all these years. She kidnapped Autumn, others...me.

I see her in my mind's eye, frantic, trying to put the Eternity Flower back together when my fury blew it apart.

Oh. My. God. *Wait.* She was so upset because she believed that I'd ruined her chances at living forever, didn't she? She said it was for pain. I thought it was an addiction. But the whole time she was trying to cheat death. No wonder she treated the damn thing like a precious baby.

My thoughts run circles in my head.

Some things slot into place. Like why she kept the flower with us. Why it was so important. It doesn't explain the kidnappings...or why she took me with her when she left Eden....but I feel those answers aren't too far from my grasp. Like they're knocking at the back door of my brain and I'm very close to turning the knob.

I give John a laser-sharp glare. "You think transplanting the flower outside this place will grant you eternal life elsewhere? That's your mission, isn't it? Did you even care a little bit about me coming back here, about me meeting my real mom, or was it all just to get gardening tips?"

"No, I don't....I didn't..." He inhales and starts again. "I'm not seeking for us to live eternally, but...normally."

"Normally? Normally isn't forever. You want to live forever outside of Eden, too."

"I want us to have the choice to live outside of Eden. I do not know what power the flower holds beyond our borders. Except that it allows us to surv—"

The bell rings again. This time it's louder than before.

"There's no time to discuss. We must hurry. The Council is summoning us." John's on the move again.

"*Summoning*? I'm liking this less and less." I snort.

My eyes go to my feet as they disappear under the carpet of fog that covers the forest floor. It's thick enough that I reach down to rake my fingers through, expecting some sort of resistance. But they slide right through the vapor as if there's nothing there.

Higher up in the trees, a trio of birds clings to the ends of the branches, making them dip from the weight. Their feathers are silver, their beaks golden. They're beautiful. I watch them for a second and a shiver runs down my spine. Because their eyes...their eyes look human. But when I blink, they're back to regular black bird eyes.

I shake off that shiver. *Get a grip, Redd.*

When we get back to the square, most of the market goers are gone and the stands taken away. John leads me directly past the large fountain of a gargoyle spitting water and up the wide stairs to the massive cathedral. Last night, it looked gorgeous lit up by torchlight. And it still is, but...also kind of creepy. Now that I'm up close I see that all along the edifice, snarling creatures are carved into the glittering white stone. The stained-glass windows aren't of angels and saints but horrific creatures with fiery eyes and tufted tails.

"This is...um...different." I gesture to the entranceway, giant wooden doors set inside a carved archway of fanged teeth.

John shrugs. "It's supposed to represent Temptation's maw. Pretty good likeness if you ask me."

"Temptation?"

"Aye. The mother snake in the Garden," he says like I should know.

"Which garden?"

"*The* Garden."

"Wait. *The* Garden. As in the Garden of Eden?" I start laughing. "You guys have a sense of humor."

Then he's opening the door and the scent of what must be Eternity Flower incense hits me smack in the face. My eyes water with how powerful it is. Leading me through the vestibule to a rounded doorway and up a set of winding stone stairs, John turns and gives me a nervous smile. "You all right?"

I remind myself why I'm here as the stairs lead me higher. I may be "summoned" by the Council, but I'm here, in Eden, because I want to be. Because I was sick of Agnes telling me what to do without ever getting an explanation. It took turning eighteen and a magical mask to wake me up to her lies.

"I'm good," I say as we enter a long room stuffed with shelves and hundreds of books. At the back is a large tapestry of a battle between angels, centered on a male angel with a mane of dark hair. His back is bloody, where his midnight, iridescent wings are hanging, half torn off. But even with the muscles on display, the blood all over, and the corpses of magnificent beings at his feet, it's the angel's eyes that have me, pulling me in like a magnet. He's beautiful beyond description. Otherworldly. His irises glitter gold, and despite his image being embroidered, his gaze feels real.

I know I've never seen those eyes before, but something about that angel is familiar. Maybe it's a reproduction of a painting

I've seen in a museum, or something I studied in school and forgot. I don't know.

"The Council meeting is here."

I pull my attention from the tapestry to where John is standing before a large, carved door. When I hesitate, he adds, "Do not worry, they don't bite." But any joke falls flat because a shadow crosses his face as he says it.

"Whoa. They may not bite, but then what *do* they do?"

"Nothing that is cause for concern."

My confidence slips. "What?"

"You are safe, Redd." He squeezes my fingers, a quick pulse to reassure me.

Shit. I'm so not reassured.

He drops my hands and pushes open the door. "I'll see you in a few days," he whispers, his breath warm against the shell of my ear. A pleasant shiver runs through my body, disappearing as soon as I step into the room.

The first thing I notice are the hellish creatures leering at me. Demons, gargoyles, and banshees of rich, jeweled tones in the round panes of stained glass. Below that is a long table, with a woman on the right, a man on the left, and John's grandfather, Dyonis, at the head.

"We thank you, John. You may go. We'll take it from here." Dyonis gives a curt nod.

John winks at me then pulls the door shut with a loud thump. Suddenly, I'm standing alone in front of the Council.

15

John

Eden: Present Day

As I exit the Devil's cathedral, every part of my body thrums in excitement. Now that Redd's shown me what she and Agnes did to make the flower grow in the Beyond, my melancholy has dissipated. It is not, as the Council says, impossible. It is that they—and the scouts who've tried to grow the flower before—have never figured out a different way to make it work.

A simple bloodletting.

Not the harrowing sacrifice required inside of Eden, but a finger along the sharp spines on the stem. We do not need to give a life. Nor do we need the Master's magic.

If Agnes had shared this knowledge instead of running with it, lives could have been saved... Why would she be so selfish? Does she hate Eden and those of us in it that much?

I shake the thoughts out of my head. It does not matter. All that matters now is that we can be saved. We *will* be saved.

I've gathered necessities from the Council storeroom to camp in the Beyond. I do not plan to go much further than the forest where Terror makes his nest. It will be private and close by and, if all goes to plan, I'll only be gone a few days. Yet experience has taught me that I must be prepared should it *not* go to plan. And that means bringing a pet. All I need is a pet and the flower, then I am ready to go.

This is it. This is what can—and will—change everything. For the first time ever, my desires align fully with my mission. For the first time ever, I'll do not just some good…but all good.

I like the feeling.

I smile into the sparkling air, then follow the wide stairs down to the square. But before I even step upon the cobbles, Clara's thin shadow darkens the path before me. Fury paws the ground between us, the midnight-violet fur of his hackles standing at attention. His fiery eyes narrow at me.

"At ease," I say.

Instead of obeying, Fury begins to snap and bark. Clara chuckles but then quiets the hound with a sharp word. "He doesn't like your mood, John."

I stick my tongue out at the hellhound. "Too bad, boy. I'm feeling good today." My eyes flick to Clara. "But he can always get his fill from you. You've got enough suppressed anger to keep him satiated for a while."

"I'd venture you'd be angry, too, if our places were swapped. If I kept getting missions through nepotism and not my own merit." Fury leans into her as she speaks. "And now you've even gotten your grandfather to allow you out on a wild goose chase."

"Planting the flower is no wild goose chase, Clara. It'll save us all."

She snorts.

"And I'm trying to decide which pet to take with me." I look down at Fury. "What do you think, boy?"

The hellhound's lips curl.

Clara smiles. Genuinely. It's something I haven't seen in a while.

"On your way to see our guest?" I gesture behind me where I know Redd will come out once the Council has finished speaking with her.

"Guest? She's victuals for Eden, John."

I used to adore Clara. I used to find all sorts of ways to "accidentally" brush her skin or touch her hair or end up in a room alone with her. Now I bristle at the snide look on her face. "Not anymore. Not once I plant the flower in the Beyond."

"A fool's errand. You'll fail. Like you fail at everything else." She lifts her shoulders ever so slightly.

A huge wave of regret washes over me. Since her father walked out of Eden, she's never been the same. For a long time, I was empathetic. I, too, lost my parents in the same way. But now, I'm just sorry. Sorry she finds the bad in everything. Sorry I no longer have the desire to help her see some good. I'm too tired of her constant dismissals. "Yet Redd is here. In Eden. Because *I* succeeded in convincing her to come."

"Ah. She fell victim to your charms, did she?" She lifts a delicate eyebrow.

I can't admit that it was quite the opposite, so instead I say, "You did at one time."

That elicits an eye roll. But she doesn't dare deny it.

"You pushed Redd this morning," I say, crossing my arms. "Over the falls."

"And?"

"And it was cruel."

"Cruel?" Her voice breaks with laughter. "How so, John? She loved it. She dove the falls several times over."

"Aye, but it should have been her choice to do so at first. She'd have died of fear alone at that push if she weren't in Eden."

"Ah, but she *is* in Eden. And she needed a push."

"Admit it: you wanted to frighten her. You enjoyed it."

"Perhaps. But she also enjoyed it." Clara moves closer and fiddles with my shirt collar, then rests her hands on my chest. Her eyes go to my lips like they've done so many times before. I know she's expecting me to lean in like I have so many times before.

Instead, I brush her hands away and step back.

Her eyes narrow. "Why should you even care what I do with Redd?"

"Because there is no reason to hurt her. Be nice to her, Clara."

Now she laughs in earnest.

"Devil's curse." I ball my hands into fists and Fury lets out a satisfied yip. "You may find this difficult to believe, but Redd would make a good friend. You have much in common."

"A friend?"

"Aye. A friend. Remember what it was like to have those?"

"I have friends."

"Who?"

She shrugs. "Brian. Henry...You."

"Interesting choices. You do nothing but insult me. You broke Brian's heart. And Henry...when was the last time you said more than two words to Henry?"

"What does it matter, John? You're off on another mission and have left the Dare girl for me to deal with." A blonde curl tumbles in front of her eye and she brushes it away. "Word is you're sweet on her."

I try to ignore her, yet feel the heat rise, unbidden, into my cheeks.

"Belial's breath! You are!" Clara's mouth drops. "But she's a Dare. You, of all people..."

My face is burning. I walk away from her, then speed up, nearly flying through the square.

"You cannot have her, John!" Clara's voice is fierce enough that it makes me falter and nearly trip on the uneven cobbles. "You'll see! She'll be given to Eden! You cannot stop what is meant to be!"

But by now, I'm no longer listening.

16

Eleanor

Eden: 1604

Virginia grew from a child to a young woman. By the time she was seventeen years of age, I'd saved her from the Fire Pit five times, each time exchanging a bit of my soul, my sanity, for her life. With each child I drowned, a piece of me shattered, the splinters of self-hatred so deeply embedded that I no longer knew the vivacious woman who'd stepped foot onto the massive ship called the *Lyon* to find adventure and freedom overseas. Now, when I looked in the mirror, I saw not the dew of youth still clinging to my cheeks despite the passing of time, nor the luxurious shine of my hair, nor the curious glow of health Eden gave us all. Nay. I saw the bloody-toothed monster that was my mask.

Now I was Eleanor Dare, hatred personified, with claws for a heart and teeth for a soul. I was the master of the sacrificial ceremonies and nearly as feared as the Devil himself.

The village would not admit this, but they liked it that way. Though Satan was our master, we all wanted to think of ourselves as holy. If I was bad, then the others could tell themselves they were good.

Winefrid Powell had now been forced to see three of her eight children drowned. Of the nine women in the village, Joan Warren was the only other miserable pup that had even birthed a live child. Her first-born was fed to Eden the second the cord was severed.

Most of the women had stopped using the petals of the Eternity Flower as a barrier to pregnancy. Whether there were twenty babes or two, one would have to be sacrificed to Eden for the village to live, and as the years passed, we all wanted to live...or rather, we wanted to avoid the fires of hell that would surely come after death.

The Eternity Flower gave us eternal youth, but now we suspected it also affected our ability to fall pregnant. It was just like the Master to ask us to sacrifice life and then impede us in the making of it.

Joyce Archard decided to go about getting pregnant as a matter of duty. She even beat Audry in how many village men she bedded, much to the chagrin of her husband, Arthur. I'd despised Joyce for her liaison with Ananias back in Roanoke, but now she held only my pity. Her stomach rounded every spring like clockwork. Yet every child she birthed was stillborn. Every single one. No matter the father. No matter a boy or a girl. No matter that she carried the babe to full term. Every single time. The ability to escape death and harm in Eden did not seem to apply to a babe in the womb. And Eden refused to accept for sacrifice what God had already called back home.

I do not know how Joyce kept on.

By 1604, there should have been a score of children running amok through Eden's streets, even with the sacrifices. Instead, there were less than a handful of youngsters under the age of twelve. And those were all Winefrid's. Whether Winefrid was an unfortunate soul, a twisted saint, or a wretched fool, I was not certain. But that woman was the sole reason we were still alive.

Virginia often descended the hill from the cottage to wander into the heart of the village and to the Powell home. She would bring the girls crowns of daisies and the boys homemade biscuits. She'd play cards with the younger children and gossip with the older ones while Winefrid put her feet up and Edward drank his ale. Their acceptance of her, however, even after all this time, was tenuous at best. Virginia was the quintessential good girl, the sweet young thing who was pleasant with everyone. She was the complete opposite of me and therefore should have been loved by all. But she was a Dare, and blood stains.

I thought she visited the Powell home because she was perhaps sweet on twenty-three-year-old Ambrose Viccars, who lived in the cottage next door to them. With his broad shoulders and brooding manner, Ambrose would have been the target of lustful gazes back in England. Yet here, it was not the case. Apart from Virginia and the young Powell girls, every single woman in Eden had watched him grow from chubby child to handsome young man. He felt like a son and there were some lines that many of us could not cross.

Except Audry Tappen, of course. As Dyonis would surely point out, the only thing she did not cross was her legs.

For several weeks, I sensed Virginia was hiding something from me. She'd come home flushed and distracted. We'd expanded the cottage once she was an adolescent, and she now had her own upstairs chamber. For the longest time, it had felt as though she was a part of me. An appendage that breathed and talked on its own. Now, she was becoming someone separate, with her own opinions and preferences...and secrets. A strangling sense of panic wound its way around my heart when I realized just how much of her life I was not privy to.

One evening, she came home from a long afternoon away and ran directly to her bedchamber. I thought I glimpsed something under her arm, and so I decided it was time to see what she'd been hiding from me. I climbed the stairs quietly and opened the door to her chamber without knocking. She was setting something on the window seat, directly in the sun. As she heard the hinges creak, she whipped around and stepped sideways. "Mama! You're to knock first!"

She tugged on a leaf of ivy that was outside the window, attempting to hide the wet undergarments from my view by making the vine grow inside.

But it was too late.

Anger drove me forward. I nudged her aside, ripped off the strands of ivy, and touched the linen. It was soaked through. "You've taken to doing your own laundry now?"

"Aye," she agreed too quickly.

"Then why is the scrub board still downstairs?"

"'Twas a minor stain, no need for scrubbing."

"Your courses?"

"They took me unawares."

I narrowed my gaze. "Odd. You finished your courses last week. I know. I'm the one who washed the rags."

"Odd," she agreed, but did not look me in the eye, knowing she was caught.

I studied her then, as a young boy might. Without her coif, her dark blonde tresses fell in thick waves, silky yet tousled enough to bring thoughts of wild nights in a bed to mind. Her lips were full and pink, her blue eyes shiny under a bridge of thick lashes. The flesh of her breasts peeked out from beneath the ties of her chemise, and her hips had rounded into womanly form. She was no longer a child. And, Devil as my witness, that terrified me.

"Is it Ambrose?" I asked quietly.

Her eyebrows came together in confusion.

"Who took your maidenhead?"

Her cheeks burned red but she stood straighter. "I'm not lying with Ambrose."

I tried to keep my voice even, to control the fear rising inside of me. "Have you been smart, at least? Used the petals as I told you?"

Virginia was familiar with the use of the Eternity Flower to avoid pregnancy. I'd spoken about it before. Men sought the pleasures of the flesh wherever and with whomever was appealing and available. It did not matter that she was a Dare and therefore unacceptable company. If status were a barrier, all the prostitutes in England would be out of a job. We called women whores, but it was men who were the true bawds.

I had given enough. There was no way I was going to give up a grandchild to the Master's twisted version of heaven. Better to have no grandchild at all.

"So? Have you?" The words were sharp enough to crack stone.

She shook her head. "I've lain with no one."

"Satan's scourge, Virginia. Stop the lies! I do not give a damn about your whoring. I care about the consequences of such." The words were coarse and foul and flew out of my mouth before I could think them straight. I did not believe her to be a whore—Devil knows I was no saint at her age—but my anger at her keeping secrets harshened my rebuke.

The blue of her eyes darkened. She crossed her arms over her chest and lifted her chin. "You may think me desperate for Ambrose's advances, but that lout squeezes breasts as if he's juicing a lemon. I've told him no and he listens. I am the daughter of Eleanor Dare, the evil witch. He fears me."

Her words both disgusted and relieved me. I swallowed down the worst of my anger and stroked Torment's fur. "Then why are your undergarments wet?"

She flopped onto her bed and sighed loudly, as if she were too tired to fight any longer. Her theatrics woke Deception, who was now big enough that we'd built a large tub for the creature to nap in, under the cool shadow of Virginia's bed. Soon, the water dragon would come into her powers, and I would refuse to keep her in the house. But for now, Deception was innocuous. She stretched her neck out and rested her head on Virginia's thighs. The puff of smoke that left her nostrils was less than that of a snuffed candle.

"I've been swimming," Virginia said as she stroked the beast's scales.

For a moment, I could not even speak. Those were the last words I expected to hear. "Swimming?"

"Aye."

"In the river?" Sometimes the villagers waded into the river, to feel the cool rush of water over their ankles, upon their shins. The riverbed was deep enough to submerge oneself if desired, but the rocks and tug of the current made it impossible to swim. The only area one could really swim would be…

"Nay, not the river." Virginia did not say more. She did not have to. I knew it was the Fire Pit.

"But it's a place of death."

"And of beauty."

"You could die there," I started. "It's the one place where we can die."

Now she sat up, ice in her voice. "Nay. It's the one place where we can be sacrificed. But I think I am safe from your murderous hands."

I turned and exited the room, slamming the door. Tears burned behind my eyes. I stopped and took in a shaky breath on the staircase, trying to soothe the pain in my heart. After all I'd done for her, Virginia still hated me.

I was losing her. She was my only reason for living, and I was losing her.

She was supposed to be mine.

Even with the help of Eden's magic, I ruined dinner that night, the fish scorched, the leeks tasteless, the pudding thin. My mind would not focus. At first, I thought of nothing but

Virginia's hurtful words. Of how my actions to save her had also pushed her away. Yet as we swallowed the soupy pudding, I sensed an arrogance in the way she held her shoulders, in the smirk she fought to keep off her face. Then I knew there was more Virginia was not telling me.

Two days later, I pretended to be busy in the kitchen as she left the house, her Devil's mask under her arm. As discreetly as possible, I followed her. Twice, she nearly saw me as she descended the hill toward the village, but luckily the trees that had been young saplings when we'd built our home were now fully grown and wide enough to hide my form. On the other side of the town square, she met Samuel Powell near the footbridge, his own mask in the crook of his elbow. He was two years her junior and still growing into his limbs. He had none of Ambrose Viccars' charm or presence. So I was taken aback when he pulled her into the shadows of a willow tree and kissed her so thoroughly it made my cheeks burn. Together, they walked through the forest, following the line of Eternity Flowers along the river, until they reached the glowing water of the Fire Pit. Two of Samuel's siblings were there. So was William Wythers. He paced the spongy moss carpet and complained about their tardiness. I stayed in the shadows as the boys stripped down to their trousers and the girls to their shifts.

Almost as one, the group put on their Devil's masks and walked into the pond. My heart beat faster as they continued, the water now up to their thighs, their waists, their chests, then over their heads. They disappeared, leaving nothing but bubbles on the surface. As the last one popped, I saw a vision of Walter

Harvie thrashing under the water, bubbles escaping his tiny mouth as my own hands pushed him under.

The vision broke and panic washed over me.

"Virginia!" I screamed. I raced through the forest and into the pond, terror squeezing my chest like a vice. "Virginia!"

I plunged under the surface, the cool water forcing Torment to release his claws from my neck. Now in the deep, I opened my eyes. The pond looked to be ringed in flames, the algae waving under the movement of the water. But in the center was only darkness. No Virginia. No William or Samuel or the others.

I scrambled towards the surface. My heavy skirts dragged as I crawled out of the water coughing and spluttering. I lay in the mouth of the pond, crying, terrified that Virginia was gone. That Eden had swallowed her just as it had swallowed those wretched babes I drowned to supposedly save us all.

I don't know how long I lay there sobbing. Long enough for the sun to have moved from one side of the forest to the other. Long enough for Torment to have resettled into his favorite spot round my shoulders, long enough for my chemise to have dried stiff around the arms.

Then suddenly there was a splash. Then another. And another. A league of demons rose out of the water, their faces menacing. Laughter came from behind those fangs and turned-down mouths. Laughter and cheers of excitement.

The first one to tear off his mask was Samuel Powell. He wore a grin that faltered the moment his eyes fell upon my form. "Eleanor Dare."

Virginia tugged the mask from her own face. Shock widened her eyes, then anger reddened her cheeks. "Mama."

"Oh, Virginia! You're alive!" My sobbing started all over again.

The group of youths stared at me as one by one they took off their masks. I imagine that seeing my form there, seeing me reduced to tears, I no longer looked like the unformidable Eleanor Dare to them, but a pathetic old woman in need of her child.

And yet, the lot of them scurried off so quickly they did not even take the time to dress. They simply grabbed their affairs from the pile at the side of the pond and ran into the forest.

That left Virginia and me alone.

"Thank the Devil you're alive," I said, wiping the tears from my face. I went to take her in my arms, but she moved out of reach.

She peeled the soaking shift from her form, her naked body pink in the glow from the water. Her clothes lay on a rock where the river spilled into the pond. As she dressed, she did not look at me or say a word. Her anger was so full and palpable, however, that within a handful of seconds, Fury was running through the forest. Once he reached us, a soft whine escaped his snout. His deep violet fur stood up on his back, the blue tips like spikes. He gently nuzzled Virginia, happy for the ire she was feeding him.

I inhaled, the scent of the Eternity Flower lining my nostrils, then exhaled, my fear finally gone. I smoothed my damp skirts and fixed my coif, my backbone growing stronger and my jaw setting.

"Where were you?" I asked. From the iron in my voice, she would know I was not to be played with.

She did not answer, instead starting back to the cottage.

"I asked you a question, Virginia." I hastened my strides and grabbed her elbow. She did not stop and so we walked in tandem, Fury squeezing into the space between us. The fog surrounded our ankles and the sunlight nearly disappeared behind the thick leaves of the gnarled trees.

I tugged again at her elbow and Virginia sighed. "We went...beyond."

"Beyond?"

She glanced up at me, then around the forest, as if she were worried someone could hear. "We found a place. A place that is beyond Eden. It smells of salt and melons and cedar."

I stumbled, stepping on Fury's giant paw. The hellhound yelped, then took off back through the woods. Virginia's words echoed in my ears. What could she be talking about?

"How?" I shook my head, remembering how I'd tried to escape all those years ago when I was first told to sacrifice Virginia. There had been no place to find. "How is that possible?"

Virginia shrugged. "I imagine it's always been there. But no one dares go into the pond. It's only because of the games we played a few years back that we know anything about it."

"You've known for *years*?" My voice rose.

"Nay. Not about the Beyond. That we recently discovered..." Here she paused, as if weighing her words. "We used to play Sacrifice, wearing the mask. One can breathe underwater in it. But 'twas not until a few weeks back that we thought about using it to swim. And then, once underneath, we saw the tunnel."

"The tunnel?" I realized I was continuously echoing her phrases, yet I could not form a coherent thought.

"There's a tunnel in the pond. It leads to a place William recognizes."

I shook my head. "What place?"

And then Virginia said the words that made my knees give out on the spot: "The tunnel leads out of Eden, Mama. It leads directly to Roanoke."

17

Redd

Eden: Present Day

The 'elders' that make up the Council look decades younger than any of the residents at Shady Pines. Even Minnie, who's the young one there, looks downright weathered compared to these guys.

I suddenly feel extremely vulnerable in this room lit only by stained glass and candlelight.

"Sit." Dyonis gestures to a heavy chair at the end of the table with a worn red velvet seat and back. He smiles, only it's not exactly warm. I get a flash, almost like a memory, of him smiling like that and placing me behind bars. I sit stiffly on the edge of the seat, shaking off the weird vision. I don't know what is going on with me. Maybe all the magic here is too much and my brain's glitching.

"We've already met, but in an unofficial manner. I am the Governor." Dyonis tugs on a pearl hanging from his earlobe, then motions to the others. "We are the Council. Or rather, a part of it. Not everyone is present today. Only Christopher,

Emme, and I. There are tasks to be done as, Devil willing, we've a Harvest to prepare."

Devil willing? Wait. That's the kind of expression—

All is good. You are safe here.

I melt back into the chair just as Dyonis' eyes shoot to the woman. "Emme? You asked to verify that she's the girl we seek. You have her now here in front of you."

"Aye, Governor." Emme is short and round, with breasts the size of small pumpkins. She's wearing a skirt and bodice over an embroidered blouse, along with a little white coif on her head. She scrapes her chair back loudly and walks across the oiled floorboards until she's standing directly in front of me. Our faces are at the same level height-wise, though I am sitting and she's standing. She looks into my eyes at first.. Then she drags her gaze to my birthmark. Her hand comes up under my chin, fingers clenching my jaw.

"Hey!" I try to pull my head from her, but her grasp is too strong.

"Terribly sorry, my dear. Must inspect." She scrutinizes my skin, rubs it hard, then lets go of my chin. It should hurt, but it doesn't.

"She's a Dare," Emme says. Her voice stays even, unemotional. I can't tell if, for her, being a Dare is a good thing or a bad one.

"I...I heard that not everyone's happy with my family." I swallow. "The Dares, I mean."

"What have you heard?" Dyonis asks.

That your family hates mine. But I say, "Just some prickly vibes."

The three of them exchange a glance. Then Emme gives me a smile. "We're such a small community, there are often petty feuds. But we're happy to have you with us." She squeezes me into a soft hug.

It's so different from the rough way she inspected my birthmark only seconds ago. I've been wanting to feel I belong somewhere for so long that this simple gesture nearly makes me burst into tears. I swallow them back as she releases me and returns to her seat.

The other man strokes his pointy beard. "My responsibility is to ready all of Eden for you. You've met some of the villagers already. Not everyone greeted you with open arms?"

"Oh, no. It was nothing. Mostly everyone was really nice."

He drags a finger over his beard again and nods. "Good. We shall have a welcoming ceremony soon. Once Eden is ready for the Harvest. Until then, we hope you'll be comfortable."

I decide to forget any bad vibes from snooty villagers. They don't matter. Because there's going to be a welcoming ceremony. For me. For *me*.

"You remember the rules set out for you?" Dyonis narrows his eyes at me.

My smile falters as I sift through my hazy memory of last night. "Not to talk too much about life outside here with the kids."

"Rather, you're not to talk about it at all," says Christopher. "Understood?"

"Yes. But I have lots of questions—"

Emme cuts me off. "You've met Clara?"

Clara/Autumn. I tap the armrest. "Uh. Yeah."

"We've entrusted her to help you get further acquainted with Eden. She can answer your questions."

"All of them? I've got a lot—"

"Aye, she'll answer them," Dyonis barks.

"And my birth mother? Virginia. When can I see her?"

"I thought Isobel told you."

"She said later today." I look to the sunlight coming through the stained glass. It should be nearing noon now.

"Then you have your answer."

The same jolt of irritation that I felt when I realized someone had gone through my backpack returns. "Virginia is the reason I'm here."

A muscle in his jaw ticks. "Aye, I am aware. You will meet her."

"Who's been raising you in the Beyond? John believes Agnes had done so." There's skepticism in Christopher's voice.

I take a breath. "Is it true that Agnes took me from my birth mother?"

"Aye." Emme nods. "'Tis the truth."

"Why? Why would she take me? And why would she take other kids? I saw...in the mask. She took children..." I'm about to say *children that are here in Eden* but trail off because a sudden vision pops into my head: me, in old-fashioned manacles.

What is happening? Why do I keep seeing weird visions?

A knot forms in my chest. It doesn't feel like a vision; it feels like it was something real. *Ridiculous*, I tell myself. I would remember.

"Agnes was a troubled soul. Had we realized just how troubled..." Emme shakes her head.

Dyonis clears his throat. "You never did answer the question of who raised you."

I'm about to tell him that it was Agnes—why would he think otherwise?—when I hesitate. Something doesn't feel right, but I don't know what. I can't cheat like I usually do and get a sense of what their motives are. So it's time for me to play with my cards close to my chest. "No. I didn't."

Dyonis blinks, his annoyance clear. But then he nods.

"You've seen the white flowers that line the river and are planted in front of every dwelling, have you not?" Christpher asks.

"Yeah. They...the scent is really powerful."

A corner of his mouth lifts into a smile. "Aye. I suppose to an outsider it would be. We've become accustomed to it."

Dyonis leans forward. "Have you seen these flowers in the Beyond?"

Again with the Eternity Flower? First John, now the Council? Do they really think it will give them eternal life outside of Eden? I see their faces. If John was telling the truth, these people have barely aged in four hundred years. I think of Agnes and the way she was looking forward to lines forming around her eyes. *They prove you've lived life as you should have,* she'd said. *No cheating.*

Maybe she *didn't* believe she could cheat death. But if not, then why was she so damn upset when I exploded the flower?

If I weren't in Eden, I'd be getting a headache. Instead, it feels like my brain has turned to bubble gum. Everything is stuck together, and I can't separate my thoughts.

A dark shadow materializes in the corner of the room behind the Council. In a matter of milliseconds, the shadow becomes the Master. He lifts an eyebrow above the sharp line of his mask and shakes his head before disappearing. I hear his voice as if he's whispering directly into my ear, *Tell them nothing. Make them squirm,* but when I turn no one is there. It doesn't creep me out as much as it should. Maybe it's because his voice is like chocolate syrup, sweet and rich and comforting.

Do I listen to the Master? I'm not sure I can trust him.

But do I fully trust the Council? Dyonis might be related to John, but he's got none of his grandson's warmth.

"Why? Why do you want to know if I've seen it outside of here? Why are you asking me all these questions but not answering mine?"

Any friendly pretext falls as Dyonis' hazel eyes bore into mine, his voice like ice. "'Tis not up to you to question our reasons nor our authority. Have you seen it or not?"

Whoa. Well, then.

I have no freaking idea what is going on here, why Agnes took kids, took me, why this place is magic or why the Master is telling me to keep secrets. But I'm done talking about that damn flower. They can figure it out themselves.

"I don't know," I say, shrugging. "Maybe? Maybe not. All flowers look alike to me."

Dyonis turns to Emme. "Fetch Clara."

"Aye," says Emme, bustling out the door.

Dyonis flicks his fingers at me. "You're dismissed, child. You can wait for Clara outside. She'll be your guide while John is gone."

I've got so many questions, but I know no one here will answer them. Maybe Clara will be more help.

When I step outside of the council room and back into the library, someone grabs me from behind, covers my mouth, and yanks me behind the angel tapestry. I know it's not Clara, because her voice comes from the stairwell. She's talking with Emme, something about her mother.

The hand over my mouth presses harder. "Don't. Say. A word."

18

John

Eden: Present Day

My cheeks still burning from the thought that Clara and others in Eden suspect I have feelings for Redd, I climb the western hills, eyes on the wild tangle of flowers and plants high up on one of the cliffs. Though I do not intend to go further into the Beyond than the wood at the other end of the tunnel, I still must bring a pet along. Just in case. While Chaos is my usual companion, he does not do well in one place. And I hope to stay near the flower. The other hell hounds are too dangerous for this type of mission and the smallest pets, like Nuisances or Suspicions, would not be of much help. A Persuasion, however, is quiet, easy to keep control of, and could be of use should I somehow cross other people.

The problem is getting one.

As I walk, I keep a wide berth from the Dare cottage out of habit. Eleanor has not been there in years, but Grandfather has always warned me to stay away. There's more than bad blood between our families; I believe Grandfather is truly afraid of the woman who led the pact with the Devil. I believe he may even be more afraid of her than the Devil himself.

I believe we all may be.

So instead of taking the shortcut past the small home, I follow a longer, overgrown path to the Garden. The Garden is one place in Eden that villagers only visit on a dare or for punishment, never for pleasure. I slap at the long grasses, weeds, and wildflowers impeding my steps until I finally find myself in front of an open set of golden gates choked with flowering vines. Inside there are dozens of trees laden with fat fruits and bushes heavy with jewel-toned berries. Errant Enticements have come here from the Caul and have woven a glittering web over the golden fencing from one side to the other, creating a ceiling of fine, silky threads that shine in the sun.

The Fire Pit is the only place we can die in Eden. The Garden is the only place where we can feel physical pain outside the days leading to sacrifice. When I was a boy, Clara, Brian, Henry, and I used to stand outside the Garden, giggling in the shadows and telling stories, hoping and dreading to get a glimpse of the prisoners. We only ever saw the shine of Persuasions among the greenery, never a face or a figure. When we were slightly older, we took our game to the next level and dared each other to step inside, to slide past the lush green leaves of the jungle of plants. A ravenous hunger rose up inside us when we set our eyes upon the apples hanging from silvery branches, the Persuasions urging us to take a taste. We timed how long we could go without reaching for cursed morsels, stopping each other before our fingers touched the fruit. Then one day,

Henry picked a rotting apple from the ground before we even had a chance to warn him.

He'd sunk his teeth into the brown flesh. And though he writhed in pain, he kept taking bites as if he were starving. And he was starving. The more one eats of the Garden's fruit, the more one wants, despite each bite causing agony, sucking the very energy of life from the body.

Luckily, in our recklessness, we'd kept an ounce of reason. While we did not wear our masks inside the Garden as it would have ruined the game, we did keep them on hand. Immediately, we pressed his mask to his face, which allowed us to pull him out. But even those few moments changed him. The always-ready smile slipped into a frown more often, and sometimes the only answer he gave to questions was a faraway look in his eyes.

The pain of starving in the Garden is real, and the torture of it is not only physical. I saw it in Henry...and I know because I've spent time there myself. When the memory of it haunts me, I snuff it out like a flame on a candle—quickly and before it can burn down the wick of my sanity.

Scouts used to be trained here for months at a time. Their loyalty tested. Clara and I both received preferential treatment; our time was limited to only a few days.

It was enough.

It was more than enough.

My heart pounds and my stomach twists simply seeing the fruit trees and flowering vines through the golden cage that surrounds the Garden. I bite my tongue, trying my best to dampen the memory of how swollen and dry it had become, my lips cracked and painful as I recited over and over, *The price of life is a soul. One life for the good of many. One life sacrificed saves us all.*

I look down at my hands, the skin there healthy and flush, blinking away the vision of the wrinkled, dry casing that covered my bones while proving my loyalty to Eden and only Eden.

I nearly turn around, nearly decide to forgo this excursion to pluck a Persuasion from the Garden. But I am here now and I know how to remain unscathed.

I squint through the vegetation to see that Temptation is coiled around the massive, gnarled apple tree in the middle of the garden. The snake is one of the oldest pets of Eden. Her scales are no longer shiny copper but a burnished brown from age. A murky film covers the vertical lines of her pupils as blindness set in centuries ago. Yet her fangs remain sharp, her forked tongue flicking out from between them to smell the air. I will not go nearer. The closer one gets to Temptation, the harder it is to escape.

There is movement in the brush behind the giant serpent. My breathing grows strained. *Devil have mercy.* Prisoners. But the greenery stills.

I stay outside the golden fence and instead eye the long branches of a sapling spilling over to the other side of the bars. Among the leaves and fruit is a small Persuasion—a copper snakelet with round, black eyes, and miniature fangs. Though it's the snakelet I want, I feel the desire to pick one of the ruby apples, my fingers already making their way between the pickets of the fence and towards the fruit. Heart racing, I yank my hand back just before my skin makes contact. A cold sweat breaks out on my forehead.

That was close.

With trembling fingers, I take my mask from my bag and press it to my face. The beauty of the garden drops away to reveal the truth underneath. The slime of Suffering coats the fruit and clings to the foliage, the Persuasions now bright and shiny amongst the dripping, sticky darkness.

"So young, but your powers are coming in nicely," I say to the Persuasion I have my sights on. "Imagine what they'll be like when you're as old as your mother."

His ebony eyes stay focused on mine, each one no larger than the size of a peppercorn. The line of his mouth seems to rise, almost like a smile. He's cute. I'll have to be extremely careful. Even wearing the mask, I reach through the barrier and nearly pluck the apple twice more before gaining control of my senses and pulling away.

Finally, I manage to focus. Just as I am about to grab the Persuasion, the leaves shift and a face fills my vision. I hold in a cry at the sight of the cracked lips, the skin pulled tight across razor-sharp cheekbones, the yellowed eyes wide in crazed hunger.

By the Devil's hand...

My breaths come in short bursts, in time with the hammering of my heart.

Despite being ravaged by years of suffering, the face before me is clearly that of Eleanor Dare. I blink and see her as she was before ever stepping foot in the Garden. Her undeniable beauty. Her uncontested power. The superior glint in her eyes, the haughty lift of her chin, the arrogant twist of her lips.

"You've come to bask in my torture, Dyonis?"

I open my mouth to tell her I am not my grandfather, but the words fail to come. I am only a hair's breadth away from the infamous Eleanor Dare. From the woman who started *everything*. Terror and awe and, I will admit, the slightest bit of admiration nail me to the spot.

Despite the outings in my youth to the Garden, despite hoping for a glimpse of Eleanor or Virginia among the leaves, I only first saw a Dare when Virginia was paraded across the village square several days ago. Eleanor I've never seen in the flesh. I've seen pictures; Agnes snuck in a camera from the Beyond at one point. When she absconded, those pictures were confiscated and they are kept in the archives. But pictures are a pale comparison to the being in front of me.

Eleanor is smaller and thinner than I am, yet she is somehow larger than life.

"Enjoy your pitiful consolation," she continues. "Enjoy my suffering. For 'tis all you have."

She leans in, pressing her forehead against the golden bars of the Garden's fence. The gate is wide open, but without her mask she cannot leave the cursed place. It is why Grandfather keeps it locked in the safe.

"I won, Dyonis. She lives. *I. Won.*"

Suddenly, her hand darts out from between the golden pickets, fingers brushing my shoulder. I startle and jump backward. She plucks an apple from the branch above me and laughs, the sound rich and hearty. But as she sinks her teeth into the rotten flesh, her face changes, once again haggard and starved. Her laugh turns to a witch's cackle.

I don't take the Persuasion I originally had my eye on. Instead, I take the closest one. One that is tiny and thin and whose copper scales are only starting to shine. I rip him from an overhanging branch, his body small enough that his head and tail barely stick out from either side of my fist.

Eleanor cackles again. The hairs on the back of my neck rise.

With the Persuasion in my hand, I run.

19

Redd

Eden: Present Day

"**S**tay quiet." Thomas whispers in my ear as he pulls me further behind the tapestry, his sweaty hand across my mouth. "Please."

He's tall and wiry, but I think I could easily beat his thirteen-year-old ass in a throwdown. That said, I like him. And weirdly, I trust him. So instead of stomping on his foot or biting his fingers, I nod.

Dropping his hands, he turns around and fits a key into a hidden door. We stumble inside just before Clara's voice grows closer.

"John told me to steal you away before Clara got you in her clutches. You'll want to avoid her for as long as possible." His wide smile reminds me not everyone in Eden is as cold as Dyonis Harvie. "Perfect place to hide from her. She will not expect you to be in here as it's secret. I am not even supposed to know it exists. So we must speak quietly."

From the other side of the wall I hear muffled voices, the pitch of Clara's familiar one. I can't make out what they're saying, but she must be talking to the Council.

"What is this place?" We're in a large room, nine circular stained-glass windows lighting the place from above. Sitting on the shelves, pouring out of chests, and spread out on the big table in the center of the room are all things I recognize. Books by contemporary authors, shiny magazines like you see in waiting rooms, racks of jeans and t-shirts and several pairs of sneakers. Neon-colored windbreakers and ponchos. A dusty Polaroid camera, a battery-operated cd-player, old iPods, and transistor radios. There's a shelf filled with potato chips and chocolate bars and fizzy cola, and even a stack of cash. This room is the first thing in Eden that feels familiar.

"The Council storeroom. It's where they keep things from the Beyond." Thomas watches me with interest. "Are these all truly items from outside?"

"Looks like it." I smile at an old cassette tape. "But some are a little outdated."

He takes a package of peanut butter cups and rips it open. "Not the food. John brings it in. No one else cares for it, so they don't keep close tabs. That means I get to eat it if I'm careful about hiding what's missing."

"Do you like it?" I smile as he shoves one whole chocolaty disk between his lips. After seeing him eat last night and this morning, I'm beginning to think this kid is a bottomless pit.

"Love it," he says, mouth full. "Want one?"

"Nah. Thanks, though. Got any coffee?" I've had a good case of brain fog ever since waking up and can't quite seem to shake it.

Thomas digs through the shelf of junk food. "Nay. No coffee. But once John brought coffee flavored sweets—"

I cut him off when I spot a certain backpack sitting on a shelf next to a rusty old lunchbox. "That's mine!" I pull it from the shelf and open it. There's my toothbrush. My underwear. And when I dig into the zipper pocket, I see that Clara's picture is still inside. It's not even ruined after five minutes in the water. I let out a relieved sigh and hike the bag onto my shoulder.

Alarm widens Thomas' eyes. "If you take it, the Council will know we were in here."

"Too bad. It's mine. They stole it from me."

"Aye, I understand. However—"

I sigh. "You'll get in trouble. Yeah, yeah. Okay. But..." I slide the picture out and stuff it into my skirt pocket. "They won't notice that."

"What is it?" he asks as I set the bag back where it was.

I begin to reach for the picture to show him but stop. No. Clara should be the first one to see. It's only fair. "Nothing really. Did you find that coffee candy yet?"

He shakes his head and goes back to looking.

While he searches, I step closer to one of the walls where a series of framed documents hangs. Talking about outdated... Most look really old, written on yellowed paper with spotty ink and letters that look more like calligraphy than anything else.

The first few are hard to read, the writing is so fancy, but I understand a sentence or two here and there: *The first councille of Eden, undertaken in the yeere 1590, consisting of these men and women.* And another one: *The names of the cheife men and women of Eden, 1640.* The documents are dated every 50 years or so, with a list of names underneath the title. I don't really pay attention to the names, but as I pass them, something makes me stop, go back, and look again. That's when I notice the names have barely changed—from 1590 on, there was always someone on the council with the name Dyonis Harvie, Emme Merrimoth, Johnathon Tydway, Elizabeth Glane, and Christopher Cooper.

I study the lists again. A couple names are on the list for a time. First Eleanor Dare, who then falls away and is replaced by Arnold Archard, then much later, he's replaced by Joyce Archard.

Eleanor Dare. She must be part of my family.

I stare at Eleanor Dare's signature, slanty and small and neat compared to many others. But the fading ink doesn't give me a clue. I look and the signature seems exactly the same fifty years later. And fifty years after that. I squint and study one document, then the next and see that it is the same with the other signatures.

"Hey, Thomas? All these names on the wall..."

Thomas glances at the documents. Then he grins. "I've something to show you." He settles down on top of the table, then pats the empty space next to him. I sit. He takes a book from a small bag hanging from his belt. "John brought it back for me. From the Beyond. So I could see how the outside views the fate of the elders. They're still writing books about them!"

He hands it to me. It's titled *The Lost Colony: America's Greatest Mystery*. I vaguely remember learning something about the Lost Colony in history class. But what, I couldn't say offhand. I open the book and read the first sentences in the introduction:

In 1587, 119 English men, women and children settled on Roanoke Island in what is now North Carolina. Three years later, they had disappeared. Even today, we are still seeking the answer to the question: What happened to them?

I page through it and stop at a list of names. Names of the 1587 colonists. I feel a strong sense of déjà vu, and that's when I realize some of these names are the same ones I saw on the walls—the names that hadn't changed for centuries. "Wait a minute. You mean this is where the lost colonists ended up?"

Thomas gives me a curt nod. "And they are still here."

"You mean they're buried here?"

"Nay. You've just met with some of them."

"Come on…" I shake my head, but after the waterfall, I think I can believe the whole flower-keeps-us-living-forever thing. "You're saying the Council is made up of the colonists?"

"Not only the Council. Thirty-three of the colonists became Eden's first inhabitants. Your mother included."

"My mom was in the Lost Colony, too?"

"It wasn't truly lost."

I'll give him that. I guess. "How old is Virginia?"

Thomas laughs, almost harshly. "She was born the same year my Uncle Walter was born. 1587."

My heart races and goosebumps pepper my skin. It's crazy, but what Thomas is saying feels *right*.

Thomas continues. "Grandfather never lets us forget it. Virginia lived. Walter died."

"John mentioned something about tension between our families. That's the source?"

"Tension. Hatred. Hundreds of years of bitterness."

I think of Dyonis and his humorless eyes, his hard words. "Your grandfather doesn't like me, does he?"

Thomas smiles a sad smile. "No need to be upset. Grandfather often does not even like *me*."

"Oh, Tom." I give his arm a squeeze. After having spent the morning jumping the waterfall with him, I feel close to him. I like this kid.

A blush spreads over his cheeks. Reaching for the book, he says, "Virginia is in here."

He scans the pages. Part of the way through, he stops—"Here!"—his smile is wide as he looks at me. "Your mother is known on the outside."

And there in big, bold letters is the chapter heading: *Virginia Dare: First English Child born in America*. Underneath it reads: *Eleanor Dare was with child when she boarded the ship to the Americas...*

I keep blinking at the names Virginia Dare and Eleanor Dare and suddenly it hits me. I learned about *them* in school. I mean, there are streets named after them. Movies filmed about them. Legends based on them. "Wait. *Virginia Dare* is my birth mother?"

"Aye." Thomas nods. "I thought you knew that."

"I did, but not... *The* Virginia Dare?"

His eyes light up. "So she truly is well-known in the Beyond!"

This is nuts. So, so nuts.

I look down at the page again.

But how amazing is that? *Virginia Dare is my family.*

Irritation flares. "Why didn't John tell me this?"

"From everything I've read, people in the Beyond think eternal life is a myth. If John had told you—"

"I wouldn't have believed it," I finish for him. Seems to be a recurring theme. But I suppose it's true. Annoying, but true.

"Do you think you could take me to meet Virginia?" I ask Thomas. I don't want to wait one minute longer. "Dyonis said I could see her later, but I don't trust him to make good on that promise."

He runs a hand through his hair, making the strands stick out all over the place. I can tell he's warring with doing what he's supposed to do versus what he wants to do. In the end, his want seems to win.

"Aye, but—"

That's when the door swings open. It's Clara, her face pink, her eyes blazing.

"Clara!" Thomas yelps.

"Thomas! You conniving worm!" She tips her head to the side, blonde ringlets falling from her coif to nuzzle the curve of her shoulders. She's beautiful—she'd be cheerleading captain or prom queen anywhere else—but right now, it's the kind of beauty that has teeth and claws.

"You've no right to be in here! Did John let you in?"

"Nay!" Thomas shakes his head.

"If not, how?" But before he can answer, she's shaking her own head. "No matter. Your Grandfather will get the answers. And you'll spend a night in the Cave of Dread for this."

Whatever that is, it doesn't sound good. A finger of guilt hooks me. "No, Clara. It's my fault. I...I was snooping around and found this room. Thomas just happened to come along after."

She lifts an eyebrow. "The room magically opened?"

"Yep." I shrug. I mean, the place is magic, right? Could happen.

She rolls her eyes but doesn't call me out on the lie. "You should not be in here."

"But I'm learning about my birth mom. Virginia." I smile and add, "Virginia Dare."

"And what has Thomas told you?"

I glance at him to make sure I don't say anything to get him into further trouble. "Uh..."

"She knows the Roanoke colonists ended up in Eden. Had you any inkling, Clara, that Virginia Dare is a celebrated heroine in the Beyond?" He holds up the book he was showing me.

"Oh, I don't know about heroine..." I start. But then I trail off, not really sure what she is. Historical figure, maybe? Except that's she's not really historical if she's still alive.

Clara and Thomas start bickering about rules and integrity. I wave my hands to stop them. "How about you fight later? Right now, why don't you tell me what this place *is*."

Thomas blinks. "Like I said, a storeroom—"

"No," I say. "Not this room. Eden. What is Eden? And how did these 400 year-old people even get here?"

There's an awkward beat of silence before Clara says, "Eden is the Master's sanctuary."

"And where does the magic come from?"

"The Master and Eden itself."

"And who is the Master?"

Clara starts to describe him physically, but I cut her off. "I mean, how did he get magic?"

"He's—" Thomas starts.

But Clara shoots Thomas a look. "That is for the Master to answer." She turns to me, her sharp edges melting away. "Now. Let us visit more of Eden."

Thomas hooks his arm through mine. "*I* was going to explore more of Eden with Redd."

Clara scoffs, tugging me from his grip, "You will not. I was tasked with her welcome."

"I can show her, as well," Thomas says.

Clara glares at him and stands her ground. "Nay, you cannot. Already your grandmother has been looking for you. Go tend to your chores while I tend to Redd."

I look at Thomas and nod. "It's okay. I'd like to spend some time with Clara. Really."

He grimaces but moves to leave. Before he does, he whispers, "Do not trust her," into my ear. As much as I like him, I'm going to make my own decision about Clara.

The second he's out the door, she bumps my hip with her own and smiles warmly.

"Come," she says. "I will show you my favorite haunts."

She doesn't make it sound like a good thing.

20

Eleanor

Eden: 1604

Virginia and I fought bitterly the evening after she'd told me about the tunnel to Roanoke.

"We're going." The second we got back to the cottage, I began to put victuals, tools, and clothing into a bag.

Virginia scoffed. "But William said we'd almost died in Roanoke. That we nearly starved there. He thought we'd now be able to grow fruit or flowers, but our magic is impossible beyond Eden. We tried."

"It does not matter. We must leave here. I will go anywhere—anywhere—to be free. For *you* to be free. We may need to forage at first," I said. "But 'tis early enough in the season to plant a garden—"

"Mama," Virginia started.

I ignored the interruption and headed to the yard, already imagining the new life we would lead. "We'll need to dig up the squash—"

"Mama!" Virginia shoved her palm against my chest, stopping me in my tracks. "We're going nowhere."

My laugh was sharp and bitter enough to make her flinch. "Oh, we are, Virginia. You've found a way out. We're leaving Eden behind."

Virginia stood her ground. "But Samuel is here! I'll go nowhere without him."

The affection in her voice made my heart catch in my throat. "Samuel Powell?"

"Aye. We...I care for him."

That gave me pause, but only for a moment. As I took the spade from its nail on the wall, I thought of the other villagers. Of Elizabeth and Emme and Dyonis—Dyonis who would never forgive me. A way out of Eden would not turn back time, but it might atone for my actions. For bringing us here in the first place. "Then we shall bring Samuel with us. The whole village can find its way back to Roanoke and out of this damned pact. I do not care if demons try to rip us apart," I said, stabbing the spade into the soil and accidentally spearing the root of the plant. "We will leave here first thing in the morning."

"If he does not come, you'll have to drag me out," she insisted.

I would if I had to. It was the only way that Virginia could live life as it was meant to be lived. Outside Eden, she could fall in love and have a family. Babies she would not need to sacrifice. She could grow old. Now that it was possible, I had to get her back to Roanoke. There, I would get her out from under the Devil's hold.

I would save her soul.

Not an hour later, William Wythers came knocking on our door. He stood with hunched shoulders, his dark hair hanging in his eyes. I knew something was wrong the minute he smiled at Virginia. It was a pained smile, as if it bore bad news rather than a greeting.

"Ginny...I..." William's brown eyes flicked to me then back to Virginia. She stepped out of the cottage, shutting the door behind her. I wasted no time pressing my ear against it.

"Samuel and his family...they've snuck out of Eden. He wanted to tell you their plans, but he dared not risk it," he was saying, his tone soft and apologetic. "He was afraid your mother would do something or say something to the Master."

My surprise was so sudden, so heavy, I swayed under the weight of it. Tears pricked my eyes. To the others, I was Eleanor Dare, the Devil's pet, forever faithful to the Master. It was what I had played at, to keep myself and Virginia safe. I do not know why the revelation shocked me so.

"Nay. Nay," Virginia's voice broke. "Why would he go? Nay. He wouldn't have gone without me."

"Aye, Ginny. He did."

"I can still catch him. It has not been long. He will be waiting for me out there, I know it. I simply must gather my mask—"

I whipped open the door. "We're going together," I said.

Her eyes narrowed to slits. "You! You're the reason he left!"

"No matter. We will follow in the morn."

"We will go now," Virginia stated.

"Fine." I was almost grateful to the young Samuel. Now Virginia would leave Eden without a fight.

As she ran to get her mask, I turned to William. "You go home. Tell your uncle where we've gone. The entire village deserves to know there is a way out of this cesspool." He had come to Roanoke with his uncle, Anthony Cage. The man had raised him as if he were his own. William was now twenty-one years of age, but Anthony ruffled his hair and kissed his head as if he were still in leading strings.

"I'm coming with you," William said, his Adam's apple bobbing as he glanced behind me to where Virginia was returning from her chamber. She may have thought herself in love with Samuel, but it was obvious that William had those same sentiments for her.

"So be it," I sighed. We'd leave a note. The village would find out when they realized we were missing. I had William pry Torment's teeth and claws from my neck. I felt so much lighter. But when William handed me the beast, Torment's soft fur a cloud in my hands, I knew I could easily get caught up in stroking his pelt, welcoming his hooked fangs into my skin once again.

"I must leave you behind," I said. He looked at me with mournful eyes and scurried off through the meadow. I turned to Virginia and William as Torment's lithe form was swallowed up by tall grasses.

"Let us go now," said Virginia. "Samuel cannot be too far ahead."

"Aye. Let us go." I did not give a damn about Samuel. But if the Master had heard about the others leaving... I shook my head. I did not know what would happen. What *could* happen.

I only knew I did not want to find out.

The moon was rising when we emerged from the water on the other side of the tunnel, the shadows around us deepening. Yet, despite the growing darkness, despite my years away, I recognized Roanoke. This beach was where I first stepped foot on the island. The trees and brush before us once hid Manteo and me as we made love. The tapestry of stars in the sky above us was where I'd once hung my dreams. The air smelled of salt and greenery and the lingering stillness from a hot day. But it was blissfully free of the heavy perfume of the Eternity Flower.

"'Tis Roanoke," I breathed as we crossed the beach. There I traced the letters C-R-O still visibly carved into the tree on the overgrown path to the settlement. "But lovely once again. The rains have come and healed this place over the years."

William ran a finger over a long stalk of grass. "I do not remember it lush like this. Though the memories I have of this place are almost dreamlike—the gnawing ache of hunger, the thin, bitter gruel Uncle Anthony forced me to swallow."

I, too, remembered the taste. "That was made with bark of the white pine. For something, anything, to fill our bellies."

For a moment we were silent, looking around us. It was beautiful now, but this place had been so full of fear and death.

Doubt made my breath quicken. Was it right to come back? Was I really giving Virginia more out here than in Eden?

Virginia's voice broke my thoughts. "We must find Samuel! I imagine they've taken shelter for the night." She pointed towards a sparse area in the tree line, where we'd once cleared a large patch of land.

William turned to me. "We found the old dwelling places when we explored, though they're barely standing."

"No one else ever came, then." I thought of Father. Had he ever made it back from England? Did he cross the ocean with supplies, excited to see me and Virginia and find nothing but abandoned homes instead? And now, where was he now? I hoped he was happily growing old, surrounded by his drawings and paints.

Suddenly I felt parched. My throat was sore with dryness. I reached for the vessel I'd filled with ale and packed in my sack, drinking more than I intended to.

It did not quench my thirst.

As we walked, my limbs began to ache.

"We must pass this way, where the brush is thinner." Virginia led us past a small inlet, huffing in impatience at the slowness of our trek through the weeds. Whole curtains of insects buzzed over the water. I waved them away and squinted in the dimness at the shape before me.

A boat, like the ones the native peoples used. Rotting and soft, but still floating after all this time. An image of Manteo with a paddle flashed into my mind and a burning wave of shame washed over me. The horror we brought here to Manteo's people, to the other tribes, was unforgivable. Much of the evil had already been in us before we ever landed here—our sheer greed and selfishness along with the false belief in our own superiority. Not even the Devil could be blamed for that. The evil of his masks could only grow from the seed that had already taken root.

I thought of how Manteo had told me to go. To leave the mask behind.

Where would we be now if I had listened?

"We can use this to get across the Sound somehow," I said, motioning to the boat and pulling out my ale once more. My thirst was making me dizzy. "We could appeal to the Croatoans. They're good people."

William peered out over the water. A hazy cloud covered the moon and the darkness was nearly total. "We'll have to wait until morning."

"We must first find Samuel." Panic seeped into Virginia's voice and spurred her to move faster towards the old settlement.

Twigs snapped under our feet and branches lashed our legs. My vision blurred. I reached out blindly, my nails scraping the bark of a nearby tree. Pain shot through my limbs, and I cried out.

"Mama?" I felt Virginia's soft fingers wrapped around my arm.

I blinked and the world cleared. The pain fell away as quickly as it had come. Apart from the moments when Eden dried up before sacrifice, it had been fifteen years since I'd felt pain like that.

"'Tis nothing," I said, my voice shaking. "Continue."

We resumed walking. A noise cut through the forest sounds, something that made my heart clench.

"Do you hear that?" William whispered. We'd reached the old palisade now, most of the thin trunks that once used to keep us safe now burned to charcoal. The clouds slid away from the moon, its milky light illuminating what used to be our settlement. Our cottages were no longer homes. Those that were not torn apart were falling apart, nature strangling every surface with vines or flowers or thorns. And from somewhere in those broken walls was the sound of weeping.

"'Tis a child," said Virginia. She and William exchanged a look then started towards the noise.

Nay, I wanted to scream. *It could be a trick of the Devil's.* But I could not speak. My mouth was so dry that my tongue felt like cotton wool in my mouth. With each step I took the ground tilted beneath me, my head spun so.

Yet the sight we came upon sobered me long enough to sear the image into my brain.

The three youngest Powell children clung to each other, their faces tear-stained and dirty, their eyes glazed and haunted. Two monsters lay writhing at their feet, their skin gray and withered, their eyes wild globes in the sunken sockets. Skeletal hands stretched toward the children, who stayed just out of reach. One monster wore a skirt, the other trousers. They thrashed about so violently that the clothing was already turning to rags.

And then I realized: these were not monsters. These writhing corpse-like beings were Winefrid and Edward Powell.

"Oh, Beelzebub's teeth," I gasped.

Virginia did not hesitate. She went to the children and began tugging them away from their parents. William followed. Virginia took the baby Brigit from young Catherine, and William rested his hands on Ann's shoulders.

"Go." It was more whimper than word escaping from the dying lips of Winefrid Powell's mouth.

But we stayed rooted to the spot.

"Winefrid." I bent down, wincing as a pain shot through my temples. "What happened here?"

"Go back," she moaned.

"Samuel!" Virginia screamed into the darkness. "Samuel!"

A flight of birds took off at the sound, but there was no answer from the forest.

"Where are Samuel and James?" William asked Ann. The girl's words were sliced through with sobbing. She was impossible to understand.

"Samuel!" Virginia called out once more.

I swayed. Black spots floated before my eyes. Pain gripped my spine, my skull, my gut. My skin felt as though it were shrinking upon my bones. And the thirst...the thirst was unbearable.

Winefrid gasped her last breath and Edward followed, his eyes going glassy and still.

William shook them but they were done moving. I watched as he turned to say something to Virginia and then...

"Mama?" Virginia's face came in and out of focus. "Mama!"

Behind her, William whispered, "Look at her skin, Ginny. Oh, Devil save us."

I tried to lift my hand, to see what he was referring to, but my limbs had gotten so heavy...it was like lifting a boulder. A veil of black obscured my vision as the pain got worse.

A vision of the Master stood over me, his silken laugh filling my ears. And through the pain, through his taunting, one thought sustained me: my Virginia. I tried to force Satan's image away with memories: The day of Virginia's birth, how little and foreign she'd seemed in my arms. The smooth feel of her skin against my lips as I kissed her forehead. The heaviness of her body when she'd fallen asleep in my lap. The melodious tone of her laughter when the fish from the river in Eden jumped directly into her hands. The soft curls of her hair, the ludicrous amount of honey she slathered on her bread, the grateful tears that lined her eyes when I'd fashioned a corset for her that accentuated her newly-formed curves.

Virginia was my life. My reason for being. *Virginia.* I meant to scream her name, tell her I loved her. Tell her I needed her. But the noise that escaped was barely a gurgle.

Then the vision disappeared, and everything jumbled together. Strong hands under my back and knees, lifting me into the air. A frantic heartbeat against my ear. The pain, oh dear Lucifer the pain, as I was jostled to and fro, branches whipping past, tearing off my coif, scratching my cheeks.

A mask was pressed to my face, its wood unforgiving and solid. It smelled like Eden, like home...like evil and greed and flowers. I sucked in a rasping breath and the mask softened to the contours of my face.

Suddenly, I was swallowed up by cool water and tugged along, a strong arm around my chest. I could breathe, but I could not get enough air, such was my panic. I struggled and twisted, the grip on my body tighter the more I moved.

Finally, I was yanked out of the water. Pebbles and sticks and muck and moss grazed my skin. The mask was torn off my face and I breathed in the overwhelming odor of the Eternity Flower. I blinked, the film over my vision clearing.

"Look!" Virginia said as William and the Powell children surrounded me, water dripping from their hair. "Oh, Mama, you're all right."

I looked down at my hands. Skin as dry and wrinkled as bark slowly smoothed out and regained its dewy texture. I closed my eyes as I felt it knit itself tightly around my form. The pain in my spine had still not receded.

"Go," I heard a voice, smooth and rich. "Bring the children to the village. I'll take care of your mother." A troupe of footsteps leading away. A soft whisper saying, "Eleanor."

I opened my eyes. The pain melted like winter snow in spring and my breathing was once again easy.

But the thirst...

The thirst was still there, still unrelenting. I cupped my hands into the pond and bent forward, ready to drink. But before I could, a simple wooden cup was thrust under my nose. The odor was fetid and familiar. Black Contagion floated on the liquid.

"Here. Drink this."

The Master crouched down beside me, not caring that his boots were in pond water. "Did you forget, my sweet Eleanor? You pledged to me your soul all those years ago when we toasted our future after Walter's death."

I shoved aside the cup to drink from the pond. But no matter how much I swallowed, my thirst would not be quenched.

He held out the cup again. "Did you honestly believe you could leave me? Winefried and Edward made that mistake...and now, instead of living in Eden, they will spend eternity in the bowels of hell."

Leaning closer, he whispered. "You cannot leave me, Eleanor. I am everywhere."

He watched as I imbibed more and more pond water.

He watched as Torment came, climbing my shoulder to sink his teeth into my skin and wrap his body around my neck once again.

And he watched, black eyes glinting as, finally, I took his damn cup of Contagion and drank.

21

John

Eden: Present Day

As quickly as I can, I sprint away from the Garden. When I no longer hear Eleanor Dare's laughter behind me, I stop and tear off my mask. After so many years in the Garden, Eleanor has still kept her spine of steel. And here I am, spine of jelly, shaking like a young child running from a Nightmare.

I lift the Persuasion so he is level with my gaze. He is too young, I see that now. Yet, he will have *some* power. Besides, there is no way in this devil's paradise that I am going back to the Garden right now.

I run a finger over the Persuasion's head and say, "I'm taking you on an adventure. I need you to do my bidding while we're in the Beyond. Agreed?"

His tiny tongue flicks out and back. I loosen my grip and he winds his way up my arm to curl around my ear. He has trouble latching on at first, but then he's a perfect fit. I smile. "Good. Now, little Persuasion, we have much to do."

At the Fire Pit, I first gather some petals to stuff into my pocket, then unearth the long roots of the most robust Eternity Flower I can find. I take an oilcloth from my bag to wrap the flower in, folding the ends over the thick ball of white petals. With a length of twine, I tie up the bundle like a package, then strap it to myself as if it were a newborn.

As I do, Secrecy comes down a tree trunk, tiny claws gripping the bark. Her tail quivers and her black eyes shine in the shards of sunlight piercing the canopy of leaves. Persuasion hisses, his tongue tickling my skin. I stroke his scales to calm him and address Secrecy instead.

"You've been around quite a bit today," I say to her. "Are you trying to tell me something? Or are you trying to get something from me? You've hoarded enough. You don't need any more." Somewhere in these woods is the squirrel's stash of confidences, whether given freely or forced.

Secrecy stiffens, her ears pricking. Then she takes off like a shot across the forest. I hear the whisper of footsteps in the underbrush and suddenly, Griffen Jones is standing before me. "Where'd that damned creature scurry off to?"

There are villagers who spend their days hunting for Secrecy's stash; Griffin Jones is the most notorious. He'll follow Secrecy for months hoping to get his hands on some juicy gossip. He never succeeds, but he tries over and over. He's been in the deep of the forest so long this time that his auburn beard is a long tangle of knots and his unkempt hair has matted into natural dreadlocks.

I nod in the direction Secrecy ran.

Griffen's eyes are bulbous, the whites visible all around the irises. Instead of running after Secrecy, he stares at me. I'm not sure if he recognizes me from upriver earlier where he disturbed the kiss with Redd, or if his stare is because I look odd, the Eternity Flower strapped to me and a neon blue bag from the Beyond at my feet.

I'm about to ask if he's all right, but I think better of it. This is the man who cuts off his own feet for amusement. Who spends more time following a squirrel throughout the forest than he does with his own family. Well before I was born, Lunacy burrowed into his brain and, to my knowledge, still takes up residence there. I'd rather not engage. I've seen people enter a conversation with Griffen Jones. It rarely ends well.

"The Council is corrupt," he says. "It would have to be with women ruling over our fates. Women! Eleanor Dare, the witch, usurped my place on the Council!" He shakes his head violently.

"Ah," I say, trying to be as noncommittal as possible. Griffen has lost track of time; Eleanor Dare hasn't served on the Council for nearly 200 years.

I busy myself with my bag, but he stays put.

He points a filthy finger at me. "What do you know of piecing things together?"

"I...uh...I am not certain I understand your question."

He carries a worn satchel, nearly black with dirt. He fumbles with its ties, lifts the flap open and digs inside. He throws a drawstring pouch at me, hitting me smack in the middle of the chest.

I open the pouch and inside is a golden-shelled secret, albeit one that's badly shattered. I'm simply amazed it's a true secret

and not a walnut or acorn in there. Perhaps he is not as crazy as he seems.

"'Tis the only one I've found. I've tried fitting shards together, but I cannot get it right."

"I'm not surprised. It looks beyond repair—"

"Nay! Nay! It simply takes a good eye!" Griffen is getting worked up now, his hands balled into fists, his eyes—unbelievably—growing wider. "Do you not see, boy? They hide truths! Feed them to that creature and carry on as if the Devil was the only evil one! We must expose them for leading us down the primrose path this whole time."

That's when Secrecy skitters past again. Griffen shouts and follows at amazing speed, leaving the pouch behind. I sigh and put it into a zipper compartment of my bag. I'll give it back to him upon my return.

Griffen is not wrong. So many truths of Eden are hidden. Even we scouts are bound to Secrecy for many things. It is one way of ensuring we cannot get ourselves into trouble.

As I put on my mask, I think of Agnes. She was a scout, so, if she was still bound to Secrecy even in the Beyond, what she could have told Redd about Eden and her role here was limited. No wonder Redd was mistrustful of her. The tidbits in Secrecy's stash stay intact for centuries. The absence of those truths, however, rots relationships quickly and to the core.

Setting my fingertips on the lip of the water, I tap out a tune for Deception. The water dragon knows my smell and my melody. She can let her guard down. But truth be told, we rarely call upon her. Her role here is to quiet the fear of a sacrifice and we haven't needed her for that for years. I hope we never will again.

As I reminded Grandfather, we may do cruel things, but we are not cruel at heart.

Persuasion hugs my ear tighter as I enter the water. With one arm cradling the flower to my chest, I swim through the pond and into the tunnel. A flame of pride warms my belly as I kick forward through the enclosed space. When I transplant the flower, no more bones will join the jumbled path of them cradled by the sediment.

I reach the Beyond. On the bank, I rip off my mask and breathe in the salty air. The sun is hot here and the air is clear as glass. But tall trees shadow the edges of the marshy beach. It is the perfect place for the Eternity Flower to take root.

I find a spot in the shade to pitch the small tent I brought with me but decide, before I do anything else, I must imbibe some nectar. I need it to keep any pain at bay. I take one of the petals from my pocket and suck the sweet liquid from its base. Then I immediately start digging. The longer the flower is out of the ground, the less chance it has of surviving.

I set the flower in the sun and stab my trowel into the sandy soil, the scraping sound a backdrop to the constant sawing from cicadas. My first hole is too close to the water. I have barely dug a few inches when it fills up like Grandfather's tankard. I'm about to try again a couple of feet further back when I hear a splash and a yip, then feel a familiar energy surge onto the beach.

"Satan's scourge, Chaos! You followed me here?" Out here I cannot see him, but there is no denying the mischief and anarchy that bubble in my gut. It overshadows the shadow of pain in my leg and the determination to plant the flower.

I'm hoping Persuasion will influence the hellhound, who is now pawing my legs and licking me with his wide tongue.

Pushing Chaos toward the water, I say, "Go back! I cannot risk things going awry with you!" But while the hound stops pouncing on me, he does not reenter the Sound.

"Lot of good you are," I mumble to Persuasion, though I realize that, when it comes to the Master's pets, the older one is, the more powerful. Chaos has Persuasion beat by hundreds of years.

Chaos nudges me with his nose and pants in my ear. I grip his fur in my fist and lead him to a large tree several feet away. "Stay!" I order, as I start to dig again. He lets out a disappointed whine, but I ignore him, concentrating on my work.

This time, while the soil is damp, the hole stays empty of water.

Until it suddenly starts growing deeper and deeper...

"Chaos!"

I reach forward to try to catch the invisible hellhound, but he bounds away from me. I dig three more holes that he ruins before finally getting him to heel.

Despite my care in swaddling the plant, the swim has left it worse for wear. Perhaps when it is not so waterlogged, it will perk up. However, now the heavy bloom of petals droops, head down like a sullen adolescent. The leaves, too, hang limply towards the ground. Even though the spiky stem is thick, I worry it will bend without proper support.

It takes me a few minutes to find a skinny branch dead enough to break off a tree. I stick it into the ground and tie the plant to the branch, taking extra care to secure the sagging head.

Thinking of Redd's insistence to be ever so careful putting the flower into the ground, I treat it as if it were made of spun glass. By the time I'm finished transplanting, hours have passed. Chaos got the better of me a few times, but in the end, it is done. Held up by the crooked branch, the Eternity Flower stands like a beacon in the dim shadows of the cedar trees.

I reach up for Persuasion, who is still wrapped around my ear. In the Beyond, he's also invisible to me. When I feel the cool length of his body, I pluck him up.

"Persuade it to grow," I say, placing him on the flower's thick stem, but the beast hisses as if burned. I feel around for him again, then place him back around my ear, gently stroking his scales.

"Fine. You may come in handy in other ways," I sigh.

Just as Redd taught me, I drag the pads of my fingers over the spiky stem. Over and over and over, until the pain is a fire in my veins. When I can bear it no more, I take another petal from my pocket, rub the Eternity nectar over the wound and bandage my hand.

As the sun drips like honey down the sky and the cicadas' song grows louder, I unroll the tent I took from the Council storeroom. With the bendable poles, a panel of mesh, and way too many zippers, it may as well be a difficult jigsaw puzzle. Add Chaos into the mix and it becomes unsolvable. I try to get it to stand, but each attempt simply ends with a puddle of bright nylon at my feet and a litany of curse words on my tongue.

For the love of Lucifer, this is ridiculous. I'll sleep on the ground. The weather is nice. Chaos' breath alone is all the heat I need. There's no reason for a tent.

I'm covered in dirt, salt blanketing my skin, exhaustion making my knees buckle. But, eyeing the white flower practically glowing in the deepening dusk, I've never been happier. This will save Eden. All is good.

Then the mosquitos arrive.

My whole life, I've lived among voracious creatures. Creatures that can eat away at your very soul. Yet Torment and Evil and Repugnance have something to learn from the insects that call the marshy part of North Carolina home. Their appetite and ruthlessness is beyond compare. And even Persuasion's quick tongue cannot catch them all.

By the time the stars have come out, I'm covered in itchy, red welts. I've wrapped my jacket around my head, leaving only the whites of my eyes open to the air. Under the sleeves of my sweatshirt, lines of blood streak my arms where I've scratched too hard. I feel as though I will lose my mind should I stay among these carnivores one moment longer. Despite what Redd told me about keeping close to the flower in the first hours after planting, I'm seriously considering returning to Eden until morning. Yet I don't dare take the risk.

At least no one is here to witness my pathetic state.

Of course, as the darkness grows heavier, the cicadas quiet down. And over the soft lapping of waves, I hear staggered breathing and sobs. Noises that do not belong to Persuasion or Chaos.

It is then that I realize I am not alone.

22

Redd

Eden: Present Day

Clara takes me through the village square, pointing at each half-timbered house that lines it and listing off the names of those who live there. We pass John's house and, right next to it, her own. It's the pale yellow of baby blankets and lemon cookies, with blue shutters and a silvery path of stones leading to the door.

"So you and John...you've always been neighbors?" I ask.

"Aye. I was still toddling when he was born, so I've no memory of a time before him." Her mouth turns down for the slightest of seconds and I wonder if maybe she *does* have a memory from before...just she can't really place it. Maybe she remembers Minnie.

I shove my hand in my pocket and feel the smooth surface of the photograph tucked there, hesitating. I decide it's still a little too early to bring it out.

We saunter down the cobblestoned street, arms hooked together. The sun is bright, but that same glittery mist from earlier clings to the village like cotton candy on a stick. What John called the Veil.

Clara nods. "The Veil of Secrets. It keeps the village a secret from others. And it keeps secrets from the village. What lurks behind is revealed from time to time. Yet now we see only happy mist."

"I don't get it," I say.

"Aye. That's the idea, Redd."

"Does everyone here speak in riddles? Like, is it a requirement?" I ask, only half-joking.

Her lips twitch. "I imagine it must seem that way."

I would have thought that having magic meant there was no physical labor. But there's a woman scrubbing some black mildew from the corner of her doorway, a blacksmith sweating in the forge, and a man polishing the leather on a whole row of shoes at a cobbler's shop.

"Keeps boredom at bay," Clara explains. "And we wouldn't want to all become like that lazy beast, Sloth, here, now would we?" She points to a fat, fluffy purple cat sleeping so soundly it looks dead.

Our first stop is Myllet's bakery, where Clara gets me a savory pie and then a berry pastry. They nearly bring me to my knees, they're so good. That Jane woman at the market wasn't joking when she said the baker's recipes were perfection.

I guess 400 years gives you a lot of practice.

Whenever we pass someone, I ask Clara their age. Despite some of the numbers being in triple digits, not one person looks like they'd be considered elderly. It's weird to be around such a young-looking crowd, since I normally spend so much of my time at Shady Pines. I feel like I'm in a renaissance fair staffed by college students and not a real village people call home.

The hound called Fury finds us later in the afternoon. There's something cute about his expression—like he's about to throw a tantrum. And I love the way the very tips of his fur are the blue of an oven light.

But when I tell him he's cute and reach out to scratch his ears, I feel a surge of rage. It makes me stumble backwards, my heart racing. Just like Chaos, this animal has powers.

I smile at the dog. He growls but leans into my hand. "Glad to know I'm not the only one with anger issues," I tell him.

Clara, Fury, and I pass a sandy, marshy bog. The odor of sadness permeates the air around it, overpowering the scent of the Eternity Flower.

I'm starting to get a hang of the cheesy way they label things in Eden. I joke, "What's that? The Depths of Despair?"

Clara eyes me like I'm half crazy. "Nay. Though I would not want to fall in. Misery resides in that quagmire. The sands sink, so it is better to give the area a wide berth."

"Uh, okay." I step further away from the quicksand.

We follow a different path up the hills than this morning, a steep one that puts us on high cliffs overlooking the village, rocky mountains soaring upward behind us. The sky is cornflower blue, except for the thick rope of white clouds choking off the tops of the mountains. They are so dense, they seem almost solid.

I think of where I came in, through the tunnel, from the Sound. I imagine you'd be able to enter Eden not only through the tunnel, but over the mountains. The thing is, we came in from the Outer Banks, and the mountains in North Carolina are way on the other side of the state. The terrain here doesn't make sense.

So where in the hell are we?

"What's on the other side of the mountains?" I ask Clara.

She purses her pink lips. "Nothing. Clouds."

"No, I mean over the mountains. Like what city or state or whatever is on the other side of this chain?"

She stops and tugs her coif from her head, shaking out her curls. For the briefest of moments I see the toddler from all of Minnie's photographs, the cherubic face, the rosy skin. Then Clara lifts an eyebrow and she looks anything but innocent. "There is nothing. Eden ends there. The clouds form a barrier."

"It can't just end. Earth isn't flat. There's no edge to fall from."

"Aye, there is no edge. Simply an end. Eden is not part of your world. Here, the rules are different. With each Harvest, Eden grows. One day, we'll get acres more, perhaps all the way down to the other side of the mountains. Perhaps that will be soon." She smiles at me, and I don't like the weird frisson it procures.

"Harvest? You mean gathering crops and stuff?"

"Something like that." She winks. "You'll see."

By now, the village is beginning to look like a toy town below us. Clara walks at a steady pace, following a well-trodden path.

"The Council told me I should ask you all my questions."

She laughs. It's a pretty sound. "And the Council told me I am to let Virginia give you answers."

"At this point, I'm wondering if I'm ever going to meet her," I say, my tone bitter.

"I can tell you are from the Beyond." She nods. "You're impatient. Things move more slowly here. But it will happen. I will bring you to her later today."

Since she doesn't answer my questions about my family, I want to tell her about hers. About Minnie. I've been wondering how to do so all day but haven't come up with anything. So, I try my best to be nonchalant as I say, "Ummm...tell me about your family."

That gets a confused look. "What about them?"

"Well, what's your mom like?"

"She's like a mother. And before you ask," her voice gets hard, "my father is no longer with us. I refuse to speak more of him."

I wish I knew her well enough to give her a hug. It's got to be so painful to have known and then lost your dad.

I try something different. "What's the very first thing you remember? Your oldest memory? Doesn't matter how vague it is."

She sighs and shrugs. "I don't know."

"Give it some thought. Like...me? One of the first things I remember is waking up from a nightmare. I can still feel the rawness of my throat from screaming, the sheets wrapped around my legs, my skin sticky with sweat." Agnes had burst through the bedroom door like a hurricane, wrapped me in her arms, and stroked my hair. She hugged me until I felt safe again. I'm so angry with her, so disgusted by all she's done...and yet...yet I feel an overwhelming wave of love at the memory.

Clara's silent for a moment, then she says, "I remember being gifted my mask. The Master handed it to me when I couldn't have been more than three or four years of age. There's a connection there, between all of us in Eden, and I remember feeling its power. I have a vague sense of being scared before that. Perhaps Nightmares. They do prey on the young. But the mask was a comfort. A healing presence. It still is."

"Have you ever been outside of Eden?"

"Aye. But I had no clue there was anything beyond Eden for quite some time. Now, where I am taking you—to the Caul—John and I used to go there as children. We were always told never to climb onto the Caul alone; only in pairs. It is my favorite place in all of Eden, but its beauty is also its danger."

"So you and John are good friends?"

She tilts her head and cuts me a look. "Do you hearken after John?"

"Hearken after?"

"Are you attracted to him?"

"Oh," I think of Shay and how easy it is for us to bond over mutual appreciation of certain specimens of the opposite sex. Maybe the route to Clara's friendship is through this. I grin. "Let's just say I have no problem looking at him."

"Aye, he *is* pretty," she says, flashing me a brief smile. She's quiet a second then adds, "You do know that John and I were promised to each other, do you not?"

"Pr-promised?"

"The Council has always wanted us to wed."

"Wait...what?" *John's engaged?* I trip over some loose rocks on the path and nearly fall on my face. Clara catches me before I do.

"Thanks," I mumble. "I...I had no idea. I mean...he never said." Then I think about how that sounds and add, "Not that he would have had a reason to say, really. Like, we barely know each other."

"So he did not tell you?" Clara drops my hand and starts walking again. Only faster.

My heart pounds and I feel tears start to claw their way to my eyes. Oh, God. Here I thought she was just a bit flirty...

But John didn't give me any indication he even liked her. I mean, he did say they'd always been close. But what the actual fuck? He *kissed* me. Like he meant it. And here I was, hoping he was one of the good ones when all along he was an asshole. An *engaged* asshole.

I should have known.

Fury yips, running further on the trail, then coming back again, tail wagging.

Clara probably hates me. She probably sensed there was something between me and John from the beginning...

"Look, Clara. About John—" I start.

"We're nearly to the Caul," she cuts me off, her voice tight.

"I had no idea he and you—"

"There." She points. "See it?" Obviously, she doesn't want to talk about it.

Ahead of us, something glitters in the sunlight: a giant web stretching across the void between two cliffs. It's football-field sized, thousands upon thousands of filaments in a perfect spiral.

"There's not a giant spider somewhere, is there?" I can't hide the fear in my voice. Insects in general don't scare me. Cockroaches. Earwigs. Moths. Ants. No problem. I want to say spiders don't bother me either, but I realize while standing here in front of this outsized doily that they do. Quite a bit.

Agnes nearly had a panic attack any time she accidentally brushed a spiderweb. She insisted we could be caught in a daydream by touching their strands. A good amount of my "training," along with holding my breath, was how to get rid of a spiderweb without ever touching it. So I could handle it. I would even say their presence rarely produced more than a disgusted frisson. But this? How freaking big is the arachnid that wove this thing?

"The Enticements are tiny." Clara points.

That's when I see part of the glitter belongs to the spiders themselves. They're relatively small, no bigger than the nail on my pinkie finger. They aren't the usual black or brown; they're like jewels. Some are clear as diamonds; their bodies shimmer and shine and reflect the colors around them. Others look like sapphires or rubies or emeralds. They're beautiful, but also probably the creepiest thing I've ever encountered. I swallow, my throat tight with growing terror. There are hundreds...maybe thousands of these Enticements busy working on the web.

Okay. I am definitely not at ease with spiders. Not. At. All. I've been lying to myself about the damn things.

At random intervals in the giant Caul are lumps: human sized forms tightly wound by the shiny, silken threads. Like trapped flies. What the...?

Clara brings me closer and I see the drop below is heart-stopping. "I can understand why you weren't supposed to come here alone. You could get killed falling from this thing."

She shakes her head. "You know by now that a fall wouldn't kill us. It would not even hurt us."

Right. I do know. But it still feels unreal.

"The danger comes from staying stuck, staying wrapped up in the Enticements' embrace for weeks or months on end. Some have lost their mind this way." Clara's voice gets bitter. "Some go so far as to decide they'd rather never live in this world again, and leave their family behind."

It sounds like she has personal experience with it. Her dad? Did he come here and lose his mind? I want to ask, but despite my growing horror, I study the web. And I notice details. Fingertips sticking out of a cocoon of sticky thread, a tuft of hair, a boot... My stomach churns. "Clara! Look, we've got to help them!"

"Oh, Redd. You needn't worry. It's no longer like it was when I was young. Like when my father used to spend time here. Now, every week, Roger Prat and his gang come to cut the stragglers free. No one is left here too long. Not anymore."

One of the forms wiggles, hands ripping at the webbing. Immediately, dozens of Enticements crawl over and spin the hole closed. I feel like I'm going to be sick, anger and dread lacing my stomach. Fury paws at my leg.

"This is horrible," I say. "I need to get out of here."

I start to move away, but Clara grabs my arm, slowly stepping closer to the edge until the toes of our shoes only inches from the mass of jeweled spiders. She puts a hand on my back and rubs it. "You needn't worry, Redd. Truly. You don't understand. We come here of our own volition. This is entertainment. It's...how shall I explain it? The Enticements' talent lies in making your desires seem real, tangible. You *experience* your wants. Like a drug or a dream. And once you have entered the Enticements' web, those needs and wants keep you inside it."

"Until someone frees you?"

"Aye. It's heady."

"Yeah. Hard pass. Why don't you just take me to see Virginia—" I start to turn away again, but Clara shoves me.

"Have fun," she giggles over Fury's howls.

And I go flying onto the web.

23

Eleanor

Eden: 1604

It had been only three hours since Virginia, William, and I had come back from Roanoke, but it felt like centuries. I had not stopped to think, had not closed my eyes, for the moment I did, I saw the Winefrid and Edward's living corpses and imagined myself succumbing to the same fate. I saw the Devil's face and heard his words: *I am everywhere.*

Brothers Samuel and James Powell were gone. Back in Eden with a warm posset made from the nectar of the Eternity Flower, young Anne had finally been able to tell us what happened. Her brothers ran off the moment their parents started changing, and as the younger siblings did not follow, they left them behind. Anne was not sure if the boys had crossed the water or stayed on the island. Anger made her small hands shake as she called them out for the cowards they were. When Samuel and James ran, they had not run back home to Eden. They were out there, somewhere...beyond. We did not know if they were alive and well, or ill and suffering. We only knew that the girls were safe while Winefrid and Edward Powell were dead.

Joan Warren had gotten up for a midnight cup of perry as was her habit and spied us through her kitchen window as we were coming back into the village. The gossip we'd hoped to keep quiet until morning had woken the village faster than wildfire. And now the villagers were asking questions. Why did Winefrid and Edward wither and die but not their children? Why had I begun to suffer after only a short time, while Virginia and William had gone out several times over the space of several weeks, staying for hours on end with no consequence? And was it possible to hope for a different future? A future outside of Eden?

Dyonis called a Council meeting so we could figure out some answers.

I had been thinking of nothing but since my return.

The meeting was long and our decisions heavy. As always, Secrecy was there to hide away our words. Once the creature had left the room, Dyonis stood. "Now it is time to call the villagers together."

The village meeting was held in the square, torchlight brightening the dim blue of early morning. First Dyonis addressed questions and set down rules. He told the villagers we believed the illness to be progressive in the youth, which was why it had not shown up immediately for those who'd already stepped outside. Yet despite this warning, and despite forbidding anyone to use the tunnel due to possible danger, there were still those who said they wanted to try. The Council's authority was not yet absolute—that would come in time—and the older youths especially were more curious than frightened.

After the meeting, there was a remembrance ceremony for Winefrid and Edward Powell. We hosted ceremonies after sacrifices—sometimes a gathering to recite memories and give thanks, other times a celebration to recognize that the child sacrificed had given us all the gift of life. But in those moments, we tried to give meaning to death; this was different. Unlike the innocents sacrificed, the Powells would not end up in heaven, but hell. And there was no greater purpose for the Powells' deaths. The village did not burst with new life now that they were gone. It burst with uncertainty. There were shouts and tears and whispered conjecture over who would now house the three girls they'd left behind.

It was custom to drink to the dead, no matter one's age, so the Council offered the villagers a deep, dark ale. Even one-year-old Brigit was given a cup.

The Council had been serving the ale to the villagers, handing out cup after cup. No one dared take a goblet from me except my Virginia. But when her fingers wrapped around mine to grasp the cup, I froze. I loved her more than anything. More than life itself. She mattered more than I did. So much more. What would be best for—

"Mama," Virginia whispered, amusement tilting her lips. "You must let go."

I lifted my gaze to hers. Her blue eyes were clear, but the edges rimmed in red. She liked the Powells and thought she loved Samuel. It was rare for her to see suffering.

"I—" but that is where my tongue failed me. It stuck like an anchor to the floor of my mouth. Secrecy had taken those words.

"Virginia," I started again.

Deception was draped over Virginia's shoulders and coiled loosely around her neck like a fat stole. The water dragon's breath filled the air in the form of a small cloud between us, the first time I'd seen true evidence of her powers. I stepped back and turned my head so as not to be affected.

Virginia sighed. "Aye, I know what you're going to say. Deception will soon have to leave us."

It wasn't what I'd intended to say, but it was true. I nodded gravely.

I still had not removed my fingers from the cup. There was so much I wanted to say, but the words would not—could not—come.

Virginia waited, eyes searching my face.

Suddenly, a hand was on my arm, warm and firm. I turned to see the Master, his black eyes sparkling behind his thin leather mask. He had a habit of appearing whenever he liked, and a ceremony always brought him round. "Is there a problem with the ale, Eleanor?"

He took the goblet from our hands and sniffed it. His mouth twisted as he did so. I could have sworn he was hiding a smile, humoring me. "Aye, it smells off. Mayhap you can find Virginia something else to toast the dead with."

He poured the contents onto the ground. It looked like a black puddle in the darkness.

"Go on, then. There is more ale across the square," he said, handing me the empty cup and pushing me towards the long table laden with food and drink. *Aye*, I thought. *The ale is better across the square.*

Turning, I nearly rammed into Dyonis, who was carrying a large tankard in his hand. Lifting it to stop it spilling, he said, "Careful where you tread, Eleanor Dare." His gaze slid from me to Virginia and the Master behind me. I held my breath, but he said nothing more; he simply stepped back and allowed me past.

I wove through the crowd. Jugs of ale lined the table the Master had pointed out, but instead, I filled Virginia's cup at the fountain. Water spilled out from between a stone gargoyle's teeth, clean and cool.

On my way back to Virginia, Emme and Elizabeth stopped me with a questioning look. While they were still unwilling to make our friendship obvious, they weren't as skittish about it as before. Emme squeezed my elbow. "Everything all right, Eleanor?"

I nodded, continuing towards the spot where I'd left my daughter with the Devil.

Only then did it occur to me exactly what I had done. I'd left her alone. With *him*.

How? How did that happen? Across the cobbles, Deception lifted her equestrian head. A blue membrane slid across her eyes as she blinked. I understood.

Her powers were beginning to take hold. And I'd been deceived.

I reached Virginia, flanked by Dyonis and the Master. Dyonis' tankard was in her hand, the sleeve of her chemise damp where she'd just wiped her mouth.

Dyonis narrowed his hazel eyes and let out an almost inaudible tut. "I saw that Virginia was without a drink."

"Happily, he had some to share." The Master smiled. Dyonis smiled with him.

I forced my own lips to bend, though I wanted to howl and spit in both their faces.

Dyonis moved on through the crowd, leaving Virginia and I alone with the Master, who stroked Deception's long snout and said, "Deception is growing, Virginia. Soon, she'll need to be in the water most of the time and a tub will not be deep enough. May I suggest the Fire Pit?"

Virginia tightened her hold on the creature.

The Master continued, "You will miss her, of course. But she's Eden's pet, and therefore yours as well. You can always call to her, ask her to do your bidding, or even put her to sleep…all by tapping out a tune on the water. She's extremely sensitive that way." And then he showed Virginia the sequences that Deception was susceptible to.

As Virginia tapped one of the tunes on her arm, the Master disappeared in a shimmer of shadow.

Virginia spied William Wythers across the square. But as she stepped forward to go towards him, I grabbed her hand. "'Tis dangerous to leave Eden. You had better not still be planning to search for Samuel."

She stiffened under my hold, looking down at the cage my fingers made around her wrist. "You are safe now. That was my only concern outside of Eden. The only reason I came back here."

"Virginia, you cannot go. You saw what happened to Winefrid and Edward."

"All the more reason to do so. Should Samuel be suffering..." She let her words die out as she blinked away tears.

"Then you would be too late."

She tugged her arm away. "You know nothing of love, Mama."

I very nearly roared that all I did was out of love for her. My every move, every breath, every thought. But she could not understand. Not until she'd had a child of her own. Instead, I scoffed. "You think Samuel loves you? He left you behind, Virginia. He did not even bid you farewell."

"He left because of *you*." Her eyes blazed. "You chased him away." She stalked off without a backward glance. A moment later she was near William, whispering in his ear. When I saw him shake his head 'no', I heaved out a relieved sigh.

I sipped my own ale and gave Torment's head a scratch. Elizabeth found me and as we made a toast to Winefrid together, I lost sight of Virginia and William.

I did not worry at first because William was no fool. He knew to go back to Roanoke now was not only dangerous, but a lost cause. I was counting on him to speak sense to her.

But as the sun rose over the horizon and there was still no sign of them in the square, I realized I hadn't counted on two things: that he loved her, and that Deception was coiled round her shoulders.

24

Redd

Eden: Present Day

Clara's still laughing as I fall backwards onto the Caul. I land on my back, the web bouncy but clingy, like a fly-trap trampoline. I yelp and flip around, hoping to crawl back to the edge of the cliff where Clara and Fury stand watching. But with each movement, I get more and more stuck in the sticky fibers. Enticements come at me, their tiny, jeweled bodies light as air, tickling my skin. I frantically brush them off and blow at the web like Agnes taught me, but there are too many and I'm too tangled. The moment I think I'm free, more Enticements come to entwine me in their gluey threads. Panic takes over.

"Clara!"

"Oh, Redd. Enjoy!"

Great. I've been stuck with a sadist. Even if I wasn't an arachnophobe, I don't know how the hell to enjoy getting mummified by thousands of spiders who suspend me with their delicate threads over a bazillion-foot drop. "Get me off of here!"

I'm not fast enough. Tiny legs scurry over me, covering every bit of exposed skin, making my spine buckle in revulsion. Ribbons of webbing cross my feet, my chest, my wrists, light as air but growing tighter and tighter. I'm wound in gossamer.

Then I feel a hand on my shoulder. I rip my head from the sticky threads to turn.

Oh, God, it's Agnes. Right here, next to me. I feel a surge of anger, but it immediately dissipates at the sight of her face. Her green eyes are full of tears, her lower lip trembling. "I'm so sorry," she says. "I should never have kept secrets. I should never have lied to you."

I feel my own tears coming on. "But you did. Why did you do that? Why did you do any of it?"

"I was on my own. I didn't know what to teach you about our past. How to teach it to you. So...I ran from it. Can you forgive me?"

Despite what she's done, I can't deny that I love her. I reach out and she squeezes my hand. As she does, something skitters over our fingers.

A spider. A tiny, diamond-like spider.

Her grip gets tighter and she changes. Her green eyes darken to hazel, and her delicate face grows tough. It's now Dyonis before me, a cruel smile on his lips. "You belong to Eden," he says. His fingers are so tight around my own, I can feel the bones breaking. "Eden will feed on your soul."

"No!" I scream, twisting away from him. I shut my eyes tight, then open them to see glittering strands sticking to my eyelashes. I swipe them away but the moment they're gone, a spider scurries over my face, a new shiny thread blurring my vision. "Clara!"

"Stop fighting it, Redd." I hear her coo. "I'll be back for you."

"No, Clara!"

Suddenly, Minnie is next to me, her plastic daisy earrings swinging as she laughs. Behind her glasses, her eyes are brimming with tears—the good kind. "I cannot believe you found Autumn. My baby. My sweet baby."

I haven't seen her this happy. Ever. It makes my heart feel so full my chest aches.

But the ache grows and my breaths come in short puffs. I glance down to see Enticements trussing me like a Thanksgiving turkey.

"Clara!" I scream, but she doesn't respond. She's left me here with no way to get out.

"My daughter." It's a new voice. I turn and see a face that looks so much like my own I have no doubt it's my birth mother.

"Virginia?"

"Ahredden, 'tis you. How I've missed you. I only held you once for a matter of minutes, but my arms have felt empty ever since." She pulls me to her. She's warm and smells like violets and the Eternity Flower and love.

Her fingers stroke my hair and she whispers, "We're together now," into my ear.

I want nothing more than for her to hold me. Everything is perfect. The sky is a pastel pink, the breeze soft and sweet, Virginia's smile so pure it feels like home. I don't know how long I stay in her arms, happy tears wetting my cheeks. Minutes? Hours? I begin to think I could stay like this forever, when I feel something get stuck in my tears. I wipe it off and see that it's an Enticement, its legs weighed down with salt water.

Ignore it, I tell myself. *Ignore it and you can stay with Virginia.* I squeeze my eyes shut and wish the spiders away, but when I open them again, Virginia is gone, only jeweled spiders in her wake.

No, no, no!

"Clara! Clara! Get me out of here!"

"You don't really want to leave, do you?" John's hair falls over his forehead as he leans over me. "Because if you did, I couldn't do this." His fingers trail up my arms and over my shoulders, leaving whispers of pleasure in their wake. His eyes stay on mine, but his hands slowly make their way down my sides until they're on my waist, hot against my skin, under my shirt. Luscious shivers gather in my core. It feels like fireworks are going off inside me. John's grip tightens and his lips crush mine.

I break off the kiss. "Wait. You're engaged."

He sighs. "That's not what Clara said. She said we were—"

A surge of spiders converges on his face. Muffled moaning comes from underneath the moving mass of shiny arachnids. I hold in a scream as I desperately try to brush them away. When I finally succeed, instead of John, I see my own face looking back at me. My mouth and chin are bound with thousands of silvery threads of webbing, my eyes are open wide with terror. The moaning grows frantic as Enticements glide over my features, their filaments sealing my eyes shut.

Panic grips my lungs. Oh, dear, God. It's me. How the hell is that me?

I rip the web from the mouth. The second I do, my own lips form the word, "Run!"

I try getting free, but every movement just gets me more stuck in. I'm never getting out. Never! "Clara! Clara! CLARA!"

A shadow blots out the sun and I see Clara looking down at me, a patronizing smirk on her lips.

"CLA—" Now the Enticements crawl over the real me, their threads a gluey mask over my face..

And that's when my panic turns to fury. I feel emotion surging through me in a way that I haven't since facing down Agnes right before I entered Eden. My rage tastes like ash and tar. It surges through my veins and burns through my skin, shaking everything around me. I hear a loud crack and the heavy shifting of rocks and soil along with the delicate ripping of threads. Air rushes past, my hair whipping about as Clara and I fall God only knows how many stories down to the valley below.

WHAM! My body is thrown onto hard-packed earth, the jolt reverberating in my bones, my teeth, my brain. The breath is knocked out of me and, once I catch it, I sit up, wincing and groaning out of an expectation of pain. But, of course, none comes. Eight-legged jewels run in every direction. They've lost their sticking power without the web.

Next to me, Clara flicks several off her skirt and blouse then looks above us with a gasp. "What in the Devil's name?"

The Caul is hanging in tatters, and half of the cliff it had been clinging to is reduced to rubble. In the distance, I hear shouts.

"I can't believe you pushed me onto there," I growl, standing. I check myself for injuries, but I have none. Not even the tiniest scratch. "I told you I didn't want to do that."

"But *everyone* wants to do that."

"Well, *I didn't.*"

Fury comes out of nowhere, pouncing on me, licking my face. Every time his tongue slides over my cheek, my anger grows. I give him a quick scratch between the ears then push him away.

"I don't understand why you're upset." Clara frowns.

"It was a fucking nightmare, Clara, that's why!" My voice echoes off the high cliffs on either side of us, drowning out Fury's happy yips. The other people who had been in the Caul and who fell along with us are glaring at us and tugging themselves free of their cocoons. They don't look happy to be free, just surprised and very annoyed. They all make their own guesses as to what's happened, huffing and swearing in their weird way.

Clara is staring at me in evident confusion. I'm still trying to shake the images that came at me while I was in the web. In all honesty, there were comforting moments...really good moments...but mostly terrifying ones. I swallow and take a deep breath. They were hallucinations, I remind myself. Nothing to be worried about.

Yet the sense of joy I felt when I arrived in Eden is warping into something else.

She stands and crosses her arms over her chest. Her eyes narrow as she says, "You were only on the Caul for three hours.

You should have been fully steeped in pleasure or satisfaction. It takes weeks before your own desires start to twist your mind."

"Obviously, that's wrong." I pick up my fallen coif from the ground and shove it on my head, pulling the strings under my chin instead of at my nape. My hands are so shaky I can barely knot the ties. "And I was there for *three hours*?"

"Aye." She shrugs, but it doesn't come off as casual. She's still looking at me like I've grown six extra heads.

"Admit it: you were angry. About me and John. And you left me there!"

She huffs. "I don't give a demon's wail about you and John. Relationships here are not as they are on the outside. We've not followed through on the Council's wishes regarding our handfasting. And you needn't be so affronted at me leaving you on the Caul. I checked in on you every hour."

"Well, that's fine then, isn't it?" I spit out. I push Fury away, as I'm ticked off enough without him adding to it.

"Apparently Eden's magic does not work the same on you. Perhaps you've been in the Beyond too long."

"Or perhaps you wanted to scare me."

"I can assure you, this was meant to be a fun jaunt, not a terrifying experience in any way." She scoffs. "If I wanted to frighten you, there are more efficient ways to do so."

My anger is starting to fade. It doesn't seem like Clara meant it to be so horrible. Is the Caul really something that everyone else enjoys? From the way the others who fell are lamenting how the Caul is ripped, it sure seems like it.

I shouldn't be surprised. Really. As usual, I'm a freak.

Even in here.

After seeing the orchard, I'd kind of thought I'd found a place where I wasn't so different.

Clara starts walking back the way we came, skirting the rubble from our fall. I don't know what else to do, so I follow her.

"What I cannot understand is how the Caul burst as it did. I've never seen anything like it. The gossamer may look delicate, but it is not."

"I was upset. That's how," I say, not adding, *I obliterate things with my anger alone*. But maybe, just maybe everyone here does, too.

"Even Fury cannot accomplish that with all the ire in Eden," Clara says.

There's my answer: I'm. Still. A. Freak.

Clara continues, "If you'd been wearing your mask...we've plenty of power in the masks. Though they seem to work even better in the Beyond. Have you used yours out there?"

I think of the visions I had, of how I felt invincible with it strapped to my face. "I've worn it a few times."

A smirk dresses her lips. "Then you know how delicious that kind of power can be."

I open my mouth to agree, but then think better of it. That kind of power may be 'delicious' but it's also a bit scary. So instead, I say, "You know that Agnes took me from here?"

The change of subject makes her slow her steps. "Aye."

"She also took kids from elsewhere. From the Beyond. I think...I think she brought them here."

I wait for a gasp or some sign of shock or denial. But Clara narrows her eyes at me. "What makes you say this?"

The photograph I brought with me pops into my mind. I could show Clara her very own baby picture. Maybe I can just tell her, point blank, that she's from the Beyond. But then I think of how devastating it was to learn the truth about Agnes from John...well, actually the mask. How I wish I had found out differently.

I haven't even known Clara a whole day. I have no right to blow up her life like this.

At least not without really weighing my words.

I'm scrambling to come up with something when I see that we've wound our way to a plateau. On the far end of a large clearing is an adorable little home surrounded by an overgrown flower garden on one side and an out-of-control vegetable garden on the other. There's a bench made of a log just next to the front door where I imagine you can sit and see the entire village below.

My chest aches at the sight of it all. It's sweet and understated and, although neglected, pretty darn perfect.

I'm just about to ask who the place belongs to when the front door opens. A woman steps out and I think she looks like an Elizabethan-era Barbie doll. Her gaze is honey brown, her lips dusty pink, and even her coif can't hide the silky blonde strands of her hair.

She stays frozen for a moment, eyes on me. Then she rushes forward, her rapid steps kicking up her skirts. She throws her arms around me, her muscles iron underneath her spun cotton blouse. Her breaths come in between gulping sobs, and soon she's pulling back to kiss my cheeks, my forehead, my nose, her salty tears wetting my face.

"Thank the Devil you're alive," she says. "I sensed you were here…already last night, I tossed and turned in my bed, a feeling keeping me awake, though I did not know why. Then, when the Council came to announce the news…. Oh, what joy! It took me all afternoon to prepare the cottage. But 'tis now ready. For you. For us."

It's her. Oh, God, oh, God, it's her.

Finally. FINALLY.

A wave of emotion flattens me. My knees turn to noodles and I ugly cry like a weirdo. "Virginia," I blubber. "Virginia."

"Aye, my child." She kisses my forehead again, her lips warm against my skin. "Welcome home."

25

John

The Beyond: Present Day

Someone else is here.

I dig my folding knife from my bag and unfurl the jacket from around my skull. "Terror," I whisper, calling to the Master's pet who guards this beach. The giant lizard may be invisible here in the Beyond, but his mere presence should have driven fear into the heart of anyone who came near. It takes a will of iron to get past such a barrier, especially when you are unaware it even exists.

In response, a cold blade of dread slides up my spine. Persuasion coils tight around my ear and Chaos leans into me, his heavy body trembling. Terror is here and doing his job. So who is the person who got past him?

"Ease up, Terror," I say, and immediately feel better. "Hold off for now."

Slowly, I creep further away from the water and into the forest. A thin silhouette is curled up on the damp ground, back against the thick trunk of a cypress tree. A woman, I think. She wheezes, each breath a struggle, and lifts the bottom of her white blouse to her nose and mouth. It comes away stained with darkness.

Blood. It's stained with blood.

I step on a twig and the sound of it cracking shatters the quiet. She turns, her face now in view under the thin streams of moonlight snaking through the leaves. I see that one of her arms is thin, the muscles shriveled. I recognize her from the glimpse I got from the window the night I searched for the mask in Redd's home.

"Agnes," I say, astonished to find her here. "What happened to you?"

Her eyes narrow, then widen. "Dyonis? How—"

"Nay. I'm his grandson, John."

"George's son?" It's a whisper. A look of longing and then pain crosses her face as I give a quick nod. I'm unsure whether it's to do with her physical suffering or my father's name. She and my father were scouts at the same time. They were both Eden's greatest successes...until they both became Eden's greatest disappointments.

Her tone turns pleading. "Did you bring a petal or two? I'm in such pain...."

I've only one petal left in my pocket. I'd brought it in case of unforeseen circumstances as I would rather not ravage the flower I'm trying to grow.

This is certainly unforeseen.

Agnes releases a relieved sigh once she's swallowed the nectar, but her countenance is just as deathly.

"You're the one who took Redd into Eden, aren't you?" she coughs. "George must be proud."

I scoff. My parents barely knew me. "I didn't take Redd. She came to Eden of her own accord."

A bitter laugh fills her mouth, then turns to a gargle. She spits blood onto the forest floor. "You fed her half-truths to get her there."

"And you fed her half-truths her entire life. Hence the reason she was willing to come."

Her mouth contorts into a hateful frown, but then she tilts her head to the side. I see some of the blood on her cheek disappear. "Who is it? Chaos?" The tiniest sliver of softness enters her voice.

"Aye, Chaos."

"Leave me alone, boy." Her eyes fill with tears. "I'm no longer your friend."

I push him away, hearing him run off into the forest. "Why are you bleeding?" I say to Agnes. "What's happened to you?"

"Something I expected to happen long ago."

I have no time for her cryptic answers. My priority is the flower. "I need your help—"

"Where's my mask?" She cuts me off and looks around as if it may suddenly appear. "I'm going into Eden."

"I discarded your mask in Wisconsin. It will find you. Eventually."

"No! I need it now." A sob breaks her composure. "I need to get Redd...And...this wound...I'll die if I don't go in now..."

From the way she looks, I believe it.

I almost plead with her to help me grow the flower when it occurs to me that her entering Eden is proof enough that the flower can grow in the Beyond. Her entering Eden would show everyone we needn't to sacrifice ever again. If she survived this long, so can we. Fate must have sent her my way. This is perfect. If only I hadn't discarded her mask...

"Redd held her breath to get inside Eden. Can you do so for that long?" I ask.

"Maybe. But I don't know if that will work. I'm not like her..." She slides up the tree trunk, trying to move to a standing position. But before she manages, her face pales. She sways, falls to all fours, and vomits dark bile. Her voice shakes as she pleads, "Help me through the tunnel. I need to save Redd. You can't sacrifice her. Take anyone. Anyone but her. She no longer belongs to Eden."

"Listen." I crouch down beside her, resting a hand on her shoulder. She jerks away. "We can save her. And we will. It is why I am here. To save everyone in Eden—Redd included. We can do this. We'll go through the tunnel. Together. Hold your breath, like Redd did."

She blinks at me and nods. Then her eyes roll back into their sockets. Before I can grab her, she lists to the side, passing out.

No amount of shaking or saying her name revives her. Tattered breaths still escape her lips, thank the Devil, but I cannot drag her through the tunnel to Eden without her mask. She needs to be conscious to hold her breath. If nothing is done, I'm unsure what will happen. I am no doctor. She said her wound would kill her.

Satan's scourge, I'm in a bind.

The only thing I can think of is to give her more nectar from the flower. It may help her heal. Or revive her. I hate to rip any petals off the one I planted. I hate to weaken it at all, but could I live with myself if Agnes died and I did not try to save her?

I limp back to where I planted the flower. Pain shoots up my leg—a testament to my stress that it is back so soon—and I'm grateful when I see the white bloom glowing under the stars. It still droops. Reluctantly, I tug two petals from it. They come away all too easily. I squeeze the nectar of one onto my tongue. The taste is sweet, the relief of pain immediate. But the usual jolt it sends through me is gone.

Only a few hours into my mission and I sense the flower is dying.

I unzip my backpack, take note of its contents. Driver's license. Money. Extra undergarments and socks. A book. Dried meat. A wedge of cheese. Drinking water. And a camera from the storage room, to take a photo of the flower once it's bloomed. If we cannot make it through the tunnel, I could take a picture of Agnes for proof. Though she is in such a state, I do not know if anyone would recognize her from an image.

A mosquito buzzes near my ear. I smack it, a spot of sticky blood staining my hand. I wipe it onto my jeans, satisfied to see the insect's corpse along with it. At least there seem to be fewer in the woods next to Agnes.

I take the water but leave my bag next to the flower. Persuasion is still curled round my ear, his scales cool against my skin. I start back towards Agnes, Chaos circling round my feet, his breathing heavy and agitated. More than once I nearly trip on his invisible bulk. "Enough!"

When I reach Agnes again, I see there's a bloody rivulet of spittle coming from her mouth. This is getting worse and worse. Gently, I crouch and tuck my arm behind her neck to lift her to a sitting position. I put the flask of water to her lips, thinking perhaps it will revive her. But the liquid just dribbles down her chin.

Chaos yips and jostles me so that Agnes falls into my arms, her blood slick on my hands. We are not far from the road here. It snakes around at such an angle that when a vehicle drives past, its headlights are so bright they blind me. It takes me a beat to get my bearings.

In that time, the vehicle screeches to a halt. I hear a door slam, then another, the slapping of rubber soles on the asphalt. As they get closer, it occurs to me that I had called off Terror. I need him to get back to work. Before I can say a word, I hear, "Hey!" coming from the darkness.

I blink to remove the white circles still marring my vision, expecting to see strangers. But the faces before me are familiar—Redd's best friend, Shay, and the old woman, Minnie.

Shay's gaze flicks from me to Agnes and then back again. Her voice is murderous when she asks, "What the fuck did you do to her, Smith?"

26

Eleanor

Eden: 1604

Virginia and William were gone. Torment's teeth dug further into my skin, his body winding tighter and tighter around my neck. Would I ever see my Virginia alive again?

I stayed at the Fire Pit, waiting. I did not sleep. Did not eat. Deception was there, too, curled into a shiny black ball in the shallow end of the pond. Virginia must have used the dragon to convince William there was no danger, but then left the beast behind. I entered the pond and the tunnel myself to go after Virginia, but I felt the illness catch up with me before I even got halfway through. There was no way I would make it to the Beyond alive. So, instead, I stood at the mouth of the pond, my eyes trained on the surface of the water, hoping and praying to the Devil himself that I'd see Virginia and William break through it.

When a day later they finally did, they were nearly unrecognizable. Their limbs were twisted and frail, their faces masks of suffering. Yet Eden's magic began to work the moment they crawled out of the water, reversing what had been done on the outside.

Once they'd recovered enough to talk, William told me he and Virginia had found Samuel and James' masks, but not the boys themselves. They hadn't had time to explore more. They had intended to search the entire island. But they were unable to do so because the illness had started. The pain was so great, it took them the entire day to crawl back.

Word traveled quickly throughout the village. Any doubts that may have surfaced regarding the danger in the Beyond were now quelled. Virginia and William had just proved the illness was real. From here on out, we would no longer worry about the younger generation believing they could escape to a better life on the outside.

For weeks, Virginia was inconsolable. She was convinced she'd lost the love of her life in the Beyond. Some days, I held her as she wept, and she begged me to stay close. Other days, she called me a witch and screamed that if I hadn't scared Samuel away, he'd still be in Eden.

I was patient. Calm. I brought her Sloth to cuddle, and a blanket made from the Enticements' web; it would allow her to dream pleasant dreams. I made her favorite meals and sang her favorite songs and told her scandalous news I heard from the ever-present fluttering Gossips who hid in our cupboards.

William came knocking on the door every few days, always with a hopeful look in his eyes. He brought her every single type of Malice pearl he could dig up and strung them together in a heavy necklace like the Queen might have worn. The memory of

England seemed impossibly long ago, impossibly far away. Yet if I concentrated hard, I could still see my hometown market filled with people, still hear the excited whispers when it was rumored the Queen would pass through. I wondered if our Queen still lived, and if England was at all like I remembered it.

A small shock went through me when I realized I would never know.

As time passed, Virginia's melancholy state began to wear upon me. I was thankful that William was a smart young man; talkative, hard-working, and determined. He manipulated Eden's magic through his woodwork. His skill was beyond compare. After carving the beams and doorways of his uncle's home, he came to ours. He wanted nothing in return but conversation and the excuse to be near Virginia.

Others in the village wanted his carvings in their homes, too. And so there were long days when it was only Virginia and me in the house, her tears our constant companions.

It was on one of these days that the Master came to visit.

He knocked upon the door and requested we sit with him for a cup of ale. While he and I waited for Virginia to come downstairs, he took off his shirt and hung it over the back of his chair, stretching out half-bare in my company. I found my eyes drawn to the ridges of his stomach, the firm swell of his chest, the raw scars that covered his back.

"'Tis inappropriate to sit at the table unclothed," I told him as I washed and cut vegetables to prepare the evening's meal.

"I do not give a demon's wail for what is appropriate, Eleanor," he said, sipping his ale. "I dare say you are only bothered by my unclothed state because it arouses you."

I scoffed and set out carrots and potatoes for cutting.

"Have you missed my company?" the Master asked. He'd left Eden after the remembrance ceremony. We had not seen him for several weeks. We knew he'd spent time in hell if, after he had been away for a while, dark circles shaded his eyes, and a frown framed his mouth. It was the case tonight.

I scoffed again in answer to his question.

He turned his tankard around in his hands and sighed. "There are souls out there made of nothing but rancor and venom. I cannot understand why Father does not smite them the moment their energy is conceived."

"And would you still be here had he done that?" My knife clapped loudly over and over on the wooden board as I cut through the carrots. I could have made it easier with magic, but the sound soothed me and, to be truthful, so did the heft of the blade in my hand.

The Master narrowed his eyes but continued, "I do not see why the Lord tortures *me* to find and punish those with dark hearts. When I bring their souls to hell, they blame me for their evil doings. As if I forced their hands. Ha! I cannot listen to them. 'Tis so exhausting."

"Oh, you poor devil," I cooed, my voice bitter. "So misunderstood."

Just then, Virginia came downstairs.

For the Master, she'd made an effort. She'd changed her chemise and brushed her hair and, it seemed, she even pinched some pink into her cheeks. It galled me, but I said nothing. Seeing her without tears in her eyes was worth keeping my tongue in place, even in the company of the Devil.

She sat at the table, her gaze caught on Satan's bare chest. "Master," she greeted him breathlessly, the color in her cheeks deepening.

"What? No lily of the valley for me today?" he teased. "I've nothing to adorn my hair."

Her eyes flicked to the flower garden she'd created outside the cottage. She'd neglected it these past few weeks. Of course, nothing was dying or brown, but the blooms were less robust and not nearly as beautiful without her magic to embellish them. A startled look crossed her face and she stood, about to go out and pick some.

"Nay." The Devil stopped her and pulled a tiny, round red pod from his pocket. "I've the seeds."

Virginia stared down at the fruit, her eyebrows pressing together. She blinked, and a sprout of green split the pod. It grew until it was adorned with long leaves and tiny bell-like flowers. The Master nodded. "You've not lost your touch."

Instead of tucking the sprig into his hair, he pinched it between his fingers as he studied her face. "So young. Adult, now, aye. Yet still so young. But you've grown, Virginia Dare. 'Tis no longer you who should be offering flowers to me. Quite the opposite." He conjured more of the flower, enough to make the room smell like spring.

As he handed her the bouquet, Virginia sat back down, a smile on her face.

Devil's curse, it had been too long since she'd smiled. I almost forgave the Master his dreadful manner. But not quite.

"You could not conjure outside of Eden, my dear Virginia. Magic does not exist out there. You realize this? 'Tis something special here." He spread his hands to indicate all of Eden.

She shrugged. "I would not care about growing flowers outside of Eden. I would only care about being with the man I love."

"Samuel?"

"Aye."

He frowned. A storm brewed in the pools of darkness behind his mask. "And he loves you?"

"Aye."

"If this is so, where is your lover?"

Her chin wobbled. "He is out there. In the Beyond. Through the tunnel."

"And why did he go?"

Now she turned to me, her face like thunder. "Mama scared him away."

I opened my mouth to speak but the Master continued, "I thought love conquered all, my sweet. Yet it did not conquer his fear."

"'Tis not his fault. His parents—"

"Hush. No excuses. The truth is that he did not love you. Or rather, he did not love you enough."

The shock on Virginia's face made me turn to the Master in anger. "Stop this!"

But he waved me away. "The boy was an insufferable clay-brained idiot. Yet he sang your praises and made you feel like you belonged. When he kissed you, you forgot you were a Dare, did you not?"

She bit her lip and stared down at her cup, not daring to look the Master in the eye.

His hand went to his mask. "When Nature kissed me, I forgot I was the Lord's unworthy son. She made me feel worthy when her lips were on mine. But she, like Samuel, ran away the moment things became difficult." He stayed quiet until Virginia stole a glance at him. Then he said, "I do not call that love."

Belial's breath. I found that, for once, I agreed with the Devil. I began chopping vegetables once more, unsettled by the thought.

"Do you love me?" he asked Virginia.

"Aye," she was quick to answer.

"Yet you wanted to leave me."

"Because Samuel—"

Satan lifted a hand to silence her. "Now your mother..." A smile grew on his lips, sharp as cut glass. "She tells me over and over how I am not worthy of her love. But the fact that she is here, that *you* are here, Virginia, is proof of *my* love. You are both mine and will always be mine. Unlike your poor sod Samuel, I care for you both too much to let you go."

"Too much to let go?" I laughed. "That is no proof of love."

"And have you always let everything you love go?" His voice was sugar, but his gaze lethal.

Torment's teeth dug deeper into my skin. Yet it was still not deep enough.

He turned back to Virginia. "You saw the Powells die, did you not, Virginia?"

She nodded, tears filling her eyes as she remembered.

"I've given you eternal life, eternal youth. You need never die. Do not waste your tears any longer. Samuel is not worth them. In fact, the boy left you behind only to eat poisonous berries and perish less than five days later of the flux."

I gasped, horrified at the image, and even more horrified the Devil shared it with Virginia so blithely. Yet she wiped away her tears and gripped the string of Malice pearls around her neck with a fist. A look of determination replaced the one of despair on her face. She nodded. "I am done mourning."

The Master's gaze softened from cold night to warm charcoal as he put a finger under her chin and dragged it along her jawline to brush the raised surface of her birthmark. "You're marked as mine, Virginia. 'Tis the most precious of gifts."

"Aye, 'tis," she sighed. I hated how she looked at him in adoration. Fear pooled, cold and sharp, in my gut. My fingers tightened around the knife.

"And one day you will give me something precious in return."

"Of course," she agreed.

I could no longer take it. I could no longer stomach the manipulative seduction in the Devil's voice, nor the veiled threats to my only child. "Nay. She won't. Before you get a thing from Virginia, you'll have to cross me."

His laugh boomed loudly in the small room. "You amuse me, Eleanor."

But I was not to be trifled with. I gripped the knife and whirled around, centering the point of the blade between the bloody scars on his back.

I was about to plunge it in, when suddenly, the chairs trembled and the air in the room jerked about as if the kitchen was its very own storm. My hair whipped upwards, long blond threads smacking me in the face. Carrot slices flew at the cupboards and the door.

The knife was wrenched from my hand by a fierce wind.

Then something hard and cold and sharp rammed itself into my chest.

The Master was now directly in front of me. In his hand was my knife, and the blade of that knife was ensconced in my heart.

"Ready to stab me in the back, were you, Eleanor?" the Devil whispered, his voice dark, his breath warm on my cheek. Do not forget who the master is here."

I knew the blade would not hurt me; in Eden we healed. But I could not dampen the terror that surfaced all the same. It wrenched my lungs and squeezed my heart. I nodded once, stiffly, and the whirlwind stopped. Everything dropped to the floor.

The Master pressed his thumb to the mark on my neck, the crescent moon of his fingernail. Then he pulled the knife from my chest and set it back on the cutting board. Blood stained both my bodice and the carrots scarlet while the wound healed as if it had never been. Torment jumped down from off my shoulders to gobble up the pieces, but the Master beat him to it.

He took a slice, popped it in his mouth, and licked my blood off his fingers. "Good."

27

Redd

Eden: Present Day

I swallow a mouthful of small ale, doing my best to force it down. This seems to be what people drink here, and I don't want my first encounter with my birth mother to be one where I admit I don't like her taste. I'll drink small ale for the rest of my life if it means I can have more time with her.

Because all that matters is that I'm here. With Virginia. I can finally figure out who I am. Why I am the way I am. And I can feel part of a true family. No more lies.

A mix of anger, incomprehension, and regret sours my stomach.

Agnes' lies messed with all three of us—me, Virginia, and Clara.

Clara's across from me. She sits as if the chair is about to burn her ass clear off and eyes the room like she's afraid something will jump out of the shadows. I'm not sure why she's staying when it's obvious she's uncomfortable here with Virginia.

But Virginia has been smiling at me since I sat down, offering ale and savory pancakes, and squeezing my hand. It doesn't matter if the ale is too bitter or the pancakes too thick or her grip too forceful. Because she's my real mother and this is all I've ever wanted. Agnes may be a better cook—just the thought of *her* pancakes makes me miss breakfast back in Hidden—but Virginia is my mother. Not someone who kidnapped me and raised me as her own.

Virginia doesn't look like the woman in my hallucinations on the Caul. My imagination had given that woman a face very similar to my own. The real Virginia isn't quite my doppelganger. She and I both have blonde hair, but mine's darker and wild and hers is golden and smooth. Where she's thin and sleek and unblemished, I have well-defined curves and a thick spatter of freckles on my face. I feel like a cow next to a gazelle, wondering how it is that we're family, how it is that everyone's been saying we look the same. But then she twists her head and I see exactly how we're alike.

With her free hand she tucks some hair behind her ear. The crescent moon of our shared birthmark peeks out from under wisps of hair that slid out of the bunch. Her mark is dark, nearly black, and looks almost painted on while mine is cinnamon brown, raised, and uneven. Essentially, though, the marks are the same.

"I cannot even begin to tell you how happy I am you're here," Virginia says to me for the millionth time, her fingers crushing my own.

My sixth sense is all over the place, so I ignore any flashes I get since the conflicting tastes and smells and sensations are more random than anything else. Virginia's hug tasted like lies while the kiss she planted upon my head felt like pure joy. Since then, all I've sensed is the overpowering odor of the Eternity Flower.

We sit at Virginia's wooden table, crumbs from our pancakes scattered over our pewter plates. I focus on the smooth surface of the tankard before me, the level of the liquid inside my own cup woefully high compared to that in Clara or Virginia's.

Countless herbs dry in bunches hanging from the intricately carved ceiling beams. The cottage has an open floor plan, the kitchen, dining and living areas all parts of one big room. The table we're at is pushed near the entrance hall, yet still close enough to feel the heat from the large fireplace that creates a transition between the eating and living spaces. There are drawings hung along the whitewashed walls, sketches of everything from landscapes to people to animals. One that catches my eye is of a man with Native American features, dressed in Elizabethan-style breeches, much like the ones the men wear here. Something about the drawing squeezes my heart. The illustration projects such a sense of love and regret, though I'm not sure how in so few strokes of charcoal.

Like in John's home, every wooden surface from the beams to the doorways is carved with miniature creatures or florals. But more light enters this place than the dark rooms of his home. A latticed window above the sink looks out onto the vegetable garden, while another larger window in the living area opens onto the flower garden. Weakening sunlight filters through the glass, its orange light slowly dying to ash.

"I've got so many questions," I say, as Virginia gets up, untwisting her fingers from mine. I nearly gasp in relief. There's no pain, but even with the magic in this place I've lost sensation in my pinkies.

"And I hope to have some answers." She takes our plates and sets them in the stone sink, then opens a standing cupboard where dozens of tiny holes decorate the doors. She lifts a tea towel to reveal a plate of cookies. They're small and look like teardrops. Setting them down in front of us, she slides back into her chair. Instead of grabbing my hand again, she taps her nails on the tabletop, a steady staccato beat. Maybe she's as nervous as I am. From what John's grandmother said, Virginia has been a hermit. Possibly unwell. Maybe me being here *is* a lot for her.

I'll need to take it slowly.

The biggest questions, the ones that have pierced my heart since finding out I was kidnapped, stay stuck to the back of my tongue. Like *did you miss me? Why did you never try to find me before?* and *Do you still love me?*

I swallow another mouthful of ale and immediately regret it. How the hell does anyone drink this stuff? I try washing away the taste with one of the cookies, the marzipan so intense it makes my eyes water. Clara is stuffing them in her mouth. I don't know how she can stomach the sweetness. It makes me think of Thomas and how he went after the food last night at dinner and breakfast this morning and snacks early afternoon. Thinking of Thomas makes me think of the book he showed me. And that makes me think of a question that is not so hard to ask.

"Is Eleanor Dare here, too?"

The name makes Virginia stop tapping her nails. "You know of Eleanor?"

I nod, about to say Thomas told me. But then I think that maybe that would get him into trouble. "No, actually. Not a lot. Just that she's your mother."

Her mouth purses and a flush rises into her cheeks. "Ah, you will meet Eleanor at one point. But not today. She and I..." She glances at Clara, who's reaching for another biscuit. Lifting an eyebrow, she says, "Sometimes 'tis not easy between mother and daughter."

Clara draws her arm back, empty-handed, and crosses her arms over her chest.

"Yeah. I know." I think of Mom...Agnes. Definitely not easy. "Why did Agnes take me from here? From you?"

Virginia squeezes my hand again, but this time I like the strength behind it. It feels solid and reassuring. "Oh, my sweet child. This may take a while." She lets go of my hand to lift the pitcher of ale. She's about to pour more into my cup when she sees it's still full and stops.

Clara pipes up. "I believe she does not appreciate the ale."

"Oh!" I'm horrified that Clara noticed but also annoyed with her for pointing it out. "It's not that, I—"

"Let me prepare a different drink for you," Virginia says.

"Oh, you don't have to—"

She waves her hand to stop me apologizing. "I pray you, do not worry. 'Tis nearly dark. I always have a warm drink before retiring."

"Agnes usually makes us a warm drink at night, too," I say. "I guess it does help me relax."

Virginia was starting to stand but now stills halfway. "Agnes?"

"Yeah."

"I am not sure I understand."

"Oh. Well, I...I thought she was my mom until recently. I mean, before I knew about you."

"Aye." She sits back down. "That I do understand. But you said she *makes* a warm drink...are you also saying Agnes is alive? The same Agnes that took you from us?"

With the Council I wanted to keep my past to myself. With Virginia, I'm willing to share anything and everything. "She's the same person."

"Belial's buttons," Clara breathes.

"Alive?" Virginia's eyes grow wide.

"Alive," I confirm.

Virginia's voice strains. "Where is Agnes now?"

I think back to yesterday—crazy that was only yesterday. She'd followed me all the way from Wisconsin to find me just outside the tunnel leading to Eden. I was so angry with her. All her lies. I'd screamed at her, actually knocking her over with my fury. "Last I saw, she was right outside the entrance to this place," I say. "But by now she's probably on her way back home."

My gut twists when I imagine her leaving Minnie and Shay behind at the auto repair shop in Ohio. When I think of how confused they must be. Are they home, too, wondering what the hell has happened? I know that Minnie will be worried sick about Agnes, but that Agnes deserves none of her worry or love.

Suddenly, I realize I can't wait for the perfect moment to tell Clara/Autumn the truth about who she is. I open my mouth to start when she looks at Virginia, her voice just above a whisper, "John was correct."

Whatever that means, from the way Virginia's mouth twists, it doesn't seem like she believes this is good news. Agnes is really *persona non grata*. Nobody wants her alive.

"She was growing the flower?" Virginia asks. "How?"

"Like any other flower, I guess. A lot of care..." I trail off. I don't know how we got off track from my own questions. I don't want to spend my time with Virginia talking about the flower. I did enough of that with John. "I don't know. I already showed John how it grew."

Virginia's face freezes.

"Was that okay to do?" I ask her, suddenly scared I've done something wrong.

"Aye, of course, my love. I only... simply hearing Agnes is alive is a shock..."

Out of the corner of my eye, I spot movement. A quick skittering over the carpet. A cockroach.

Virginia presses her lips together, then looks at Clara. "Clara, dear, while I speak with Redd, would you mind preparing a posset in my place?"

Clara hedges, "A posset? I'm not certain I make a good one."

"Nonsense," Virginia says. "It will be perfect, so long as it's strong. I've most everything you need in the kitchen cupboard and the garden. Gather the lavender fresh. Then run over to the Harvie household to see if the Governor has his special honey for the drink. I've none on hand."

I shake my head. "Oh! That's way down the hill! Don't bother on my account—"

"Hush." Virginia cuts me off and for the slightest of seconds the tone in her voice makes me recoil. But then she smiles and pats my shoulder. "'Tis no bother, my child."

She turns back to Clara. "Take your leave."

Standing, Clara heads outside.

From the corner of the room, two more cockroaches cross the floorboards and scurry towards Virginia. Without looking down, she lifts a foot and crushes them both with her boot. She turns to me and smiles. "So. What can I tell you?"

"I...I want to know about Agnes."

Her eyes go to the fireplace. Only a charred log remains, embers glowing from inside its cracked surface. "Where shall I start? The beginning?" When I nod, she continues. "I considered Agnes like a daughter—"

"She was your daughter?" Shock makes my words loud.

Her mouth purses at my interruption.

I shift in my chair. "Sorry. Go on."

She clears her throat and starts again, "As I said, Agnes was *like* a daughter. She was a good girl. Strong. Loyal. Even those who did not like her could not deny how devoted she was to Eden and all of us here. And then—" she pauses, thinking "—and then she began to lose her mind."

I think of everything Agnes said and did while I was growing up. Then all the things she did before I was even born. Losing her mind could be an explanation. Maybe this whole time, she was mentally unstable—like seriously mentally ill. "What do you mean?"

"She and Eleanor, your grandmother, became obsessed with the Beyond." She stands and moves towards the fire. The cockroaches aren't dead; they lie flattened on the carpet, legs uselessly waving in the air.

Grabbing a tinderbox from the mantle, Virginia takes out a long stick and touches it to the dying embers. No flame forms, just black smoke. Then she passes her hand over it and the tinder stick flares to life. From that she lights the drippy remains of candlesticks in a candelabra and two sconces on the wall, bathing the room in a yellow glow.

Clara comes back inside, out of breath, a basket in her hands.

The purple cat I saw earlier enters behind her, his steps slow. I smile at the fat little beast, but Clara scolds him. "Out! Sloth, how did you get in?"

"Aw, he's so cute," I coo.

Virginia says, "I'll allow Sloth to stay. Redd, you may hold him."

Clara pulls a sprig of lavender along with glass containers of liquid out of her basket. As she begins mixing stuff together, I try to pick up the cat. It's harder than it seems. Despite being a big, round fluff, he's as loose and limp as wilted lettuce. Finally, I get him settled like a baby in my arms. I sit back, fatigue settling over me as Sloth lets out a rusty purr.

Virginia pulls a chair closer to the hearth. "Your grandmother has always been adept at making enemies. At forcing others to pay for her mistakes. Eleanor made some choices early on that would not allow her to leave Eden, while Agnes was one of those who could pass through without getting too ill."

"Like John," Clara interjects as she hangs a pot of milky liquid over the fire.

"Aye." Virginia frowns, but continues, "Agnes passed back and forth between the Beyond and Eden. However, the entire time, Eleanor was grooming the girl to see this place as a prison. To believe those of us in the village were evil, rather than questioning Eleanor's own motives. Once my belly was swollen with life, your grandmother convinced Agnes the baby in my womb was in grave danger here in Eden."

"Was I?"

"The Dares...*we* Dares"—she says it as if the word leaves a bad taste in her mouth— "have enemies. They want to see Eleanor suffer. Eleanor saw this as a threat to you and Agnes acted upon it."

"By taking me out of Eden."

"Aye." Virginia nods. "Eleanor is locked away for her part in it. But Agnes got to spend her life with you—my daughter. How is that right? How is that just?"

"It's not," I say.

"Now, I can assure you, I've spoken with the Council at length. You needn't be afraid because of what Agnes did. You are safe here."

"Well...I thought it was impossible to get hurt in Eden, anyways? What would they do to me?"

"One does not need to break bones to be hurt, dear Redd. Suffering comes in many forms." As she says it, something cold settles in my stomach.

But then steam rises from the pot over the fire. The soothing scent of lavender, vanilla, and something sweeter fills the cottage. It calms me. I stretch my legs out, careful not to disturb Sloth. I'm feeling extra sluggish, but it's been a long day.

Clara pours the liquid into cups and Virginia continues, "Agnes is also responsible for William's death. He went after her. But he could not pass easily into the Beyond. He lost his life in the process. You'll never have the chance to know him."

"My father?"

"Agnes never spoke of him? He and I were married nearly four-hundred years." She says it matter-of-factly.

John told me that my father was dead. But I didn't realize Agnes had something to do with his death. It doesn't feel like I should be surprised. I should know how horrible the woman who called herself my mother for the last eighteen years really is. But still, a part of me wants to deny it. Deny everything. How can it be possible? How can the woman who gave me kisses and cut coupons with me and made me stacks of blueberry pancakes be this monstrous? This selfish? How did I not really know her at all?

"And the kids Agnes kidnapped?" I kiss Sloth's fuzzy head as I wait for Virginia to respond. The conversation makes my stomach turn and yet...yet...I'm so comfortable here. I could stay here in front of the fire, doing nothing forever. Absolutely nothing.

Virginia smiles as Clara hands us each a cup. "A lavender posset. My favorite. Thank you, Clara."

I look down at the murky liquid and sniff. It smells sweet and has the consistency of syrup. It's already more appealing than the ale.

"Drink up," Clara says as she pulls up a chair.

I swallow a hefty mouthful. It warms a path from my throat to my belly. "That's really good."

Clara beams at me. "I was worried it wouldn't be. I pray you, have some more."

I want to make her my friend, so I take another gulp.

Stroking Sloth, I can barely keep my eyes open. My lids feel like lead weights. "Did you know about the kids? The ones Agnes took?" But as I say it, the whole conversation feels like an effort. I don't even want to think.

"You look fatigued." Virginia sets her teacup down untouched. "'Tis getting late, my dear. We can continue talking in the morning when we break our fast. I've prepared a chamber with fresh linens for you. I am so happy you are here."

I have more questions, but she's right. I'm really tired.

Really, really tired.

Why am I so tired?

I look down at my empty teacup, dread pooling in my gut.

Virginia turns to Clara. "Clara, would you mind staying and getting Redd settled into the chamber near the stairs while I go thank the Governor for the honey? I shall be back shortly." She heads out the door, Sloth jumping from my lap to follow her. The second the cat is off my knees, I feel lighter, less lazy.

Of course. *Sloth.*

I laugh, relief flooding me. It was the cat, not the drink.

Clara studies me. "Is everything all right?"

"I'm fine. Just...that cat. He was turning me into a couch potato."

She blinks, then gives a short laugh and leads me up a set of stairs, the banister carved into a flowering vine. "Ah! Sloth. I cannot tell you how many times I've wasted away hours due to that creature."

We reach the guest room. A small window looks out over the flower garden, the night sky lit with stars. A bed in a simple wooden frame is tucked into the corner. God, I'm tired again. I look at the bed with longing, but first want to tell Clara the truth. I sway as I feel for the glossy square in my skirt pocket. "Clara."

"Redd?"

It takes me a minute to get my fingers to wrap properly around the photograph, but when they do, I shove it towards her. "Virginia isn't the only reason I came here. I also came for you."

Despite the wall sconces, it's dim in the room. She squints at the photo, her lips twisted in the exact same way Minnie's twist when she's concentrating. "Who is this?"

"It's you. As a toddler. You were only a little over a year in that picture."

Her frown deepens.

"You...you have a mom," I say. "In the Beyond. She's a friend of mine. And she's been looking for you for nineteen years."

"I...My mother is here. I am a daughter of Eden."

"You were kidnapped, Clara. By Agnes. Like me...only the other way around. Your real name is Autumn. Your mom's name is Minnie," I try to make it come out softly, with empathy. But my tongue suddenly feels like a lead weight. My words begin to slur. "Agnes took you from her when you were only a baby. She's missed you every day of your life." It comes out *sheeezzzzmisssseduuuueverydayovvvyurliiiiiiiife.*

Clara stares at the picture between her fingers. I can see the thick edges shake in her hands.

For a moment, the only sound is our breathing. "Clara," I start. I shake my head. That sets it spinning.

A sound of a door slamming and voices come from below.

"Who's that?" *Whooooozaat?* I'm having a hard time getting the words to roll off my tongue. "Clara?"

She does not take her eyes off the picture until I say her name once more. Then she crumples the photo into a ball and shoves it in her skirt pocket. Her voice sharpens. "That will be the Council, here to talk about the ceremony."

"My welcoming ceremony?"

Her smile is a sharp blade. "Aye, a ceremony to truly welcome you to Eden."

And for the third time in a matter of hours, Clara shoves me backwards. I land on the bed, its mattress lumpy. "Time to sleep," she says.

I'm so tired I can't even lift the blanket.

"Wait—" I start, but it comes out a weak gurgle.

She doesn't wait. Instead she leaves the room, shutting the door behind her. There's a metal scraping, like the sound of a bolt sliding into place. My heart rises into my throat, and I roll over, intending to get up.

But I don't even make it off the bed before everything goes black.

28

John

The Beyond: Present Day

The ambiance in the vehicle is volatile.

The four of us—me, Minnie, Shay, and Agnes—are inside a van with the words SHADY PINES FOR INDEPENDENT LIVING (AND GREATER FREEDOM!) painted in block letters along the sides. There's room for at least eight people, with a long bench at the back. Minnie took the keys from Agnes' pocket then directed us to set Agnes on that bench. We are now heading at terrifying speed towards the hospital. I do not know how I ended up here. No. Not true. I do know. Both Persuasion and Terror failed to do their jobs, and Chaos excelled at his. That, and I was caught off guard with Agnes' blood on my hands. Because Minnie does "not trust me as far as she can throw me," the moment I entered the van to help them place Agnes inside, she and Shay activated the child locks so I could not get out and Minnie began driving.

Despite my arguments and pleas, neither Shay nor Minnie fully believe that I found Agnes in the forest coughing up blood and did not cause her injuries. They're also having a difficult time understanding that because Redd stayed in Eden, she can't simply call them from someone's cell phone. Minnie is two seconds from taking me to the police to arrest me on suspicion of both battery and kidnapping. It's only the vital need to get to the hospital first that is keeping her from doing so. She and Shay even left their own car behind so that I would be outnumbered in this van.

Shay is in the passenger seat, eyes narrowed, holding something made of bright orange plastic out towards me. It looks vaguely like a knife in a cocoon. She found it in the glove compartment, and from Minnie's comments, I believe it is a seatbelt cutter. But Shay tells me she's not afraid to use force and "if I make one little move, she's going straight for the throat".

I have no idea what the consequences would be should she use the knife cocoon on me, but I sit very still. My only movement is to uncurl Persuasion from my ear so he can perch on one of theirs. Perhaps he'll be more effective that way.

At the moment, Chaos is panting from the heat. Minnie looks at me in the rearview mirror, a frown on her face. She shakes her head and tells me I breathe like an "obscene caller."

Changing lanes, she turns sideways to look for oncoming traffic. At the sight, I feel a shiver down my spine. From this angle I can clearly see Clara in her. Hard to believe I hadn't noticed it before.

I wonder what would have become of Clara had Agnes never taken her from Minnie. Joyce Archer is not a bad woman. And she has not been a bad mother to Clara. Yet she has not been a good one, either. It was Clara's father, Arthur, who kept a smile on the girl's face. But he spent too much time caught in the Caul and his mind could no longer separate reality from fiction. Grandfather told me once that Arther Archer had lost two boys—one in Roanoke and one to sacrifice—and never recovered from the grief.

Much like Grandfather himself.

Via the rearview mirror, I study Minnie. Under the pink lipstick, her face is pleasant, but there is a sadness in her eyes. Has she recovered from losing Clara? According to Redd, she hasn't. According to Redd, she cannot. A strange lump forms in my throat. I try to swallow it down, but it will not budge.

And what of Thomas, I think. Do his birth parents still grieve for him?

As a scout in training, I learned that bringing children to Eden was a gift. Never was it mentioned that our acts may hurt those in the Beyond. What happens in the Beyond is of no consequence to us. We are not to care.

So why do I?

"Redd told me your daughter was taken from you. Is that true" I ask. Even though it was Agnes who kidnapped the babe, I feel some guilt over it because I am a scout. Because I, too, was trained to take children. Because I, too, will be expected to supply them to Eden if I cannot help the flower thrive out here.

"What the fuck kind of question is that," Shay growls.

Minnie's knuckles whiten on the steering wheel. But she answers. "Yes. She was. Nineteen years ago."

"Yet you continue living without her."

In the mirror, I see her blink back tears. "I do. I move forward. But not on."

"Does it still hurt?"

Shay swears and brings her weapon closer. "You want to know what hurts, Smith, I'll show you—"

Minnie stops her with a gentle touch and a quick shake of the head. Her voice is whisper soft. She is no longer the angry, yelling woman she was when she locked me in the car. "It still hurts like a spike through the heart," she says.

The lump in my throat is sharp and prickly now, like the casing of the nut on the tree of doubt.

I could tell her that Clara is alive and well. That she needn't worry or grieve. I could even arrange a meeting between mother and daughter here in the Beyond.

But it should be Agnes or Redd who tells Minnie about Clara. Either the one responsible for taking her...or the one responsible for finding her. It is not my place to do so. Nor my priority.

The cool slide of scales against the skin on my wrist makes me gasp. Persuasion did not find a perch on Shay or Minnie. Satan's scourge. I wish I'd have taken an older snakelet.

Ahead of us an exit sign looms, POLICE in large block letters. Minnie slows as she nears the offramp.

"Chaos," I whisper, my tone urgent.

That's when a little convertible comes from out of nowhere, cutting Minnie off from the right. The nose of our car is only inches from the other and I feel my heart jump into my throat. I'm catapulted violently to the side, the seatbelt a vice over my chest, as Minnie quickly veers left to avoid a crash. The movement sends her back into the main lane so she misses the exit. It also jostles the orange weapon out of Shay's hand and into the void between the two front seats.

"Dammit!" Shay swears as she tries to retrieve it with no luck.

"Jackass!" Minnie hollers to the other driver and presses her foot a little harder on the accelerator to catch up with traffic. Her face has gone white.

Beelzebub's teeth. I scold Chaos under my breath, though not sharply. His method was risky, but he did his job.

Now it is back to Persuasion. I lean forward and drop him onto Minnie's shoulder. She tilts her head as if she feels something but does not brush him off.

We drive past the next exit sign, and she enters the lane marked HOSPITAL.

Good job, Persuasion. Minnie trusts me.

As if reading my mind, she says, "I still don't trust you, John. But from how much she told you, it sounds like Redd might." She purses her lips and nods. "Now let's see what Agnes says about you. Until I know you didn't hurt her, I'm not letting you out of my sight."

29

Redd

Eden: Present Day

I'm out for only a handful of minutes before I come to with a start. There must have been some Eternity Flower nectar in that drink Clara made me. I know because suddenly I can sense absolutely everything—from the particles in the air to the cockroaches in the walls to the myriad of emotions from the people downstairs. The one and only time I tasted the nectar from Agnes' river flower this is exactly what happened. Sensations crowd me, I taste them, feel them, hear them. My gut heaves. My whole body convulses. I squeeze my eyes shut and bite my tongue, the taste of blood filling my mouth.

Voices from below bubble up, snatches of conversation thrown at me. The words pile up, one on top of each other, each like a sledgehammer to my brain. It's not painful, but maddening. So much so that I can't handle one more second.

I'm about to scream when a different voice—a honeyed voice—whispers directly into my ear. "Pull yourself together, Redd."

My eyes fly open to see the Master standing over me.

The sounds, the feelings, the sensations, fall away. I run a shaky hand over my face and exhale. "Thank God," I say.

"Oh, I wouldn't thank Him," he chuckles. "God has nothing to do with this place. He stays very, very far away."

Slowly, I sit up. The small flames in the sconces glow brighter as the Master lifts a hand, lighting the small room. The ceiling is covered in black spores of a strange mold, tendrils of it reaching down the walls. Hundreds of tiny holes cover the ceiling beams, sawdust falling from them as a white worm burrows in and out.

The Master scoffs as some of that wood dust falls to the bed. "Abandon. He'll ruin even the most beautiful of places. Eleanor would be furious that this house has succumbed to the beast."

I scurry backwards until I hit the headboard. I really don't want that stuff on me.

"We're going to have to stop meeting like this," the Master says, a smirk on his lips. With his chin, he motions to the now shuttered windows and the closed door.

And then I remember: Clara. She gave me something to drink. Locked me in here.

No. She wouldn't have locked me up. That makes no sense. I stand, my legs slightly wobbly, and make my way to the door. The metal knob is cool under my touch and seems much newer than anything else in this room. But when I attempt to turn it, it doesn't budge.

The Master sits on the bed, watching calmly as I push and pull and nearly break my wrist trying to twist the thing. It's only when I lift a fist to bang on the wood that he stops me. "I wouldn't draw attention to the fact that you're awake, Redd."

"But this is a mistake—"

An eyebrow shoots above his mask. "Listen."

All of a sudden, I can hear the voices from the rooms downstairs again. This time, though, the conversation is as clear as if I were standing there.

"—gave her triple the dose. She'll be out until morning." I recognize Clara's voice.

"'Tis a pity we had to do this now. I was beginning to enjoy myself. I could have gone on like this for weeks. What a delightful diversion from the day-to-day." That from Virginia.

"Everyone has found such excitement in meeting her and treating her like any other," answers a man. I think it's the Christopher guy from the Council. "The novelty, the experience shall tide many over for years to come."

"Aye, well, we've had enough excitement. She was never here to stave off our boredom." Dyonis, John's Grandfather. "She was brought back for one purpose only. Indeed, I should not have given into John's whims. I never should have taken her out of the holding cell in the first place. But I had not anticipated the possible complication of the flower—that Agnes could have made it grow."

There are several grunts of agreement.

"And now we must force the Harvest or risk everything," a woman says. There's a long pause then, "We'll need the entire village to help."

"I will call everyone together," Dyonis says. "Keep the girl locked up. There is nothing in the chamber upstairs she can use to escape?"

Virginia tuts. "Nay. I've chained the shutters closed from the outside."

"Good. And her own mask is locked in the safe box." I hear the pop of a cork. "One drink and let us get on with the business of hastening the Harvest."

"The price of life is a soul," chants a woman. Then I hear the clinking of glasses. "Finally, the Dares get their due. May the girl's death bring us a century of life. May Eden feed to satiety."

The Master snaps his fingers, and the voices fade to nothing. The only sound now is my rapid pulse beating in my ears.

It's true. Clara. Virginia. They gave me something to knock me out and locked me in here. On purpose.

"No." I can't help my voice from breaking. Virginia's betrayal hurts more than I ever thought possible. She was supposed to be the piece that plugged the hole in my heart.

My body starts to shake, and my teeth begin to chatter as I realize the truth. The woman I thought was my mom kidnapped me. The woman who gave birth to me drugged me and locked me away. They don't love me. They never did.

I'm all kinds of fucked-up.

"What do you think of Eden now?" the Master asks. "Is it still so beautiful?"

A memory hits clear and in technicolor: Dyonis handcuffing me as soon as I arrived. And John was there next to him. John looked right at my manacles and told me they were "pretty bracelets." I believed him.

I've been so stupid.

How? How did I not see it?

John never meant to help me. No one here did.

The Master lets out a long-suffering sigh. "Finally. You're no longer under Deception's influence. I was beginning to wonder if that feisty Dare character had skipped a generation. Virginia is somewhat gullible but far from weak. She simply lets her heart take precedence over her head. And Eleanor's cunning meets my own. You should have at least a bit of brimstone inside you."

But I don't understand any of it. "Why? Why would they do this to me?"

"I can answer that." He crosses his arms in front of a broad chest. "With a story."

Wait. What?

"Once upon a time," he starts, his voice smooth and soft as a lullaby. "There was a pathetic little group of colonists living on Roanoke Island. Among them was a woman named Eleanor Dare."

As he talks, I go to the window. I open the glass panes to get to the shutters, but they're impossible to budge. I try with magic. Nothing. "I know this story," I say through gritted teeth.

"No. You don't." His voice is sharp enough to make my spine stiffen in fear.

In one fluid movement, he grabs me and sits me down next to him so our eyes are level. "Eleanor had, shall we say, a special relationship with the Devil. A relationship she tried desperately to deny. When she was still a young bride in England, her father was set to go to the Americas. She begged for passage on the trip over with her father and husband. Naïve and pigheaded, she imagined the Devil would not find her in the New World. She tried to escape her tie to him, but it had become a part of her. One cannot flee oneself."

While he explains, the scent of him fills my nostrils. Autumn leaves, winter wind, and something else. Something darker. Something that makes my stomach curl in fear despite myself.

"The Devil had a chokehold on Eleanor. She was his. The sharp point of his thumbnail had marked her—"

He suddenly thrusts his hand under my chin and wraps his fingers around my throat, pushing into my skin. His thumbnail pokes the exact spot where my birthmark is. He taps it hard. Once. Twice. "—it had marked her right here," he says.

My muscles are still like soft butter from whatever Clara gave me, so my attempt at pushing him away is weak. He squeezes once, cutting off my breath for a second. Then he drops his hand and stands again, his eyes on his fingers as if there is some message there. A tight ache encircles my throat.

He continues, still looking at the tips of his fingers. "The colonists came to Roanoke. There, they died horrible deaths. Starvation and disease ate away at those who were not killed by their enemies. Eleanor lost her husband. Her lover. Her friends. Yet the remaining colonists still fought to stay alive. Death would have been merciful for most of them, but they were terrified of dying. Eleanor was no exception, though in her case she had good reason to want to live; she'd given birth to a child after her arrival on Roanoke. A little girl. A girl that gave meaning to Eleanor's very existence. Little Virginia Dare." He looks at me and lifts the corners of his mouth into a wry smile. "Your mother."

The words send a wave of longing and hurt through me.

"She, too, was marked with the Devil's print upon her jaw. That terrified Eleanor—to know the Devil had extended his reach to her flesh and blood. You realize mothers will do anything for their child? Anything."

I scoff at that.

He ignores me. "Amidst all that death and disease, Eleanor did what she could for her baby to survive. When all other options were lost, she called out to the Devil. She pleaded with him to keep them alive. Now say what you want about the Devil. But he is not like God, too busy to hear your pleas. If the Devil is called upon, he answers. Like any good master."

Realization dawns and I feel the little hairs on my arms stand at attention. Despite my brain telling me it can't be real, my gut tells me the truth.

The Master.

The Devil.

All those weird expressions people use in Eden finally hits home. Oh, shit.

"You," I whisper.

"Me," he responds with a smile.

I scan the room, looking for something to smash the shutters with. *Get out of here, Redd.*

A spark lights the dark orbs behind his mask. "I saved Eleanor and Eleanor saved Virginia. And that saved the others—though many, with their fantastical views of God in Heaven, would disagree. Many did, in fact, but the deed was already done. I gave them the opportunity for what may be eternal life.

"Yet even I cannot give something for nothing. Even my magic has limits. As long as Eden is fed, this small paradise will stay beautiful and lush. So for generation after generation, there has been a price to pay."

"What price?" I ask. Now I'm wide awake and alert, adrenaline pumping through me.

"A sacrifice, of course. We call it the Harvest. Over hundreds of years, every family has sacrificed several of their own. Every family."

He stops. Looks me in the eyes. "Every family but the Dares."

It's like I'm underwater. Everything slows down, floats about. I can't take a breath. My lungs burn like they're ready to burst.

He bends down, his face near mine. "Amazing how after hundreds of years of never conceiving—of never allowing herself to conceive—Virginia found herself with child. Of course, the Dares were expected to pay their due; the choice to sacrifice you was made before your birth. But then Agnes stole you away to the Beyond. Did you know that she'd taken children from the Beyond to keep Eden alive? Agnes is no Dare—not of blood, anyways—yet she put that family before everything else. She expected others to die for Eden, but not you. She, Eleanor, and Virginia made their own rules." He smiles an indulgent smile, as if impressed by their rebellion.

He continues, "Yet there are families who do not forgive generations of spared life. Families who have lost more than intended."

The Master tilts his head and I can clearly see his eyes. They're deep black vortexes with a powerful pull. Those eyes make you want to share your deepest secrets and confidences. They make you want to take risks...on him. And even though they are not the gold of the eyes in that cathedral tapestry, I know that was him because they have the same hypnotic power.

Here, before me, is Lucifer, the fallen angel.

"Prove to me that you are not powerless. That the blood running through your veins is worthy of so much more than a simple sacrifice." He flicks his wrist and his body turns to vapor.

In the time it takes me to blink, he's already gone.

30

Eleanor

Eden: 1607

True to her word, Virginia no longer mourned Samuel. Or rather, she acted as though she had. Every once in a while, I would catch her deep in thought, a look of such regret upon her face I turned away.

But no matter. With Samuel gone, our quarrels lessened, and she grew closer and closer to William. She would often go to wherever he was—whether it be carving in the Devil's cathedral or in someone's private home—and bring him a cool drink or a pastry. Sometimes, they would go for long walks, picnicking in the meadow. Other times, they spent evenings under the stars, hands clasped, taking turns as Enticements wove them into the Caul. They danced together during village festivities, and he showed up nearly every day at the cottage with freshly brewed ale or some thick, liquored syrup made from the Eternity Flower. He supped with us; his uncle was now courting Audry Tappan, and William felt a third wheel at their dinner table. I made sure to not make the same mistake, as I did not want Virginia to feel out of place in her own home. I shared conversations with them and played cards with them, but also gave them the privacy they needed. I spent more and more time on the bench outside the cottage, with Sloth on my knees and Torment round my neck, knitting or sketching to keep boredom at bay.

Even after months and months of spending time with Virginia, William still looked at her with absolute adoration in his eyes. I knew it was only a matter of time before he'd ask her to marry.

I was correct.

The ceremony was held on the day Virginia turned twenty years of age.

It was the second handfasting ceremony since arriving in Eden. Jane Pierce and Humfry Newton had tied the knot two years earlier, but they were the only ones. While there were plenty of wifeless men in the village, in a community where marriage was encouraged but not necessary, and children were wanted whether they be born within or outside of the bonds of matrimony, the women of Eden did not see the point. Joan was too severe for long-term companionship; Audry—though now with Anthony—enjoyed the freedom to hop in and out of different beds; Emme and Elizabeth seemed to prefer each other's company to a man's, and I had no interest in marriage or the act that often went with it. Before Eden, I had sought out the pleasures of the flesh, roused by the broadness of Ananias' shoulders, or the shadow of a beard upon Manteo's jaw. The men of Eden, however, roused nothing but my derision.

Apart from Virginia, that left only the three Powell girls, all under the age of twelve.

So Virginia and William's wedding was an excuse for a celebration in which everyone took part. For once, it did not matter that Virginia was a Dare. Today, she was part of the community, and today no one gave her black looks or turned up their nose as she walked by.

Across the river, past the fruit trees and in the meadow behind the farmland in the easternmost part of Eden, all had been set up for the festivities. Eternity Flowers created an archway for guests to pass under, where a flutter of Braggarts with bright pink wings peppered the air.

A long banquet table held a bounty of food—from meats to jellies to pies. Clement Tayler was serving his conjured ales and sirups and wines, each one tastier than the last. The amber fizzy wine was especially popular, the bubbles like tiny explosions upon one's tongue.

Fury and Evil lay pouting near the footbridge. Today they would have little anger or malice to fill their bellies. Chaos panted, tongue out, tail wagging. His coat changed color with each breath, and his ebony claws dug into the soil. Someone had been smart enough to tie him to a tree just far enough away from the festivities for him to do little damage.

No longer bound to the sumptuary laws of England, and free to conjure the cloth we liked so long as we had the basics, we fitted ourselves out for the occasion. Virginia had helped me conjure an outfit of tinseled satin, with silver embroidery on the latticed partlet and sleeves. I'd given Torment a bath, his fur for once smelling of lavender instead of self-loathing.

The men wore lace ruffs and decorated their jerkins with fancy buttons and elaborate trim. William kept scratching his neck and tugging at his sleeves, but the fashion suited him well. Yet no one was more stunning than my Virginia. We'd been preparing her gown for weeks, starting by collecting a large grumble of Ignorance. The wriggling larvae grew into flies of Suspicion, their newly formed bodies a shimmering gold. Suspicions now studded a delicate overskirt woven by Enchantments that Virginia wore on top of her silver silken gown. A crown of Eternity Flowers sat upon her head and cascaded like a veil over her long, blonde locks. The sight of her made my heart wrench. I'd created this beautiful young woman. I'd loved her. Raised her. Saved her. William was a good man. But, Satan's scourge, I did not want to give any part of her away.

I stood apart from the crowd, under the shade of an apricot tree, watching but not yet taking part. To make small talk with the others, to dance and laugh...it was a day of celebration, aye, but it also felt a bit like a day of mourning to me.

Our relationship was going to change.

"You cannot hide from the party forever, Eleanor. Not a soul is missing the spread upon the banquet table. Look at Cutburt White, sucking down pickled eggs and plum pie." William's eyes were nothing like the Master's dark, piercing jewels. William's were a warm brown that belied his gentle nature. It was impossible not to smile up at him.

"Cutburt White never misses an occasion to stuff himself on other people's recipes. Even mine."

"Come, let us fatten ourselves up as well," William said.

"Fine." I followed him into the crowd and to the table, fingering the Malice Pearls sewn into my skirts. Truth be told, I was grateful to William. Virginia had talked about building a cottage in the center of the village. That would leave me alone up on the hill as I refused to live among the others; not after how I'd been treated. So I proposed we increase the size of Virginia's bed chamber and add a door to the hallway leading to my own chamber in the cottage up on the hill. I could still be part of the household but in a private wing. I could cook for them, clean for them, allow them to spend their days in leisure. All I asked in return was their occasional company.

Virginia, of course, was against the idea. She believed me needy.

But William got her to agree.

I overheard him talking to Virginia one day in the garden. He'd been whispering and checking over his shoulder, but he did not realize I was in Virginia's chamber upstairs where the wind carried his words directly to my ears.

"I cannot imagine what 'tis like for her. She has very little, Virginia. You are too young to remember, but 'tis not like the early days when we had faith in being saved. Nay. We are here forever. *She* is here forever. And she will forever be alone. No man in Eden will take her on as a wife, and even the women who are closest to her keep their distance." William held Virginia's elbow while he spoke, as if holding her upright.

I wished someone were there to hold my elbow, because the truth of his words made my knees turn to water.

He continued, "She loves you, Virginia. You are the one thing she has. I'd rather not be the one to take that away from her."

"You call it love," she sighed. "Yet it does not feel like love. It feels like a heavy net that impedes any movement she or I want to make."

He took her in his arms then, and murmured words that were no longer clear. But they stayed with me. Aye, the hallway was lengthened, and a heavy door separated my chamber from the rest of the house, but we were still together.

Once the sun was high in the sky, William and Virginia stood in the glittering tent and repeated their vows in front of the entire village. Dyonis, being Governor, officiated the ceremony. The Master stood behind him, a simple band of leather covering the gash in his face. He was dressed in an embroidered velvet jerkin and cloak, silver buttons polished to a shine, Malice pearls swinging from his ears.

As Dyonis tied the knot round Virginia and William's hands, the screeching of birds nearly drowned out his words. They dove at us from above, their wings brushing roughly against our heads. The ground shifted, throwing us all onto our hands and knees.

The glorious tent, sparkling like jewels in the sunlight, suddenly went up in flames. A crackling noise filled the air as the web was singed and burnt into nothing but ash. A cloud of gray smoke obscured everyone and everything and, despite the knowledge that we could not die, my heart pounded in panic.

The Master stepped out of the smoke in front of Virginia, his hair swirling like snakes upon his head. "You're mine," he said, holding her face in his hands, his fingers digging into her skin.

I screamed until my throat was raw, but no sound came from between my lips. I scratched at the earth with my nails, trying in vain to pull myself forward. Then as the Master traced her birthmark with his thumb, I closed my eyes, salt stinging the lids.

But when they opened again it was William who held Virginia's face between his hands. The tent was still glittering above us and sunlight streamed through it, illuminating everything in a buttery light. The Master stood calmly behind Dyonis, a benevolent smile upon his lips.

"Wife," William said to Virginia, "I shall take care of you."

I took a breath, trying to ground myself in the here and now.

What had I just witnessed? Was it my imagination? My fears playing tricks upon my mind? I studied the others in the crowd, searching for looks of confusion on their faces.

But there were none. I was the only bewildered one here. The only one with visions of the Master gone mad. Perhaps the fizzy wine had been too rich for my blood.

"Husband," Virginia said to William, her voice shaking just a bit. "I am perfectly able to take care of myself." She gently removed his hands from her cheeks and laced her fingers through his. "However, I will enjoy your company."

Her words were a balm to my worry. That was my Virginia. She wanted marriage, but she'd have it on her own terms. She'd changed so much since Samuel left, tail between his legs. Eden had forced my girl to be strong.

No man held sway over her, I told myself, not even Satan himself.

It would be a very long time before I realized just how wrong I was.

31

John

The Beyond: Present Day

We sit in hard plastic chairs under a harsh set of fluorescent lights, surrounded by the sounds and smells of pain. Hospital staff walk past in brightly colored uniforms and ugly rubber shoes. It's been hours, but I have been unable to leave. Somehow, Shay and Minnie have talked one of the security guards—one that is roughly three times my size—into making sure I do not run. I wonder if Persuasion is working against me rather than with me since the giant guard hasn't taken his eyes off me, never leaving me alone for a second. His name is Joel. He drinks sludge from a machine that's labeled coffee but tastes like dirt and stares at me from over the rim of the paper cup.

Shay and Minnie's trust is precarious at best. But perhaps Persuasion is working both with *and* against me. Or perhaps the snakelet's burgeoning powers are too uncontrolled. Because, aye, I have been unable to leave. But, on the other hand, the police have not yet been called to come and drag me away.

I look at the clock. Devil's curse. We've been here too long. Agnes has been in surgery for hours. The clock hands keep advancing with no word from the doctors.

A crash sounds from down the corridor. I grit my teeth. Chaos.

The hellhound is loose somewhere in the hospital, and I can only imagine the havoc he's wreaking. Already, the vending machine has spit candy bars across the room, three patients have run past, naked buttocks on view for all to see, and the elevators have stopped at all the wrong floors. No matter how many times I call Chaos, he does not come. There's too much here for him. A smorgasbord of mayhem and confusion. I'd rather he use his powers to help me out of this situation, but it does not seem that will happen until I can get my hands on the idiotic beast.

Shay's gaze goes from me to Joel and back again. Both she and Minnie have relaxed a bit in my presence, and I want to keep it that way. So I try to disarm her with conversation. Now that she no longer has that weapon pointed at me, she's less threatening. "Odd that you were only coming round to find Agnes tonight," I say. "Didn't she leave you yesterday?"

"We started back to Wisconsin but worry got the better of us. Ms. Winter—Agnes—wasn't answering her phone. My dad was able to find the Shady Pines van through a tracker they use on all company vehicles. So, once we knew where Ms. Winter was, we turned around," Shay explains.

"And happened upon me as you arrived."

She and Minnie share a glance, blush rising into both their cheeks. Shay gulps down the rest of her coffee and Minnie lets out a defeated sigh. "We'd been driving around there for hours."

"You had?"

Shay crumples her cup and tosses it into the large metal bin at the end of the row of chairs. "We knew she was there because we saw the van..." Her voice trails off. She shifts and turns to Minnie. "Why didn't we follow?" she whispers just loud enough that I hear.

Minnie's eyes are red from crying and her bright pink lipstick is smudged. A look of confusion crosses her face at Shay's words, then the harsh lines around her mouth deepen. "I...I don't know. There was something frightening..."

Two strong women, loyal friends. Loyal enough to stay nearby rather than run far away. Yet Terror had done an excellent job. Wonderful beast. The fear he forced upon them kept them from entering the forest despite knowing Agnes was there. If I hadn't called him off, they never would have happened upon us.

I let out a breath. Satan's scourge. What bad timing. At least I know that Terror is back on duty now, protecting the flower.

A doctor in a white coat and sky-blue shoes comes up to us. Her eyes go directly to Minnie as she says, "May I have a word?"

The two of them head down the hallway to stand next to a painting of green and orange leaves. In the glass covering it, I can see their reflections. Whatever the doctor is saying makes Minnie frown even further.

Joel grunts and goes to the machine for another coffee. The man has had at least six since I've been here.

"I don't know what to think," Shay mutters. Now that she's no longer nursing a coffee of her own, she has one leg bent over the other and is shaking her foot like it's on fire. "This whole scenario is a fucking mess. My dad's beyond pissed. At Minnie. At Ms. Winter—Agnes. At Redd. At me." She shakes her head. "I don't think Redd and her mom will have a job at Shady Pines after this. That is if...if Ms. Winter is even okay."

I don't say anything. I honestly do not know what it means for Redd, for me, for Eden, if Agnes is not all right. If Agnes cannot come with me to prove the flower grows out here, the flower needs to thrive on its own. And with me here instead of coddling it on the beach, I've no idea if it will.

"Why didn't we just go into the woods when we saw the van? We should have." She swipes her eyes angrily and shoots me a look. "And I really don't know why I'm talking to you instead of forcing you to speak to the police. Like, why, after all of this, am I trusting you?"

Because Persuasion is holding his own. Good little snakelet.

"Because I'm trustworthy."

She scoffs but doesn't push any further. Instead, she says, "Redd...did she get to meet her birth mom?"

"She hadn't when I left, but she will." As I say it, I hope it is true.

"You know, Redd seems naive. A total pushover. Like she's always so nice and sweet to the residents at Shady Pines and she does her best to disappear into the shadows. She's good at pretending she doesn't even exist. She tries to make herself as small as possible, but it doesn't matter. She's got a weird kind of pull. People are drawn to her. There's something there, simmering under the surface. Almost like a power."

I think about this. It's true. She's a Dare and therefore I should have tried to destroy her. But here I am, smitten by her. Here I am, trying to save her along with the rest of Eden. "Aye. I agree. If I believed in witchcraft, I'd say she bewitched me."

Shay rolls her eyes. "Oh, that's such misogynist bullshit. Women don't 'bewitch' men. It's not her fault if you've got a hard-on for her. Seriously."

Heat rises into my cheeks. "What I meant to say was that I felt that pull. And from what I know of her, if Redd had power to bewitch, she'd use that power for good. Not to manipulate."

Shay's foot stops shaking abruptly. She grins at me. "Well, maybe she'd manipulate a *little*. She does cheat like hell at cards."

We both laugh at that. It's a nice respite from the tension of the past few hours.

She sighs, uncrosses her legs, then crosses them again. This time it is her other foot that shakes, the plastic tips of her laces rapidly tapping against the leather of her shoes. "Finding out Ms. Winter kidnapped Redd? That's, like, darker than dark. I had to help Redd run, you know? How could I not? She would have done it for me. But I hope I didn't make a mistake."

"I promise you that Redd is fine."

"Right, but just so you know, despite seeming naive, she's not. She can be totally bad-ass. She can take care of herself."

"Aye, I believe she can."

Shay blinks furiously, as if fighting off tears. "Still. It might be harder to meet her birth mom than she ever thought it would be."

"She was enjoying Eden when I left," I tell Shay truthfully.

"And why exactly did you leave?"

"I have a task out here. But I will go back to Eden. Very soon. I must speak with Agnes first, however."

She narrows her eyes at me and I try not to fidget under her scrutiny. How long can Persuasion keep her believing my half-truths and lies?

I glance at the clock on the wall again. This has gone on too long.

Shay bites her lip, then finally points her chin to the doctor and Minnie. "What are they talking about?"

As if she hears, Minnie nods at the doctor then comes back our way. She lifts her glasses to wipe the tears from her eyes. "Oh, dear Lord. I can't believe it. She...oh...the doctor says the internal bleeding is too much for them. That they've never seen anything quite like it."

"What?" Shay jumps to her feet. "What does that mean?"

Minnie lets out a sob. "It means she's dying."

My head jerks back, the words a physical blow. It's not possible.

She cannot be dying. What does that mean for us?

Is this a fool's errand, as Clara said? Or can I bring the woman back to Eden?

Shay's voice rises. "That's not possible! She was fine only yesterday!"

"There was huge trauma to the gut. They don't think it will heal."

"What trauma?" Shay asks, nearly yelling.

A medic comes running with a gurney, jostling the three of us hard enough to nearly knock the women to the floor. I steady them, hoping Persuasion has not been trampled underfoot.

"What trauma?" Shay asks again.

Minnie shakes her head. She's no longer trying to wipe away the tears. They're coming in rivulets. "There's no outward bruising or obvious injury, which the doctor said was odd. They can't figure it out. But she said it was possible when I suggested maybe Agnes had gotten hit by a car."

Shay's eyebrows come together. "But what car?"

There's a pause, then the two women turn to me. Persuasion's powers must be losing hold, because I can see in their eyes that they're about to accuse me of running Agnes down.

"Joel!" Minnie calls. The giant throws his coffee into the bin and steps closer to us.

That's when I hear a familiar canine yip and a piercing alarm. In a forceful spray of cold water, the sprinklers turn on, soaking us all. Shouts fill the air, doors down the corridor fly open and people run out of exam rooms half-dressed to head towards the main entrance. A child takes an umbrella from the stand near the doors and opens it, the water running off the pink material in a sheet. Medical staff shout orders, and more than one person wearing those odd bright-colored shoes slips, bones cracking as they hit the tiled floor.

I'm swept along with the crowd, separated from Minnie, Shay, and Joel, pushed out of the indoor rain shower and into the outdoor heat. It's nearly sunrise, the sky that unnamed shade of gray that happens just before the dark turns light. Behind me, both a fire truck and two police cars arrive, parking right under the lit EMERGENCY sign.

The lights in the hospital flicker and a man in a half-open hospital gown takes a fire-extinguisher from near the entrance, spraying everyone near him in white foam.

Chaos! That hellhound lives up to his name.

I must find Agnes. I must bring her back to Eden.

I turn around to see Minnie and Shay coming through the mass of people dripping water onto the concrete drive. Joel is right behind them. He looks up and catches my eye. My stomach drops at the intensity of his gaze. I turn on my heel, ready to run, but he's fast. Before I can even take two steps, he's got his hand around my arm.

"Ah, ah, ah…" he says. "Ready to talk to the police?" Though he states it as a question, the iron grip of his fingers tells me I have no choice.

He pushes me towards one of the police vehicles, the blue lights still flashing.

I do not have time for a police officer's questions. I must call upon Chaos and Persuasion to get me out of this. I make a clicking noise by putting my tongue behind my teeth. But the din around me drowns it out. I have no idea if the Devil's pets will hear.

Joel talks to the officer, who opens the back door of his car. I swallow worry as I see the worn beige seats ready to carry me to the station. My mind races. Forget Agnes. I must run. Run and go back to the beach where Terror guards the flower—

The same doctor that was talking to Minnie earlier comes up to us, out of breath and in a rush. Her glasses are askew and her cheeks red. "Agnes, well, it's unbelievable—absolutely unbelievable—but she's conscious. She's...um...quite upset," she says, hands on knees, panting. "And she's demanding to see you."

"Of course," says Minnie. She and Shay begin to turn back towards the hospital while I'm pushed into the police vehicle.

"No." The doctor shakes her head before they get too far. Then she points to me. "Not you. Agnes is insisting on seeing him."

32

Redd

Eden: Present Day

The Devil. The Master is the freaking Devil. That's why these people can live so long. That's why there's magic here. They made a pact with the Devil and they sacrifice children.

What a cliché.

If it weren't real, I'd laugh. If it weren't real, I'd roll my eyes and tease them for a lack of imagination.

But it's real. All. Too. Real.

John fooled me.

Virginia never loved me.

Agnes stole children. Stole me.

Clara...Autumn...drugged me. Lied to me.

They want me to be their sacrifice. They want me to die so they can live.

The worst part is that right now, I want to die, too. I want to curl up and disappear. I want to stop the agony. The straight-edged razor of betrayal buried in my heart.

Hot tears slide down my cheeks. I stay in the bed, wallowing. The cathedral bell rings, and even behind the thick shutters, I can hear commotion in the village, like rhythmic swipes coming from every direction. Hours pass. The flames in the sconces die. Sunlight creates fine lines where the shutters meet.

When I have no more tears to cry, I watch that worm—Abandon was what the Devil called it—eat away at the structure of the ceiling beams.

Abandon. Abandon. Abandon.

Is that what I'm doing? Am I abandoning everything? Everyone?

Not everyone has wronged you, Redd.

If I let myself die here, if I never go back home, Shay will wonder where I am. She was the last one to see me. She'll either think I abandoned her, or she'll worry something horrible happened to me. And, knowing her, she'd feel responsible. I can't let that happen.

And Minnie...

Minnie doesn't deserve to lose someone else to this place. She also deserves to know what really happened to her child.

It's not all about me.

I wipe my tears and sit up. *Get yourself together. Stop being so selfish.*

I've got to get out of here and back to Shay. Back to Minnie. But how? I'm locked in.

There must be something here I can use to wrench those shutters open. I start the search, yanking open the chest of drawers, ripping the paintings off the walls, every second that goes by my panic and rage growing larger. I feel it burning through my veins, igniting my soul.

Nothing. No knife or fire poker. Not even a paperclip to pick open the lock. The room looks like it's been ransacked and I'm still empty-handed.

The hairs on my arms stand at attention and the creaking of the stairs sounds loud in my ears. Someone is coming.

And that's when it hits me: my anger. I can use the power of my anger. The same way I did on the Caul. The same way I've done, unintentionally, so many times.

There is a quiet knock at the door. "Redd?" Clara whispers.

I don't move, don't breathe as I wait for the bolt on the other side of the door to slide open, wait for the lock to click and the knob to turn.

I wait.

And wait.

Nothing happens.

Finally, I hear the stairs creak again, and I exhale.

I turn back to the shutters. I think of everything I overheard, of what the Devil told me, of my stupid hopes and dreams of finding out my truths. Those horrible truths.

They don't love you.

They want to kill you.

My insides boil over, my anger as hot as lava. I can feel it burning through my blood, singeing every nerve in my body. Evil, evil anger. The pain feels good. That intoxicating pain of self-indulgence. I let my fury take over. It becomes its own beast, claws its way out of me, and lets loose.

The window glass and shutters turn to powder, just disintegrate like they were made of nothing, like they never existed. A low laugh escapes from my mouth at how easily it happened. How easily I can bring about ruin.

I'm a monster. And, damn, it feels good.

I jump out the window, landing directly in a rosebush in the garden below. The roses are beginning to wither, their blooms browning at the edges. The thorns tear at my skirts as I break free.

Eden looks different than it did earlier. It seems to be changing. The lush grasses of the hill are now brown, the leaves on the trees and shrubs dry and brittle. All the Eternity flowers in front of the house have been cut down. From up here, I can see the village below. Dozens of villagers are there, hacking the heads off flowers with machetes.

I don't take time to even wonder what they're doing. I'm just glad most everyone is down there and not here. I need to get out before anyone knows I'm missing. I run as fast as I can down the other side of the hill and towards the woods.

Towards where I know the tunnel out of Eden lies.

33

Eleanor

Eden: 1625

For nearly a quarter of a century, Eden was a true paradise.

The crops flourished, the flowers bloomed, and the river ran clear. Not once did we see a brown leaf or a withered apple, and yet no sacrifices were necessary. Not a one.

Torment was lighter on my shoulders, Evil had been losing weight, and Repugnance was quiet, no longer croaking so loudly from his muddy hovel.

The children grew. All three of the Powell girls married. Ann and Catherine seemed to have inherited their mother's fecundity, both giving birth within months of their wedding dates. Even Joyce Archard managed to keep a baby to term, the boy born in the autumn of 1620—now the youngest—and most spoilt—child in all of Eden.

The Council started a new tradition and made sure each child was baptized in the name of Eden. A private ceremony for the newly-born, with only the Council present, held in the basement of the Devil's cathedral. All children were to be baptized the very day of their birth. To welcome them into the fold...or, need be, to prepare them for their death.

A small comfort, but a comfort all the same: innocents could not be sent to hell, so at least the souls fed to Eden were not tortured souls. We hoped they gained some peace after death.

Yet by the time 1625 had rolled around, death was far from our thoughts. As was sacrifice and suffering. A quarter-of-a-century is long enough for one to forget the essentials, but short enough to surprise one in its passing. Those years go by in a blink.

Of course, Satan knew just when to strike.

It started slowly. The black spores of Contagion that we scrubbed from our homes every day stuck more and more stubbornly to the walls. The first, sweet bite into a pear had an aftertaste of something sour. The chirping of the birds sounded more lament than exultation. These tiny things were easy to brush off as nothing important. For, after so long without a Harvest, we'd fooled ourselves to believe it would never happen again.

Finally, one summer morning I woke to a changed Eden. I knew before I even opened my eyes, as hunger was already gnawing at my belly. When my lids did open, I saw a long trail of black Contagion stretched across the ceiling. The mottled spots made the hairs rise on the back of my neck. Torment had been sleeping in a ball at the foot of my bed. Now he scurried up my legs and across my torso to settle in his familiar place upon my shoulders.

With trembling hands, I threw off my quilt and looked out the window. Eden was bare. Our garden was nothing but brittle dry stalks. The trees naked, snarling beasts with leaflike hair, rooted to the ground; the sheep that grazed on the hill below us had disappeared, only tufts of wool in their wake. The glittering mist that usually surrounded the village had become a dense gray fog.

I put on a kirtle over my chemise and hurried downstairs. An ache began to form near my temples as I threw open the cupboards. Our stores had either turned to dust or rotted to a vile sludge. Try as I might to conjure something with the remains, nothing edible appeared. Even the pump at the sink spit out thick blood instead of water.

Eden's magic had withered like everything else in this damned place.

With every passing second, pain and hunger and thirst needled their way further and further under my skin before finally anchoring themselves to my very bones. I could barely stand, I was so overcome.

How could we have ever thought that we'd beat Eden?

The stairs creaked, Virginia shuffling down. Her face was a pasty white, dark circles under her eyes. She walked with her arms around her belly, half-bent, a grimace on her face. Seeing her suffer was worse than my own pain.

"Mama, the Harvest," she whispered. "I'd thought...hoped...it wouldn't happen again."

I nodded, the movement pounding nails into my head. "I as well. We should have known. We forgot how evil the Master truly is."

"The Master did not orchestrate this," she said, sliding into one of the kitchen chairs.

I scoffed at that. "Your precious Master is the Devil, Virginia."

"Fine. Even if he did, 'twas nothing you did not agree to."

I did not understand how she reasoned so differently than I. Or perhaps, I did not understand how she could be so astute and yet so accepting of our circumstances.

Finally, a realization hit. Horror widened her eyes. "Who will it be?"

But I could not answer. That was something the Council needed to decide together. As if on cue, the bell of the Devil's cathedral tolled three times. A call for the Council to meet. Immediately.

It took me longer than usual to descend the hill to the square. I had to stop several times to catch my breath for the pain. When I arrived in the Council room, my brow was slick with sweat.

I was not the only one. Everyone in the room looked as though they'd aged fifty years. But it was not simply the pain that did it. It was the weight of what was about to transpire.

There were no good choices for a sacrifice. At eight, seven, and five years of age, the children of the village were not new and unaware and unattached. They were all old enough for us to know them by their individual personalities. They were old enough for us to see them as human.

And they were old enough to suffer from the terror of the experience. Old enough to understand the betrayal as I pushed their head under the water.

It was too cruel. Even for us.

And yet...we had no choice. Or rather, we had already made our choice. There was no escape. For anyone. Only eternal life or death.

If only we could give them a draught or a tonic to make them sleep peacefully so they would not realize what was happening.

But sacrifice did not work if the offering was unconscious.

As we fought back and forth across the cherrywood table about who it would be, I could no longer bear it. I turned and retched onto the sapphire carpet, a mixture of magic and hand-weaving done by Joan Warren a decade earlier as a gift to the Council. As yellow bile seeped into its fibers, I put my head into my hands and sobbed.

"Enough, Eleanor!" Where normally Dyonis' voice would boom across the entire room, it now crackled like a dying fire. His chest heaved with raspy breaths, his face contorted with pain. "'Tis far too late for regrets."

"You perform the sacrifice. I won't do it." I shook my head. "I refuse."

"We could choose Virginia instead."

Now I laughed. But it was a pathetic hiccough of a laugh rather than the true thing. "She's no longer a child. And Eden feeds off youth."

"Aye," Dyonis said. "But Eden will take what we give her. And Virginia is young enough. Her death would give us something, whether it be weeks or years, I do not know. However, I would be willing to find out."

I do not know where my strength came from, as two seconds earlier I was as limp and useless as a rag doll. But now I jumped off my chair and hurled myself at Dyonis. All of my rage, my regret, my fear came out as I rammed my fist into his face. I felt the hard line of his jaw and then his cheekbone and then his nose as I punched him again and again and again. While I still could not kill him, I could make him hurt. In the days before a sacrifice, when the magic was lifted, we became vulnerable to that kind of pain once again.

And for all that was unholy in this Devil's paltry paradise, seeing the blood spurt out of Dyonis' mouth, feeling the crack of his bones against my knuckles, hearing his grunts of agony…it was divine. I soared on the rush of my own anger, and soon enough both Fury and Evil were howling outside the Council door.

It took the strength of every single Council member to pull me off him. And by the time they did, Dyonis' face was nothing but a bloody pulp. Perhaps the old Eleanor of England would have felt guilty. Perhaps the old Eleanor of Roanoke would have been appalled at herself. But Eleanor of Eden thought it a beautiful sight.

Dyonis' mouth contorted into what was supposed to be a smile. "Go tell Joyce Archard she can finally give to Eden the babe she'd always hoped to."

Twenty minutes later, I informed the Archards of the Council's decision. Joyce and Arnold took the news with stony faces and even stonier hearts. Arnold's jaw tightened but he said nothing else. He spat on the floor and headed upstairs, leaving Joyce and I alone.

Joyce peered into the room where her child lay, hands gripping his stomach, hunger and pain raging through him. The boy called to her, begged for her, but instead of going to him, she quietly shut the door. I reached out to touch her shoulder, a meager gesture of comfort when I knew there was no comfort to be had.

Joyce pulled back as if burned. "Save your pity, Eleanor Dare. Alexander was conceived for this very reason," she told me. "Because of the vile pact that *you* made."

I knew her words were masking her true pain, as her hands were balled into tight fists and her brown eyes blinked back tears. What would she tell Alexander as we all donned our masks that night? How would she spin it for him to come happily?

And how would I drown him once I saw his rising fear?

"We will come later. Best you do not fight it," I choked out.

As I made to leave, she hissed, "Ananias hated being wed to you."

Though I had been about to step out of the cottage, I now stopped and turned around, ignoring the white-hot pain surging through my muscles.

Joyce added, "'Tis the truth. He told me many a time that he preferred my lips to yours."

At her words, Torment licked my ear. The same feelings of shame and worthlessness washed over me as they did when first seeing my husband with Joyce back in Roanoke. But I shoved back both Torment's greedy tongue and my insecurities. Ananias' infidelity had led me to Manteo, and, no matter how we came together, I would not take back a single day with that man.

I knew it was Joyce's fear of losing her son that was speaking. I understood that completely. And yet, I could not help but respond, "No surprise, Joyce. Ananias always did prefer to take the path well-trodden."

Virginia, William, and I helped each other don our furs and masks for the ceremony. As was typical, we all regained a measure of strength and vigor when we pressed the wooden faces to our own. But even with its power surging through my blood, guilt gripped my heart as I knocked on the Archers' door, every adult in the village wearing masks and holding torches behind me.

Little Alexander was frightened. He clung to his father's leg, eyes wide at the sight of us monsters. Stoic, Joyce forced the necklace of drooping wildflowers over his head, her hands steady. As Joyce and Arthur tied their own masks to their faces, Alexander began to fret and bawl. We hummed, one long disturbing note, while Joyce took his hand, half-leading, half-dragging the boy to the Fire Pit.

There, the Master waited. He was in his beastly form, more imposing and disturbing than ever. The hatred I held in my heart for this being was such that I often dreamt of holding his own head under the water. And as he lay a clawed hand upon Alexander's small shoulder, as Joyce stepped back, as I saw the fear in the boy's eyes deepen to terror, as his cries reached a fevered pitch, something overtook me.

"Nay," I told the Devil. "We never agreed that the sacrifice had to be frightened."

Satan did not stop me as I grabbed Alexander around the waist and settled him on my hips. He was big enough that his weight was uncomfortable, and his legs dangled all the way to my knees. But I held him close and whispered, "I have something wonderful to show you."

Using one of the same sequences the Master showed Virginia and I long ago, I tapped on the water. The glass-like surface of the pond began to swirl, and seconds later, Deception's massive equine head crashed through the surface. She had grown so much that even I gasped as she soared higher and higher, her serpentine body seemingly endless.

But then I said, "You are safe, Alexander. You are happy. And when I push you under the water, 'twill be fun and do you no harm."

Deception breathed a cloud of smoke his way and he giggled. He stroked her scales, then got down on his knees in the water all by himself.

When I held his head under, he gave no resistance.

None at all.

After the pond had swallowed his body and Eden took his essence, I felt the warmth of Virginia's hand upon the small of my back. An act of forgiveness for all that I'd wrought. "That was good of you, Mama."

And as the flowers began to bloom, the grasses grew underfoot and the trees filled with birdsong once again, the villagers let out a sad but relieved cheer. A magical feast would be waiting for us all in the square when we got back, and already our aches and pains had evaporated.

Yet I did not move from my spot at the lip of the pond as the others left. I tapped out a tune on the water, and Deception slipped back under, ready to sleep.

I had not noticed that the Master was still there, leaning against a tree, his fangs and claws retracted. "Smart girl," he said to me. "Smart, smart girl. I cannot wait to see how you react to further complications in the future."

It took all my willpower, but I ignored him, waiting until he disappeared. Only when he was gone did I let out the breath I was holding and cry.

34

John

The Beyond: Present Day

When I arrive in Agnes' hospital room, I wonder if Chaos has concentrated all his efforts here. Agnes is screaming at the top of her lungs to "see the boy who brought me here." Two nurses, one a man bigger than Joel, the other a woman small as a child, are both trying to calm her down. The gown she's wearing is dry, hanging limp on her thin frame, but wet hair sticks to her forehead and cheeks in spikes. A clear tube taped to her arm connects her to a rolling metal pole with a pouch of liquid hanging from it. The mattress from the bed is overturned, the sheets soaking up wetness from the floor. Water drips from the ceiling and sits in a puddle where there is a dip in the linoleum.

The moment I step into the commotion, she stops screaming. A look of relief passes over the woman's harried face, but the man doesn't flinch. Agnes' shoulders drop and she lets out a sob. Purple circles shadow her eyes, and there's a blue tinge to her lips. She looks on the verge of death.

I've never been in close contact with serious illness or injury. Inside Eden there is no illness, all injuries can be healed, and sacrifice is the only way to die. Suffering only takes place in certain parts of the village, and while one may *want* to die...there is no fear of it truly happening. If what Minnie said is correct, Agnes is dying. It's terrifying. I want to run from the room and right back to Eden. Why even plant the flower here if we become so vulnerable? It never truly occurred to me that it might be so easy to die so young.

But I take a breath and remind myself why planting the flower here is important: *sacrifice*. We must be able to choose to lead life without the need to sacrifice another. We must be able to live on our own, out from under the Devil's thumb.

I shoot one last look at Minnie, Shay, and Joel standing in the hallway, then nod to the nurses. "I believe she wanted to speak with me."

The woman pulls two chairs from the side of the room and motions to them.

"I want to speak with him alone." Agnes does not take her eyes off me.

The man shakes his head. "That's not—"

I hold up a hand. "Please. I beg of you. Leave us be. I take full responsibility for my own safety."

After a bit of hedging, the nurses finally step out of the room. The door glides closed behind them, leaving me alone with Agnes.

Her green eyes follow my progress over the wet floor to the side of the empty bed frame. I tip the plastic chair so that the water pooling in the seat falls to the floor. Then I sit, wiping my sweaty palms on the damp fabric of my jeans.

She does not say hello. She sways then steps forward to sit. I half-stand to help her, but she ignores me and instead falls into her own chair without draining it of water. I see the wetness gather on the cotton of the hospital gown. "Do you have the nectar?"

I nod.

"I need some. Just a drop. Anything..."

I unzip my bag and take out the wilting petal I'd shoved in there. I hesitate, cursing myself for not having brought more. I will need nectar in a matter of hours to keep my own pain at bay. But the petal's gone before I can reconsider, as Agnes snatches it with a shaky hand, opens her mouth, and squeezes the liquid onto her tongue.

She breathes a sigh of relief, tears streaming down her face. She wipes them with her stronger arm.

I glance at the withered muscles in her other arm, wondering just how long she'd endured without the nectar before.

She notices my gaze. "Ten full days when I first left Eden. I thought I was going to die. The flower...it was near dead when I picked it. It took so long to revive." She coughs up blood.

"I'm taking you to Eden." I stand, ready to scoop her into my arms.

"No. Don't." She touches my arm to hold me back. Her fingers are colder than winter snow.

After a beat I ask, "How did you get hurt? A car?"

Agnes shakes her head.

"They think it was me—"

Her mouth twists, blood still coloring her lips. She ignores the question and leans forward. "What's your name?"

"John."

"Harvie?" In the pitch of her voice is the history of our families—four hundred years of feuding.

"Aye." No use denying it.

"You're George's son." She takes in a breath and lets it out. "You have a sister?"

I shake my head. "No. A brother. Brought in from the Beyond."

"Oh." For some reason, the answer seems to bring tears to her eyes. She blinks them back and asks in a broken voice, "How...how is George?"

I ball my fingers into a fist, feeling the bite of nails into my skin. "Gone. Dead. He and my mother chose to leave Eden. Leave me." It comes out with more emotion than I intended it to, my resentment evident.

She closes her eyes and drops her head to her chest. She stays like that for so long, I worry she's died right in front of me. But finally she whispers, "The sacrifice. It was too much for him. Too much for them."

I scoff. I do not care why my parents abandoned me, only that they did. I'd woken up one morning and they were gone. Forever.

There had been no indication they were planning to leave. I was only four years of age, and if there had been signs, I did not see them. Momma tucked me into bed with the same efficiency as always—a quick kiss on the forehead and a reminder to keep the Nuisances from nibbling. Pa did not always come into my chamber before bedtime, but it was not unheard of. Therefore, him coming to tug my blankets tight did not raise alarm bells in my head. If I think back hard, I can see how defeated he looked. His shoulders hunched, the spark missing from his eyes. He was still scouting then. It was unusual for a married man with a family to do so. But Grandmama once explained to me that Agnes was his replacement and after she'd absconded, the Council had had difficulty trusting someone new.

I can, perhaps, imagine the toll scouting had on him. If, as Agnes had said, it was "too much" to bring children to Eden, I could almost understand. Eden does something to people to make them believe death might be easier. Like Clara's father, gone insane after too much time in the Enticements' web. Or Lindsey Little who, as a child, fell into the sinking sands where Misery resides and had never truly gotten past the trauma.

But understanding is not forgiving.

Just then there is a knock at the door. It swings open. The same nurses from earlier enter the room. "A clean, dry bed for you, Agnes," the woman says. She and the other nurse strip the soaking sheets from the plastic-coated mattress on the floor, then set it back into its frame. They make the bed with new sheets and tell Agnes they need to get her into a dry gown.

Agnes orders me not to leave. She then allows the nurses to pull the curtain to help her change and tuck her into the clean bed.

During this time, the janitor comes through with a mop and as I watch his movements, a thought occurs to me. A thought that had never once crossed my mind before, a thought so dizzying I grip the chair to keep my head from spinning. *If Agnes was able to leave and grow the flower...Belial's breath...*

When the janitor and nurses leave, I turn to Agnes. "Perhaps my parents, too, had the flower! Perhaps they are still alive out here."

"No. Not possible." Her voice is as sharp as a demon's fingernail. "They did not have the right blood to make the flower grow."

At that, my head does begin to spin. "What? What are you saying? There's a special blood to make it thrive? Redd told me how to grow it, she said nothing of—"

She coughs again, lifting her elbow to her mouth. The blood that coats her arm is bright and thick, shiny under the lighting.

I've had enough conversation. I slide one arm behind her head and the other under her knees and lift. She is lighter than I expected. "I am taking you to Eden—"

My progress gets stopped as the tube connecting her to the pole with the liquid falls over, setting off some sort of alarm. Agnes sucks in a breath of pain, and I see that the tube is connected to a needle stuck under her skin. Blood stains the gauze around it.

I set her back onto the mattress and pick up the pole. The female nurse comes running in, flipping a switch on the machine near Agnes' bed and fiddling with the needle. Her frown deepens as she applies new gauze.

When the nurse has left, Agnes motions to the wound on her hand where her skin is beginning to shrivel and darken. "Look. I'm dying from Eden's illness. It...my injury was too much... I won't make it to the beach, let alone the tunnel. You want to save Eden? Get Redd out of there before the Harvest happens."

"If I cannot get you back to Eden, you must help me grow the flower. That will save Redd." I look at the machine, ready to turn it off so when I unhook Agnes from the tube there is no alarm.

But her words stop me. "I can't," she says. "You can't, either. As your parents couldn't. We don't have the right blood."

"I don't understand. You—"

"It's Redd's blood that has been sustaining the flower all these years."

For a second, I feel like I am in freefall. I shake my head. "You're trying to trick me."

"No. But even if I were, are you willing to risk it?"

"You're lying. Redd told me—"

"Redd doesn't know." She sets her head back on the pillow and closes her eyes.

"I don't believe you."

Her eyes flick open, her gaze like fire. "Then don't."

The challenge there speaks more truth than anything else. The thumping of my heart sounds like a drum in my ears. Suddenly, things make more sense. Much more sense.

Redd's a Dare. The Dares have always been special in the Master's eye. I hadn't realized just how special. But it explains why Redd could trigger my mask. Why she can replant the flower. And Agnes...the only reason she ever survived living as a Dare was that she was not truly of their blood. It never ran through her veins. The Council decided her life was not worth sacrificing.

A renewed energy courses through my muscles. Eden can go on without sacrifice.

"I'm sorry, Agnes. That you're ill. That…" I cannot say *you're dying*. "I'm sorry that it ends like this."

"Save Redd." A tear slips out the corner of her eye. She looks even smaller and weaker than she did only seconds ago, as if the effects of the nectar are already wearing off. "Tell her I love her. And that nothing is her fault."

She pales even further, her face contorting in pain. I wish I had more nectar to share. To ease her suffering. But I don't. I hesitate to leave her like this, but she clenches her teeth and grinds out, "Go!"

Joel is gone. Minnie and Shay's bags sit on the plastic chairs outside the room, but the two of them are down at the end of the hallway. They are deep in discussion with a tall man who has the same nose and chin as Shay. His face is a mask of anger. The three of them make grand gestures with their arms, their voices rising. Quickly, I rummage through Minnie's purse to find the keys to the van, then slip around the corner before any of them see me. I do not have time for more complications.

Over the scent of antiseptic and stagnant water is the odor of wet dog. Chaos is near. And, since no one disturbed me leaving Agnes' room, my guess is that Persuasion is also close by. I click my tongue to call them both to me.

A moment later, I feel Chaos' bump against my leg and Persuasion wrapping his lithe body around my ankle. I lift him to a safer perch around my ear. "We're going to save Eden," I say to them.

Or, more accurately, Redd is.

35

Redd

Eden: Present Day

I reach the pond, the orange algae glowing like embers of a fire. The Eternity Flowers around it still stand tall. I guess the villagers decapitating the things with long blades have not yet made their way this far downriver.

As I step into the water, the giant black water dragon rears her head. She breathes out smoky vapor and, for the slightest of seconds, I stop. *I'm safe here,* I think. *It's beautiful here.* But I shake the thought loose and swear at the creature. *That's* what happened when I arrived. That's why I hadn't realized what danger I was in. Like every other animal I've encountered here in Eden, this dragon has powers.

But with the anger running through my veins, her powers are no match for my own. "Get back!" I command the beast. And unbelievably, she does. She unfurls her long, serpentine body and disappears under the surface of the water.

I disappear under the water, too.

Holding my breath is second nature. I begin to count as I swim. *One, two, three, four...* I cut through the swirling waters in the deepest part of the pond, aware of the dragon in the shadowy depths, her beaded pupils following my progress. When I pass through the tunnel, I notice what I hadn't coming in: the bones. The human bones decorating the muck at the bottom. Proof that the Master—the Devil—was not lying when he said they sacrifice people here in Eden.

Get out, Redd. Get out.

I speed up, swimming harder and faster than ever before. Not even a full three minutes pass before I get to the end and break through the surface of the water on the other side where I take a deep breath, the salty air filling my lungs.

I got out. I got out and away from that place. Those people. The Devil.

I trudge to the shore and fall onto the ground, the sandy muck holding my shoulders and hips and head like an embrace. I blink up at the bright sun, the blue sky. I listen to the sound of the breeze through the leaves and the happy chirps of birds and allow myself to cry. I sob, tears pouring down the sides of my face. I cry until I can barely breathe and have no more tears left before sitting up and wiping my eyes.

That's when I hear the sound of footsteps in the brush. I squint into the forest as a shadow makes its way through the trees. My whole body tenses, thinking first of danger. Then I think maybe the person coming my way has a phone on them. Maybe I can call Minnie or Shay. Maybe I can get out of this mess faster than I thought.

When the person steps out into the sunlight, though, my breath catches and my heart jumps into my throat. It's John.

What the hell is wrong with me? This is the guy who took me to Eden to sacrifice me, and my stupid body reacts with, *Oh, hey good-lookin'.*

I've got issues.

John's face brightens like he's happy to see me here and alive. "Redd! You're all right."

"No thanks to you, asshole," I say. My fingers twitch and my anger builds. I ball my hands into fists to stop myself from strangling him.

But he doesn't even seem to hear me. He's rambling on about how worried he was. Then he goes on and on, pointing to a sad-looking Eternity Flower down at the edge of the beach.

I don't listen. I start walking. I've got to get out of this forest.

John's yelling for me to stop. I don't. He tries to grab my arm, but I pull myself free and put one foot in front of the other, keeping my anger in check. I could hurt him. I could *kill* him. I know I could. So I count my steps and breathe. *One, two, three, four, five...*

"Terror!" John yells.

Fear burns like ice crystals in my stomach. Sharp and cold. It's enough to make me gasp and stop my progression forward...until I realize that John has just called one of those magical pets on me. "Don't you dare," I tell him. My voice is not my own. It's evil. It's anger. It's horror.

I see John's Adam's apple move as he swallows. "Ease up, boy," he says, never taking his eyes off of me.

The fear falls from my bones. But now we are standing amongst the trees, the two of us only inches apart, facing each other. "You lied to me. About everything," I say. "You brought me to Eden to die."

He blanches. "Oh, Redd. You must understand…I did not…well, aye, I did, but then… I tried to keep you away…" He runs a hand through his hair and shakes his head. "It's horrific. And complicated. And I cannot explain it all now. We haven't the time. But I do pray you'll forgive me one day." The pathetic Eternity Flower planted near us doesn't make a dent in my sixth sense. His emotions wash over me. Guilt. Regret. Longing. Hope.

I focus on the shards of sunlight piercing the foliage, on the woody scent surrounding us, and push everything else away. "Don't count on it." I start walking again.

"I need your help. To save Eden," he calls out to my back.

That makes me stop. Incredulous, I turn around. "You've got to be kidding me. No way in hell am I doing anything to help anyone in that place."

"Not even your birth mother?"

I let out a bitter laugh. "You mean Virginia? You mean the woman who welcomed me into her home, pretended to care about me, fed me all sorts of stories—God only knows what was true—and then drugged me and locked me up? The one who was going to hand me to the Council? You mean her?"

His surprise hits me hard. Stings my eyes. He frowns. "Virginia did that? That…I find that hard to believe."

"Well, believe it." I start walking again.

"Then if you will not help Eden, help Agnes. Bring the Eternity Flower back to life. You're a Dare. You have the power to do so."

"What do you mean 'help Agnes?'" My anger flares again.

"She's hurt. Badly." He scrubs a hand over his face. "She's in the hospital."

And suddenly my emotions go haywire. I should hate her. I *do* hate her. But dread grips my heart at the thought of anything happening to her. She did some awful things. But now I know that she was also trying to protect me, to keep me from the Devil and from Eden. As John explains which hospital, I cut him off. "Will she be okay?"

I can taste the sorrow on my tongue before he even answers. He shakes his head and I growl, "Give me your car keys."

He takes a step back. "No. Not until you make the flower grow—"

"GIVE THEM TO ME!" I scream it, my fury an explosion. He goes flying backward, landing with a heavy thud on the dirt. With a moan he sits up, blood dripping from his nose and mouth.

Goose bumps pop out on my skin one after the other until my whole body is chilled. *I did that.* I'm about to help him when I remind myself that he brought me to Eden for sacrifice.

His eyes grow wide. "You. You're the one who hurt her."

I hold out my hand. "Give. Them. To. Me."

He fishes the keys out of his pocket. I snatch them from him.

When I turn towards the forest, he says, "She needs the nectar. From the flower. She cannot survive without it."

Horror makes my scalp tingle. "What? What do you mean? You said it was for eternal life."

"Aye." He nods and wipes the blood from his face. "Inside Eden, it is. But here, in the Beyond? We need the nectar for the pain...and...to stay alive. Too long without and—" He cuts himself off with a deep cough.

I think of how she coddled that thing. Like it was her lifeblood.

Oh, God. *It was.* That's why she acted like an addict....and I destroyed that flower when I was back in Wisconsin.

What have I done?

I walk out of the forest and back to the Eternity Flower he planted. It's curled in upon itself, its stalk withered, its petals slick and laced with what looks like black mold. It gives off a rank odor, rather than the syrupy sweet scent I'm used to. I drag my fingers over the stunted spikes along the stem until my skin breaks, blood staining my hand. I then press my palms to the dirt that cradles the roots. Nothing. The rotten petals are not replaced by healthy ones. The stalk doesn't straighten.

John crawls up behind me and breathes, "I don't understand."

"It needs time," I say. "It always takes time."

"You don't have time," he responds. "Agnes is dying."

At that, I rip a handful of petals from the withered bloom and break into a run.

36

Eleanor

Eden: 1687-1987

I stopped performing the sacrifices.

Once Virginia had passed her one-hundredth birthday, I knew she was no longer at risk of being fed to Eden. Therefore, Dyonis lost the ability to force me into doing the burdensome task. Truth be told, he gave in easily. By then, it no longer mattered who sacrificed the offering, because I was, and always would be, the main target of the villagers' hatred and guilt. Though I no longer shoved the children's heads under the water, their blood was still on my hands.

Even with Deception lulling the older ones into the pond, every sacrifice was heart-wrenching.

Also, we were learning.

What grave and horrid discoveries we made.

We already knew that the younger the sacrifice, the longer we had before the village decayed. But we also discovered that a child of those who came from the original Roanoke colony was worth more to Eden than that of a descendant.

Yet with each passing day, it was less and less likely that any of us original colonists would conceive more than sporadically. Some gave it their best effort, such as Lewes, who may as well have walked around without breeches for how often he dropped his trousers, and some, like me, the so-called village witch, gave it no effort at all. Some did what came naturally, although even among the Powell girls, birthing had been reduced to a trickle. And some stopped nature before it could take root—Virginia heeded my advice to avoid pregnancy and I made certain there were always fresh Eternity Flower petals near her bed for precisely that purpose.

The babes of Eden were few and far between.

The Council, thinking of the future, became desperate.

It was no longer a suspicion that the presence of the Eternity Flower affected our fertility. It was a certainty. So, hoping to rid our home of this sweet-smelling plague, we decided to cull every single Eternity Flower in Eden. Even with everyone in the village lending a hand, even with magic making the work easier, it took nine whole days.

Eden starved within a second of the last stalk being cut.

That sacrifice was especially difficult, as we had brought it upon ourselves. From that moment on, we knew we could no longer continue as we had been. Even if the youngest generations gave us more births, the village was small enough that there were few families to intermix. We needed new blood if we wanted to survive.

Eventually, there would be no soul to sacrifice.

If we could not leave, we needed others to come.

The Council set up a secret room in the underbelly of the Devil's cathedral, just around the corner from where the baptisms took place. While the rooms above ground were illuminated with stained glass, the area below was nearly pitch dark. Stone arches bled dampness. The air smelled of decay. And no matter how many torches we lit, goosebumps prickled our skin with cold. But it was the perfect place to create experimental potions and powders, as it was a breeding ground for Contagion. We scraped the black rot from the deep crevices of rock where it retreated between sacrifices. We knew now that the Eternity Flower was the source of life inside Eden and Contagion the source of death outside of it. Yet we were not sure what reaction the nectar might have on those who left.

Once we thought we'd figured that out, we tested its effects on the youths themselves. The trials were known to only the Council, both Secrecy and Deception helping to keep it that way.

First, we tried the "youth" who'd entered Eden with us. But they were all well over a century old now, and even the Eternity Flower's nectar could not stop time from catching up with them almost immediately. The suffering nearly killed them. They were back in Eden within minutes.

The next youths sent out—under thirty years of age—came back within hours, the aging less of a problem, but the pain and suffering too much to handle. Gradually, however, we were able to increase the amount of time they could last. From hours to a day, then to two days. Their bodies did not go through the illness provided they had fresh nectar at the ready. But it was a delicate balance. And we nearly lost a few of our own in trying to get it right.

No one lasted long enough to do more than explore the uninhabited forest near the mouth of the Sound. The flower petals themselves were more robust than the youth.

Then we thought that it was perhaps our choice of youth.

Dyonis called a village meeting. By now the surface of Eden had grown. The ring of fog circling us got wider with each sacrifice, but despite the ever-expanding acres, we still met on the cobbles in the square.

I knew what Dyonis was going to say, but stood with the others, Virginia and William by my side, while the Governor shouted from the cathedral steps. "Eden has made itself heard. We are bound to this place and must obey. To leave is sure death for most, if not all, of us. 'Tis here in Eden where we are safe. 'Tis here in Eden where we are amongst family and friends"—here I could not help but scoff—"and we must remember that. Aye, life here requires grave sacrifice. But those of us who have lived on the outside know that these sacrifices are nothing—absolutely nothing—compared to the hardship that awaits us through the Beyond."

Dyonis bowed his head, took a deep breath, and again lifted his face to the crowd. "Yet we must endeavor for a select few to survive there, if only for a short time. We believe we have found a way to do so. 'Tis the Council, and only the Council members, who will determine who can and cannot attempt to step through to the Beyond. Our choice will be prudent, based on the youth's health and strength of mind."

"You've found a way to survive outside?" Virginia crushed my upper arm with her fingers and said in a broken whisper, "Why now, Mama? Why did the Council not seek a way to do this immediately after we lost the Powells? If you had, Samuel might still be alive."

"Samuel?" I could not help but shake my head. "Why in Satan's sullied name do you even have a thought for that boy after all these years? He made his choice, Virginia. And 'twas a poor one. Besides, the survival outside of Eden is only temporary."

"He could have lived." Tears glistened in her eyes. Next to her, William looked at the ground. The years were beginning to blur into one long mass, but it was somewhere between 1850 and 1870. So more than 200 years they'd been wed. Yet Virginia still uttered Samuel's name in a way that made William's cheeks flush red.

It was young Tim Taylor who was chosen to visit the Beyond. He was fifteen years of age. The Council had good reason to choose him. A secret reason.

The reason offered to the village, however, was simply his physique: he was a strapping boy who looked as though he could withstand anything put before him. We gave him a blooming flower, the nectar sweet and heavy when a petal was pulled.

Even so, we doubted he'd stay more than three days in the Beyond.

He was gone six.

Eagle-eyed Joan was the first to spot him when he came back. Immediately, she ran to ring the cathedral bell. Virginia and I had been speaking with Michael Millet, bartering an exchange of several of our enhanced herbs for his homemade bread. But at the first gong, we, like everyone else, stopped what we were doing to turn towards the path leading from the pond to the village.

The boy tumbled forward, pale, dirty, and much thinner than when he'd left, his eyes wild with the vestiges of pain. He fell to the ground, his breathing rapid and rough, his limbs spindly and withered, his right foot twisted the wrong way. Over his shoulder was a sack filled with books, a few trinkets, and what he called a broadside. *December 20, 1860 THE UNION IS DISSOLVED* was written in large type across the top.

Virginia, always attentive to others, knelt next to Tim and stroked his sweaty forehead. His breathing smoothed and color returned to his cheeks. Eden was working its magic to heal. After a moment, he sighed an extremely deep sigh for a boy of his age and, with Virginia's help, sat up.

All eyes fell upon him, curious.

"So many people. Amazing. Dazzling. Yet dirty and uncivilized." Tim patted his bag of books. "But the inventions they have. I saw them. Read about them."

Everyone began to talk at once, hurling questions at the poor boy.

Dyonis held up his hands and the crowd quieted. "Tim will speak with the Council before anyone else. Please return to whatever 'tis that you were doing before his arrival. He will be back to satisfy your curiosity soon enough." Dyonis turned to Tim. "Come. Time to give your report."

We questioned the boy for three hours straight, wanting to know everything there was to know about the effects of the nectar on the 'illness' and the world outside. After Tim had finished speaking, we sent him off with the order to stay tight-lipped for the moment. Then, once he had closed the door behind him, we rifled through the books, studied the broadside, and played with the small sticks—called matches—that started fire. We looked through the items in awe and disbelief.

The world had moved on without us in it.

It had changed so thoroughly that most of the words on the printed pages did not make sense. As I read, I could not quell the sense of loss. What would my life have been like had I made other choices?

"You look at these things with such a longing in your eye, Eleanor." Elizabeth tapped a book with illustrations of something called a *steam locomotive* that was in my hands. She leaned closer and whispered, "If we were not here in Eden, we would be long dead by now."

Then she added, "*Virginia* would be dead."

I slammed the book shut. "Quite right."

Now that we'd figured out a way to allow the youth to spend days at a time in the Beyond, we had to train them for a specific task: to find young babes and bring them back to live...or die...with us.

"Young orphans?" I leaned forward, looking into Dyonis' hazel eyes. I remembered the ragged waifs from the orphanages in England. Even Eden seemed better than those dens of despair.

He shook his head. "The ones we train, the scouts, they will not have time to go find an orphanage. And we need the newly-born, if possible. Better for sacrifice or for raising here. A child who remembers their family, their past, could be troublesome. I want none of it. Nay, the scouts will take the first appropriate child they come across. 'Tis the only way."

I fell back into my chair, my breath leaving me in a sharp huff. It was...horrific. Yet no surprise. The longer we lived, the easier evil became. "We've been killing our own youth. Now we would be stealing and taking the lives of the babes of others! 'Tis so very wrong."

His eyes sparked. "That did not matter to you when you took Walter's life."

In fact, it had mattered greatly. But nothing could bring Walter back, so there was no point in denial.

"We cannot do such a thing," I insisted. "We cannot."

Christopher snapped, "Then what do you suggest, Eleanor? How will Eden continue if we do not?"

I could come up with nothing. "Let us at least make sure the ones taken are unwanted. Not ripped from those they love."

"Beelzebub's teeth, Eleanor. Now is not the time to grow a conscience." Dyonis was scratching down a list on parchment. Ink stained his fingers and the ruffled cuffs of his sleeves black. "We will need the Master to conjure new masks for the children taken. 'Tis the only way they'll make it through the tunnel."

"But will he?" Emme chewed her bottom lip.

"And what will be the price?" I asked.

There was only one way to know.

Dyonis called his name, and the Master appeared as a column of smoke that quickly took the form of a man. "Did I hear correctly?" he teased. "Seems it has been centuries since you've called."

Aye. We called upon the Devil as little as possible. Nothing from him came without strings.

As we laid out our request, his eyebrows arched higher. "By my father's black heart, you've become monsters."

Once again, he'd spoken the truth.

There was a moment of quiet, where we all squirmed in our seats, guilt and horror and hope clamping our lips shut. But then the Master laughed, the sound of it a glorious symphony. "Oh, my pets. You needn't hesitate. Of course. 'Tis why I am here."

I found my voice. "And in return?"

"Such a pesky question." He pulled a chair away from the table and sat, nudging my elbow with his boots so he could set his feet on the armrest of my chair. "But I'll answer. Yes, you may procure children from the outside to expand Eden or to feed Eden. However, this does not make your own children exempt."

"I-I do not understand. What do you mean by t-that?" Johnathon had a habit of stuttering in the Devil's presence.

"I mean that the Council and the others who entered Eden from Roanoke all those years ago still must see their own family blood drowned. Not for every sacrifice. Not even for every other sacrifice. Occasionally."

For a moment none of us breathed. Then Elizabeth spoke. "Master, the infertility in the village...we cannot seem to have children—"

"Oh, you can. And you will. The infertility is...frequent but not constant. For some, your descendants will come soon. For others"—here he looked directly at me—"it may take decades."

I lifted my chin. Never. I would never allow myself to be with child again while in Eden. And I had taught Virginia well when it came to children. I wasn't worried about her.

A warm chuckle built in Satan's throat. His smile grew. "I told you all you could govern yourselves. Therefore, I shall leave you to it." He disappeared as quickly as he arrived.

Now we set about planning for the future. We had never met God and knew we never would. So instead of revering the Almighty, we played Him.

Young Tim was perfect for the task. Yet we were not sure if future recruits would be as resilient. Therefore, scouts would be chosen at birth and baptized accordingly.

But there was still the problem of loyalty.

"How will we trust the scouts to return, Governor?" Emme was rubbing her fingers over and over a textured cloth Tim had brought back. "Once we've allowed them to survive outside. They can only last as long as the nectar does, but who's to stop them from planting the Eternity Flower in the Beyond? What if it takes root there?"

"If the scout is able to plant the flower outside Eden, why not let him?" Dyonis said. "'Tis something we should know. But before we try it, before we do anything, we ensure the scout is loyal. Every scout. Beginning with Tim."

"Tim? He seems like a good lad—" I started.

"Nay. We *ensure* it. It must be part of the training from here on out. Loyalty to Eden above all else." He pushed back his chair, the legs screeching on the polished wooden floor, covering the patter of Secrecy's approach.

As the critter slid inside the room to gather our confidences and carry them away, Dyonis looked us each in the eye, his voice low and stern. "For the next couple of months, the boy will see me and only me. Once I am assured of his devotion to Eden, we allow him out to secure us a new child."

We did not see Tim Taylor for three months. Though the Council informed the villagers that Tim was training to survive on the outside, only Dyonis knew exactly what that training entailed. We as a Council had gotten extremely powerful over the last century. Dyonis as Governor even more so. His decision was law. Rarely did anyone voice doubts about his opinions or edicts. And those opinions and edicts became darker and darker.

Evil had long forgotten me; now the hellhound was nearly inseparable from our governor, taking up a permanent spot in front of his hearth. Dyonis began to smell like the beast, the sweet scent impregnating his hair and clothing. I breathed it in deeply as he neared me, memories of childhood linked to that particular perfume. I was not one of the younger, brighter souls who paled as though the odor turned their stomach.

It was Evil's unmistakable scent that I followed one morning, determined to know where Tim was and what Dyonis considered training for a scout. The trail led all the way up the western hills to the Garden. I squinted against the bright sunlight glittering off the delicate roof woven by Enticements. Trees heavy with fruit and flowers bursting with nectar filled the area inside. Among them, I could barely glimpse Temptation's tiny snakelets—the Persuasions—their copper scales hidden among the leaves. Temptation herself stayed wrapped around the gnarled apple tree in the center, her massive head lifting as I stepped past the open gate and inside.

I'd been smart enough to take my mask with me. Though Eden was not large, it was larger than it had ever been, and there were places in Eden where one could suffer. Wearing a mask could keep one from losing one's mind. The worst of the places were the Cave of Dread and the Garden.

Both were forbidden to all, and only used as places of punishment. Eden was a paradise, not a hell. It was the Devil's paradise, however, so there was always ample room for darkness.

Pressing the wooden mask to my face, I felt it grab hold. Now the lush fruit and flowers appeared as they truly were, rotting and covered in the sticky slime of Suffering. I walked through the Garden, careful where I tread. My heart pounded in my chest; the mask would keep me from harm, but what of young Tim?

I found him under a tree surrounded by dozens of apple cores. Persuasions curled around the shells of his ears, and a long, red welt lined his cheekbone where Temptation had struck him with her forked tongue. This boy, who only three months earlier was strapping and healthy, was now nothing but skin and bones. His brown eyes protruded from his skull, his lips were cracked and white, his ribs evident under his dirty, thin chemise. I knew that each bite of the forbidden fruit would make him want more and the more he ate the more he'd starve. It was Temptation's favorite trick.

Tim would know it, too. But knowing and resisting are two very different things.

Tim's eyes closed, his body drooping, an exhaustion I hadn't seen since Roanoke obvious in the limpness of his limbs.

Leaves rustled and as someone moved closer, I slid behind a tree.

Dyonis. Like me, he was wearing his mask, its wicked face in a permanent snarl. "No sleeping!" he barked.

Tim's head jerked up, his eyes blinking open.

"Who are your masters?" Dyonis stood over the young man, his shadow obscuring Tim's expression.

"The Council and the Devil." Tim's voice was weak, but the conviction behind it was not.

"And who do you love?"

"Eden. Eden above all else. What we do, we do for the good of Eden."

"We need a child, Tim. In fact, we need several."

"The price of life is a soul. One life for the good of many. One life sacrificed saves us all."

"Aye," said Dyonis. "That it does."

I could take no more of it. I stepped out where Dyonis could see me, my anger making my mask tighten.

Dyonis sighed. "Eleanor. Why is this not a surprise?"

"You call me a witch, yet here you make the Devil look benevolent."

That made him laugh. "Tim, Eleanor Dare is here to see us. What do you have to say about that?"

Tim's mouth twisted into a grimace as he chanted, *"Eleanor, Eleanor, murderous witch."*

I became my own monster, the hatred and anger and shame inside me spilling over. I ripped apples, then pears, then peaches from the branches of the trees around me, firing them at Dyonis and Tim. The soft thud the fruit made as it hit flesh spurred me on until the two were covered in pulp and juice.

Tim began to scrape up the remains from off his chemise and eat them.

Tears pricked my eyes. Devil save me, what was I doing?

Dyonis wiped the mess from his shoulders and tugged off his mask. He was still as handsome as he'd been a couple hundred years ago, except now there was an emptiness in his eyes. "He's ready, Eleanor. Tim's ready. We have his loyalty."

I shook my head. "I resign from the Council."

"As you wish. We no longer need you."

"You cannot do this. You cannot—"

But Dyonis scoffed. "Oh, Eleanor. You know as well as I do that we will always do what we must to survive. And you know that this is better kept secret than shared, aye?"

I could have threatened to expose his cruelty. I could have run and announced it to the entire village. But I felt the cool scales of a tiny Persuasion resting just behind my ear and instead agreed.

For years, I told myself that was why I'd given in to Dyonis. Why I quit the Council. Why I didn't fight to find a different way for us all to survive. That the tiny snakelet bending my ear was the reason.

But I had not removed my mask; Persuasion had no power over me while I wore it.

I had simply given in to Dyonis because I was tired of fighting. I was tired of living in suspicion. Of living full of fear and hatred. I wanted to live simply, thinking of nothing more than how to best Virginia and William in a round of Maw or what to conjure for the evening meal.

And I wanted Dyonis to be the villain for once.

Outside of the Garden, Tim regained his perfect health, standing tall and strong once again. But if one looked closely, one could see his shoulders stooped slightly now, as if he carried an invisible weight.

Dyonis was correct: Tim was ready. For the next several years, Tim returned to the Beyond over and over, bringing new children to Eden. They dressed in simple materials such as calico and wool, with a bit of braiding for embellishment. Their regard seemed haunted, but only months after their arrival, it was as if they'd always been a part of our community.

Arnold Archard was offered my seat on the Council. I was no longer privy to the Council's doings. Even after copious amounts of perry or ale or liquored syrup, Emme and Elizabeth stayed tight-lipped on anything other than idle village gossip.

Yet I knew how the Council thought and made my own guesses as to what decisions they were making. Each scout got too ill to continue returning to the Beyond once they reached twenty-five years of age—something the villagers accepted as a quirk of Eden. Something I guessed was more a quirk of the Council's. It did not matter as I would never set foot outside of Eden, but at every ceremony, every celebration, I sniffed my food and drink, and always checked for Malice pearls under my pillow. Who knew if the Council would find a way to befoul us all inside the beautiful walls of fog that kept us imprisoned.

As the years passed, new scouts were trained and new children were sacrificed or brought into the fold. Those children grew, married, gave birth and the cycle started again. Eden grew—both in population and size. The fog was pushed back to reveal mountains and woodlands and meadows we could now explore.

Over that time, every family gave to Eden. At least every family had given a child once, if not several times. Every family except mine.

I was waiting for Dyonis' wrath. Or for the Devil to threaten Virginia, William, or me. Life seemed bearable—almost good—and so, of course, I was waiting for the tide to turn.

Instead, it got better. We were given a gift.

37

Redd

The Beyond: Present Day

I leave John on the beach, any stupid worry about him being hurt eased by the knowledge he can just swim back to Eden to heal. I hope he goes there. And stays there. With all the others who betrayed me. I find the Shady Pines van, Shay's car, and John's rusted piece of crap parked off the side of the road. The keys John threw at me are for the van. I hop in and drive it to the hospital as fast as I dare.

When I arrive, the place is a mess. It looks like someone hosed it down. Half the people inside resemble shipwreck victims, and the staff is even more harried than I would have expected. A woman lifting sopping pieces of paper off the central desk gives my outfit a strange look, but tells me how to find Agnes' room.

While in the elevator, I'm at war with myself. My anger destroyed the flower that Agnes so carefully planted every time we moved. The flower that I had no idea was keeping her alive.

But what really gets my heart racing is the last time I spoke with her. I see it play out in my mind's eye. I see myself, blasting her with my fury, see her flying backward in pain, just like John did.

Is it my fault she's here? Is it my fault she's hurt? All because I got angry?

I know now that she truly was trying to protect me. She did so many bad things, she lied about so much...but that, that was real.

As I step out of the elevator onto the correct floor, three faces turn my way. Minnie, her nose red, her mascara smudged, her usual smile a deep frown. Shay, her nails bitten to the quick, her cheeks stained with tears. And Shay's dad, his usual stern expression morphed into one of worry and confusion.

"Redd!" Shay wraps her arms around me, nearly knocking me to the floor. "Oh, my God, Redd! I'll never leave your side again!"

"Shay," I say, trying not to cry myself. "It's okay. I'm okay."

"What are you wearing?" she lifts an eyebrow at the colonial gear.

But before I can answer, Minnie plants a kiss on my forehead. She doesn't say anything, just squeezes me like I'm an orange she's juicing—so thoroughly, I'm nothing but pulp by the end of it.

Shay's dad nods at me. "Redd. Glad you're alright." And while I can taste his relief that I'm okay, I can also feel his animosity like a tiny electric current. I dragged his daughter half-way across the country and got her to lie about the whole thing. He's not going to forgive and forget within the first minute of seeing me again. If ever.

"She's in there," he motions to the door with a quick jerk of his head. "She'll be happy to see you."

He then shepherds Shay and Minnie down the hall as I push open the door to Agnes' room.

One look at her and my legs nearly give out from under me. Fighting back tears, I grab the doorframe, tasting bile.

Agnes...Mom....is almost unrecognizable. She's always been thin, but now she's skeletal. Her skin is a dull gray. The muscles in her arms are shrunken, and her collarbones are sharp blades. She looks more like a corpse in a coffin than a woman in a hospital bed.

Yet her green eyes spark with life when she sees me. "Thank you, Lord," she whispers before her own tears start falling.

The second I step forward and the door snicks shut, she reaches toward me, desperation in her voice. "Do you...do you have any petals?"

"I do." The muscles in her face relax, but the tears come harder.

My body feels like gelatin, all wobbly. I slide into the chair next to her bed and take the petals from my pockets. An odor of rot fills the air.

She recoils, shaking her head. "No! It won't work like that!"

"It's...it's all I have." My throat closes up. *It's all I have because I destroyed the other one, the one you used to survive.*

She presses her face into her hands. A long howl leaves her, making the little hairs all over my body stand up.

Please, please let John be wrong. "Are you dying?"

From behind her hands, I hear her croak. "Yes."

I burst out in tears and my breath comes so quickly my ribs ache. I can barely get my words out. "Did...did I do...this to you...when I...got mad?".

"No." She wipes the tears from her own eyes. "No, you didn't."

I can smell the lie.

"I...didn't...mean to...hurt you. I never...meant—"

Her voice is soft. "I know. And you didn't do this. I did this to myself, Redd, by keeping the truth from you. You're not at fault. Not in the least."

I can sense the sincerity and love in her words. But it doesn't absolve me. How can it?

If I'd have just listened. If I had just held myself in check...she might not be dying...if I hadn't ruined the flower, too—

"The flower! John planted it on the beach. We can get there, get you healed."

Intending to help her out of bed, I yank back the sheet, revealing her torso and legs. Her legs are thin as twigs, but also twisted, the bone curled into ribbons underneath skin so thin and gray it's nearly blue. Part of her right leg is missing. It has literally turned to dust.

Oh, God. Oh, God, oh, God, oh, God.

I bend over and vomit right into the wastebasket next to the bed.

"We need help!" My voice rises as panic takes over. I search for the button to call the nurse, but Agnes has it in her good hand and is not giving it over.

"We have to get you help—"

"No, Redd!" Her voice is so sharp and strong, so unlike her physical state, that it stops me.

I straighten up, mopping the tears from my face with my sleeve. "Please. Please. Let's just get you to the flower."

But she shakes her head. "It wouldn't have saved me anyway, only helped with the pain. Because even the flower can't help this kind of wound."

"This is my fault. I'm so sorry. So, so sorry—"

"I told you it wasn't."

"I can't believe—"

"ENOUGH!" The word is a thunderbolt. "What I need from you is a promise: that you'll never go back to Eden. Ever".

"I won't," I blubber, meaning it. There's no way I ever want to step foot in that place again. I know now why she took kids to Eden...but... "Why...did you do it? Why run away with me?"

"I promised I would save you. I love Eleanor and Virginia. And you." She wraps her fingers around mine, her skin already cold as death. "My God, how I love you."

My heart feels like it's been wrapped in barbed wire. "I don't want you to die. I can't—"

I'm cut off by the beeping of the machines. Agnes grips my fingers tight as her body convulses. This time I scream as loud as I can for a doctor.

The door flies open, and two nurses enter. They try to push me away, but Agnes will not let go of my hand. She looks at me and says, "Virginia would be so proud of you."

I feel more tears coming, both out of fear for Agnes and from Virginia's betrayal.

"You look exactly like her," Agnes continues, even as one of the nurses is wrenching my fingers from hers. "Exactly. Except for the eyes. Her blue eyes."

And then a nurse wrenches my hand from Agnes'. I'm hustled out of there as a doctor rushes in. I can't see much from outside the door through the rectangular bit of glass. But there's a muffled scream, then a lot of swearing and confusion and frantic movement around the bed.

Shay and Minnie join me in the hallway, their arms around me, their words soft and warm.

But only minutes later, we're given the news.

Agnes—Mom—is dead.

38

John

The Beyond: Present Day

Devil save me, I am unused to this level of pain. Every breath burns. It is as if a red-hot fire is charring my lungs and gut. As if Agony has stuck his fangs into my flesh and clung on.

Redd. Redd did this.

She is a Dare. I knew the Dares were powerful in their own way— that the Devil favors them, that the village fears them—but I hadn't known about this. True power outside of Eden.

I want to give it more thought, understand it—understand Redd—and, for the love of Lucifer, why the fact that she blew me backwards with the power of a cannonball makes her even more attractive to me than before. I want to puzzle it out, but my priority is to get proof that the flower grows out here back to Eden. I look over to the Eternity Flower I planted yesterday.

The petals stay the color of rust, the stalk soft like overcooked asparagus.

The sight of it in that state hurts me more than the pain scorching my insides. I must stay, wait for it to bloom. Devil willing, I won't need to stay too long. I am not sure how much more of this suffering I can endure. And if my injury is anything close to Agnes', I must get into Eden to heal.

But it seems as if the Devil has other plans for me.

The sun inches its way upward, and even this close to the water, the heat is unbearable. It exacerbates the pain.

I can tell Persuasion is exhausted from the way he droops listlessly over my ear. Chaos licks my cheeks and forehead. I run a hand through his fur. He's well fed from the pandemonium in the hospital, so staying calm comes easier for him. I feel the weight of his head against my shoulder. The three of us lie in the shade, the sand and mud acting as our cradle.

An hour passes. Two. More.

I begin to cough up blood.

At one point, the pain is so bad I black out. When I come to, the sun is high in the sky. I take a breath. It is a knife scoring my lungs. But over the briny scent of the water is the sweet smell of the Eternity Flower. Squinting against the brightness, I turn toward it. The plant that was dying earlier in the day is now full of life. The velvety white petals shiver in the breeze, the stalk strong, the leaves bright green.

By a demon's tongue and tail. It worked. It worked!

"Look!" I say to Chaos and Persuasion. The word brings up more coughing and blood, yet happy tears fill my eyes. "It's beautiful."

Chaos barks. Before he can do any damage, I order him to stay put.

Gritting my teeth against the pain, I rummage through the bag I'd left in the sand to find the camera. Lining up the flower in the tiny window, I make certain the Sound and beach are visible behind it. The machine spits out a glossy square. When the image takes form, a full minute of joy blots out all pain.

I did it. I saved us from further sacrifice.

No. Not me, Redd. *Redd saved us.*

Tucking the picture into my bag, I tug a petal from the flower and let a drop of nectar fall onto my tongue. It tastes sweet and familiar. It gives me strength, but does not completely heal my wound. I put on my mask and enter the water, the Devil's pets by my side. The fire still burning in my chest forces me to stop every few feet; I do so with impatience. In only a handful of minutes, I can share the news with everyone in Eden. No more sacrifice! We can start by leaving Eden...slowly, one person at a time. Then, more people. More flowers. We can have Virginia use her blood and gardening power to grow an entire field in the Beyond.

Finally, I see the orange-scarlet glow at the end of the tunnel. Deception's breath makes the water churn, loosening bones from the silt. A skull floats past me as I kick my way into the Fire Pit. *No more. No more bones will fill this pond*, I tell myself. *Eden's centuries-long nightmare is over.* Breaking through the surface of the water, I fall onto the riverbank and rest my cheek against a spotty carpet of moss.

I whimper in relief as the pain recedes. Whatever Redd did to me, Eden is able to fix. Thank the Devil for that. Chaos yips, then bounds off. I close my eyes tight, reveling in the moment. Persuasion slithers into my backpack, the scrape of his scales along the canvas loud in the silence.

That's when I realize there is no birdsong.

I open my eyes and take in my surroundings.

A few blooms still shine like mini-moons in the shadow of the trees, but others are curled up like witches' hands, withered and skeletal on the forest floor. The mud bubbles, belching steam. I can scarcely believe it. It should not be like this. But there's no denying that over the scent of the Eternity Flowers hovers the odor of Contagion and rot.

The Harvest will soon start.

My heart drums. Only yesterday, Eden was perfect.

In the distance, I hear the constant swooshing of blades over vegetation.

During my training, Grandfather told me of a time the Council inadvertently hastened the Harvest by culling the Eternity Flower. They discovered that doing so induces early decay.

My stomach clenches. This isn't happening naturally. Grandfather did not wait for my return. I must stop this, stop them before the Harvest truly starts, or we will be too weak to reach the Beyond. And even if we did, one flower would not be sufficient for us all.

The path along the river back to the village is nothing but a carpet of beheaded blooms. Thousands of Eternity Flowers have already been culled.

"Stop the culling!" I yell as I sprint over the hill and past a group of villagers slicing the blooms off stalks in a large field of

Eternity Flowers, the glorious blossoms falling to the ground like bodies in a massacre. Sweat runs down their faces, their forearms bulging with each sweep of the blade. "Stop! Now!"

One or two of them drop their machetes, but most heed me no mind. I am not of the Council and therefore my words hold little weight. I must find Grandfather. By now, Fury has sniffed me out and is running by my side as I enter the village itself. Even here, the flower boxes hold nothing but headless stems. By the time I find my Grandfather, I'm shaking with rage. He and Grandmama are behind our house, snipping down the last Eternity Flowers that remain in our garden.

Grandmama's face is filled with relief when she spies me. "You're home!"

Grandfather does not pause in his work. "John."

I forgo the greetings. "What is this? You promised to wait for my return—"

"Nay," he cuts me off. "I promised nothing. I only said preparation for the Harvest takes time."

"You wanted me gone. So you could continue without my interference." I grit my teeth, livid. Fury yips and licks my hand, his tail wagging.

I cannot believe he would want this.

I take the photo out of the waterproof pouch in my bag and shove it in his face. "You must stop the culling."

He tugs the picture from my fingers and turns to my grandmother. "Isobel, I need a word alone with John."

Grandmama nods. She squeezes my shoulder as she steps past me to the kitchen door. Once we're alone, Grandfather asks, "What is this?"

"The flower is blooming. In the Beyond. You see? This is a photograph of it."

"This photograph is not something the villagers are familiar with, John. 'Tis of no use to us."

"Perhaps the villagers aren't familiar with photographs, but the Council is. You are. Look closely. You'll know this is not in Eden."

But he pockets the picture and takes a knife to the next bloom. "Nay. The Dare girl will pay."

It should be no surprise. The hatred in his heart for that family goes deeper than anything else. But I am taken aback. "You will put your revenge above new possibilities for the village?"

"Go inside. Prepare yourself for the Harvest. We will sacrifice the Dare girl and then talk about the flower."

There are only a handful of blooms left standing. I do not look at him but keep my eyes on the snowballs of petals as I say in as calm a voice as possible, "Stop, Grandfather. Stop. You do not want to hasten this Harvest. You cannot sacrifice her."

"I can and I—"

My voice rises. "She left Eden!"

"Who?"

"Redd. The Dare girl. She's gone."

Grandfather stills and narrows his eyes at me. The malice there is frightening. Terror himself would take a step back from that look. "Satan's scourge. What have you done, John?"

39

Eleanor

Eden: 37 years ago

One dark night, when the moon was but a slit in the sky, Emme Merrimoth knocked on our door at an unseemly hour.

Virginia, William and I had dragged the table directly in front of the hearth to play a round of Maw. Yet, as usual, one round never sufficed, and it was well after midnight before we even looked up from our cards. The knock startled us enough that I jumped at the sound of it.

Like all us elders, Emme's physical appearance had never caught up to her age. Her auburn hair grew out of her head like an unkempt garden, the wild hair of youth. Her round body was plump and dewy. Only her eyes and a small crease between her eyebrows belied the fatigue of her years.

"Virginia, William." She nodded at the two of them from the doorway. "Young Hugh's come home from his errand into the other world. The Council's met, and we've decided to deliver his package to you."

She stepped aside, and there stood a tiny dark-haired girl of maybe two or three years, eyes green as the moss growing on the river rocks. She was wearing an odd outfit of stretchy stockings without feet and a tight top with blue rabbits painted on it. The other world had changed so much, I found myself wishing dearly to step out and see it.

I still did not approve of taking children from their homes to raise here, but turned a blind eye to it. It was no longer my burden to feel that guilt. Except now there was a young girl looking scared and lost on our doorstep.

For a moment I could not find my voice. It was William who ushered Emme and the child inside. "I pray you, come sit by the fire."

"We're...we're to keep her?" Virginia asked as Emme perched on the edge of a chair, picking up the girl and holding her stiffly on her lap. The child's cheeks were stained with tears and her tiny mouth was turned down, the bottom lip trembling.

I stepped forward, my voice bitter. "What does the Council want from us? Why in the Devil's paltry paradise would they give anything to this family?"

Emme answered me but looked at Virginia. "After all these centuries, yours is the only family that has yet to add to the village population. To carry on the Dare name."

Though Virginia had married William hundreds of years before, the villagers still considered her a Dare. Eleanor and Virginia Dare. My name stuck to her like feathers to tar. I felt William shift on his feet, his annoyance loud in the small gesture. "Wythers. Once married, a woman takes on the husband's name. 'Tis Wythers."

We all ignored him. I crossed my arms and spoke to Emme. "You bring her to us with the intent of forcing us to give her to Eden."

"Eleanor, we may no longer be on the Council together, but we are still friends. And friends are honest when they can be. So, the truth is that Elizabeth and I insisted the child be in this home. We know you've suffered for your doings and want to see happiness here. There are other children, younger children, who would be chosen to offer to Eden first. And since this child is not of your blood..." She shrugged and pressed her lips together.

The rest of her words stayed unspoken. But I knew what was unsaid—when we gave to Eden, it would be from my family blood. Not an orphan's.

"You insisted and the rest of the Council agreed? I trust no decision by the Council."

"Do you deny the child a home?" Emme's voice was sharp.

"Nay. I said nothing of the sort." Despite the hard shell I wore, I felt soft underneath. Faced with this young child's tears, I was as gelatinous as a mollusk.

I wondered if Dyonis had softened as well. He'd finally married again; his wife Isobel had been taken from the Beyond more than a century ago. Together they'd had a daughter, Alice, given to Eden in their first year of marriage. Five years ago, they gave birth to a son, George. Once it had been determined that the boy was not to be sacrificed, Dyonis seemed to have recaptured some of his humanity.

"What do you know of her?" William asked Emme as he looked at the child. "When did Hugh bring her back? From whence did he take her?"

Emme shook her head. "'Tis not your business to know these details. Nor mine. All I can tell you is that she comes from the Beyond, and she needs our help."

It was the Council's refrain, one that forged the moeurs of the village. Outside of Eden, the world was a dark and dangerous place. It was a place of greed and suffering. A place of hatred. A place of death. We'd all heard it enough that even I was beginning to believe it to be true.

"She's a child in need of a family, and your family has been chosen," Emme continued. "You know the rules: she must think she's always been part of the village. You mustn't tell her she came from elsewhere."

"We're aware," I said, unable to keep the flint from my voice.

Emme frowned. "I should call upon Secrecy—"

"No need, Emme. You know I can hold my tongue." My gaze held my meaning. She knew just as well as I that there were many confidences Secrecy did not bury, yet ones that I had never brought to light.

Had it been anyone else on the Council, they would not have let it pass. But Emme had once been a very good friend. "Aye."

The little girl was sucking her thumb. There were several round marks on the fleshy part of her cheek, marks the size of fingertips. An unguent had been rubbed over them. The skin was not broken, just slightly pink. She must have been hurt very recently for the traces to still be there. Eden healed quickly.

"What happened here?" Virginia knelt down and pointed to the marks. The girl flinched, terror in her eyes.

Emme answered all too quickly. "'Twas there when Hugh brought her in, so we treated it. 'Tis nothing. Children are always bangin' themselves about at such an age."

"Indeed," I agreed, my voice cold. My guess was that she'd fought back when they tried to 'baptize' her.

When Emme finally left, Virginia, William and I stood dumbstruck, blinking at the girl. I asked her, "What is your name, child?"

The girl's mouth tightened, her green gaze traveling over the three of us. She shook her head, refusing to say a word.

I pushed down the questions I had—whether young Hugh had ripped her from a loving family or not, how the Council had treated her when she arrived, if she'd ever be able to forgive any of us for what they'd done. Instead, I nodded. "Aye. Your name from the past is yours to keep secreted away. We'll call you Agnes. I've always imagined if I had another girl her name would be Agnes. Unless you'd prefer something else?"

The girl said nothing, so we called her Agnes from that moment on.

Virginia shared a bed with Agnes that night. The three of us tucked the girl in and wiped the tears from her face. Between those tears, she asked for "Daddy." We hugged her and opened the chamber door so Sloth could lie like a violet puddle at the foot of the bed. We did what we could to make her feel safe. I could not imagine what she had been wrenched from; I could not imagine a world where little children wore shirts with colorful rabbits painted upon them.

Once the girl was sleeping and we were back in front of the hearth to discuss the future, I said to William and Virginia, "I hate the idea of lying to this child, despite Council rules. She should know she is not a child of Eden."

Virginia's eyes widened. "Such cruelty! She cannot go back. Let her believe she is one of us. Let her see the beauty in Eden."

"Beauty?" I scoffed. "Eden kidnaps children. Where is the beauty in that, Virginia?"

"Taking an unwanted child and offering her a home is not kidnapping, Mama."

I scoffed. "Oh, Virginia. Of course she was kidnapped."

"Enough." William slammed a hand on the table. "Enough. What's done is done. Agnes is here now. All these years of never daring to have a child. Of thinking we'd pass eternity without that gift. But now she's *ours*, Eleanor. And I intend to love her. I will do nothing to give her reason to doubt my love."

Virginia wrapped her hands around his. "Nor I."

I stood, grabbed the long metal poker and stabbed at the dying embers in the hearth. "'Tis not easy to love a child in Eden."

"Mama, you tell me all the time how much you love me!" Virginia sounded exasperated.

I rehung the poker and gathered my skirts to make my way up to my chamber. "Aye, I do. I love you more than anything. But 'twas never easy to do."

Upstairs, I peeked in on Agnes. She whimpered and twitched in her sleep, fresh tears wetting the pillow and her hair. Her skin was several shades darker than my own, her hands several sizes smaller. Her mouth was pursed into a tiny rosebud and one perfect foot hung over the edge of the bed.

She was a stranger. Yesterday, I hadn't any idea this child existed.

Yet when I looked at her, something inside me felt like a wound unhealed.

I knew that my love for Virginia had not always sent me down the right path. That I made so very many mistakes. Mistakes that had eternal consequences.

I was hoping Agnes' arrival would steer me towards a better route.

40

Redd

The Beyond: Present Day

M innie, Shay, and I sit in the hospital cafeteria, hands wrapped around paper coffee cups, trying to deal with the shock of Agnes' death. I go from anger to grief to disgust to despair. I don't know everything about who Agnes really was, but I do know that she loved me in her own way. And that I didn't appreciate her love, not until it was too late.

But she also left a secret behind her. A horrible secret.

Now I need to be the one to reveal it.

Shay's dad went back to his hotel, with Minnie promising to bring Shay there before evening. Even though I may have gotten on his bad side, he knows I can use her friendship right now. And he's too good of a guy to keep it from me.

So both Minnie and Shay get to hear the truth. I figure I'd better start with Eden first.

The doctors were baffled at the state of Agnes' body. They had no explanation for how she shriveled up over a matter of hours. They asked to do an autopsy to understand. But they'll never understand. Not unless they enter Eden. Not unless they see that the Devil is not a myth and there's truly a place where sacrifice keeps people alive forever.

I tell Shay and Minnie just that. "What I'm going to share with you is unbelievable. But it's real. It's so, so real. I need you to hear me out." I tell them everything. Well, almost everything. I don't get to Clara/Autumn just yet. But it's a start: I go from the mask to the village to the Master to Virginia to every conversation with John. When I'm finished, I feel empty. Worn out. And crazy.

The silence coming from them is deafening.

The two of them squirm on their chairs and refuse to look me in the eye.

"What? You don't believe me?"

Shay comes around the table and puts her arms around me. She holds me like that for a moment, then sits back down. "Redd, your mom—Agnes—told you she'd kidnapped you, then died in a horrific way. It's normal that you might...well...not be ready to face reality."

My heart sinks as I look into her dark eyes. Shay has always backed me up in everything. I trusted her enough to tell her about Agnes' messed up behavior, to give her an intimate view into our lives. She was behind me then. So, I thought...I thought at least she would believe me, despite the supernatural aspect. Despite the weirdness of it all. I mean, I wasn't the only one to see Agnes disintegrate into a pile of ashes.

The threat of tears makes my throat burn. "You didn't listen to anything I said."

"Redd—" she starts, but I turn away from her. I know I'm not being fair. Only a couple of days ago *I* would have thought I was crazy. But it still hurts to have Shay look at me like I'm a little kid who doesn't want to hear the truth about Santa Claus.

"It's hard, losing the ones we love," Minnie says. "You've just lost—"

I need them to understand. I cut Minnie off. "Ever wonder why I'm so good at cards?"

I reveal it then. How I read their emotions, how I 'cheat.' They still don't believe me.

The cafeteria has emptied out, so we're the only three in the large room. I tell them to get under the table.

"Uh..." Shay lifts an eyebrow. Minnie looks genuinely worried. But they both humor me and get on the floor.

"I'm from Eden," I say. "And because of that, I have powers. Want proof I'm not making this all up?"

I turn away from them. I find my fury. It's balled up inside me like a tight fist, and I pry it open bit by bit. Anger. Frustration. Confusion. Rage. Rage. Rage.

"Ah, Redd..." The Devil's voice. I don't even need a mask to hear it anymore.

I hate how alluring it is. How much I want to listen to it. How much I want to please him. Make him happy. Make him proud.

I close my eyes and let my emotions loose. I hear furniture crashing against the walls, sense the window shattering, feel bits of glass tumble onto my shoulders from the light fixtures above.

It's both draining and energizing. Like the way a long run leaves you wiped out, but on a high.

I open my eyes. The cafeteria is a disaster: the tables overturned, broken chairs, pictures in frames smashed to bits, sugar spread out like snow on the floor. I'm wet with sweat, my blouse and skirts are soaked with it, my hair sticking to my neck in dark strings.

A siren is going off and shocked employees are emerging from behind counters and doorways.

I turn back around to Shay and Minnie, who are hugging each other under the only table that hasn't been touched in the entire place. "Believe me now?" I ask.

They both nod, mouths open wide enough to admit small aircraft.

"Okay, then let's find a quiet spot. Because I have something much worse to say."

And then I take Minnie's hand and tell her the truth about her daughter.

41

Redd

The Beyond: Present Day

The three of us stand looking out at the darkening sky over the Sound, the waves crashing at our feet. Tears stream down Shay's face. She's already late getting back to the hotel. Her dad will be beyond pissed off, but she doesn't make a move. I can barely breathe for how much my chest is hurting. Minnie is shaking from head to toe, which has nothing to do with the cool evening air or the fact that she's soaking wet. She's still processing the truth about Autumn. Clara. She's still grappling with the horror of Agnes' lies and all the lost years, while also clinging to the news that her daughter is alive and very close by.

And yet...she is unable to reach her.

After I broke the news, Minnie's rage made what I did look like a windstorm next to a hurricane. But then she moved into action. And it was all about how to get to Clara. It didn't matter if she was going to step into the Devil's own lair. Minnie was going to get her daughter back.

Minnie got us past Terror. The beast's power was no match for her determination.

She rented scuba gear since she can't hold her breath for five full minutes. Fearless, she entered the water after one short lesson from the store manager. But she got only a few feet into the tunnel before the water spit her back out. Over and over and over. Some invisible barrier was keeping her from entering Eden. And after more than two hours of trying, she's finally dropped the equipment onto the beach, defeated.

In all the years I've known Minnie, I've seen her grieving, seen her angry, seen her full of despair...but I've never seen her like this. This has broken her. The fact that her daughter is on the other side of that tunnel, in a world of the Devil's making, and she cannot even enter, has emptied her of every bit of life that makes her who she is.

She drops to the ground and lets out one painful sob. It's a sound unlike anything I've ever heard.

It breaks my heart.

Shay and I try to hug her, but Minnie is lost to us. Her eyes stare blankly out before her, her face slack.

"Minnie." I wipe away the tears falling from those empty eyes then swipe at my own.

Nothing.

The heavy odor of the Eternity Flower wafts over us. The plant that was dying earlier in the day is now full of life. The velvety white petals shiver in the breeze, mocking me. I turn away to look instead at the dark expanse of water before me, and fear brings a knot to my gut. I know what's on the other side. I know what they want to do to me there.

I promised Agnes I wouldn't go back. And I don't want to. I really and truly do not want to.

Yet I'm the only one who can.

Clara probably won't listen to me. I might even die before I get the chance to talk to her. But I owe it to Minnie to try.

"Don't do this," Shay says when I put a foot into the water.

"I have to. You know I have to."

Shay's beautiful face crumples. "Redd."

"I love you guys," I say.

And then I dive under the water to head back into Eden.

42

Eleanor

Eden: 34 years ago

As Agnes grew, we discovered that she was an intelligent child, one who learned quickly. I taught her to fear the Master, despite Virginia's insistence that she love him. In moments alone with Agnes, I was adamant; Virginia's love for the Master was irrational, misplaced, and dangerous. I did not want Agnes to fall under the Devil's spell.

Agnes fell under no one's spell. She viewed the Master as the monster he was in his horrid wooden mask. She viewed his pets as just that—the Devil's pets—meaning she fully understood their powers. She often looked at Torment with slitted eyes as she spoke to me. Evil she found unbearable. She only cuddled Sloth when she had nothing important to do, and she laughed at Chaos and spent hours with him in fields but was wary when he was too near our home. When Nightmares got her or when she seemed to think too much upon her past, she would head to the pond to visit Deception with Virginia. The water dragon kept the melancholy of doubt at bay. Fury was the only pet she sought out consistently; she would whisper angry and fearful thoughts in his ear and bury her nose in his fur. And yet she was not an angry child; not in the sense of one who is insolent or one who strikes out at others. Her anger brought her to action. So did her fear.

So did my own.

When she about five or six years old, she came upon me, William, and Virginia preparing for sacrifice. Only adults participated in the ritual, and only adults knew exactly what happened during the ceremony. Children were meant to be given a sleeping draught and tucked into bed to wake to a new and glorious Eden, supposedly none the wiser. It was a ridiculous rule as, despite what the Council thought, children were not fools. They saw the change in the village, they felt their hunger subside, and realized one of their own was now missing.

I had prepared Agnes' tea but, apparently, she'd let it grow cold on her nightstand, because as we were strapping on our skins and masks, she slipped into the sitting room.

"What are these for?" she asked, pointing to our outfits. Of course, she already had a mask of her own. It had allowed her to enter Eden. But, apart from that moment, she'd never worn it again. We kept it in the old Bible box—the Bible long gone—the one that I'd inherited from Ananias' relatives back in England. The one with the Dare family crest embossed on the front.

Virginia gave a start and put her hands over her heart. She smiled sheepishly, then shook her head. "Agnes, my sweet. You startled me. I thought you were sleeping." Her voice wavered. "These masks are for a terribly boring ceremony. Be thankful you're but a child and need not attend."

I snorted. Virginia was always skirting the truth. "The masks are vile, child. Vile and powerful. Stay away. Go up to your chamber and do not descend until the sun has once again lit the sky."

The girl pouted but did as told, shuffling upstairs and slamming her chamber door.

After the ceremony, the three of us stumbled back home, drunk on liquored syrup, our bellies warm and full, our hearts cold and empty.

In the earliest hours of dawn, there was a frantic knocking at the cottage door. I waited to see if William would answer, as he always woke early for a walk. But he must have already left because the knocking continued.

I blinked sleep from my eyes, threw on a dressing gown and opened the door to see Dyonis Harvie standing there.

"Dyonis?" My gaze dropped as he shoved Agnes in front of him. She was covered head to toe in dirt, tears dripping from her cheeks and chin. "Agnes! How...why are you not in your bed?"

Dyonis glared at me. "The question is why was she not given a sleeping draught last night? You could have saved her a night in the Cave of Dread for flouting the rules."

The Cave of Dread was a place of torture. A cave where insects and arachnids and worms burrowed into one's ears and nose and mouth. A cave of pitch darkness: stone walls pressing in, creatures crawling, panic twisting like a blade in the gut.

I ripped Agnes from Dyonis' grasp and wrapped my arms around her so tightly that, had we been elsewhere but Eden, it would have broken a bone.

"Virginia! Virginia, now!" I yelled. My daughter came running, her white nightdress falling off one shoulder.

She gasped at the sight of Agnes, but took her from me, covering the girl's head with kisses. "Oh, my poor Agnes!"

As Virginia stepped back inside, I growled at Dyonis, hatred burning my blood. "I'll kill you. I'll have Eden eat your entrails. Watch your back, Dyonis." He and I both knew it was impossible to inflict any pain upon the man, yet the venom in my words was potent enough to make him flinch.

It was the tiniest of victories, but I would take it.

He cleared his throat. "Keep the girl in check, Eleanor. You know the Council can do great damage if necessary."

"As can I," I said before slamming the door in his face.

Withholding my love had not helped Agnes. It was time to give it freely.

No more treading lightly on thin ice. I was ready to crash through it, ready to sink down if need be.

And, if need be, I would take all of Eden with me.

That night, I told Virginia and William, "We shall raise Agnes with love, but that love will no longer be blind. She must know Eden is not what we all pretend it to be. You must stop lying."

"Oh, Mama." Virginia looked up from her drawing. She'd found my father's old box of drawing things and taken a liking to sketching everything around her. She, like me, had talent. She turned to paper and paints when she was troubled. And since Dyonis had brought Agnes back home, Virginia had gone through several sheets of parchment. "I spent so many years hating you when I was young for just that reason: you opened my eyes to truths about this place that I did not want—nor need—to know. Truths we can do little about. Allow her to be a child."

"She spent the night in the Cave of Dread, Virginia! I believe her illusions are already shattered!"

"Eleanor," William said, his voice a near whisper, his eye to the ceiling above us. Aye, I needed to keep my voice down. I did not want to wake Agnes.

In a calmer tone, I added. "I am not suggesting we don't allow her to have fun. But at some point, she must know from whence she came. She must know to be just as wary of the Council's edicts as she is of the Master."

"She should be on guard. I'll give you that. I have nothing against teaching her what to fear," William agreed.

Virginia shook her head. "Teach her what you will. But I shall say nothing against the Master."

I should have noticed the glint in her eye, the pitch of her voice. I should have paid attention. But I was already making plans to protect Agnes from the evils of Eden.

I'd made my mistakes with Virginia in the past, yet I had protected her. And now Virginia was a grown woman, centuries old. She no longer needed my protection.

Devil knows, I was wrong.

43

John

Eden: Present Day

The alarm has been sounded, the bell a constant ringing in the background. The villagers looked everywhere in Eden but, of course, Redd was nowhere to be found.

The entire Council has now gathered in our great room. A fire rages in the hearth while they rage at each other. Jonathon Tydway's usual calm is gone as he swears. Christopher Cooper is so upset, sweat drips down into his eyebrows. Joyce Archer has lost her icy exterior, emotion dotting her cheeks pink. Accusations are made. There is talk of negligence all around. And they intend to search all of Eden again.

They refuse to hear the truth about the flower while sacrificing Redd remains a possibility. I cannot convince them Redd has left Eden. Even Grandfather accuses me of lying when he opens the safe box and Redd's mask stares back at him. "See!" He points inside. "She could not have absconded without her mask."

"She has," I insist.

"Impossible," Elizabeth Glane shakes her head. "Let us look again in the mountain caves".."

So often in Eden, we are made to keep quiet. Keep secrets. We are compelled to do so, whether out of loyalty or through coercion. Not as often, we are asked to tell the truth. *Compelled* to tell the truth. Now no Devil's pet wields its power to make me speak, but the looming Harvest unpins my lips. "For the love of Lucifer, listen! Redd can hold her breath for five full minutes!"

All eyes turn to me.

"She entered Eden without her mask on," I admit. "She does not need it to breathe for her."

"You lie." Emme Merimoth's round chin trembles.

I stand straighter. "I do not."

Grandfather's face turns purple. "You knew this all along?"

My silence says everything.

That silence turns into a deafening roar, their shouts and anger bringing Fury to howl outside the door. Elizabeth calls for me to be thrown in the Garden. Christopher suggests Misery's sinking sands.

Before they discuss my fate further, I cut in. "My punishment can be decided later. We must get the villagers to the Beyond before the Harvest is fully upon us." I turn to Grandfather. "Show them the photograph. Show them the proof. They must know of this new possibility."

His jaw tightens and his eyes narrow, but he pulls the photo from his pocket. The glossy square passes from one Council member to the next. Each frown deepens as they behold what the picture means.

A Worry scutters along the floorboard, its shiny exoskeleton reflected in the firelight.

I start, "We haven't much time. You've culled so many flowers the Harvest could soon start. We must tell the villagers. There is a choice now—"

Christopher snarls, "Too risky a choice."

"Aye," Emme nods enthusiastically, almost as if this is good news. "We will soon be weakened by the Harvest. One flower for all of Eden is not an assurance of survival."

"Then let Virginia free. She's a Dare and a gardener. She has the blood and power to grow more." I look at the Council, one member after the other. "It has come full circle. Do you not see? A Dare damned us. Now a Dare has saved us. And another can keep us alive."

Grandfather laughs. "The only way we would release a Dare is for her to see own blood sacrificed."

The photograph has made its way back to him. I reach out to take it, saying, "You're blinded by hatred. Let the villagers decide for themselves."

He pulls his hand back. "'Tis the Council that decides, John. Always has been." And then he throws the photo into the fire.

I dive forward to snatch it from the flames. Christopher shoves me to the side, and Jonathon steps in front of the fire. I fight, elbowing one man then sweeping the feet out from under the other. In the hearth, the photograph curls, letting off a sickly smoke. But before I can grab it, six pairs of hands are pulling me down to the floor. I thrash and kick and swear. Grandfather swears right back at me, taking a pair of heavy manacles from a cupboard and clamping them to my wrists. "Devil's curse! Stop!"

"Why? Why would you do this?" I'm still fighting. My right foot connects with Christopher's jaw. When he screams in pain, the others all freeze, surprised and horrified.

It hurt him. It should not have hurt him.

Lucifer save us, the Harvest is starting. The culling brought it on so quickly.

I take advantage of everyone's surprise to break free of their grip. I must tell the villagers they can leave and still live. No one would choose to make the sacrifice if they did not have to. Even without the photograph, without the Council's backing—

I only make it halfway to the door before they are on me once again. This time, I aim to hurt and strike out with my bound wrists, my feet, my head. I've yet to feel a thing, but already both Jonathon and Joyce have joined Christopher in their cries of anguish.

"Thomas! Grandmama!" I yell. "Tell the villag—"

A white, hot pain turns my words to a scream. The smell of cooking skin overtakes that of woodsmoke and rot. I lurch back to see Grandfather with the fire poker, the tip burning orange. My forearm sizzles where he scorched me and my vision blurs.

"Come to your senses, John. Would you truly risk all our lives for this uncertain dream? We must go forth with sacrifice. 'Tis what is best for all," he spits.

I fall back onto the carpet, almost glad for the physical agony. It is what I deserve. I should have done more. I failed. Saving us all was within my grip, but now it is too late.

The price of life is a soul.

I failed.

I pull my knees tighter to my chest and think of the Dorrel girl and her giggle. The Hewett babe and his smile. One of them will be given to Eden. *No. It cannot happen. I will not—*

"It is upon John's head that the Dare girl escaped," Joyce says, tucking her hair back in place after the skirmish. The color has gone out of her cheeks and her eyes shine with pain. She turns to Grandfather. "And upon your head that you allowed the girl out of chains in the first place. So, despite there being younger blood to give, 'tis your family that should pay."

He rubs his temples, then the red Malice pearl hanging from his ear. His voice is so quiet, it is near a whisper. "Ah, but we are not the only ones who let her out of our sight."

"Nay, not Clara."

"And not John."

"Thomas, then."

Fear grips my heart. "NO!" I sit up, a wave of dizziness striking me sideways as I do. "Grandfather, you cannot allow this!"

"Thomas is not your true brother, John. Not of your blood," Joyce says, as if it makes the tiniest bit of difference in my love for the boy.

"Take me instead," I say. "I beg of you."

"Enough!" Grandfather barks, his voice cracking. "We will sacrifice neither you nor Thomas. It will be little Clarence Hewett. Joyce knows that. We all know that."

The others murmur their agreement. Joyce moves to the window and rests her forehead against the glass as if she can barely hold her head up.

I struggle to stand. "No, Grandfather. Not the Hewett babe. I go willingly to sacrifice—"

That's when Joyce gasps. I follow her gaze to a moving shadow by the Archer home. In the growing dusk, it is hard to make out, but the form looks feminine. Joyce turns and shakes her head at me, her face twisted in disgust. Her skirts rustle as she runs out of the room.

Emme goes to the glass to see for herself.

"By the Devil's hand," Emme breathes.

The others crowd around the window. I cannot see beyond the backs of their heads. Grandfather begins to shout orders. Emme gathers Virginia and Eleanor's masks from the safe box. Christopher, Jonathon, and Grandfather grab me and, despite my fighting, manage to put me in the holding cell in the root cellar. As they lock the door, I hear Grandfather say, "Time to prepare the ceremony!"

44

Redd

Eden: Present Day

When I come out of the water into Eden, I think for a minute that I'm in the wrong place. It hasn't even been a full twenty-four hours since I left, but it's unrecognizable. Instead of the treacly scent of Eternity Flowers, it smells like rot. The flowers all around the pond are gone—nothing but withered stems or slimy, black stalks remain. There's a weird sound in the air, almost like wind through branches, but its pitch is all wrong. It sounds like moaning and—I swear to God—it's coming directly from the trees themselves.

I crawl onto the cracked mud of the riverbank, cutting the palm of my hand on a sharp rock. Not only does it sting like hell, it doesn't immediately heal.

I'm about to make sure I am truly in the right place when I hear a familiar yip. Chaos comes crashing through the dry underbrush to wet my face with his fat, green tongue. He's big and fluffy and despite the weird fangs and fiery eyes, he's adorable. I scratch him behind the ears and pat his sides. His fur changes color with every breath, but the spots where I touched him stay dark. I look down at my hands, worried the cut is worse than it feels.

Every bit of my skin, my clothes, everything, is red. But there's no way this is from my small cut. I turn back to the Fire Pit and see that its usual orange glow is turning more of a deep scarlet. The river that rushes into the pond is now like a severed artery, with blood gushing instead of water.

This cannot be good.

Chaos doesn't seem to mind, as he keeps licking my face. I feel the slightest urge to do something crazy, but his power isn't overwhelming like it was before. "Okay, boy, that's enough." I gently push him away.

He sits—tail wagging, tongue out—while I stand and squeeze out my hair. It looks like blood dripping from an open wound.

"Which way to Clara's?" I ask Chaos. While the area around the Fire Pit is illuminated due to the glowing algae, the forest is dark with dense fog. I can't even make out the hills and fields I know are somewhere just beyond the tree line.

Chaos starts trotting in a direction and I follow. It may not be the smartest thing to follow a dog whose power is bedlam, but he's my best bet to finding my way out of the forest.

We don't come across anyone until we reach the village. I sneak through the crooked streets, darting out of sight any time someone is about to cross my path. I'd wanted to approach Clara's house from behind, but a group of women holding a furious discussion blocks my way. Without the Eternity Flower everywhere, my sixth sense is back on high alert. The acidic taste of panic fills my mouth, along with the odor of fear and anger.

I stay in the shadows created by naked hedges growing between Clara and John's houses. Candlelight glows from several windows of John's house, but the angle of the setting sun and the gray wisps of fog make it impossible for me to see inside. The shadows end, and there's nothing to hide me if I want to run to Clara's front door. How am I going to do this?

That's when Chaos bumps my hand with his nose.

He doesn't speak, yet it's like I can understand him; he's ready to help and has an idea.

I like this dog.

"Okay," I whisper and pat his rump.

Chaos takes off to the other side of the square and slams directly into a group of people, one of whom is holding a lantern. The lantern goes flying and smashes onto the ground in front of a stout half-timbered house. A wind comes out of nowhere and the tiny flames feeding on the brittle blades of grass immediately blaze into an inferno.

Pandemonium. Villagers run to grab whatever they can to put out the fire. Bright embers rise into a column of smoke, like orange stars in a midnight sky. I take my chance and sprint around to Clara's front door.

I don't ring the bell hanging from the frame. Instead, I try the knob. It turns easily. In one quick movement, I slide right into the entrance hall. It's dark in here, but sconces are burning, creating two small halos of light.

The house is grand, with tapestries and paintings hanging on all the walls and lush carpets laid over oiled wooden floors. I need to find Clara. Alone. And I need to convince her not to give me away and instead come with me to meet Minnie.

It's a huge ask.

I'm not sure where to start. I tiptoe past a carved staircase and peek into the first doorway. A fire roars in the fireplace, illuminating a sitting room. The chairs look like something for royalty, with high, steepled backs and intricately carved armrests. Candelabras sit on side tables, and a simple chandelier hangs from the ceiling. On one of the whitewashed walls are two masks like the one that brought me here. The black and white and red hair hangs in stiff clumps, the wood so worn it shines. One has fat square teeth, while the other sports thin, pointed fangs. The black pools of the empty eye sockets seem to watch me.

I'm about to search further for Clara when a wave of pain nearly knocks me over. A saw to my stomach. A blade to my back. I grip my belly and try to catch my breath as the wave subsides. My throat goes dry. I'm suddenly so hungry, so thirsty. It's unlike anything I've ever experienced.

I hear a noise down the hallway and turn to see a feminine form in the shadows. I think I've found Clara, but when she steps forward into the light, I see it's Virginia who is standing there. I let out a gasp, but she seems unsurprised to find me here. "Oh, my dear Redd! We've been searching everywhere for you, my child. In all the wrong places, I see. From the looks of it, you've either been in the Fire Pit or skinning calves."

"I left. Then came back."

"I'm so very glad you did. I was worried it was something that I'd done."

The taste of her deception does not kill the hunger gnawing at my gut. "Hell, yeah, it was something you did. You drugged me."

"A simple posset to help you sleep—"

"You can cut the bullshit, Virginia." My voice sounds so much stronger than I feel.

The smirk on her face combined with the sudden smell of satisfaction makes me take a harder look at her. She's different. Her hair has gone lackluster and her face is gaunt. She looks like she hasn't eaten in weeks, like a shell of the woman she was yesterday. But it's something else that makes my skin pebble: her birthmark—the crescent moon that resembles mine—is smudged, the paint a long shadow under her jaw. And then I look at her eyes. Really look. They're brown.

Agnes said Virginia's eyes were blue.

I put a hand to the wall to steady myself. This woman is not Virginia.

She never was.

Even the hunger and pain can't stop my rage from building. "Who are you?" I whisper.

The front door flies open. The smell of smoke and rot roll into the hallway, along with Clara's voice, "Mother! The river has run to blood—" At the sight of me, her mouth drops and her eyes widen. "OH!"

The woman I thought was Virginia sneers. "The Dare girl is back, Clara."

"You're Clara's mom," I say, just to get it clear in my own head. But even though I'm reeling, it makes sense. Too much sense.

She lifts her chin. "Joyce Archer."

This whole village played me. And I was so desperate for explanations, so desperate for family, that I let them. Gladly.

I swallow; it's sharp as razors. "Is Virginia even real?"

"Aye. That she is. And she is your mother." Joyce chuckles and grins. "Although I thought my performance was well done."

Her eyes flick to Clara. "Give word that Redd is here."

As Clara reaches for the door, I say, "I came back for you, Clara. For Minnie. Your birth mother. She couldn't get into Eden. She tried. She just wants to see you. That's all she's ever wanted since they stole you from her."

Clara hesitates and I see her chest rise as she pulls in a long breath. She looks at Joyce.

"Clara!" Joyce snaps. "Sound the alarm. Now!"

"Minnie is waiting on the other side of the tunnel," I croak.

Clara's gaze shifts to me. "Run!"

45

Redd

Eden: Present Day

I shove Joyce aside to get to the back door, then crash into the backyard with no idea where to go, just away from everyone. Black smoke replaces the usual glittery mist as fire makes its way around the village. Here, it's dry kindling just waiting to ignite. Dead rose bushes, brown grass, skeletal stalks. I head for a break in the tangle of thorns, but there's a loud bark and Evil comes bounding right over the bushes. His massive paws slam into my chest and I fall backwards, the breath knocked out of me. Before he can pin me down, I roll to the side and scramble away. But Fury is suddenly there, eyes blazing, drool hanging in thick strings from his maw.

Now Joyce and several others are closing in. I'm blocked on all sides. I knew it was risky coming back. Even so, I really wasn't expecting to be caught only minutes after my arrival.

The only thing I can rely on to help me is my anger. And seeing everyone surround me makes me furious. That ire draws the canine Fury to my side, now guarding me instead of attacking. I focus the last bit of strength I have on destroying whatever I can. The windows of the house shatter, splinters of glass slicing my skin, in sharp, stinging bites. But it's nothing compared to what the others feel, as they're a lot closer to the house. They scream as glass showers over them.

Chaos tears through the yard, giving me an out. Now I've got two hounds watching my back. I take my chance and run, jumping over hedges and squeezing between houses to follow the winding path out of the village. Common sense tells me to run back to the pond and get the hell out of Eden—again. But when I want to turn in that direction, a wall of fire stops me. Yesterday I could have probably walked through the flames unscathed. Today, just the heat from the blaze is enough to make me back off. Today, I can get hurt here.

So I head the other way. The grass is dry and crackly under my feet. The smoke spreads, creating a sea of black in front and behind me. Ash falls from the sky like sooty, gray snowflakes. It becomes nearly impossible to take a good breath.

Behind me, I hear shouts, the thud of footsteps.

I cough and wheeze, zig-zagging to lose my pursuers, running blindly in the smoke. That's when the ground turns to jelly beneath my feet. I try to catch myself, move, but wet sand weighs me down, and I sink first to my knees, then to my waist, then up to my chest. It's like drowning in a cold vat of oatmeal.

I struggle, feeling desperately about me for anything to grab on to. There's a dry clump of grass just within reach. I'm just about to grasp it when I feel a slick tentacle wrap around my ankle. A wave of despair washes over me. It's useless. I'll never get out of this quagmire. I'll never get out of Eden.

I start to cry.

The air next to me shimmers and the Master is suddenly standing over me, hand out.

"Ah, Redd. Feeling sorry for yourself?" He smiles, his lips in a perfect upturn. He's wearing a simple band as a mask again, but no shirt or shoes. Almost like my tears tore him away from reading a novel on the couch or napping in a hammock. "Need a hand?"

I hate to give in, but I nod. He pulls me out just before the sands reach my chin. I crawl onto the dry ground, sandy muck dripping from every part of me. The misery I felt only a moment ago lifts. Now I'm annoyed. And angry.

"I know who you are," I say, wiping my eyes clear of tears. "You're the Devil."

His laugh echoes as if we're in a cavern. "Ah! I can keep no secrets from you!"

I don't like the tone of his voice. It's mocking. And yet something about him draws me in. Makes me want to approach him, curl up in his arms like a baby.

"Up!" he orders. Without even thinking about it, I obey, back on my feet.

He sweeps an arm out and the air clears. In the distance, orange flames dance through the village, a brightness in the darkening night. "That is your doing?"

"Yeah. It is. And God help you, if you hurt me—" I start.

His laugh rings out into the air again. That sweet, smooth laugh. "God? You speak of God as if he would protect you."

He turns slightly then, flashing me the thick, knotted lines of skin along his back. "He did this to me. I was a pulpy mess for hundreds of years before it finally healed. And even here, in my own personal paradise, the marks never disappear."

I see the bits of bone poking through his skin, am held captive by the stain of scars there. Horror loosens my muscles. "I'm sure you deserved it," I say, my voice a whisper.

His entire body stiffens. He blinks behind the mask, and suddenly his eyes are glowing hot embers. His hands bunch into large fists, the knuckles white. When he speaks, his voice is low and warped, like someone's slowed down a recording.

"I deserved it? You know nothing of me. Nothing! You think I am but darkness, yet I was born of light. Circumstance brought me to this position. I keep order in the world; I take loathsome souls and I punish them. You may not think it a noble employment, yet it is essential. Regardless, I had no choice. When the Good Lord rips off your wings, you can no longer fly!"

My heart rate kicks up and I try to keep my body from shaking.

"Did I deserve it? No more than you deserve to die for the village. And yet you shall. Because that is the way of things—bargains struck, pacts made, loyalty lost, and lives broken. You are like me, little Redd. You will get the opportunity to suffer for sin. Lucky for you, the suffering will be over quickly enough. I have been steeped in it for centuries."

He steps towards me, the heat of his body practically scorching me.

"All the evil, all the pain inflicted in your name all over the world—" I start.

But he cuts me off, his dark eyes blazing. "If that is your argument, then you must confront God as well. Many more evil deeds are committed in his name than in mine."

He shakes his head. "The longer one stays in the dark, the harder it is to adjust to the light. You believe yourself so righteous. Yet where do *you* come from, Redd? Do not judge without first examining your own soul."

His words make my stomach queasy. Does the fact that I was born in Eden make me bad?

Does it make me evil?

No. *No.*

We glare at each other, and I feel my own fear and rage build up inside me. His eyes stay on mine as he steps forward. Terror crawls over me, making my skin itch. I don't move a muscle, but I feel my power building and building. It crackles in the air between us.

"So unfair, Redd. So very unfair. The villagers cannot use their magic at this time. Neither shall you." He gives me a satisfied grin and snaps his fingers. With another laugh, he disappears.

My power disappears with him.

I try to gather my fury into a weapon, concentrating as hard as I can. Nothing. Absolutely nothing.

Then the back of my neck prickles and I know someone is behind me. I swallow and turn around.

A group of monsters stand only inches from me. The tallest one leers, his filed teeth and crooked nose straight out of a nightmare. I step back. But before I can go any further, he whips out a hand and grips my arm so tightly it throbs. "No more running," he says, and drags me away.

46

John

Eden: Present Day

I am locked in the cage in the root cellar, my wrists in manacles, my arm a fevered, blistering wound. I stand on the lumpy mattress to look out the tiny window set into the dirt-packed wall. A blaze rages through the village, devouring the dry grass, hugging leafless trees, and licking the timbered houses. There is much shouting and screaming...along with happy barks from Chaos. Twisting my neck to get a different view, I see that down the alley, little Magdelyn Pratt is crying. From the looks of things, her hands are burnt. She's never lived through a Harvest. No one ever taught her not to touch fire.

I keep my eyes on the scene outside the window, searching for answers as to how my plan with the flower went so awry. Why is the Council resisting planting them? I cannot believe they'd rather sacrifice another child than attempt to cross into the Beyond.

The scrape of a bolt sounds, and the main door opens. Thomas comes into the small room. The sight of him brings me hope that I'll get answers so I barely notice that his eyes are a painful shade of red, or his face paler than I've ever seen it.

I pelt him with questions. "Tom! What's happening? Is it true they're preparing the ceremony? I must go! I must stop them from sacrificing little Clarence—"

"The Hewett babe is not in danger," he says, his voice wooden. "Redd's back. They're chasing her."

The shock renders me silent for a moment. But then question after question rolls off my tongue, "What? Why in Lucifer's name would she have come back? She's not yet in the Council's clutches, then? She's running?"

Thomas has none of the answers.

"Then how about a key to this cage?" If anyone knows where an extra key is hidden, it is Thomas.

But he shakes his head. "There is only one."

It is a blade to the heart. "And Grandfather has it."

He swallows hard. "John, I heard."

"You mean with the Council? You eavesdropped? Then perhaps you've heard something more that—"

"We're not brothers." He cuts me off.

A jolt of panic shoots through me. Devil's curse, I'd forgotten Joyce said that amidst the whole mess. We've never told him he was taken from the Beyond. Now I truly look at him, take in the red eyes, the pale face. Despite his lanky form, he looks tiny and vulnerable standing before me.

"Oh, Tom," I try to reach for him, but the cage and my manacles hinder my effort. "You are my brother. Blood makes no difference."

His lip trembles. "Then why would you offer to sacrifice yourself instead of little Clarence Hewett? Do I mean nothing to you?"

I'm taken aback. "You mean everything to me. Everything."

"If I mean everything, then why would you willingly die? Why willingly leave me alone? Your life is not worth less than anyone else's."

"You don't understand. I failed—"

"You did not fail, John. You succeeded. I knew you would." He's crying in earnest now, tears turning his eyelashes into auburn spikes. The sight of it makes my heart ache. He swipes at his nose and frowns. "You do not have to die for me. For the Hewett babe. For Redd. For anyone. If you truly see me as a brother, do not leave me. Do not give up now."

I think of my parents. How they gave up and left me behind. I will not do that to Thomas. I will not leave him. And I will not give up. We can create a new Eden on the outside. I only need to bring the Council to their senses.

I begin to kick at the cage. I must get out of here. I must stop everything. The Council must listen. The villagers must listen. They *must*.

But no matter how hard I try, there is no way out of this cage. Not unless...

"Tom! Go get my backpack. It has my mask inside!" The mask still has power, even during the Harvest. It can free me from this jail.

With Thomas gone, I pace. I will not let Redd die. And I will get us to the Beyond. The Council cannot deny us all the chance to leave Eden. Do they truly believe it is too great a risk? Redd can make the flower grow. Why sacrifice her when she is much more useful to them alive than dead?

When Tom opens the door once again, black tendrils of smoke enter the cellar with him. "Soon everything will burn," he says. "You may not be safe. Even here."

I would not die. But I would suffer. If the burn on my arm is any indication of the pain, I'd much rather not.

Tom begins to lift my mask out of the bag, but only gets it halfway before he stops. "The hair is stuck in the closing," he says, fiddling with the zipper of the inside pocket. As he does so, Persuasion slithers out of the backpack.

"Come, boy! We'll make them listen," I say. The snakelet makes his way into the cage. I squat and pick him up. He settles onto his perch behind my ear.

Thomas is still trying to free the mask from the zipper.

Impatience makes me stroke Persuasion's scales and bark, "Hurry, Tom!"

The snakelet must be gaining in power, because Thomas tugs so hard at the zipper that when it finally loosens, both the mask and the bag go soaring. Thomas scrambles over to pick up the mask. Instead of running it back to me, however, he freezes.

"Tom! Come on! Slip it under here," I say, indicating a small gap at the bottom of the cage between the floor and the iron grid.

Instead, he bends down, picking up something off the ground. He holds it up. It is the secret Griffen Jones left with me. The glossy shattered shell reflects the orange flames outside the small window.

"You've a secret?" Thomas asks.

"Not mine. I've no idea what it holds. It's broken," I say quickly. "Come! Give me the mask."

Thomas slides the mask towards me, but his focus is on the splintered secret. With deft hands, he fits the broken pieces together. Just as my fingers curl around my mask, he gasps.

"What is it?"

"The secret...it's Eleanor Dare's." He opens his hands to reveal it.

It explains everything.

47

Eleanor

Eden: 19 years ago

For hundreds of years, Secrecy squirreled away each confidence we gave her, one by one. Thousands upon thousands of nuggets were buried in stashes all over Eden. The creature was not careless, so sometimes I wondered if she did not have Chaos' taste for bedlam, as every fifty years or so a villager would find a lone kernel of truth. It would be something directly affecting that person—a cheating lover's lie, a jealous friend's gibe, a sneaky child's fib. Just enough to sow discord, but never enough to shatter lives. For fun, parents told their children bedtime stories, weaving all sorts of fantastic tales about secrets found and lives turned upside-down, but they were just that: stories.

Until one of my secrets got found.

One evening, I came home after an afternoon of exploring the newest part of Eden—a glacier of blue ice—to see Gossips fluttering about the house, trying to get in through the cracks in the windows. I regularly shook out our clothing and emptied our cupboards to keep the disgusting little moths from hiding in our cottage. Luckily, the vile things had poor hearing and poor eyesight, so when they went on to other homes, any rumors they carried they often got wrong. However, it was no good to take chances. But there, along with the Gossips was Fury, scratching at the door and whining.

My first thought was of Agnes, both because she may have brought something of interest to the Gossips and because Fury had become something of a friend of hers. By now, Agnes was nearing twenty years of age and her relationship to the village had changed. She'd been inducted as a scout a few months earlier. From the moment I'd told her the truth about her past, she wanted to know more about the Beyond. The Council was tight-lipped about the details of how to survive on the outside, so any unauthorized visits were thwarted. That meant to get out, Agnes needed to be a scout. How she managed to convince the Council to make her one, I did not know, though it may have pleased them to know she would suffer in the Beyond. She had not been chosen for scouting at birth like the others, so the pain was likely near unbearable. Yet Agnes was determined.

The Council sent her out into the other world to do their bidding. To take items. And to take children. Even before a new child was introduced to the village, I already knew the days that Agnes had taken a child. Her face was ashen, her hands shook, her light dimmed. Yet it was a means to an end: she intended to learn the secret of survival outside Eden. She intended to leave the village for good one day. It both pained and gladdened me.

Yet she did not know *how*. Several scouts had attempted—and failed—to plant the Eternity Flower in the

Beyond. At first, I thought this was a lie of the Council's making. But Agnes herself had tried to no avail. It needed the Devil's hand for planting.

When I asked the Master to have pity upon the younger generation, to help the flower grow outside Eden, he laughed in my face. "*Now* you have pity on the younger generation? Nay, I will not help. This is your blunder, not mine. Acts have consequences."

Indeed, they did. It was not something I was likely to forget.

Agnes shared stories of the Beyond with Virginia, William, and me. It was strictly forbidden for scouts to do so, and were she caught, she would have spent time in the Cave of Dread, the Garden, or perhaps even a night in Terror's nest.

"They have people who are elders," she told us, "but whose faces tell the story of their years. They're beautiful. Frail, but beautiful."

I remembered the way skin wrinkled and thinned when it was old in the Beyond. No one there had described it as beautiful. But it was natural. And that in itself was a kind of beauty.

Agnes brought back miraculous items from the outside. Some were strictly for the Council, others she snuck in. She told us of radios, telephones, and items that played music directly into one's ears. Like the other scouts before her, she showed them to the Council, who attempted to recreate them without success, as our conjuring was limited. The telephones and radios did not work here, as whatever connected them to each other did not pass through the barrier to Eden. But the boxes of music, watches, and even cameras worked in Eden until the batteries went dry. The camera was what intrigued me most, so she gave me one, the photographs coming out of the machine the moment you took them. It was magic like I had never seen. Strange and uncanny and truly miraculous.

As long as I kept others from seeing the camera, I could keep it. So I used it. And loved it. I had pictures of us wrapped in linen and hidden in the back of a drawer. I would pull them out occasionally to remind myself that life in Eden had its good moments. That I had people I loved.

William adored the clothing Agnes brought, though he could not leave the house in anything but his homemade breeches. But while he slept, he wore pants from the Beyond, made from a stretchy material, soft and light. Virginia hoarded the writing and drawing pencils Agnes gave her. She sketched so often that the pencils were practically nubs.

Therefore, I imagined the Gossips and Fury were now at our doorstep because Agnes had been found out sneaking things to us. My heart raced and my breath caught. I ran to the cottage, shooing the silvery moths away, tears already blurring my vision, imagining Agnes' slender wrists being clamped into manacles.

But what greeted me as I burst through the door was infinitely worse.

Virginia sat near the hearth, her eyes a violent red from crying, her cheeks blotchy, and a furious downturn to her lips. There, in her hands, was one of Secrecy's cache.

Fury had bounded through the door when I opened it, and now settled at Virginia's feet, foamy drool dripping from his maw.

"Virginia?"

She turned to me, then looked at the shell in her hand. With a flick of her wrist, she rolled the nugget towards me, across the dining table. I caught it before it fell, the golden husk already cracked open to reveal the meaty fruit inside.

Devil have mercy. It was a very old secret. Four hundred years old.

The secret was from 1604—after the Powells had shriveled into living corpses out in the Beyond. After Virginia and William had raced back to Eden with my own withering body from our attempt to escape to Roanoke. This secret was the nugget of the Council's discussion that night. The decision that had shaped our entire existence here.

Warmth spread out from my hand up my arm and into my chest and head. There, in a flash of a vision, my own secret was spread before me:

The Council met in an upstairs room of the Devil's cathedral behind a heavy, wooden door. I sat at the long cherrywood table, watching the reflection of candle flames dance in the oiled wood. Dyonis brought the meeting to order, then all eyes turned to me as I had been the one to go out of Eden and come back.

I gave no preamble. I had the answers we were seeking. "When we made the pact with the Master, that night he gave us a special drink laced with Contagion. It has bound us here. But the children are not bound. Nor are they part of the pact. They never have been."

The moment Lucifer had put the cup to my lips upon my return to Eden, I understood. The memory of that fateful day when I'd drowned Walter to save Virginia had come back to me. He'd refused Virginia the brew he'd forced upon me. At the time, his words meant little, but now I understood. 'Even I am not so cruel as to bind a child to Eden for something a parent chose.'

The candle flames flickered and swayed as we discussed this. "They could leave," said Emme. I lifted my gaze to see color fill her cheeks. "William, Robert, Ambrose, Catherine, Ann, Brigit"—here she caught my eye—"and Virginia."

An ache filled my chest, a mixture of hope and terror.

"So my Walter and the others...they died for what?" Dyonis' voice was thick with hatred. In the past few years, he'd taken to decorating his ears with the most volatile of Malice pearls—a red resentment in the right and a black rancor in the left. I'd heard, too, that not only had Evil become his familiar, but that Dyonis also had a soft spot for Grudges, those slick, wriggly creatures that latched themselves to the skin.

I looked around at the others. They, too, had changed and hardened since arriving in Eden. I knew I had. A sticky mass of black tar filled the place where our souls used to be.

"They died for nothing." Dyonis sneered.

"Nay, not for nothing," I said. Torment's paw slid down my collarbone and I stroked the soft fur. "They died for us."

Twenty-six adults. Twenty-six of us had made the pact with the Devil.

Over fifteen years, five children had been sacrificed to keep twenty-six of us alive.

And now...now two adults were dead.

Twenty-four of us left to save or let die.

Seven children—a few of whom were now adults in their own right—who were still here in Eden. Seven children who did not need saving. They only needed letting go.

The question was...would we let them go?

We were quiet a moment, contemplating this. Dyonis leaned forward. "All this time, we've been gnashing our teeth, lamenting our predicament. Yet there is good in what we have. We have yet to acknowledge that. We live fully. Healthily. We could let the young ones go through that tunnel. Let them live pitifully short lives where, with each passing year, their body deteriorates. Mayhap 'tis what we should do, were we still God-fearing souls. Yet we are not. And let us not pretend that the world outside is heaven."

"I, for one, wonder if heaven truly exists," I said.

"We had thought it here when we first arrived," said Emme, a wistful tone in her voice.

"Until the sacrifices." I ran a hand over my face, pained by the memory.

"Aye, the sacrifices." Christopher Cooper's brow pleated. "Were we to send the youth back into the world, they would not need to sacrifice their children as we must do here."

Emme nodded. "And—"

Christopher held up a hand to silence her and continued, "Yet they would face hardship. Hunger. War. Pain. Illness. Their children may die of the pox, or the plague, or of fever. Is it not worth the price—for every single one of us—to live eternally? To be young and healthy and never ill?"

Jonathon stroked his beard "Aye. 'Tis not simply to save our own lives that we sacrifice to Eden. 'Tis to give this gift to all."

"What you say has merit." Elizabeth wore a delicate shawl woven by Enticements. She tugged it tighter. "One sacrifice for the good of many."

"One for the good of many," Dyonis repeated. "The price of life is a soul."

Emme shifted in her chair. "Are we all in agreement, then, that 'tis better for the children to live here in Eden than to send them back through the tunnel and to the...the...Beyond?"

I shook my head, astonished that their opinions of this place had changed. "Are you telling me that you see Eden as a gift now instead of a curse?"

Jonathon shrugged. Emme and Elizabeth looked at each other. Christopher nodded. And Dyonis simply narrowed his eyes at me.

A bitter laugh stuck at the back of my throat. "You've shunned me. You've despised me. You've made my and Virginia's life hell. And all this time you've been thankful for landing in Eden?"

"Oh, Eleanor, you're mistaken," said Dyonis, his voice soft and calm. He fingered the Malice pearl hanging from his right earlobe. "No one here is thankful for what you've done. And no one here will ever forget that 'twas you who forced our hand. We are simply doing our best to deal with the losing cards you've given us."

He gave me a smile that turned my blood to ice.

"As I said, there is good in what we have." He then turned to the others. "We must keep the children here, or there will be no future for anyone in Eden. Winefrid Powell is no longer among us. Let us hope her offspring are as fertile as she."

"And what do you propose we tell the villagers?" Christopher lifted a bushy eyebrow. "I am not certain the truth will do."

"The truth most certainly will not do," scoffed Jonathan.

"We tell them we believe the adverse effects simply happen more slowly in the young. But that there is no avoiding it," Emme *suggested. "That even the children must be wary. To leave is certain death."*

"So we lie," I scoffed.

"'Tis not necessarily a lie, Eleanor." Elizabeth frowned. "They would die, eventually. And they could be affected by leaving. We do not know."

"We know. And the youth, they've been there. They know."

"Then what do you propose? That we let them choose? Do you want Virginia to leave you behind, only to die in six months from a rotten tooth?"

Elizabeth knew well how to dig under the crusty scab I called my heart. As much as I wanted her free of this place, the vision of Virginia out there alone, possibly in danger, or ill... It gave me pause. What, in the end, was best for my Virginia? Was it eternal life in Eden or was it freedom from Eden for a few years before natural death?

And did I want to live forever if she was not by my side?

By now my pulse was drumming in my ears.

"What if..." Dyonis cleared his throat and tilted his head. "What if we made the lie true?"

Emme frowned. "How?"

There was a moment of silence, a simple beat, when understanding reached us all.

"Ah," breathed Jonathon at the same time Elizabeth said, "Oh."

"The Contagion may not work the same if we give it," Christopher pointed out. "We're not the Master."

"But well worth the try," responded Jonathon.

"Nay. We cannot," I said. "'Tis unconscionable. 'Tis one thing to lie, but this... We must give them the choice to stay or leave."

"And if we do? If one child leaves here, then another, then another? If we have no more children to give? Where do you see yourself in five years, Eleanor?" Dyonis asked. "I'll tell you where—in hell. I agree with you on one thing, there is no heaven, at least not for us. The moment we cease to exist here, we'll find ourselves in a darker place. We'll be those poor souls the Master complains about. The ones he tortures so thoroughly that even his celestial body becomes fatigued."

For the second time, silence blanketed the room, though this time that silence was thick with fear. We'd all seen the Devil come back from months away, shattered and moody, horror clinging to him like a ghostly cloak. Whatever he had seen, wherever he had been, we wanted no part of it.

"It comes down to this," Emme said, her voice soft, then gaining in intensity. "We can allow the children to leave, condemning ourselves and the other adults to hell. Twenty-four souls we'd condemn. Or we can continue as we have been. A child here and there to leave their vitality to Eden. At least those souls are spared eternal torment. They go back to God."

"Do they? Are we certain of that?" I asked. "Or has the Master been fooling us?"

That opened the floor to shouts and insults disguising sheer panic. If we wanted to maintain the tiniest bit of decency, we had to believe what we'd been told.

If so, then perhaps the cruelest option was to let the children go.

What was I to do? Could I acquiesce and still somehow save Virginia from Eden? Did I want to?

"So we agree?" Dyonis leveled his gaze at each of us, one by one, until he had our assent. "No more discussion is needed."

Just then, there was scampering on the roof tiles. Secrecy's brown-gray head poked through the one unglazed square of the easternmost stained-glass window. She gathered our secret into a tight ball and carried it away in her cheek.

Dyonis stood. "Good. I'll call the village together. We'll make our own truth out of Contagion and feed it to them in the ale."

I set the golden nugget down on the dining table and felt shame wash over me. The Contagion we'd given them had worked. It grew inside them like a voracious cancer when in the Beyond. Yet all traces of disease disappeared in Eden.

Even worse, what this secret did not reveal was what we had done so many years later. We mixed the Contagion we gathered with varying amounts of nectar from the Eternity Flower, hoping to find the perfect solution for our problem: we needed to slow the effect of the Contagion in the youth if they stepped out of Eden.

Slow it, not cure it.

Baptisms were nothing but the Council giving each babe their dose. Less for future scouts, more for the others.

I looked up to see fury in Virginia's eyes. It did not matter that she did not know it all. She now knew enough.

Virginia and I had had our share of fights. I dare say she hated me when she was an adolescent. But never had I felt the absolute revulsion that came through her voice now.

"You poisoned us." Her words were slow, each one punctuated with a pause. "All of us who'd been children when we arrived here...we could have been free of the pact hundreds of years ago. But you poisoned us to keep us here. So the elders could live."

"Not only so we could live," I said carefully. "So *you* could as well. And if we hadn't...if we died...we'd go to hell. You've heard the Master's stories. You've seen his face when he comes back from there. You wouldn't want us elders in hell, would you?"

She scoffed. "Do not ask what you do not want an honest answer to, Mama."

A lone Gossip had made it inside, and as it fluttered in front of me, I clapped, flattening its body between the palms of my hands. The gesture wouldn't kill the creature, but it would wreck its ability to spread rumors.

I wiped its tiny form and the residual wing powder from my hands, then pulled a chair near to hers. When I sat, our knees nearly touched. The fire was roaring, the heat of it uncomfortable. Sweat immediately formed a slick on my forehead and a stream down my spine. I took off my coif and patted my face with it.

"You would be long dead, Virginia, had you not stayed in Eden. By now even your bones would be dust."

She did not look at me, instead keeping her eyes on the flames. "You did not give me—nor any of us—the opportunity to choose."

"I did try to tell you. I did! I tried to warn you not to drink the Contagion! Secrecy held my tongue." I reached out to wrap my fingers around hers, but she jerked them away. "Do you remember? At the Powells' remembrance ceremony? I held on to your cup? The Master watched over you as I went to get you some water instead of the infected ale. But you drank it while I was gone. 'Tis he who's to blame."

"Oh, come now, Mama! You've never trusted the Devil. Do not expect me to believe you did that once."

"Aye! Aye, I did!" I was nearly shouting. "I was addled at the time. Deception breathed upon me and—"

"Enough!" She ripped her gaze from the fire to blink at me, her eyes so bright with hatred they rivaled the flames.

I dragged my tongue over my lips, which felt dry as sandpaper, and lowered my voice. "I was going to tell you so you could have a choice. But then...it was too late. You'd already drunk the ale."

"I could have gone with Samuel," she breathed, her words catching. "We could have been together."

The screech of my chair legs on the wooden planks cut through the cottage as I stood. I could scarcely believe what I was hearing. After four-hundred years, Virginia was still harping on about that simpleton, Samuel? For the love of Lucifer. She had a husband who cared for her—nay, who worshiped her—and yet her thoughts still went to that skinny fifteen-year-old child?

I needed perry. Something strong to ease my nerves. I went to the cupboard and poured myself a glass of the pear liqueur, relishing the burn at the back of my throat when it went down. "You were children, Virginia. He was a *child*! He was not worthy of you. Had you given him a fortnight in the Beyond, you would have realized that. You would have been together, aye, but you would have been *dying* together from some horrific disease.

You're too young to remember life outside of Eden, but the illness, the fear of death, the suffering..."

I poured myself another glass, the bottle clinking against its rim, my hands were shaking so much. "Besides, you have a good man now. Be thankful. What you had with Samuel was not love. Not at all."

She turned on me then, letting out a scream so guttural and loud that it even drowned out Fury's happy howl. She stood and ripped the nut from the table, throwing it to the floor and stomping on it until the shell was fractured into pieces. She kicked the secret across the room and the broken shell fell through the floorboards.

Had she not done that, she could have shown it to others. But now it was unlikely she would fish it out and piece it back together before Secrecy came to hide it away once again. The rest of the village would be none the wiser unless the words came from her own tongue. And no one would believe a Dare over the Council.

I'm ashamed to admit what a relief that was for once.

But the relief was short-lived, as my own pain from Virginia's agony and anger replaced it. Tears rolled down my face as well as hers. As she yanked bundles of herbs from the ceiling, threw down the paintings from the walls, knocked over the cupboard of crockery, I put my hands together.

"I beg of you, Virginia. Forgive me. I love you. Everything I've done, I've done out of love for you."

She wrenched a sconce from the wall and hurled it at me. Her breaths were ragged now, her cheeks a violent pink, her hair a tangle of wheat-blonde strands. "Stop using your love for me to excuse your selfish, vile acts!"

I sensed the prick of Torment's claws gripping tighter on my shoulders. "What can I do, Virginia? Anything, I pray you. Tell me! I never wanted to hurt you."

"'Tis too late, Mama." She grabbed her cloak from the peg on the wall and tied the ribbon at the neck. As she stepped out the door, she said, "From here on out, you will no longer dictate what I can and cannot do. From here on out, you will no longer dictate who I can love or cannot love, nor how I do so."

A leaden weight filled my chest at her words. I called after her, but she ran down the hill and away from me.

48

John

Eden: Present Day

I stare down at the open shell of Eleanor's secret, unable to move for the ache in my chest. It is the worst kind of pain I've ever experienced, and I wonder why they have not found a more violent term for it. "Heartbroken" is too gentle.

I fear if I look up, I will fall apart.

Grandfather and the Council did not simply betray me today. They betrayed the village centuries ago. And they've been lying to us, murdering their own blood, ever since.

They never wanted another choice. They wanted us to stay stuck in Eden forever. So they could live. While their children died.

They do not love us. They only love themselves.

"John," Thomas says quietly. "Do not give up."

Finally, I look up and lift my mask to my face. Its power is unchanged. The cage and my manacles both click open. "I won't."

49

Eleanor

Eden: 19 years ago

Virginia said no more about our fight. It was as if it never happened. Fool that I was, I believed this meant I did not have to worry. That she had done nothing rash.

Life returned to normal. Weeks passed where Virginia and I sketched in the meadow or played backgammon or made liquor from the nectar of the Eternity Flower or lazed about with Sloth stretched out on our knees. Agnes was in and out, sometimes walking with me and keeping watch as I took photographs, other times forcing us up to the snowy plateau on the mountain where we made snow sculptures in the cool mouth of a cave. William spent his time whittling, working on the farm, and laughing at the pub on the square with his friends. Evenings, the four of us played cards or dice in front of the hearth. Sometimes, we locked the cottage door, fastened the shutters, and listened to the little box of music Agnes had snuck in. We were a family. And for pockets of time, it was enough.

But, in Eden, nothing is ever truly enough.

I hadn't paid attention to Virginia's changes.

I'd been distracted, as Agnes—who for the past few weeks had been happier than I'd ever seen her, despite her onerous tasks as a scout—was suddenly moody and withdrawn. She would not tell me who, but it was a man. Of course it was. Nothing like a man to ruin a woman's good humor. It had taken me decades to realize how little we needed the male sex. And in this place where pregnancy was a curse rather than a blessing, we needed them even less. But Agnes had yet to come to this realization. I spent days coddling her, making her praline pies or warm tea or telling her stories from my long-ago youth. I'd been so focused on Agnes that I hadn't seen the warning signs coming from Virginia as to what was about to transpire.

It was autumn, a beautiful season in Eden, when the leaves on the trees turned red and gold and amber but did not fall until the snow came. I'd collected sap from the forest, which I boiled down to a sweet liquid that was perfect for making candied pecans or drizzling over puffed cakes. I set a cauldron of it to boil, the steam thick as fog in the kitchen. William was out playing cudgels with Ambrose and his other friends. Agnes and Virginia had been upstairs in Agnes' bed chamber and then the bathing room all morning, their whispering more frenzied than the fluttering of Braggarts' wings. They'd ignored my calls to come to the kitchen to help.

I sat on the log bench in front of the cottage overlooking the village. Tendrils of steam escaping from the windows made Torment's fur stick wetly to my neck. I pried him from me, enjoying the cool slip of air on my skin, and embroidered flowers onto the sleeves of my favorite chemise. Never far, Torment's whimper broke my concentration, and I looked up to see Virginia and Agnes both come out of the cottage and over to me. Virginia held something in her hand. The line between her eyebrows was pronounced, the pout on her lips exaggerated. Agnes looked positively ghastly, her usual glowing skin a dull pallor.

My belly twisted like a screw at the sight of them. What now?

I set down my needle and thread. Torment took it as a sign to return to his regular perch, and within seconds my shoulders felt weighted down once again. "So now you will speak with me?" I grunted. "Agnes, I could have used your help with the syrup. You're the one whose magic works best in the kitchen."

She shrugged. "I've no doubt your syrup will be perfect."

The two of them stood there, in front of me, never quite meeting my gaze. I waited, but when neither moved nor spoke, I barked, "Out with it, then. Why are you both looking so grave?"

Agnes settled down on the bench next to me, Virginia beside her. "We've something to show you," said Agnes. She opened her hand and Virginia gave her the stick she'd been holding. Agnes passed it to me.

I frowned. I turned it around, trying to understand just what it was supposed to be, but without success. It was small and white and had a tiny window with two red lines in it. Something from the Beyond, that was clear. It was made of the hard substance Agnes called plastic. A substance we could not conjure here.

"I'm at a loss. This means nothing to me."

She then tugged a small, flattened box from her skirt pocket. Bold, blue lettering read *Are You Pregnant? Results in Three Minutes or Less.*

I grabbed the edge of the bench, the wood hard and rough under my fingers. Though I was sitting, I felt certain I would tumble over and that the ground beneath my feet would disappear. My breath caught in my lungs and the whole world tilted. "Nay. Nay. What is this?"

"Ginny's with child." Agnes had stopped calling Virginia "mother" years ago, ever since she understood exactly where she'd come from. Instead, she used a familiar form of Virginia's name and it had never seemed out-of-place. But as Agnes said it now, it made Virginia sound like a child herself.

I leaned forward to look at her. She was sitting with her eyes shut tight. Just as when she was young, thinking if you did not see it, it was not true.

I closed my own eyes for a moment. *Please, for the love of Lucifer,* I thought. *Let it not be true.*

"Virginia knows better than to get with child here in Eden," I started, then glared at my daughter. "And she's a four-hundred-year-old woman whose courses slowed a century ago!"

"Slowed, not stopped, Mama." Virginia opened her eyes but did not look at me.

"No other woman in the village over the age of three hundred has gotten with child. Nay. You're saying this"—I held up the white stick— "This...thing knows when a woman is pregnant? How? You got this from the Beyond. 'Tis not to be trusted."

"We can trust it." Agnes swallowed and leaned her head against the cottage wall. "And Ginny has said all the signs are there."

"Nay. I will not put my faith into this odd magic from the Beyond. We must know for certain. And here, there is only one way to do so." I steeled myself and stood, gritting my teeth as the world tilted once more. "Agnes, prepare a basket. Virginia, grab a blanket. We're going on an outing. A family picnic. Nothing that seems out of the ordinary."

Ten minutes later, the three of us headed towards the Fire Pit, the autumn sun unusually hot upon our heads and backs. Once we'd set the blanket down on the lowest part of the hill, not far from the pond, and placed our bread and cheeses out for show, we searched the surroundings to make sure we were alone.

Virginia stripped down to her shift and, knife in hand, waded into the water. The orange glow illuminated the pond under the shadows of the trees, Virginia's legs a white haze below the surface.

Agnes and I sat on the blanket, our elbows hooked. My breath came quick and short. A sheen of sweat spread across my forehead.

"What is Ginny doing? How will we know?" Agnes whispered.

"She is giving Eden a taste. We'll see if its appetite is whetted or not."

"That makes little sense."

As Virginia brought the tip of the blade to the skin on her inner arm, I explained, "Virginia will feed Eden her blood. If she is not pregnant, her blood will spill and do nothing more than drip into the pond. But if she is with child, Eden will taste and enjoy, even though it is not currently hungry." I tried to keep my voice even. "Eden may even lick the plate."

Virginia dragged the knife downward, lengthwise from her wrist to her elbow. A curtain of blood cascaded out of her arm, falling into the water at her feet.

My heart pounded, sweat now stinging my eyes. Virginia stood, arm out, watching her skin knit together as the scarlet liquid spread before her.

Suddenly, the water itself rose up all around her and yanked her down. Bubbles frothed at the surface where she'd been, but everything else was calm.

"Nay!" Agnes screamed, about to run to the Fire Pit.

But I pulled her back. "The wound is healed. There's no more blood to taste and Virginia herself is no infant. Eden has no use for her. Like I said, Eden is but licking the plate."

The pond heaved forward, spitting Virginia upon the bank. She coughed and sputtered, orange bits of algae stuck in her hair. Both Agnes and I ran to her, assuring she was well.

Her face was pasty. Her body shook. Her blue eyes were full to the rim with tears.

"Satan's scourge," I said as I took her into my arms, my heart nothing but an ache inside my chest. "You're with child."

The walk back to the cottage was silent. Virginia shivered the whole way despite the warm air.

Once we were inside, I went straight for the bottle of perry. I poured the diluted liquor into glasses and set them out on the table.

Seeing as the rules of Eden were different inside the womb, we had a window of opportunity to change things. If the pregnancy was new enough, it could be ended. "There is a brew we can make to rid yourself of—" I started.

"Nay!" Virginia snapped her head up. "This babe will grow to term."

"And then what, Virginia? The Fire Pit?" I shook my head. "You do not understand how horrible it is to live with that kind of death upon your hands. And here, in Eden, Satan makes sure that guilt never fades."

"But perhaps the baby will not be slated for sacrifice," Agnes said. "Perhaps he or she will grow to live a thousand years. George Harvie and Margrit Spendlove are set to have a child soon—"

I scoffed. "Oh, Agnes. Dyonis' grandchild? Nay. That child will not be chosen over Virginia's. This is what Dyonis has been waiting for. This is what the *entire village* has been waiting for. We are the only family who has yet to lose one of their own. And if Eden were already sated, I wouldn't put it past Dyonis and the Council to cull every Eternity Flower in Eden to force the Harvest."

Virginia shook her head. "The Master will not allow it. He loves me."

Even after all these years, Virginia's blindness to the Devil's evil surprised me. "Do you truly believe he loves you so much he'd save a baby of yours?"

"He saved *me* when I was a baby." Desperation thickened her voice.

"He did not save you! *I* did!" I shouted.

I took a deep breath, trying to calm my pounding heart. "Think, Virginia. The Master may want to put that infant into the Pit even more, solely because it is yours. Because we are of the same lineage. Have you thought of that?"

Virginia's skin paled even further. "Nay. Nay he—"

Agnes cut in. "He is the Devil, Ginny. You always seem to forget that. Despite the pain he causes."

"We needn't decide what to do today. We have months." Virginia's voice was barely above a whisper.

"Goes faster than you can imagine," I said.

"I pray you, Mama. Say nothing of this to William. Not yet."

I nodded. I could give her that.

Silence rose like dough in the room, the yeasty mass of it nearly choking us. But we were all thinking the same thing: how in Satan's sullied name could we save this babe?

50

Redd

Eden: Present Day

Creatures form a semi-circle around me, each demonic face contorted in hatred. In desperation. In hope. Long, yellowed teeth poke from black gaps of mouths and stiff, matted hair tops wide cliffs of brown foreheads. Their bodies are covered in shaggy fur, the stink of wool and sweat and evil coming off them. Above them, the air twists and bends like a warped mirror, as if the power of their combined dark intentions is so intense it is almost visible. A sharp nail of fear pierces my chest.

"'Tis your moment, child," the one who grips my arm says. His voice makes every hair on my body stand at attention.

A mask. He's wearing a mask. But it seems so real, despite the crooked nose and the sheep's fur for hair and the fat teeth filed to sharp points. It's transformed into so much more. The man wearing it is now a monster. An evil, angry beast.

A different monster, one with a fanged mouth stretching from ear to ear, growls, "She will save us all!"

The invisible blanket of energy above them buckles and shifts with such violence it creates sparks over their heads. A raging wind lifts, then descends upon us. The force of it batters me like massive invisible fists.

Furry, clawed hands grab at me from all sides. The stench of the beasts is almost unbearable and my throat spasms. I kick. I struggle. I bite. At one point I even growl and the sound is so animal it shocks me. But none of it matters. A set of manacles is slammed onto my wrists and the masked villagers pick me up as if I weigh nothing. Their combined power is immense.

They drag me. The moon has fully risen and it's huge and red and round. Bony, spiked animals pop out of steaming pockets in the ground. They make a noise that sounds like laughter.

This is what Eden looks like without the Veil.

We go through the dried-up fields in the direction of the pond. Torches sizzle at the front and back of our procession. I stumble and suddenly I'm surrounded, tightly packed in the middle of the group. Their claws puncture the skin on my arms, my shoulders, my waist. It hurts, but every scratch is a reminder that I'm still alive, still here, still fighting. The beast on my left looks at me, says something unintelligible under his breath and when I feel his mouth next to my ear I stifle a scream. The masks – I know they are just masks – the masks have become so real they've fused with the wearer and move and breathe with them. The villagers are now beings, not people. They are the demons you read about in horror stories.

In front of us, running ahead, then backtracking and watching us with their tongues out, are Fury and Evil. Chaos is nowhere to be seen, but I imagine this is the kind of party you don't want to invite that particular creature to. Evil snorts out smoke and keeps his flaming eyes in my direction. Fury nudges my legs. Anger shoots through me the moment he does, but it turns to despair when he trots away.

The air smells like wood smoke and dust and rot. The wind thick with debris from the inferno devouring the village. Ash and dirt clog my nostrils and mouth. I feel weaker and weaker the closer we get to the Fire Pit.

I swallow a soreness that has lodged in my throat. This is where I come from. These are my people.

Kidnappers. Murderers. Liars.

Agnes did it. Eleanor did it.

I did it.

Maybe the Devil was right. Maybe I can't judge.

The hill flattens out a bit and there before me is what used to be a field of Eternity Flowers. They've been beheaded, their shriveled blooms on the ground. I'm pushed forward. Every time I step, the treacly scent surrounds me, reminding me of Agnes, of our life together, of the moments she angered me...and the moments she loved me. There are so many moments of love. The memories are like a pulled thread, undoing a set of stitches. I feel myself coming apart, my knees giving way. Agnes needed this plant to survive, and I destroyed it. Then I went and hurt her with my anger. I hurt her beyond repair. No...

I killed her.

I killed Agnes...Mom.

She's gone and it's all my fault.

This time, when I stumble, no one holds me up. I fall face first, scraping my forehead and cheeks on broken, dry stalks poking out of the caked earth. Dirt lands like dust in my mouth. I don't move. I stay there with my face in the ground, feeling desolate.

I killed Mom.

Why even bother to try to live? I totally deserve to die.

Claws grip me. Yank me to a standing position and carry me forward. I feel like a rag doll, floppy and insubstantial.

We reach the edge of the forest, where the black smoke gives way to gray fog. I'm pushed through it, past deformed trees. Every little hair on my body stands on end. My heart races. Sweat forms on my forehead and scalp and drips down my temples.

I want to gather my anger into a weapon, but even it has left me. I'm empty of all emotion.

The rushing of the river sounds in front of us. Already from several feet away, I see the unnatural darkness of the water, smell the metallic scent. When at last all of us are standing in front of it, I watch as the torrent of blood bleeds past us. I feel the demons' hands tighten on my upper arms and I know. I know this is where I'll die.

Drowned in blood.

But instead, they push me along further, until the smoky fog surrounding the pond parts and my feet are near the edge of the water. In the moonlight, the algae shines a reddish-orange, the circular form of the pond glowing like embers from a fire.

The crowd has stopped, but there's movement at the back. Above us, the air still shimmers with some sort of dark power, swirling and buckling like it's agitated. I hear the sound of chains as well as muffled voices. That's when several masked monsters burst through the pack, two unmasked women in their clutches.

The woman is slight, her hair knotted and her dress so dirty I can't tell what color it's supposed to be. A plump ferret or maybe a mink is curled around her neck, its black eyes shiny, its mouth clamped to her shoulder. The woman commands attention: an invisible aura of power surrounds her despite the fact that she's chained and gagged. The entire crowd moves a step back when she's pushed forward, as if they're afraid of her touch. But even so, one monster spits at her face, then another, until almost everyone has a go. They chant:

Eleanor, Eleanor, murderous witch.

The other woman is pushed to the front of the pack. I'm almost grateful for the clawed hands holding me up because I nearly faint at the sight of her. Apart from the fact that she's not covered in freckles and that her eyes are blue instead of brown, it's like looking into a mirror.

There is no doubt she's my birth mother.

"Virginia." It's a whisper coming from my mouth, but she turns and sees me.

"Ahredden!" she screams, "Ahredden, my child!"

Breaking free of the monsters holding her, she lurches forward, nearly reaching me before being caught, claws around her waist. Chains clanking, she frantically extends her hands. I reach out, too, and manage to just brush her thin fingers with my own. I can smell her panic, feel her terror. But at her touch, the warm, sugary taste and feel of her love coats my tongue.

Tears pool in her eyes and she says my name again before the monsters pull her away, gagging her with a thick cloth like they did Eleanor.

The man in the mask with the crooked nose approaches, walks in a circle around Eleanor and Virginia. His back is straight, the tips of his sharp teeth lining up like the smile of a jack-o-lantern. Glee. His horrid face is full of an evil kind of glee.

"Eleanor Dare," he says, bringing his face close to my grandmother's. "Finally. The time has come where I will have my vengeance. You've taken my kin. Now I take yours. I want you to watch and remember. I want you to have the same nightmares as I. Nightmares of seeing your own flesh and blood suffer right before your eyes."

It's Dyonis behind that mask. He yells, "Summon the Master! Summon the Beast!"

A thick, bitter odor fills the air, stinging the lining of my throat. What sounds like thunder is actually tree branches cracking. The ground rumbles underneath my feet. From nowhere to right before me, is a furry, fanged creature with such malice in his black eyes that I freeze.

His mask is weathered, making his skin ridged and rough as bark. His fur is black and brown and blond and creates a mane around his head. Four fangs—two very long on top and two slightly shorter on the bottom—stick out of his snarling mouth. His arms are muscled underneath the fur. His claws are black and shiny and sharp.

He brings his face so close to mine that I see the wormholes in the wood of his mask as the pores of his skin. "Redd," he breathes. I expect his breath to reek like death, but instead it smells like wet earth and decaying leaves.

That's when I realize this animal is the Master. The beauty and charm of before is gone and only a monster remains. Lucifer. Satan. The Devil. The Beast.

Virginia is struggling, trying to say something from behind her gag. She's pleading with her eyes, looking at the horrid creature in front of me.

He turns. But his eyes move past her and settle momentarily on my grandmother, Eleanor Dare. For the briefest moment, something changes in his face, his stature, his size. It's brief enough to make me wonder if I saw it, but I know I did: *Love.* Everything beastly about him melts away for that moment.

The moment does not last.

But it's a moment that reminds me that there are reasons to live. Despite my anger at Agnes, under her every emotion, every choice—good or bad—there was one constant: love. What she did, she did to save me. I can't roll up and die so easily. I won't go without a fight.

The Devil took my power to destroy; he didn't take my desire to rebel.

The blood on the surface of the pond glows crimson from the phosphorescent plants below. The water bubbles slightly and the fog creeps in closer. The giant dragon stays hidden below. The Master moves nearer, his dark eyes burning with excitement. He takes one of his long talons and taps me on the nose. "Entertainment," he whispers to me. Then he bows his head and shouts, "Eden is hungry. We have a pact to fulfill!"

I'm shoved from behind and I stumble into the pond. The water...the blood...is thick and warm.

Dyonis wades through the bloody water to stand in front of me. I glare at him through that horrific mask.

"We thank you for your sacrifice," he growls, and then before I know it his claws are on top of my head, shoving me under the blood. I barely have a chance to take a breath.

More monster hands add their strength to Dyonis'. My face is pushed to the bottom of the pond. Sharp rocks scrape my cheeks. Silt fills my nostrils.

Fight it, Redd. Fight them. They don't deserve for you to die for them.

I use all my strength to dislodge the hands from my body, but any movement on my part just makes them shove me down harder. I count the seconds, knowing I can hold my breath, but that each number closer to three hundred is one second closer to my death.

Panic takes over.

I'm going to die. I'll never hear Shay swear again. I'll never get to tell Minnie I'm sorry or give her one last hug or see her reunited with her daughter. I'm going to die here and no one will have any idea what even happened.

The hands dressed in clawed gloves push me even harder into the bottom of the pond. I flail around, trying in vain to turn my head, my shoulders straining against the pressure.

I must get free, if only for a matter of seconds. Just long enough to take a new breath and swim through the tunnel. I try lifting my head, kicking my legs, turning on my side. Nothing helps. The hands just shove me further and further down.

My mouth opens and grit flows through my lips.

Then all of a sudden, the pressure on my head and body lets up. I get on my elbows and knees and lift my head above the water line, spitting and coughing out silt. Bloody water drips into my eyes. Rocks bite into my knees and palms.

"—to stop!" John is shouting. He's standing at the edge of the water, the eerie orange glow of the pond lighting his face. A copper snakelet is wrapped around his ear, and I have the strangest feeling that it's compelling me to listen. Next to John, Thomas holds up a shiny sphere that vaguely resembles a walnut. "The Council has lied to you! They've been lying for centuries! We can be free!"

He gently eases it open and the crowd gasps.

Like a vision, a story plays out before our eyes. A horrible vision that riles up the crowd.

"How dare you!" screams someone.

"Villainy!" shouts another.

And then they are all at each other's throats.

The dark energy cloud above us that held so much power crackles and disappears. The monsters are no longer monsters, but people in masks. Pathetic people in masks. Accusations are thrown, hatred spewed, anger ignited.

Now's my chance. No one is looking at me. I take a breath and prepare to dive under when sharp claws dig into the skin of my shoulders and jerk me back.

"Not so fast, Redd." The Devil grins, his fangs shining red. "There is one more secret you should be privy to."

51

John

Eden: Present Day

Suddenly, we are drowning in the truth. The horrible, evil truth. And it enrages everyone.

Now everyone knows: Only the original colonists who made the pact were ever bound to Eden in any way. The Council took away our choice. They poisoned us to keep us here with them. They lied to us.

They sacrificed children so they could live beyond their years.

Sacrifice was never needed to live. Only not to die.

The Council members slink backwards, eyes darting as if there is an exit to be found.

The villagers take off their masks, their faces etched with shock.

"Traitors!" cries Marie Little.

"Wretched cowards!" screams Timothy Spendlove.

"Now you see! Now you know who the true devils are!" yells Griffen Jones, his pitch full of righteous satisfaction. "The Council has betrayed us all!"

I look at Grandfather, a lump in my throat. He falls to his knees, shoulders slumped.

"Enough!" I yell. "Enough!" And somehow my words get the villagers to fall silent. "The Council's betrayal is horrific, aye. But the point is that we have a choice; we can choose to no longer sacrifice a life for survival. The flower grows on the outside. We are not bound to Eden."

"*You* are not bound. We are. Those of us who made the original pact," Elizabeth Glane says. "Eden or hell. 'Tis no choice for us."

Goodwife Warren's face is pale as moonlight. "Aye, in Eden we die without sacrifice. And we cannot survive outside. How is that a choice? "

Grandfather raises his gaze to meet mine "We do not deserve hell. Think upon it, boy. Your choice will damn us, John. Do you want to damn those who raised you?"

My heart is a mass of sharp thorns, killing me from the inside. Devil's curse, I do not want Grandfather to suffer. When I imagined us creating a new Eden on the outside, I imagined him there, along with Tom and me and Grandmama and every other villager. I imagined a new start, not a dark end. I do not want to be the one to take away his chance at eternal life. I would do anything so that Grandfather could live...

...anything but sacrifice someone else.

Cutbert White puts his mask back on. "I refuse to die. I've given too much to end this now."

"As have I," Joyce Archer agrees, lifting her own mask to her face.

"As have I!" shouts Christopher Cooper. Then Lewes Wotten. Then Lizzie Viccars. One after the other, the original inhabitants of Eden place their masks back onto their faces. They turn to the Fire Pit where Redd is on her knees, the Master directly behind her, his massive claws upon her shoulders as if he is holding her there.

"'Eternal life." Grandfather's mask grips his skin, warping his voice. "'Tis for eternal life!"

The Master grins. "Eternal life!" he shouts, then shoves Redd's head under the water. The others hurry forward to add their clawed hands to his. Within seconds, a dozen of them are holding her there.

52

Redd

Eden: Present Day

The Master whispers a horror in my ear.

I find out who I am, where I'm from, and why I'm different.

I don't want to know.

I wish I didn't know.

So when first one set of claws, then another and another, hold my head under the water, I don't even resist.

Not. One. Bit.

53

John

Eden: Present Day

I fight like I have never fought before. I choke. I maim. I hurt. With the Harvest here, it is possible to do so. I fight my way through the throng of masked villagers surrounding Redd, until I face only the Master.

But it is too late.

He lets out a hardy laugh and lifts his hand. Redd's body floats to the surface. My mouth to hers, I desperately try to breathe life back into her, my heart so loud in my ears I cannot hear the jeers of the others around me.

But it does not work. Nothing works.

My very soul feels like it has shattered into thousands of pieces, each one sharper than the next. *She was free! Why did she come back?*

Then: *You did this, John. Redd died. And it is upon your head.*

54

Eleanor

Eden: Present Day

I cannot move for the chains binding me. I cannot speak for the rag muzzling me.

But I can see. And I can feel. Oh, Devil save me, I can feel.

Next to me, Virginia sobs, her body limp.

I watch as the Master drowns my granddaughter. I keep my eyes wide open, taking in the horror wrought from my choices over centuries. And what a horror it is. My own blood murdered in the way I killed so many. My daughter in pain, and the impossibility to change it.

I think back to eighteen years ago. We'd won then. Love had won. For once.

And now I am here to witness its loss.

I close my eyes and make a plea to the being I've yet to encounter in my long life. If there ever was a time for Him to listen, I beg Him to do so now. *My lord God,* I pray, *do not continue to forsake us all.*

55

Eleanor

Eden: 18 years ago

Frost laced the latticed panes of our windows, and icicles hung from the roof. A fluffy carpet of snow spread before the cottage and down the hill to the village, where the scent of spiced wine mixed with woodfire. However, violets and tulips and pansies had begun to poke through the snow. Tiny bits of soft, green leaf could be spotted on tree branches, and my winter cloak was already feeling too warm.

By now, William knew Virginia was with child. He vacillated between caressing her growing belly with a dreamy expression on his face, to spending long afternoons staring into the hearth with terror in his eyes.

Virginia, too, went from happiness to fear within a span of seconds, over and over throughout the days. Sometimes she stood at the front door, squinting into the distance, as if waiting for someone. But it was a quiet time in the village, with the cooler weather keeping everyone indoors. Even the Master had not set foot in his own paradise for months now.

Throughout the winter, I'd been working on a cure for the illness the Contagion created in the Beyond. If it worked, I told myself, I could send Virginia outside with the babe to save it. I added an outbuilding on our grounds to work in, mixing concoctions of the Eternity Flower and Contagion and hoping to find a solution that would last more than a week or two. I found no cure, but with Agnes' help, we did figure out that if fresh plant nectar was taken daily, health could be sustained indefinitely. The problem was that we were unable to transplant the Eternity Flower outside the village borders, unable to make it grow there. Scouts had tried and failed. Anyone who went out was still obliged to eventually return or die.

In the meantime, Virginia kept her pregnancy hidden.

But Gossips were a problem now that Spring was approaching. It did not matter how often I emptied the wardrobes or dusted the drawers, there was always the chance that one would go missed.

And, apparently, one did.

Dyonis Harvie's twin grandchildren were born on one of the last days of winter. The news came in the form of a knock on the door by George Harvie himself. Agnes had been the one to answer, and when she came back into the cottage to tell us what she learned, there was such a painful twist to her mouth that I knew, in that instant, that George had been the boy who broke her heart. Of all the people in Eden and the Beyond, she had chosen to fall in love with a Harvie. Oh, the poor girl.

Perhaps we Dares and Harvies were destined to always hurt each other.

"He asked after you, Ginny." Agnes said. "I worry they suspect you're with child. If so—"

"If so, there'll be no more hiding possible," I finished.

But it was worse.

A few weeks later, when the snow had melted and the breeze was warm, Dyonis Harvie, Christopher Cooper, and Joyce Archard came knocking. They pushed their way into the cottage and demanded to see Virginia. I refused, hurling insults while William and Agnes blocked the way to the stairs that led to the sleeping chambers. But after a while, Virginia took it upon herself to end the charade and come down.

Her belly was now so distended there was no denying she was to give birth.

Dyonis pulled out a sheet of rolled parchment and set it into her hands. Leaning heavily against the large stone of the hearth, she unrolled it. I watched as she read, her eyes searching the document desperately.

I stepped next to her and scanned the page, bile rising higher into my throat with each word. "What is this?"

"A simple contract, Eleanor. Or mayhap you could call it a reassurance that everyone in Eden will at one point pay their due. Even the Dares," Dyonis said.

William gently eased the paper from Virginia's hand to read it. "This is unprecedented. Since when does the Council create contracts regarding future births?"

"Since a Dare got pregnant." Joyce narrowed her eyes at him.

"Wythers!" William nearly shouted. "Her name is Wythers now. Has been for hundreds of years."

As usual, no one paid him any mind. A Dare was always a Dare.

"I must see the Master. He has the last word on what happens here in his domain." Virginia's voice was thin as broth, no real meat behind the words.

For once, I agreed, though I doubted it made a real difference. Yet in the moment, I was ready to grasp at anything to stay afloat. "Aye. If there is a dispute about a contract, the Master has the last say."

"You'll note that the Master has already put his mark upon the page." Joyce pointed to the dot and crescent moon at the bottom of the paper—the Master's thumbprint—with obvious glee in her voice. "'Tis approved."

"But he does not know...he would not have... " Virginia's words tumbled away as tears streamed down her cheeks.

"He cannot choose favorites. That was our worry. That was why we drafted this contract in the first place. The next child born of original blood is the next child to go to the Fire Pit. It secures our future. 'Tis what we all agreed to when we arrived," Christopher said, taking back the contract. "'Tis what *you* agreed to when you had your first masking ceremony."

"But there is no need! Eden is prospering! The trees are lush and filled with fruit. The crops are plentiful." William stood half in front of Virginia as if he could protect her.

"It will not be like that forever." This time it was Dyonis Harvie who spoke, his low voice coming from the shadow of the room.

"Demon spawn!" I wrenched the contract from Christopher's hand and ripped it—once, twice, twenty times—until it was nothing but confetti falling into the burning fire in the hearth.

The pieces curled up around the edges then, with a slow hiss, they came together, the contract immediately reconstructing itself.

Dyonis walked over and put his hand in the flames, pulling out the contract. He blew ashes off its surface and told the others it was time to go. "It's binding. Even the Master cannot change it now." His eyes glinted as he walked out the door.

Later that night, we sat in front of the hearth, feeding the fire so the pops and spits were loud enough to cover any thoughts muddling our minds.

"The Master knows, then," Virginia said, her voice shaking. "He knows I am with child. And yet he signed that contract."

"Of course he did. Why wouldn't he? He's the Devil. Did you truly believe you could charm the Master into any special treatment?" I picked up my embroidery hoop and poked the needle through the material with extra force. "And Dyonis is so very pleased. To sacrifice a child of yours, the Devil's favorite. One of the very first members of Eden. That child will be worth tenfold what any other child would be. A sacrifice worth generations to the village..."

"One life for the good of many. But this life is worth so many years." Agnes' voice was barely audible over the popping of the fire.

"Every villager will want to see the child go to the Pit," William said.

I threw down my embroidery. "If only we could leave here."

"Without a cure for the illness"—William scrubbed his hands over his face—"or without the Master to plant the flower in the Beyond, *no one* can leave for good. Not even the young."

"Ah!" Virginia gasped. "We remove the child from Eden before any harm comes to him or her."

Agnes shook her head. "Not possible. The babe would become ill."

"Nay," Virginia said. "Nay, the babe would not. Because the babe is not infected."

And then she told Agnes and William the truth of the illness and Contagion. About how only the original adults were bound to the Master, yet the Council and I decided to infect the youth to keep them in Eden.

Torment licked my ear as they listened. For the longest time, no one said a word. I kept my back straight, my gaze on the floor. When I finally lifted my head, I saw the hurt and anger in William's eyes. He stood, then sat, then stood again. Finally, he took his hat from the peg near the door and stepped out. "I need some air," he said.

But I knew it was that he could look at me no longer.

Agnes, on the other hand, laced her fingers through mine. "Oh, Eleanor," she said, pity and understanding evident in the timbre of her voice. That terrified me more than if she'd spat in my face. What atrocities had Agnes seen and done that she did not harbor hatred for me because of this?

We sat in silence long enough for the fire to finally die down. Agnes uncurled her fingers from mine to gather her shawl about her shoulders.

"If I could find a cure," I said to Virginia. "Then you could run with the child…"

"Nay."

"I shall work day and night to do so. I'm so very close—"

"You are not close, Mama," Virginia said. "You know you are not."

"Give me a—"

"You should have searched for a cure centuries ago!" Virginia shouted. "'Tis too late and you know it."

I swallowed back my arguments. She was correct, I should have been trying to remedy my mistake this whole time. And I was nowhere near finding a true cure. "Then we shall make the flower grow in the Beyond. You'll survive on the petals."

Agnes shook her head. "Eleanor, you're grasping at straws. You know we are unable to make the flower grow outside of Eden."

"We find a way—"

"It would not matter. I am too old. Agnes took me into the Beyond months ago. My reaction was so violent…" Virginia' face flushed, fear darkening her eyes at the memory.

Agnes added, "It would take more than a few petals of nectar to keep her alive. At least in the beginning, she'd need more. Unless we could plant an entire field and get it to grow immediately, Virginia would wither away."

This revelation struck me as painful for all the wrong reasons. They went into the Beyond together? Without telling me? I had no words, for this betrayal stung more than I wanted to admit.

Virginia clapped her hands, a sudden idea brightening her face. She turned to Agnes. "You could do it."

"Do what?"

"Save the babe." Virginia's voice strengthened. "You've taken children from the Beyond to bring to Eden. But now you could take a child from Eden to the Beyond. A balance of sorts. A restitution."

"Absolutely not!" I shouted. What was happening here?

But Agnes blinked at Virginia. She lifted her chin and said, "I'll do it."

I could not believe it. "Devil knows what the Council would do with you when you came back to Eden. They could sentence you to years in the Garden for such an act!"

"Then I won't come back."

"The babe would survive, but you would die out there without the flower. You were poisoned."

"Then I'll die. No matter."

"Do not be ridiculous!" I spat. The determination in her voice filled my belly with fear. I loved Agnes, and as much as I wanted this babe to live, I would fight for Agnes' life over the child's.

Agnes wouldn't listen. "I want to. I want to do something good for once."

"Nay! I forbid it!" I turned to Virginia. "Tell her! Tell her what folly this is!"

Virginia's eyes shone with emotion. "Mama...I think it may be possible for both her and the babe to survive in the Beyond. They can bring a flower out. Grow it there."

"This is madness. Has Lunacy burrowed into your brain? We have no way to make the flower grow. You said so yourself." By now my breaths were coming so quickly I felt faint.

"Ah, but I hadn't given a thought to the babe's own blood," Virginia said, passing a hand over her belly. "To the father's blood."

"I'm at a loss here, Virginia." I threw up my hands. "How could William's blood help?"

"William isn't this child's father, Mama." She held my gaze, so she could see my face as her next words tore through my heart. "The Master is."

56

Redd

Eden: Present Day

I am the Devil's daughter. Everything makes sense now.

Death takes me to the heart of Eden. Here lies suffering, evil, destruction, darkness. It cradles me, shadowy hands pulling me in, whispery voices telling me to join my father in his rule. I, too, could command chaos. I, too, could sow sin and reap doubt. I could be part of a family. His family. We would be together. And we would be unstoppable.

I close my eyes and let the shadows soothe me. They seep into my belly, into my blood.

Join him. Join him. Join him. This darkness is where you come from.

But then...then I open my eyes and see other possibilities. So many other possibilities.

Yes. This darkness is where I come from.

But it is not who I am.

57

Eleanor

Eden: 18 years ago

It took me a week to recover from the news that the Master was the father of Virginia's unborn babe. Her admission that she had coupled with him willingly because she "loved him and always had" nearly drove me to madness.

How? How was it possible?

My sole objective since saving her from the Fire Pit was to save her from the Master. And yet I suffocated her with my love. So much so, that instead of saving her from him, I sent her to him.

I was not the only one devastated by Virginia's revelation. William still loved Virginia. And he was still a good man. But he, too, was deeply hurt. No one could be expected to stay faithful for more than four hundred years. Extra-marital relations were accepted, the way of things in Eden. He'd had lovers before. I assumed, so had Virginia. This, however, was different. The Master is not just any lover.

But no matter how much we wanted to, we could not weep or fret or hold grudges or rage against the situation for long.

The baby was coming. Of that, there was no doubt. Virginia, William, Agnes, and I went round and round, trying to accept the reality and figure out what to do next. If the child was, in fact, Satan's, why not sacrifice it? Did we truly want his tainted blood in our family tree?

Yet Virginia would not hear of it. Devil's spawn or not, the child was growing inside of her. And already she loved the babe.

In the end, Virginia won. We would try to save the little being. But if we were to succeed, we needed to be prepared.

Virginia's assumption—that the child would have the Master's blood and therefore be able to make the flower grow—was just that: an assumption. The only way to know the truth was to wait until the babe was born. As Virginia was a gardener, it was hard to know if the flowers she touched flourished from her magic or the baby's blood.

It was of utmost importance that we kept the actual birth secret for as long as possible. The Council would descend upon the cottage the moment Virginia began to go into labor and would sweep the child away for a dose of Contagion before the afterbirth had even been expelled. We needed time—even just an hour or so—to send Agnes out with the babe. But I was still terrified it would be a death sentence for her. I wanted proof Nephilim blood would work on the flower. We'd need to see if the child could even spark the tiniest of growth in the plant.

We also had to be on guard should the Master show up. The fact that he had signed that contract sentencing Virginia's child to sacrifice meant that he would not help—father or not. Perhaps he *wanted* to put his own flesh and blood into the Fire Pit.

Yet we needed him. We needed a mask for the baby if Agnes was to take her through the underwater tunnel. It was the only way the child would be able to breathe. Virginia thought perhaps the babe, like the Master, could use any mask. But again, there was no way of knowing ahead of time. Better to err on the side of caution instead.

We went out of our way to be cautious.

The Master had a way of knowing our feelings. He often said he could taste our lies or smell our fear. The reason he'd planted the Eternity Flower everywhere was that it dulled his sixth sense. There were moments he simply wanted a respite from the overwhelm. However, if he wasn't in proximity to the flower, our emotions were an open book.

In case he came knocking, we cut dozens of them and placed them in vases all over the cottage, replacing them with fresh ones daily. Should he ask, we'd say it was our way of preparing for the upcoming birth, as the scent was relaxing to Virginia. Hopefully, it would be enough to mask our nervousness and deception. We did not want to tip him off that Agnes was planning to steal the babe away.

As spring turned toward summer and the birdsong became constant, each day required vigilance. Every morning, a Council member came by the cottage under the guise of well-wishing. Whether it be Emme or Elizabeth or Joyce or Dyonis himself, they always lingered long enough to get a good look at Virginia, making sure she hadn't shoved a pillow under her kirtle and hid the babe somewhere away from their reach.

She would have if she could have. But there was no hiding in Eden.

On the longest day of the year, Christopher from the Council came to drink his morning ale at our table. He drank slowly, making small talk with me and Virginia. Thank the Devil it was not Emme or Elizabeth, women who'd witnessed enough births to sense when something was happening. Christopher kept his eyes on Virginia's bulging belly and swollen breasts, so did not notice how she clenched her teeth and gripped the edge of the table until her knuckles were white.

The moment I shut the door behind him, Virginia let out a cry.

It was happening.

I got her up the stairs and into her chamber, where she settled on the birthing chair William had carved for the occasion. Agnes sat behind her, rubbing her back and wiping her brow. We kept William busy in the kitchen, heating water for soaking flannels. I used them as a compress, hoping to lessen any tearing when the baby came out.

Tears kept blurring my vision, as my heart wrenched with the thought that my sweet baby was now having one of her own. When I had birthed Virginia, death was not only a possibility, but likely. Back then, in the Beyond, pregnancy was as dangerous as battle. As the day wore on, Virginia's howls of agony grew louder. It was a relief to know that, in Eden, she would survive, no matter the pain. But it did not make it easy.

The labor was long and arduous, but as the sun was dipping below the horizon, Virginia finally gave birth to a girl. A healthy girl with a cry so strong it made the room shake. I hugged her to me and calmed her, trying and failing to stop love's grip from becoming an iron fist around my heart. One look at the squirming child's form and I knew it no longer mattered who her father was. She was, and always would be, a Dare.

While Agnes helped Virginia into her bed, I wiped the babe clean with a soft cloth. Uncovering the tender spot where the baby's jawline ended, I let out a gasp.

"What? Has she talons?" Virginia started, her eyes wide. "Or wings?"

"Nay," I said, running my finger along the raised crescent moon on her skin. "No wings. The Devil's fingernail. He's marked her. Like you and me."

I gave the babe to Virginia, who kissed the stain. "She is one of us, see? She is not evil."

"She's not *him*, I'll give you that," I said, then smiled. "But 'tis obvious she's part angel."

The girl suckled at Virginia's breast then dozed off, her pink mouth still latched to the nipple. Wincing, Virginia eased her away, and tugged her chemise over her chest.

Agnes touched the downy hair covering the child's head. "She's perfect. What's her name?"

"I was going to let you name her, since she will be yours," Virginia said, her words barely above a whisper. "Here. Hold her."

Agnes bit her lip, then took the blanketed baby into her arms. As she did, the shadow that always darkened her face fell away, and a cautious brightness took its place. "Ahredden," she said. "*Rescuer.* She'll rescue us both."

The room went silent for a moment, the only noise a squeak from the child. I wiped the knife I'd used to cut the umbilical cord clean, ready to prick little Ahredden to see if her blood would make one of the many flowers in the vases around the room spark with new life. But then William knocked on the open door of the chamber. His eyes were dark with worry. "Ginny?"

"I'm good, William. As is the babe. She's barely a fistful of minutes old and already she's burrowed her way deep into my heart. I regret we must send her away."

He stepped inside and gingerly sat on the bed next to his wife. Wonder replaced the worry in his eyes as Agnes passed the girl to him. "Amazing. You made her, Ginny. You made another human being."

"Aye, that she did." A column of smoke appeared, and suddenly the Devil was before us, his broad form filling the doorway. "Yet you must admit it, Virginia. You had a bit of help."

He was but a silhouette, the setting sun in the windows of the room behind him, his hair wild, the ends tinged with orange light. It looked like his head was aflame.

"Master," breathed Virginia. "You came."

"Did you think you could keep secrets from me?"

"Do not pretend you did not know."

"Ah, but I'd hoped to hear it from your own sweet lips."

Tiny dots of fire lit Virginia's cheeks. "You've not been around to share any news with. For months."

"Aye. True." The Master tilted his head. "Nine months to be exact."

I set the knife back down and put a hand to the wall to steady myself. Now there was no doubt that he was the father. I glanced at William. He, too, seemed upset at this confirmation of fact.

"Why is your bedchamber full of the Eternity Flower?" the Devil asked, a frown on his face.

"The scent puts her at ease," I responded, almost too quickly. "Had you had the foresight to make childbirth as painless as nearly everything else in Eden, perhaps relaxation would not be so important at a time like this."

"Always ready to remind me of my shortcomings, aren't you, Eleanor?" His hard gaze found my own, and I stared back without blinking, hoping I would give nothing away.

"Save our daughter. Keep her safe," Virginia begged him, a sob behind her words. "They want to sacrifice her!"

"Does that surprise you?" Satan took the baby from William and held her up, his long fingers behind her head, his thumbs hooked under her armpits. She was tiny and fragile in his hands, and I suddenly feared he would crush her.

Then he spied the mark near her jaw. "Not only is she mine, she's marked as such. What a wonder."

"You cannot want to see her die," I said. "Keep her safe."

"Do not tell me what I want!" A quick wind snapped through the room, snuffing the candles. Immediately, they all lit up once again, the air too still, the room too quiet. The Master's inky eyes settled back on the babe in his hands. "Every family in the village must give."

"Master, I beg of you—" Virginia could not hold the tears back. "She's your child!"

The Devil dropped the girl into her arms. "Do you love me, Virginia?"

"Aye, I do." She nodded vigorously. I saw William flinch at the words.

"You say you love me, yet 'tis that long-dead boy named Samuel who still haunts your dreams. You say you love me, yet you share your bed and name with William. You say you love me, yet for too long you allowed your mother's poisoned words to taint your image of me." The Master sighed and threw up his hands. "You say you love me, Virginia, but what would you do to prove that love?"

"Anything, Master." Her voice broke. "Anything."

His words turned sharp. "Sacrifice the child. No fighting."

Virginia blanched.

"Nay!" I said, stepping in front of the bed to stand between the Devil and my daughter. "You shall not have this babe."

"Do *you* love me Eleanor? Do you even think you could?"

"Nay," I said. "I despise you with all my being."

He sighed. "Then there is little I can do."

"Do not hurt the baby. Hurt me," I said.

"But this will hurt you. And Virginia. And 'tis so easy." He flicked his wrist and a worm-eaten, wooden mask appeared. "The girl is special. Therefore, she will need a mask for the ceremony. I want to have made a true connection with this child before she is swallowed by Eden."

The mask: the first thing we needed for Agnes and the child to leave. He was giving us the key to her freedom without knowing it. I felt the pride of victory straighten my spine.

But then hunger bit into my stomach and pain shot through my veins. I could barely stand the intensity. Nay, it never happened this quickly. Never. It normally took hours, even days before progressing. I looked outside. The leaves on the trees were gone, the grass brown and withered.

In the blink of an eye, Eden had died.

The Master chuckled. "Surprised, Eleanor? Did you think Eden would wait? Not when your family's blood is on the line. Time to prepare. Dyonis and the council will soon be on their way. We all know 'tis not for well wishing." His lips lifted into a sardonic smile as he dissolved into nothing.

The moment all trace of him was gone, I turned to Virginia. "Hurry! We must see if Ahredden can make the flower grow." The moment the words left my mouth, I realized every Eternity Flower in every vase was now nothing but a rotted black stalk. Ahredden would not simply need to make a flower grow. She would need to revive one.

Agnes was already running to her own chamber where she got her pack and mask. Then she took Ahredden from Virginia's arms and swaddled her in a long cloth that she strapped to her own body in a makeshift sling. Sweat shone on her forehead, and her breath came in raspy bursts. She dismissed me when I reached for her. "I'm used to pain, Eleanor. Don't worry. I can make it to the Beyond with the baby."

"You cannot go! We've no idea if her blood is powerful enough." The ache in my head was making Agnes' form swim and sway before me.

"Let's find out," she said, taking the knife from the bedstand.

The four—five, with Ahredden—of us went downstairs, pain reverberating up our ankles and into our legs with each descending step.

Agnes tugged the baby's tiny arm out from the sling, dragged the blade along the skin. The child screamed as blood dripped onto the rotting Eternity Flower that the Devil had given me when I'd built the cottage.

We watched.

Nothing happened.

Absolutely nothing.

The sky was darkening to a smudgy purple outside, but in the distance, I could just make out bits of bright orange from torches. A procession was gathering in the town square. Soon they would make their way up the hill. No need to baptize Ahredden with Contagion. They were sending her directly to sacrifice.

Agnes blinked at the dead Eternity Flower. "I'm going. I'm giving her a chance."

I refused. No matter how much I wanted this baby to survive, Agnes was family. She was not blood, but she was part of our hearts all the same.

But she would not listen. "Ever since I was taken from the Beyond, someone in Eden has been forcing me to live a certain way. To do certain things. Everything has been chosen for me. Now it's finally my time to choose. I choose this."

"Agnes—" I started.

She put a finger to my lips, tears filling the mossy green of her eyes. "Quiet, Eleanor, I beg of you. Have faith in something other than the Devil's false promises. I will get through this. I will save her. And I may even save myself."

William took the pack from Agnes' shoulder. "I'm accompanying you through the tunnel. To make sure you succeed at getting out."

"Do not leave as well, William," Virginia sobbed. "You do not have your youth to sustain you should the flower not grow immediately. You'll die."

"He'll come back. He'll turn around before age catches up to him," I said, but William shook his head.

"I've lived long enough," He turned to Virgina. "Ginny, I was glad to have spent most of my life with you, but now I'm tired. So tired. Like Agnes, I want to do some good before I go. So I will help her escape. With any luck, 'tis God who will have me in the afterlife instead of his wicked son."

Virginia bawled and begged him, but, like Agnes, he was determined.

By now, the torches from the procession were an orange tail slowly snaking our way.

Agnes and William snuck out into the night towards the Fire Pit. We'd given Agnes a wet cloth sweetened with honey for Ahredden to suck on to keep her quiet. We hoped it would work.

As their shadows melded into the darkness, Virginia and I hugged each other and wept, fear filling the deep holes that once housed our hearts. I did not want to voice my worry that it all would be for nought. That Agnes would not survive, and neither would the babe.

When the villagers came for the child, already in their masks and furs, ready for sacrifice, we stalled. Virginia locked herself in her chamber, and it took several minutes for them to knock down the door. By the time they realized the baby was gone—as were Agnes and William—it was unlikely they could catch up with them. Scouts would be sent to scour the Beyond. But without the power to make the flower grow, they could only search for a few days at a time.

The sacrificial procession turned, instead, into the spectacle that was our arrest. The Council stripped us of our rights and our possessions. They sentenced us to life in the Garden.

Black thoughts filled my mind as they clasped manacles over my wrists. I saw Agnes in the Beyond, dying. I saw William, nothing but dust. I saw the baby, Ahredden, left alone in the middle of a forest with no one to hear her cries.

I should have fought harder to make them stay. Torment's teeth hit the bone where my skull and spine met, and I fell to my knees in despair.

And that's when I spied the potted Eternity Flower, now a shattered mess of dirt and clay on the floor. Its stalk lay brown and limp, its roots pale and sickly.

But there, where the stain of the baby's blood still colored a leaf scarlet, was a minuscule shoot, the hint of what would become a bud.

She could do it. Ahredden could make the flower grow!

"Virginia," I breathed, my eyes on the flower. "Virginia."

Virginia saw the plant and understood, her own legs giving way from underneath her.

The Master entered the cottage in full sacrificial regalia and took in the scene. Yet despite his fur-clad body, the sharpened fangs, the pure malice that made his eyes burn like coals, I was not afraid. Not in the least.

"You've failed," I laughed. "I've finally bested you, you black-hearted swine. You failed!"

The Devil let out a snarl. It shook the walls and created swirling storm clouds even darker than the night outside the door. "What have you done, Eleanor?"

When my only response was a laugh, he turned to Virginia. "Why?"

The delicate skin under Virginia's eyes was bruised purple, her lips dry as desert sand. Already, she looked as if she'd been starving for decades, not hours. But the strength of her gaze was like iron. "Because I wanted her safe," she said. "Safe from all of you."

Neither she nor I mentioned to the villagers that Ahredden was the Devil's child. Neither she nor I begged for leniency. We faced our sentence with stony faces and stony hearts. It enraged them all even more. Dyonis swore revenge. Joyce spat in my face. The Master's anger made a torrent of storm clouds blot out the moon.

Virginia and I shared the briefest of smiles before we were shoved out of the cottage towards the Garden. We stayed tall, chins lifted, backs straight. We had won. It was a small victory. But it was a victory all the same.

The Council and the Devil could take our masks, limit our magic, and lock us up. They could sully our names and torture us. They could make every day seem like hell.

But for what mattered, they were too late: Agnes and Ahredden would be free.

Make haste, I thought. *Go far. And never, ever return.*

58

John

Eden: Present Day

Eden gives no immediate sign that it is satisfied. The water does not run clear. Nor do the trees grow back their supple leaves, nor does the sky drip gentle showers onto our heads. Grandfather and the others look perplexed, their demon faces stiff and cold, waiting for the sign that will give them all cause to celebrate. They cheered once Redd was floating lifeless in the pond. But now their voices grow weaker, their cheers less hearty. Why hasn't Eden acknowledged the gift?

The energy that was in the air earlier is now replaced by an undulating blanket of fear. It smothers us.

"You have ruined everything," Grandfather whispers to me in a controlled voice. "Everything."

I look at the Master. His beastly form is unnerving; his sharp teeth and piercing claws terrify me to the bone, yet I yearn to be ripped to shreds by them. Anything to assuage the guilt and sorrow that is killing my soul.

The Master grins, his fangs opening wide as a joyous, satisfied laugh escapes from the vast cavern of his mouth. "You all are in for a treat!"

He leaves Redd to float and moves to the side of the pond, motioning for us all to sit upon the bank. We settle onto the cracked dirt, wary and confused. He drags his claws down the length of a tree, long scratches marring the trunk, then uses those claws to remove his mask. For a split-second he is simply a man. I see the gaping wound between and around his eyes before he swipes a hand over his face to create one of his coverings. Everyone else's masks fall to the ground, though Virginia and Eleanor remain gagged and chained to a tree. Virginia's eyes are dark with despair. Eleanor's burn with anger.

The Devil snaps his fingers. White and red striped cartons appear in our hands. It is so jarring here, so out of place, that it takes me a minute to recognize the containers of movie popcorn from the Beyond. Only a few of us would know it. I seek Clara in the crowd. She is not near those who drowned Redd, nor is she dressed in skins. She sits in the back, a wretched look upon her face as she blinks down at the popcorn.

The Master stays standing but shoves a large handful of the snack between his lips. Mouth full, he watches the Fire Pit and chirps, "How I love to be entertained."

We follow his gaze and soon enough, we cannot believe what we see.

Redd died. There is no doubt.

But now...now a soft glow emanates from her, starting in her belly and radiating out into her limbs. The brightness gathers in intensity until it is blinding. I shade my eyes against it, yet there is no dimming this light. Redd is radiance incarnate, no longer a woman but a luminous being. She stands, the bloody pond water changing as she does so, dripping from her in clear, crystal drops. Massive pearly wings sprout from her back, the iridescent feathers reflecting rainbows.

She was always beautiful.

Now she is dazzling.

In one grand swoop, Eden comes to life, more colorful and lush than ever before. A flock of birds flies overhead, their wings sparkling in the silver rays of a giant, glowing moon. Grass grows beneath me, a green carpet where there was only brown dirt. Leaves burst from buds and flowers bloom in rapid succession, a veritable fireworks display.

Redd's looking around her as if discovering everything for the very first time. When her eyes find mine, I can barely catch my breath.

I know now that it was never because she was a Dare that the flower grew. That the mask worked. That I was drawn to her like a bee to honey. It was the other blood flowing through her veins.

The blood of an angel.

59

Eleanor

Eden: Present Day

A hredden rises, bringing true light to Eden. It is not the glittering Veil of devilry that hides its rot. It is pure and perfect. It is magnificent.

The Master laughs as if enjoying a diversion, but I have known him long enough to hear the edge in that laughter. He is taken aback. He was expecting something, but not this. As her radiant wings unfurl to their full glory, his eyes flash and his jaw tightens.

Behind my gag, I smile.

He was expecting her to rise in darkness, not light.

He was expecting her to be his from the moment she was reborn.

No wonder he wanted to sacrifice her as a babe. He would have been able to mold her as his own, bend her ideas to his own, use her power as his own. And now... His influence has been so absolute for so many centuries that he's forgotten there are still some with free will.

Aye, the Devil's blood runs through Ahredden's veins.

But so does the blood of a Dare.

60

Redd

Eden: Present Day

Everything has changed. Colors shine brighter, emotions taste sweeter. My heart doesn't feel heavy anymore. It's weightless but full. Energy hums through my veins, warm like liquid sunlight. Hell, it might actually *be* liquid sunlight, because I'm shining like a spotlight or an oversized glow stick or...well...the sun.

The villagers of Eden surround me. Their faces are flush with life where before they were pale with death. I look into the eyes of those who drowned me. I sense their relief at Eden's renewal, taste their lingering hatred, feel their fear. One by one, they step back and break the stare first, gaze sweeping downward. All except Dyonis, whose hazel green eyes stay glued to mine. It's obvious he can't believe what is happening.

YOU'RE surprised, Dyonis? I didn't think it was possible to come back from the dead. Let alone to come back like this... Up until this moment, I never believed in angels. And now here I am, winged and sparkling.

Me. An angel. I can't help it; I burst out laughing.

The villagers take another step backward. That just gets me giggling more, enough to bring tears to my eyes.

I blink and my vision shifts, sobering me. Now the world around me is suffused in a shimmering light. No, not the world, but every being. Each has its own special shine.

I realize that shine is their soul. This is nuts. This is unbelievable. But I know in my gut it's real: I can see everyone's soul.

Some flicker, some glow, and some burn. Smoke-like shadows of darkness curl around several, hiding the light. But I lean towards the brightness. The beauty. The darkness doesn't interest me, not anymore. Only light and love and goodness.

My gaze travels around to land on John. At the sight of him, my cheeks heat up. He was always nice to look at. Now, with my new eyes, he's freaking gorgeous. I wasn't sure I could forgive him. But his soul is a white fire, radiant and warm, that outshines any shadows within him. I want to be close to that light.

"My sweet!" The Master's voice breaks my concentration. That voice is made of velour and satin and silk, with a hint of steel. He comes forward, a grin on his face. He's back to his charming, devilish self, no longer in beast form. I like how he looks at me like we've got a special secret, like it's us against the world. I feel his pull, the desire to please him, the desire to make him proud. Devil or not, he's my father. And God knows I've always wanted one.

"Join me, daughter," he says. "We can be together. We'll make an unstoppable team."

I look down at his outstretched hand and my fingers twitch. It would be so wonderful to be part of a team. Part of a family. So wonderful.

I feel a stare burning into me and turn to the two women chained to the trees. Virginia and Eleanor Dare. My mother. My grandmother. My family.

Virginia's soul shines like a beacon. Eleanor's is tired, the light waning. The smoky darkness is so opaque that it nearly blots out the rest. Nearly, but not entirely. The spark inside could one day catch flame.

I exhale. Virginia and Eleanor's chains fall to the ground.

"Ahredden!" Virginia calls. Before she can say another word, the Devil holds up a hand. It silences her just as the gag did.

But she can speak without words. I feel their unspoken intensity reverberate in my being. I can taste them on my tongue.

"Join me," my father urges again. I look at him with my new eyes. His flesh is beautiful—so beautiful—even with his wounds. But his soul... His soul is cold ash.

He played me. My suffering and fear were entertainment to him. *Everyone's* suffering and fear were entertainment to him. Still are.

Maybe one day, I'll help him find a spark among the ashes of his soul. Maybe.

I think of Shay and how she'd be able to give him an answer that sums up all her feelings in only a smattering of words. It makes me smile. So, I do the same.

"Not today, Satan. Not today."

61

John

Eden: Present Day

"**I**nsolent child!" the Master screams at Redd. With his words, the beauty that she brought into Eden is destroyed. "This is *my* paradise. You will have no power here."

A wind crashes through Eden, ripping branches off trees, sending grit and debris into the air and pummeling us all to the ground.

Then the suffering starts again. My throat is made of sand and my body flayed by rusty blades. I reach out to Tom. He grips my fingers as if they will keep him alive.

All around me, the others beg the Master to save them. Stop the pain. I'm almost ready to give in as well. But I cannot. Not when I know the flower is growing in the Beyond. Not when we can choose to leave. Choose to live otherwise. I gather what little strength I have left to call the villagers to follow me. To where we might have hope if Redd will follow, too.

"The Beyond," I shout with every ounce of my being. "Come!"

Lightning strikes overhead. Trees burst into flame. Somehow, Tom and I manage to stand and take a step toward the pond. Then two. Then three.

The Master growls our way. "Where are you going?"

I open my mouth to respond but the Master beats me to it. "You intend to lead everyone to the outside," he says. "You do realize some are required to stay? Some made a pact that cannot be broken."

"Let them go!" yells Redd.

He ignores her demand except for the tightening of his shoulders. "I'll tell you what? Let's play a game." A grin cracks his face. "Let's see how many you can get out before the tunnel collapses."

He turns to the villagers. "Ready? Set. GO!" He laughs, then snaps his fingers. In the distance, the mountains rumble. Under our feet, the dirt cracks. Thomas and I are separated as others push between us to get to the pond.

"Tom!" I shout, the effort scraping my throat raw.

Redd grips my shoulder and presses my mask to my face. "Hurry!"

"Thomas—"

"Just go!" she urges. "I'll find him."

But I cannot let her. "You must lead everyone through. One flower isn't sufficient. We'll not survive if you do not grow more."

She looks to where the Devil is laughing. He lifts a hand and the world shakes again, only stronger. The ground splits, a dark fog escaping from the crevasse. Through the murky curtain I see her nod before she dives into the pond.

"Tom!" I shout again. But now it is utter chaos, with villagers shoving their way into the Fire Pit. I'm jostled to the point of falling several times, finding myself on my knees in the bloody water. I do not stop calling for my brother. To no avail. My heart rises into my throat. Where is Thomas?

The inky sky grows even blacker, crackling like a roaring fire. A torrent of embers spills down, burning my head and shoulders. I dive under the water to avoid the scorching raindrops. All around me, others do the same. The Fire Pit is full of masked, swimming bodies. I turn around and around, searching for Thomas' lanky form. Devil's curse. Has he already gone into the tunnel?

Another quake hits. Even Deception is restless. She slides out of her dark burrow, her breath agitating the waters. The villagers are terrified and unsure how to navigate under Deception's flinty gaze and in the swirling waters. I search one more time for my brother, the hope that he's well ahead of me spurring me on. The others have never entered the dark length of the tunnel. Redd has led the first ones through, but I must herd the rest inside. It is only wide enough for one person at a time. With each quake, the gaping hole loses bits of sand and rock. With each quake, the opening gets smaller. I calm those who are too terrified to swim into its blackness, hoping every last soul will make it through. When only Deception lurks in the Fire Pit, I swim to the surface, hoping to make one last sweep for Thomas. But while the atmosphere only resembles flames under the water, it is truly a firestorm outside. I see nothing but light and smoke. Bullets of flame pierce my skin the second I am above the waterline.

I can do nothing but dive back under.

I'm almost through the tunnel when the final quake hits, this one strong enough that a web of fissures race through the ceiling. Rock and silt shower down, muddying the water. I kick, swimming as fast as I can towards the murky light. A boulder crashes down, clipping my left leg. Blood rises in the water as the searing pain makes me cry out behind my mask. Under my ripped pants, my shin is a pulpy red mess, the sharp point of my bone protruding through the gash.

Using only my arms, I try to swim forward. A wave of dizziness washes over me along with the pain. Just a few more feet and I'll be through. I continue to inch forward, fighting not to lose consciousness along the way. I can see the moonlit glow of the Sound at the end of the tunnel. I can already sense the weight of its brackish water.

But more rubble falls. The glow is filled with shadow.

I'm stuck inside here, between worlds, between life and death.

I squeeze my eyes shut and grit my teeth against the terror and pain. I'll never see Thomas again. Redd will never forgive me. The Master will take me to hell—

John? John!

I hear the words inside the mask. My eyes fly open. There before me is an ugly monster, with crooked fangs and a shock of tri-colored hair. His skin puckers and wriggles as if worms have burrowed their way under the surface.

It is a face I see every day, leering at me from the mantle. A mask hung next to mine and under those of Grandmama and Grandfather.

Thomas' mask.

Tom!

He wraps two strong hands around my forearms and pulls me toward the light he was blocking. Even behind the mask I can taste the salt of the Sound. We hit the surface and he takes me into his arms.

I remember the day he was brought to us. Emme handed him to Grandmama, a smitten smile on her face. It was impossible not to fall in love with the boy bundled in a blanket, that chubby wad of a baby with a tuft of untamable auburn hair. I was five and already felt the immediate desire to shelter Tom from anything and everything. To save him whenever he needed saving.

I never imagined he'd be saving me.

Now in the open air, I see the blanket of stars above me and the carpet of flowers below. Dozens and dozens of white blooms, on the beach and even in the adjoining forest.

Thomas sets me onto the ground, rips a petal from one of those flowers and squeezes the nectar between my lips. "We did it, John. We made it. And it's beautiful here."

The nectar dulls the pain but does nothing for the bone splitting my shin.

Thomas rips off his mask. He eyes my wound, his mouth turned down. Then he shouts, "Here! Over here!"

"Oh, gross!" The voice is Redd's. I look up to see her standing above me, her hair a tangled, wavy mass, her clothes covered in muck. She doesn't radiate light here, and her wings are invisible, but her eyes still shimmer gold. And she's still beautiful. So beautiful.

"He's hurt," Thomas tells her.

"Yeah. I can see that." She purses her lips. "Ugh. That's...um...that's a biggie."

"There's a hospital—" I start.

But Thomas cuts me off with a laugh. He shakes his head. "We don't need it. We've got Redd." Then he grins up at her.

"I used to destroy things. I was really good at it." Redd squats down next to me. She puts a hand over my leg and closes her eyes. Warmth pools in my shin and radiates up my leg. It is as if we were back in Eden. My bone slides back into place, the skin knitting together over it.

Redd drops her hand and the warm sensation turns tepid. But my leg looks and feels perfect.

"Now...I can heal," Redd says, lifting her shoulders into a shrug. "It's probably a more helpful skill."

"Thank you," I say to her, my heart swelling. "Thank you. For planting the flowers. For helping us. For everything."

"It's not over yet," Redd says. Her jaw is set, and I see the rapid pace of her pulse through a thin vein at her temple. Her gaze suddenly burns into mine and it's as if I'm jumping the waterfall with her once again. The same swooping of my stomach, the same rush over my skin. There's so much I want to say to her. So much I want to atone for. But the words get caught in my throat.

Thomas helps me sit up. I lift my mask from where Tom discarded it, and it turns to ash between my fingers. The small beach and the forest beyond it are heaving with Eden's escapees. They let out a collective gasp as their masks wither away as well.

Tom's eyes grow wide with worry at this loss of link to Eden. "We're missing people."

"The elders," I whisper.

"Aye. Those who made the pact."

"The original colonists?" Redd asks. At my nod, she stands. "I don't need a mask to enter Eden. I'll get them."

"The tunnel collapsed. You cannot get through," I tell her.

"Just watch," she says and dives into the water.

But no matter how hard she tries, she cannot. Eden is out of our reach.

The elders, the original Roanoke colonists, are now as it is written in history books.

Lost.

62

Redd

The Beyond: One Year Later

"I'm all in," I say, dropping everything I have onto the table. Coupons for soap, foot cream, disinfectant. A reduction code for several shopping sites. And a gift card for Roasted.

Whispers of excitement rustle about the common room. Everyone at *Shady Pines Senior Home for Independent Living (and Greater Freedom!)* is present for the annual Coupon Poker tournament. Even Gigi the parrot, who's currently sitting on top of my head. Gigi squawks out a cuss word and grips my hair harder with her talons. She apparently doesn't agree with my play.

Thomas fidgets on his chair. He looks at his cards, then at me, then his cards again and nods.

We set down our hands.

"You've got to be kidding me!" I huff.

Minnie throws her head back and laughs, a joyous sound. "Been waiting for this!" She removes my picture from the bulletin board under the banner *Reigning Champion* and replaces it with his.

Thomas grins at me. That boy is some kind of lucky. With all the nectar he takes, I can't get my sixth sense to work on him. So he manages to beat me in every game there is. Maw. Go Fish. Bullshit. Hell, he even kills it in the Bingo tent.

I've realized that after winning for so many years, I'm a sore loser. I shove my stash towards him with more force than necessary.

Bernice has already sidled next to Thomas to siphon his winnings. She's a lot faster now that she doesn't have to lug her oxygen tank around with her. All of the residents are. When Mrs. Wilson looks at her watch and yells, "*Antique Hunters* is on!" They all race to the TV room like a bunch of grade-schoolers let loose at recess.

Now that we use the Eternity Flower nectar for sweetener, the seniors at Shady Pines aren't aging as fast as they used to.

When there are only a handful of people left in the room, John and Virginia come out of the kitchen carrying a sheet cake topped with nineteen candles. Along with everyone else, they warble out Happy Birthday and set the cake down before me.

Hard to believe that I only became an adult a year ago. I feel like I aged three thousand years in that time. Not in bad way. Just, I'm older. In ways that I never expected.

My eyes fill with tears as they finish the song. I'm so grateful to have Virginia. She's gentle and loving and unbelievably forgiving. After Shay, she's become my best friend. Yet I miss

Agnes, quirks and all. She wasn't always easy to live with, but she loved me in her own way.

And she did bake a damn good cake.

"Make a wish," John's lips brush my temple as he settles next to me. I tuck in my wings—invisible here in the Beyond, but still bulky—so he can wrap an arm around my shoulders. The pad of his thumb traces tiny circles into my skin. I lean into him wondering how, even after a year, his touch always feels new.

I blow out the tiny flames in one breath. I wish for answers.

A year ago, we couldn't get back into Eden to save the original colonists—minus their kids—who made the pact. I tried. God, I tried so hard. But the Devil is an expert at destruction. Even my powers were useless against the rubble barring the way.

Twenty-three people are still stuck in Eden. Including John's grandfather. Clara's second mom. And my grandmother—Eleanor Dare.

I didn't know Eleanor. But for the past year, Virginia has been telling me stories. She tucks me in like Agnes used to do. She pulls the sheet and blanket up to my chin and lifts the baby hairs off my forehead, then launches into memories. Every bit of me aches with longing to know my grandmother.

But for now, I just want to know she's okay.

I want to know they're all okay. Because I feel partially responsible for leaving them behind.

"What did you wish for?" Clara asks. Her curly hair is cut into a short bob, and a shiny gloss colors her lips. She looks so much like Minnie, but that's where the similarity ends. For all of Minnie's wild earring choices and hearty laughs, Clara is classic pearls and restrained smiles. It's not easy for her. Like me, she lost the mom she knew to Eden but found a new one. Grief and anger and sorrow and joy battle to lead the ball all the time. Clara is still trying to figure out exactly who she is. I know, because so am I.

"She cannot tell." John's chin rests on my head so I feel his jaw work as he says it. "Or it won't come true."

Clara rolls her eyes. That eyeroll holds everything unsaid, mainly that we're still on shaky ground. It's taken this long for our friendship to feel half-way okay. I may have the ability to see goodness and light in everything, but I'm no angel. Well, technically I am, but only half. That other half of me tends to hold grudges and needs a good smack upside the head every once in a while. Clara dropped her attitude early. But even with her dating Shay's brother—it took Tyler all of five minutes to stop flirting with me and fall for her—and doting on Minnie and making amends with John and winning over Shay, I was hesitant. It wasn't until Thomas finally accepted her friendship that I knew I was being petty.

Sometimes I wonder just how much darkness I inherited from my father.

"Time to open gifts," Tyler says, shoving a perfectly wrapped box towards me. I know that wasn't his handiwork, so must be Clara's. The two of them are practically joined at the hip.

"Nope!" Shay bats Tyler's gift away to put hers in its place. "Mine first!"

I laugh. I don't think those two will ever stop fighting.

By the time Virginia and I get back home, it's late. The house Agnes rented held too many memories, so when Lisa, the owner of Roasted, got married and moved from the small apartment over the café to a house a few streets away, we snapped it up. There's something to be said for always waking up to the smell of coffee and scones. And it has a cute little balcony with room for a row of potted Eternity Flowers.

I follow Virginia up the back stairs leading to our apartment door, then bang right into her when she abruptly stops two steps from the landing. Even though she practically bathes in the Eternity Flower nectar, I can feel her shock like an electric current under my skin.

And that's when I see it: the metal box, embossed with a snarling beast, three crescent moons and the name DARE.

Virginia blindly reaches out behind her until she finds my hand, squeezing her fingers around my own. We stare down at the box, frozen, our rapid breaths the only sound in the hall.

My father hasn't tried to contact me once this entire year, and I've been glad of it. The only reason I'd want to speak to that fallen angel is to find out what he did to the twenty-three souls we left behind. To find out what he did to my grandmother.

I release Virginia's hand and squat down in front of the old Dare family Bible box. I run the pad of my index over the curly leaf work decorating the metal, outline the raised claws of the angry beast.

I know inside is my Devil's mask. I can hear it calling to me. I can feel it breathe. Inside is the link to my father. The link to Eden. Inside are the answers to my questions. But to open it is a risk.

Yet I'm stronger now than I ever was. I don't fear my father.

"Some secrets should stay buried," I whisper.

Virginia responds. "Aye, some should."

We stare down at the box some more. What happened to the original colonists? What happened to Eleanor?

"But maybe not this one," I say. Virginia nods.

I lift the lid.

63

Eleanor

Eden: One Year Earlier

The Devil's tantrum subsided.

The tempest of fire stopped. As did the wind and the quakes. The Master's darkness slipped around us all, the black fog of malevolence clinging to our skin. We were too spent to weep. Too desolate to move. We lay with our cheeks to the cracked ground, our bodies frail and hurting. It was as we'd feared all those years ago: Our loved ones escaped to the Beyond while were left behind in Eden.

Ahredden saved Virginia. Saved many. But she could not save the rest of us. Those of us who made the original pact.

It was more painful than I could have ever imagined, to be left without Virginia. To know I'd be without her forever.

"'Tis just us, now, my pets," the Master cooed. "Almost like the old days."

The cycle would start again. Against all odds, there would be a child born. It would feed Eden...and over and over again, we would keep sacrificing to stay alive. Nay, to stay out of hell. We would do so for eternity if we must.

Virginia. Oh, how I already missed Virginia.

My love for her had always been the justification for evil acts. From drowning little Walter to poisoning the youth with Contagion, I'd done it all to keep Virginia close. But now, after seeing her freed from Eden, after seeing my granddaughter sprout the wings of an angel, I knew there was no excuse for them. And there never had been.

"Have you not tired of this game, Master?" I peeled myself from the dirt and stood, my long skirts hiding my trembling legs. "Always playing with us, like a cat with a mouse?"

He lifted an eyebrow. "It amuses me."

"But it's been centuries. We've paid our dues many times over. Let us go. Belial's breath, we've nothing left to give you."

"Oh, Eleanor! You delight me. So naïve. I thought you cleverer than that. You have much to give me: your desolation, your fear, your self-loathing."

Yet I knew him. By a demon's tongue and tail, after more than four-hundred years, I knew him. I heard the uncertainty in the timbre of his voice. I saw the doubt in the lackluster shine of his eyes. Ahredden's refusal had cut him to the bone. In fact, I sensed that she'd broken the black, rotting lump he called a heart. Yet his love was so twisted he could not understand why he'd failed to earn her affection.

I summoned my courage to ask my next question, for the last time I'd asked, I'd set up centuries upon centuries of suffering. "There must be something to do. Something to exchange to let us go."

"There is nothing. 'Tis impossible for any of you to step back into the Beyond," he said. Darkness turned to a fine white mist, sparkling under a bright yellow moon. The pond gurgled; the bloody water suddenly clear. Moss grew under my feet, flowers bloomed along the riverbank, and birdsong filled the air. But a thick fog choked out the mountains and fields. Even without seeing it all, I knew that Eden was smaller, much smaller, than it had ever been.

Our pain fell away. We were once again healthy and young. The others sighed and whimpered in relief. As I resigned myself to never being able to change our pact, the Master tilted his head and turned to me, "Perhaps, however, I could allow you to live here without sacrifice—if the exchange is worthy."

My heartbeat quickened. "What is it you believe a worthy exchange? What can we give you?"

His lips quirked. "'Tis what *you* can give me, Eleanor. What *you* can give in exchange for you *all* to have life in Eden with no sacrifice."

"Me?" I swallowed. A trickle of sweat snaked down my temple. I looked at the others, from my oldest friends, Emme and Elizabeth, to my fiercest enemy, Dyonis. I looked and saw the pain I'd wrought from pride and desperation. They'd sacrificed much. They all had sacrificed family.

Mine family was safe. A Dare has never been sacrificed.

I did not want to sacrifice anything. I was no saint. No heroine. Yet I knew it was time.

"What is it I must give?" I asked the Devil. "What do you want from me?"

The Master stepped closer, eliminating the space between us, and lifted my chin with one finger. When our eyes met, he dragged that finger over the crescent stain that marked me as his. "Are you that blind? I want what I've always wanted from you, Eleanor."

I frowned, not understanding.

So he leaned in, his lips against the shell of my ear, and whispered, "I want your unfettered love."

My heartbeat became a crashing in my ears. A scream climbed up my throat, clawing for me to release it. Nay. It was not possible. I could never. Never.

The Devil's voice was silken. "Vow to love me, Eleanor. Do so, and life in Eden will be a true paradise."

Some vows are meant to be broken. And some vows are meant to break us.

This vow was the latter.

But how could I refuse? I had the others' salvation in my grasp. I simply needed to utter a word. One word.

"Aye." I let the word slip from my lips, because I am a Dare.

And nothing—nothing—will ever completely break me.

END

That's the complete duology! **Want to know Agnes' story?** Get the prequel novella, *The Lies That Bury Us*, for FREE when you join my newsletter here: https://subscribepage.io/TLTBUfree

Thank you for reading

Word of mouth is crucial for an author to succeed. If you enjoyed *The Vows That Break Us*, please consider leaving a review or rating; it would be greatly appreciated. Thank you!

Want to know Agnes' story? Get the prequel novella, *The Lies That Bury Us*, for FREE when you join my newsletter here: https://subscribepage.io/TLTBUfree

About Katie Hayoz

Katie Hayoz was born in Racine, WI, but ended up in Geneva, Switzerland, where she lives with her husband, two daughters, and two cats. She loves to read and devours speculative fiction like she does popcorn and black licorice: quickly and in large quantities.

Connect with Katie:

www.katiehayoz.com

Facebook page: katiehayoz.author

Instagram: @katie_hayoz

Join Katie's newsletter on katiehayoz.com

Books By Katie Hayoz

Katie writes for kids, teens, and adults. Below are some of her books for teens and adults.

You can find a full list on katiehayoz.com

Join Katie's newsletter on katiehayoz.com for updates, freebies, and fun! Get a free short story for joining.

The Clockwork Siren Series

Immersed (Adventure One in the Clockwork Siren Series)
Melusine Doré slays monsters for a living. The grim and gruesome don't frighten her; she can take on a cyclops or a three-tailed dragon without even breaking a sweat. But falling in love? Falling in love terrifies her. Because love has the power to reveal a secret dark and dangerous enough to completely shatter her world.

Submerged (Adventure Two in the Clockwork Siren Series)

When Melusine and Levi go hunt a beast down South, Melusine's deepest fear becomes a reality as she finds herself in exactly the place where all her troubles began: home. There, Melusine must face the dark secrets and lies of her family's past—and the very real possibility that she is more monster than maiden.

Surfaced (Adventure Three in the Clockwork Siren Series)

When Melusine and Levi discover that someone is trapping and torturing monsters, they're led on a journey to a traveling freak show. A simple investigation quickly turns into a tangled mess. Levi goes missing and Melusine must tap into all her unusual talents to find and rescue her lover. This time though, Melusine won't be the deadliest fish in the sea.

The Clockwork Siren Series Box Set (Adventures 1-3)

Get adventures 1-3 at an advantageous price.

Ensnared (A Prequel to the Clockwork Siren Series)

In a dark and dashing Victorian Chicago, Levi Cannon fights sirens, family expectations, and guilt from his past. Levi was raised to be a gentleman. Yet he prefers unseemly weapons and inappropriate women. Compared to his brother, Amos, Levi is a disappointment. Or so Levi's Pa says. When Amos is captured by mermaids, Levi gets the chance to become the man his father wants him to be. The question is, will Levi do what is proper, or what is right?

Devil Of Roanoke Series

The Curse That Binds Us (Book One in Devil of Roanoke Series)

Redd longs to understand her past. And with a mysterious box showing up every year on her birthday, she's certain the answers she seeks lurk within. But with each new appearance, her mother takes them on the run from the 400-year-old artifact. After finally discovering the antique before her mom, she's determined to learn the truth. But her actions awaken a link to the evil her mother fought to keep dormant.

The Vows That Break Us (Book Two in Devil of Roanoke Series)

Redd has finally made it to Eden, where she seeks to know more about the place of her birth. Enraptured by the splendor and magic of this ancient village, she doesn't realize its beauty comes from a vow of sacrifice. Soon enough, the veil is lifted, revealing the true horror of the place. Only now she's locked in.

The Quatrefoil Chronicles

Of Wicked Blood (Book One in The Quatrefoil Chronicles) Co-written with Olivia Wildenstein

When Slate Ardoin steals a ring, he unwittingly unleashes a series of deadly curses. Sure. He might die and the future of the whole world is at stake, but at least the lovely Cadence de Morel is forced to fight by his side. As each curse gets darker and more dangerous, Slate and Cadence find themselves falling for each other.

Of Tainted Heart (Book Two in The Quatrefoil Chronicles) Co-written with Olivia Wildenstein

It was over. Or, it could have been. But nothing irritates a perfectionist more than a job unfinished. When Cadence plunges

the crew back into the race to assemble the Quatrefoil, she is sure it will be quick and easy. But she should have known better.

Stand Alones

<u>Untethered</u>

Sixteen-year-old Sylvie has the ability to leave her body and astral project. While it could be like a superpower, for her it's a curse. That is until she embraces its dark side and opens herself to evil. But her newfound power quickly spirals out of control. An Indie B.R.A.G. award winner and a finalist in the Mslexia YA novel competition.

www.ingramcontent.com/pod-product-compliance
Lightning Source LLC
LaVergne TN
LVHW042342190726
843493LV00005B/894